Antoinette Brown Blackwell

Studies in General Science

Antoinette Brown Blackwell

Studies in General Science

Reprint of the original, first published in 1869.

1st Edition 2022 | ISBN: 978-3-37504-596-8

Verlag (Publisher): Salzwasser Verlag GmbH, Zeilweg 44, 60439 Frankfurt, Deutschland
Vertretungsberechtigt (Authorized to represent): E. Roepke, Zeilweg 44, 60439 Frankfurt, Deutschland
Druck (Print): Books on Demand GmbH, In de Tarpen 42, 22848 Norderstedt, Deutschland

STUDIES

IN

GENERAL SCIENCE.

BY

ANTOINETTE BROWN BLACKWELL.

NEW YORK:

G. P. PUTNAM AND SON, 661 BROADWAY,
OPPOSITE BOND STREET.
1869.

To the

RELIGIOUS TEACHERS OF MY YOUTH,

INCLUDING

MY AGED FATHER AND MOTHER,

AND

TO THOSE WHO GENEROUSLY ASSISTED AT MY ORDINATION,

This Volume

IS AFFECTIONATELY AND RESPECTFULLY

DEDICATED BY

THE AUTHOR.

PREFACE.

THE following *Essays* are a summary of the conclusions arrived at after a lifetime of more or less steady devotion to the subjects under consideration. My aim has been to make each article as complete and distinct in itself as the nature of the topic would allow; and yet to connect them all in a progressive series of thought.

In each separate *Study*, I have endeavored to bring myself into such a relation to the topics treated of, that I could clearly *perceive* every position at the time it was taken; and thus, going forward in these statements, step by step, with open eyes, I have hoped the better to enable others to keep progress with me in immediate mental vision. With this single purpose in view, I could pay only so much attention to style as would give clearness and directness of statement, and would allow me to be almost wholly absorbed with the special matter in hand. This method necessarily involved some repetition, frequent reference to parallel points and analogies, and a continual coördination of thoughts in harmony with the supposed coördinations of things; yet, perhaps these almost unavoidable repetitions and allusions, with their slight differences, arising as seen from different stand-points, may not be too frequent, at least for general readers.

Preface.

As these studies are the product of more than twenty years of an otherwise exceedingly busy life, through which, however, there has run a continuous thread of reading, thought, and observation upon these and kindred themes, it is at this time impossible always to give credit to the different authors from whom many various thoughts have been derived. When it seemed desirable to do so, I have tried to give authority for every statement of fact or scientific theory; and when this has not been done, such statements have been derived from reliable scientific sources, it is believed, in every instance. How far the system of thought which the book contains was derived by the author directly from the universe itself and how far from books, it would be impossible now to determine; nor is it really of much importance. If one can perceive a truth, it matters very little whether he got it at first hand from God's book, or from man's; and whoever should choose to lay claim to prior discovery is therefore quite welcome to it.

Making no pretensions to a practical scientific knowledge, these essays claim to be nothing but studies of principles in their general grouping and mutual coördinations, as everywhere illustrated in things.

The more metaphysical portions were the special studies of early youth, when everything pertaining to mental philosophy was eagerly devoured; with such imperfect digestion as youth has for abstract theorizing. The theological and moral topics, though the constant food of childhood, yet pertain more especially to early womanhood, in an Orthodox Theological Seminary, and subsequently, as Pastor of an Orthodox Congregational Church; bound to the discharge of the usual duties of that position, in addi-

Preface.

tion to the more general demands of the lecturing field, — a period in which, while trying with reasonable faithfulness outwardly to meet the just expectations of others, for myself, I studied first to reconcile revealed and natural religion, and afterwards to learn what the basis and the doctrines of the one absolute religion really are. The remaining more generally scientific portions of the work, with the labor of grouping and harmonizing the whole, were carried on in mature life; but while those earlier studies were hindered by duties which few women attempt to shoulder, the later ones were impeded (perhaps in both cases I should say aided) by duties which no man ever performed — those which devolve on the mother of a young family, all of whom are still in childhood.

All these things are stated not in egotism, but yet frankly, as friend might speak with friend, to that generous public upon whose indulgence I must rely in its judgment of the many deficiencies and faults which must necessarily appear in the present volume. Yet my hope is that the work may prove to be a reasonably good illustration of the truth that it makes very little difference to the student of things where he begins to study, or what part he learns first, since each portion is replete with interest and important to every other; so that everything true is corroborative of all other truths; and all alike point upwards to the common Author.

TABLE OF CONTENTS.

GENERAL STATEMENT.
PAGE

All Events are Coördinated — Creation a System of related Rational Principles, realized in Absolute Substance and Property — Properties of Matter Quantitative — Properties of Mind, also Sentient or Qualitative 1

THE TEXT-BOOK.

The Actual Universe is the Source from whence all Truth must be derived 12

PERCEPTIVE FORCE.

Perception Cognizes by Direct Intuition — Sense-Perception is Presentative like all other Perception — Perceptive Force coordinated with the Objective 19

CONSTRUCTIVE FORCE.

Deduction the Process of perceiving Abstract Principles — Conception the Creation of Possible Principles — Hypotheses — Originality not possible in Philosophy — Method . . . 28

PERCEPTION DISTINGUISHED FROM CONCEPTION.

Perception presupposes an Object to be known — Conception is a Subjective Process — the one Discovers, the other Originates — Classification — Abstraction 35

WE PERCEIVE THE REAL OBJECT.

The Representative Image or Idea — Reid — The Objective presents Itself 45

x   *Table of Contents.*

WE PERCEIVE THE SUBSTANCE OF BODIES.

PAGE

The Common Belief versus Authority — Dr. McCosh — We perceive Substance as manifesting Phenomena — Intuition Itself our only Witness 48

WE PERCEIVE BODIES AT A DISTANCE.

Theory of Sir William Hamilton — Material Media relating Mind and its Object not Representative of the latter, but Co-operative with both — Sensation the Result of Objective Action on the Mind — Perception, of the Mind's Action on the Object 53

MENTAL AND EXTRA-ORGANIC COÖRDINATIONS.

Organic Modifications are Extra-mental — Mind competent to testify only as to its own proper Experiences — Perpetual Interaction between Mind and Matter generally; and the Results 59

WE MAY PERCEIVE THE RATIONAL PROPERTIES OF THINGS.

The Ox perceives Quantitative Properties only — Man perceives the Abstract Principles of these Properties, perceives the Rational or Thought Constitution of Things as existing and operating 67

THE CONSTITUTION OF MATTER.

Definitions — Matter is constituted by Extension — Everything is extended in a Special and Definite Manner — The Properties of all like Atoms are Identical — Allotropy — Catalysis — Crystallization — Modes of Motion and Force — Divisibility — All Modes of Material Force Correlated — Action and Reaction equal — Quantity — Time — Space — All Properties and Processes Coördinated — All Process Progress, and proceeding by established Gradations 74

MIND.

The Forces of Matter are Unsentient and Quantitative — The Forces of Mind are also Sentient and Qualitative : the one is Lifeless, the other Living 109

Table of Contents.

WE MAY IMMEDIATELY PERCEIVE MINDS; THEIR SUBSTANCES, PROPERTIES, AND PROCESSES.

PAGE

Mind has no Appreciable Properties of Extension — We perceive it as Coöperative with its Organism, as we perceive a Molecule of Matter acting in the Mass — Self-Consciousness — We perceive our own Minds in the Exercise of Mental Processes — We perceive other Minds manifesting similar Processes in connection with their Organisms 116

COÖRDINATIONS OF MIND AND BODY.

Mind and its Organism are mutually Dependent — Either can Originate Disease — Idiocy — Insanity — Sleep — Mind and Body coöperate Quantitatively — Definition of Life . . . 125

THE CONSTITUTION OF MIND.

Each Mind is constituted by Sentient Properties — It is Living, Personal, Indivisible — All its Processes are Personal Experiences — There are many Modes of Sentience, related not by Extension, but by Intension — Coördinated with Pleasure and Pain — Correlation of Sentient Modes 138

COÖRDINATIONS OF GROWTH.

All Organic Growth is conducted by similar Processes — Organic and Inorganic Processes contrasted — Sentient Properties stimulate and direct Coördinated Organic Growth — Active Sentient Experience is coördinated with Quantitative Processes — Various Processes of Organ-forming — The Mind as Created — Mental Development — Hereditary Traits — Different Modes and Conditions of Organic Growth . . . 154

DIFFERENT TYPES OF MIND.

Sentient Properties are common to all Living Beings — The Character of the Sentient Nature determines the Character of its Organism, and the Organism is indicative of the Indwelling Life — The Sentience of Plants — Sleep of Plants — Each *Class* of Mind is constituted by Special Sentient Properties — Coördination of Vegetable and Animal Processes — The Consciousness of the Plant Subjective — that of the Animal both Subjective and Objective — Variety and Value of Vegetable Sen-

xii   *Table of Contents.*

PAGE

tience — Animals in a Common Organism — Special Instincts
— Theory of Instinct — The Irrational Mind 184

AN ECLECTIC DEVELOPMENT THEORY.

The Gradual and Progressive Nature of all Processes — The
Growth of Species not an Exception to this Universal Order —
One Type of Sentient Being cannot be developed into another
— Whatever the Material Beginning, each Mind must ultimately build up its Coördinated, Typical Organism ; beginning
from the Simple Cell — Variations — Hybrids — More Philosophical to suppose an Organic Matrix for all Higher Animals
than a wholly Inorganic Origin — Darwin — Theory of " Pangenesis " 232

THE "STRUGGLE FOR EXISTENCE."

The Scheme which requires all Highly Organized Tissues to be
built up from preceding Tissues is a Scheme of highest Economy and Beneficence   246

THE RATIONAL MIND.

A Rational Mind is a Mind possessing Appetencies for Rational
Principles — It can perceive the intrinsic relative Values of
Things ; and choose accordingly — Moral Principles the Outgrowth of Coördinated Sentient Relations — The Moral Being
may perceive these from an Impersonal Stand-point   .   . 253

THE RATIONAL MIND AS CAUSE.

The Rational Mind may produce new designed Events by new
Coördinations of Substantial Elements — It may also cause
new Sentient Events — A Rational Cause must work with the
Principles of Things — Qualitative Events superior to Quantity   260

MEMORY.

Memory an Appetency which brings Past Experiences back
again into Present Consciousness — The Conditions for Remembering — It gives only the Subjective Elements of Events
— Memory of Principles and of Feelings compared — Memory is the Immediate Perception of Subjective Facts   .   . 272

Table of Contents.

LANGUAGE.

Language as a Mental Property is an Appetency for the Expression of Subjective States — Feeling expresses itself in Sound and other Natural Manifestations — Representative Language — Written Language embodies the Thought of the Writer; which Thought is Presentatively perceived by the Reader . 279

CONSERVATION OF MATTER AND ITS PROPERTIES.

All Matter is Indestructible — All its Forces also are conserved — Every Atom, with all its Properties, is perpetually Existent . 287

IMMORTALITY.

Life opposed not to Dissolution, which pertains to the Body, but to Annihilation — Life is Perpetual Sentient Existence, and Indestructible — Belief in Immortality, Universal and Intuitive — Immortality demanded by Moral Fitness and Beneficence . 291

SELFISHNESS IS A QUANTITATIVE VICE.

Quantities, which can belong to but One, lead to Avarice — The Grasping Spirit is intrinsically debasing — To drag down another to the Domain of Irrational Values is Infamous . . 301

UNSELFISHNESS IS A QUALITATIVE VIRTUE.

Rational or Qualitative Values may be possessed entire by any Number of Persons at the same Time — Giving here does not impoverish the Giver — A Many Fold Increase — Qualitative Values lead to Unselfishness — Social Influences — Relative Sentient Values — The Appetency for the Intrinsically Best . 306

LAW AND ITS SANCTIONS.

Laws are either Principles inherent in the Nature of Things, or they are Factitious Enactments — The *Laws of Things* are all Immutable — Their Sanctions are Legitimate Results, which cannot be remitted — Human Laws, Enactments, whose Penalties may be remitted — Repentance and Reparation — Forgiveness, its Nature and Conditions 314

SOCIAL PROGRESS.

Conditions of Progress — Relations of External Stimulants and Internal Appetencies — Social Aids — A Process may be an

xiv *Table of Contents.*

PAGE

Irregular Advance, or even, for a time, Retrograde; but it must ultimate in Unending Progress 328

SUBSTANCE AND FORCE AS UNCREATED.

We arrive at Absolute Being by Abstraction — We know only that Absolute Substance and Property are and must be . . 336

CREATION.

Creation a System of Related, Unchanging Facts and Coördinated Changes — Is a Scheme of Realized Thought — Unity of Creation as evidenced in all Departments of Science — Oneness of all Rational Principles of Things 338

NATURE OF THE CREATOR INFERRED FROM THE CREATION.

Only two Classes of Cause — Rational Cause — The Creator, Rational Cause of the Universe — Rational Causality necessitates a Personal Mind — Omniscience — Omnipotence — Moral Perfections — We know the Creator only through His Creation — Providence — Finite Mind unable to fully comprehend the hend the Infinite — The Creator as evidenced by our Sentient Appetencies and Needs 348

GENERAL STATEMENT.

WE find ourselves living in the midst of a perpetual series of coördinated events. Everything is so obviously related to ourselves and to everything else, that mankind has been ceaselessly impelled, from the first, to believe that all things known to us are allied in a general unity. As a better estimate has steadily unfolded an ever wider range of relations and correlations, and a more accurately defined knowledge has gradually accumulated, there has arisen an almost unanimous verdict, that the whole existing *Cosmos* is essentially a Universe. It is found to be more than a simple mechanism; but, apparently, it is not more than a complex, all-comprehensive mechanism, whose innate motive forces are all mutually and quantitatively coöperative, and in part, also, living or sentient self-determining powers, also quantitatively coördinated with the general whole.

Existence, or *Being absolute* and *uncreated*, must comprehend all self-existent substance, everything which exists and persists in its own right, independent of everything else. That absolute Being is necessarily an absolute unity is not to me self-evident. Every ultimate atom, if literally self-existent, that is, if permanently existent, independent of time and of every power or possibility whatever, would be an absolute, an uncreated atom, though myriads of other similar or like atoms might coexist and be even co-related. It would still be *absolute* as to its existence, necessary and indestructible. *Substance* and *Property* are both regarded in the present essay as self-existent, or absolutely and necessarily existent;

General Statement.

and both together are understood as comprising the whole of *Absolute Existence* or *Absolute Being*. Every *property* of things would be a nonentity, or at most it could be nothing more than an abstract pure principle, except as actualized or existent in substance; and absolute substance, totally without properties, is at least incredible, if not impossible. If all absolute substance were self-existent without properties, then from such an absolute existence nothing relative could ever have arisen. Self-existent substance and property, therefore, together comprise absolute Being.

Property is a general term comprehending both the *forces* and the *capacities* of things. *Force*, one mode of *property*, has been determined by science to be as self-existent and indestructible as substance; it is the absolute and persisting motive power of all substance; and *force*, it is evident, could be literally nothing except realized in and through substance. What absolute substance, its absolute *force*, or absolute *capacity*, are, *per se*, further than that they are all self-existent, I do not attempt to say. With this absolute or uncreated existence we have comparatively very little to do in the present series of *studies*. It may be interesting and useful to speculate as to the possible nature of even uncreated Being — to try to decide *negatively* what it is not and cannot be, or at least cannot be thought to be by finite intelligences like ourselves; but to attempt to dogmatize or settle anything positively in regard to the *absolute* would be futile, since the absolute is acknowledged to be eminently above and beyond the grasp of our present human faculties. It might be equal folly to determine, in advance, that we can know nothing whatever of the absolute, the infinite, or perfect; for these all are surely to be studied until we are entire-ly satisfied as to how much and how little the incar-nated human mind can know about them; and if we must finally be content with very little positive knowledge,

General Statement.

it will yet be a great point gained to have fathomed the depth of our own subjective powers, and to have found the boundary line into the unknown or but vaguely known *beyond*. Even if a "learned ignorance" must for the present suffice, we may still hope that the eager, ever-seeking mind may find a yet higher reward in some further stage of progress. Meantime, there is assuredly some possible conception of the absolute as distinguished in thought from the relative, of the infinite as discriminated from the finite, of the perfect as separated from the imperfect ; but all this is to be held in abeyance.

Our first inquiries relate simply to the relative, the finite, the created — in a word, to the *existing universe*. While substance and property are both regarded as necessarily absolute and self-existent in themselves ; yet all their established, coördinated modes and processes evidence so unquestionably a necessity for the highest conscious thought in determining their countless beautiful adjustments, that I hold them to be most evidently created ; and by no conceivable possibility as admitting of self-existence. The adaptation of all preëstablished changes, and the fixed, definite relations invariably subsisting between them, cannot pertain to a self-existent necessity. Here is realized thought or *creation*. The present universe is regarded as having received its existing constitution through a preëstablished, adapted system or rational scheme of created modes and processes, actualized and harmonized in self-existent, absolute *Being*. The whole existing constitution of things is held to have been created, — that is, to have been both conceived or planned in ideal, and realized in the actual. Creation is assumed to be an established, preadjusted scheme of pure principles, literally applied and made operative in things. Though all ultimate *force* and *capacity* must be self-existent in its own substance, yet their coördinations or mutual perpetual adaptations are so obviously the prod-

General Statement.

uct of rational thought, that such preadaptations could not have been self-existent; but must have been originated by a rational thinker. Absolute Being may or may not be outside of our present cognizance; but the scheme of rational adaptations, now actualized and operative in things, is maintained to be decidedly within the field of human cognition. It is this perpetually operative immutable system of fixed and definite adjustments in all the modes and processes of things, sentient and unsentient alike, which necessitates a Rational Designer and Establisher of so preëminently rational a system. One may be put down if he attempt to dogmatize on the absolute, which is certainly outside of direct perception; but I do not well see how he can be answered when he appeals to the testimony of that which is self-evident, and may be immediately perceived, in its many widely ramifying relations, by every rational mind which will take the trouble to look for itself.

Our inquiries relate chiefly to the present constitution of the universe. This constitution is definitely established and immutable, though rigidly and mathematically adjusted in all its parts; while all its processes are evidently the result of prevision and prearrangement. Properties, abstractly, are simply rational principles; and, independent of their substances, in the nature of things, they could be nothing more than this. They may be regarded subjectively as thoughts, concepts, ideas, but from their rational or immaterial character, they are then dependent upon the thinking or perceiving mind. Objectively, neither a force, a capacity, nor any mode of existence could be *realized* or made *actual* except through an alliance with substantial existence. Thus, the *concept* of *motion* is solely an intellectual thought: there can never be an actual motion-producing force, unless there is a substance possessing such force, and never an actual motion, unless there is a substance which is

General Statement.

moved. The *principle* of a circle is the pure thought-construction of a possible circle. No real circle can exist unless a real substance takes on this pure mental form. So there can be no actual extension without something which is extended; no actual bitterness unless there is something which produces the special effect upon the palate which we call bitter. In this last example, there is a whole series of delicate adjustments requisite to produce in the conscious mind the sensation and perception of that quality of experience which we call bitterness. These fixed preordained adjustments of all things, in all the actual and possible processes of nature, cannot be intelligently conceived of as existing of necessity or through any irrational chance. They cannot be self-existent, they must be the product of thought.

We find that we ourselves are so constituted and so co-adapted to everything about us, that we are unable to construct even the simplest thing except by realizing in it our own rational ideas, subject always to the preëstablished principles of nature. An old wife's knitting-work and the child's first pinafore for her doll are both records of thought and purpose actualized. The rational plan is expressed, substantialized, as an accomplished fact. Thoughts are thus embodied by men in every species of art and handicraft; the inventor realizes his ideal in his invention. The artisan repeats his in his craft, and thus systems of thought, more or less elaborate, are everywhere expressed, as it were incarnated, in things. Any one, looking at several new machines — say a subsoil plough and a windmill — could, by studying them intently enough, easily discern the principle on which each was designed to operate. He would perceive that the iron share of the subsoil plough was not intended to whirl round in the air, and that the sails of the mill were not designed to burrow in the earth; then, if he saw them in actual operation, the ploughshare moving on buried under ground,

6 *General Statement.*

and the mill-sails turning rapidly about in the wind, he might discover the plan upon which each of these machines was constructed, and its adjustment to the forces through which it was designed to work. Given the machine, some rational plan or scheme of its structure and operations is a necessary antecedent. The thought-plan is originally distinct from the machine; yet it is indispensable that it should first exist, and finally be expressed, crystallized in the very structure of the machine.

"The universe," as one class of philosophers now so stoutly maintain, "is not a machine," — that is to say, it is a great deal more than any dead, unsentient mechanism could ever be, even if it were infinite in its comprehensiveness; nevertheless, the machine and the universe may both possess this one common phase of which I speak, — they may both embody properties whose new relations and combinations originate new and designed modes, processes, and results. Absolute principles may exist as innate, necessary properties of things: there may be absolute *force* or motive-power; and absolute *capacity* or receptivity for being extended, moved, or divided; but no self-existent, irrational necessity could create a related, rational scheme of pure coördinations, each dependent on all the others; and could *substantialize* this or establish it in active coöperation, through the use and exercise of *absolute substance* and its *absolute properties.* It is, in part, the old argument: if we see a watch, we know that there must have been a watch-maker, — though we do not therefore know that there is no absolute substance and absolute force, which, being self-existent, had no maker; but which have, nevertheless, been so coördinated in this watch, that the watch, as such, is inherently proved to be a new creation, a creation not of the absolute but of the relative. So far as we can determine, there must have been absolute force from the beginning; for there is nothing within ourselves which can credit the belief that

General Statement.

something could ever have been made literally from *nothing;* but it is not, therefore, certain or credible that any of the present modes of force, such as gravity, heat, light, electricity, magnetism, or chemical affinity, could have existed from the beginning, or could have existed at all, if there had been no *intelligence, will,* and *executive ability* adequate to originate and establish them. Energy may be self-existent ; but a definite system of correlated, inter-changeable modes of energy, sentient as well as unsentient, coördinating thoughts, feelings, purposes, and all possible living personal experiences with all the other modes of force and capacity now coöperative in the universe, is necessarily created ; and, as it seems to me, it may be shown to be so from an intrinsic rational or intellectual necessity. It is not proposed to answer the child's question, " Who made God ? " or even to attempt to enter so intimately into his wisdom and power — which to us must be as inscrutable as our human works are to the lower irrational animals — as to try to describe his original creative processes ; but we must try to comprehend and state the nature of the processes which we see everywhere going on about us in the creation as it now exists. We see that the universe is constituted after a perfected, rational, persisting plan, which connects all things in orderly, preëstablished processes. It is not even necessary to attempt to state *how* this plan got itself into the existing universe, since there it is, the irrevocable nature and constitution of things — at least to change it is utterly without the reach of human effort. Who originated this scheme of things, or whether it was ever originated at all, are questions which cannot affect the fact that here it is, actualized and in active operation.

Describe the present related modes of anything which exists, and you inevitably portray a more beautiful series of rational concepts than it would enter into the heart of man to conceive. Look at the harmonized structure

8 *General Statement.*

of every bird — a delicate adapted frame-work of slender bones, some of which fill with air, and thus by lightening its specific gravity, in connection with the strong muscles of the wing and the slender anterior part of the body, enable all birds who possess such a structure in perfection to indulge in rapid flight. Let these facts be pointed out to a little child, and it receives a new and charming group of thoughts ; but they are thoughts which have been ossified in the very bones of every bird since the world began. Whether or not some mind first conceived this admirable plan of bird-structure, yet the plan exists, and is registered in every organism of the whole feathered race. The savans have disagreed widely as to the origin of the undeviating, law-abiding nature of things ; but they are unanimous in portraying its admirable fitness, beauty, and persistence. Often, too, they are unconscious witnesses, intent on statements entirely foreign to this ; hence the added value of their unwitting testimony. May we not, then, accept the fact that there is a rational scheme of things, which can be perceived as realized in the things themselves — a scheme which may be stated in words so intelligibly that most minds can apprehend it, and be able to verify its truths for themselves ; and that this scheme of coördinated existing processes is the essential nature or innate constitution of all known substances?

Principles can be applied, and practically related only in and through substances. This is a universal proposition. The converse is also true ; substances can be relatively constituted only through the application and operation of related principles. So much the Universe and the machine possess in common.

Without correlations or adapted modes of property, Being might still be veritable absolute being, doubtless ; but it would be, to our apprehension, chaotic existence, nothing more. Being, without thought adaptations, without a relational constitution, the result of an unintel-

General Statement.

lectual necessity or chance, would be something, indeed, whose nature is so without the province either of our perceptions or conceptions, that we can only regard it as something to us incomprehensible. Our intellectual natures are coördinated with Being as it is now constituted; exercising and manifesting correlated properties, and presenting itself to us through definite related modes and processes. A *mode* of Being is the form under which any substance exists and acts, and all modes are perpetually changing. Thus, we perceive bodies as having extension, form, size, color, resistance, and other like correlated modes, and recognize them as possessing various interchangeable modes of force, which mutually act and react upon each other, according to the most rigid mathematical laws; while, by predetermined, definite processes, thus resulting, there arise these changing manifestations of extension, form, size, color, resistance, etc. The amount of force (and also of capacity), as a whole, is found to be unvarying, being neither more nor less under any change of conditions; and this is true not only as regards substance in general, but also as to every least particle. Each atom, it is believed, possesses a fixed amount of special force (and capacity) of its own, which is inseparable from itself; but whose various established modes are all mutually interchangeable, and are also so correlated to similar modes in other atoms that any given mode of force in action will excite a coördinated mode in every other atom upon which it acts; while the atoms acted upon react, also, quantitatively, and under equally well-established coördinations. The properties, modes, and processes of matter are all found to be rigidly quantitative, and the action and reaction between them is always exactly equal, so that they all exist and act strictly according to the mathematical principle of precisely so much for so much. The properties of matter are all, therefore, strictly mechanical; and there is evidence that they are,

General Statement.

also, unsentient, or simply and unconsciously mechanical.

The properties of mind, on the contrary, are all held to be sentient or living properties; and though they, also, are quantitatively coördinated with all the modes and processes of matter, and are under the law of equal action and reaction as to all activities in conjunction with matter, yet the properties of mind are also related in quality or kind and intensity of modes. Sentient properties are modes of sensations, perceptions, thoughts, purposes, self-determinations, and though these sentient modes never ignore or contravene the laws of the unsentient, to which they are allied, yet they have, in addition, coördinated laws and principles of their own, of a wholly unlike and higher character. Mental *forces* are all *appetencies*, and mental *capacities* are all *sentient capabilities;* hence, while matter is substance constituted quantitatively only, by related unsentient properties, mind is substance constituted both quantitatively and also qualitatively by sentient properties. Our cognizance of *Being* is therefore cognizance of substances possessing mutually adjusted and adapted properties; so that all our knowledge of it turns upon a knowledge of its rational constitution. The very existence of differentiated substances is directly dependent upon a mutual adaptation of all modes and processes — the whole existing cosmos hangs upon it, and would fall into anarchy if one single modification of any property were destroyed. Though we know that absolute Being cannot be dependent upon the present constitution of the universe, but that this constitution must be dependent upon the absolute Being for its actualization in the present creation; yet this rational constitution is to our cognizance its only life, beauty, and value. Thought has been applied to things, and each atom, whether matter or mind, is allied to its own immutable properties, with their wide diversity of coördinated modes and processes, which are forever turning and overturning, but always developing more fully the preëstablished order of things; moving molecules, moving worlds; quickening minds, developing races; lighting, warming, evolving, organizing, animating, ennobling, developing; till the result is before us — the physical and mental universe, one and harmonious. Force, the mover, the evolutionist, the one energy made effective through many correlated modes, is not only the persisting property of each unsentient atom, but of each sentient mind; and the entire coördinated plan continues in unresting operation. With our finite minds, we may not expect to perceive at once the whole scope of this all-comprehensive hypothesis.

THE TEXT-BOOK.

PHILOSOPHY may be defined as the science of substances, their properties, modes, and processes — that is, a science embracing the sum total of all the facts of existence. Is a true philosophy, then, possible to mankind with their present endowment of faculties? Evidently a completed or perfected philosophy is not attainable by men in the present stage of human development; yet such a philosophy, such a determinate science of everything, assuredly does exist, and is realized or made actual in the established nature of things. It may, then, be directly perceived by whoever has powers of perception adequate to the task. The universe *is*. What is it? This is the ever-recurring question. Perhaps the most comprehensive answer may be, It is something knowable! We have already learned enough of it to perceive that it is written in characters clearly cut and immutable; there needs, then, only a competent reader. If there be an Infinite Mind, He has read all things; this, too, whether He himself has written the whole record or not; that is, whether it was He who created all the facts or whether they otherwise originated. Omniscience must comprehend all knowledge; and I hold it to be a self-evident truth, that *whatever is*, of inherent necessity *is knowable as it is*, provided there be a mind capable of comprehending it. All knowledge is accessible to whoever has powers adequate to find it. We perceive that objective truth is coördinated with our intellectual powers, so that all knowledge of it is intuition, is derived immediately from the object. Mediate knowledge is only belief or inference.

The Text-Book. 13

Nature has all her facts stereotyped. Suppose the naturalist wishes to understand the modes by which she has built up her extensive ranges of mountains; he is curious as to the materials she used, the processes which she employed, and the time which she occupied in perfecting her work. Where shall he look for information? History is silent, for men have no record of the early times before the mountains were made. He must question the mountains themselves; he must study each outcropping rock, and penetrate by hammer and shaft into a long series of orderly records. Thus the geologist has been enabled to find in various parts of the earth's crust a sufficiently plain and legible science of the earth; his reading is still incomplete, many pages seem to him misplaced or wholly wanting, and doubtless he often misinprets the facts and reasons falsely upon the insufficient data before him; but, as a whole, the record is so self-evident that no one can intelligently doubt its fundamental truths. Nature writes her events, often, upon the most fragile plants and flowers, on the very winds and waters, and all the most evanescent and changing forms, as well as upon the most permanent. Her record is always as enduring as the phases of the object upon which she writes; and, sometimes, as if fearing both would be lost, she petrifies the whole and leaves it thus to endure for ages. She has often preserved in stone the history of her frailest leaves, her most ephemeral and minutest insects and infusoria, the record of her ebbing and flowing tides, of the piles of dust blown together by her winds, the footprints of her smallest birds, and of her rain-drops falling upon the sands. Shall she be thus careful of her most transient modes and processes, and not have ordained the conservation of the permanent properties of things, by a still more scrupulous arrangement?

All the possible modes of property, the most obvious and the most subtle, are alike coördinated in substance;

14 *The Text-Book.*

and there alone must we search for them. When a chemist would discover the nature of an alkali, he must bring forward his alkali and interrogate it. He must test it, compel it to witness in its own behalf, cross-examine it, entice it into a large number of possible complications with other things, till he has looked so deeply into its nature that he can tell with certainty what it will do and be under very widely different conditions. The properties which control his alkali are enthroned within the alkali, as immutable and enduring as the substances to which they are wedded. He cannot invent or originate them ; they exist already, and therefore can only be discovered. If Sir Isaac Newton seeks to know the laws which regulate the fall of bodies to the earth, the revolution of planets around the sun, or any other facts as to motion, he, too, must study properties as he finds them at work in nature. Observing motion under a large variety of conditions, he can see that all bodies in our solar system, and so far as observation or analogies reach, that all bodies in the universe, gravitate towards all other bodies in a grand mathematical procession. The law of gravitation is but the expression of one persisting fact in the general constitution of things — a statement of the mode of action in one coördinated process. It is a truth obtained by induction, which is only far-reaching, related perception.

All mental properties, all social, moral, and religious principles, are also registered in the natures of the beings possessing them ; they are incorporated in these natures as constitutional elements, indestructible like the natures themselves. A *law* of things is not a statute, propounding and enforcing a truth ; but it is simply the expression of an established fact as to some mode or process. All the laws of relative processes and obligations are of this character, and are inherent in the substances which possess the modes of property described. Where is the natural and legitimate substratum of all social and moral

The Text-Book. 15

law? Evidently in social and moral natures. A social law is the statement of a predetermined coördination of mental natures ; in other words, it is the expression of a social fact as it was planned ideally in the creative scheme. A moral law is an expression of the ideal adjustment of moral facts, an expression of the highest fitness of things, and therefore of the most obligatory process to a self-determining actor. This highest fitness of all moral facts or possibilities is to be found, directly, only in connection with moral natures. It is neither my design to touch the great question as to the Christian Revelation, revered as the authorized exponent of Moral Law by all Christendom, the supposed revelation of the one hundred and eighty millions of fighting Mohammedans, that of the propagandist Boodhists who have quiescently absorbed more than one third of all the peoples of the earth, — or of any other possible sacred teachings. The Author of the moral universe, first writing his record in things, may or may not afterwards explain it in books, or by the mouth of inspired teachers ; but the point to be made now is, not how we came by a knowledge of the current moral truths which we all recognize ; but, where are those truths to be found at first hand, if one has power to discover or verify them for himself. Moral laws are not substances, to be manufactured from something going before, as we weave broadcloth from the yarn ; but like all other natural laws, they are expressions of the permanent constitution of things. But as applied to natures which are sentient and allied to varying qualities of experience, I assert their claim to be regarded as the ultimate, noblest facts of moral natures. Moral laws are the highest rational principles, made real in the coördinated constitutions of living moral beings. One can learn Botany in a grammar-school just as consistently as he can learn Morals, Religion, Æsthetics, or Metaphysics simply from the teachers and thinkers, or

16   *The Text-Book.*

from their second-hand writings ; for the roots of all these
sciences are alike in things.   The dry, scientific nomen-
clature of the botanist overflows with life and poetry in
the open air, in the midst of the beautiful realities which
it represents ; and even hair-splitting metaphysics become
one masterly system of live fact, full of the muscular and
nervous energy of your own noblest life, within its own
adytum of truth.

Again the *immutable* elements of the universe are
doomed to no buried Herculaneum of mutilated and de-
faced records — they are as perfect and active now as in
the oldest time.   The physicists announce to us the conservation of all substances and forces, yesterday, to-day,
and forever ; and they are studying hitherto unread pages
with their whole souls in their eyes, till they are nothing
but eye-sight, — of course they will find what they are
searching after so diligently.   Students of the highest
social and moral science need have no fear that the established, orderly adjustments of the unsentient world will
not be equaled and excelled in the sentient.   As living,
conscious existence is of more worth than anything else ;
so all those mutual adaptations of social interests, which
coördinate all living experiences, it will be found, are not
less carefully prevised and preadjusted.   Modes and processes change perpetually ; yet even they are all coördinated and perpetually interchangeable in the world of living activity as in that of merely mechanical processes.
Life with its sentient properties is as radically indestructible and immutable as any other class of being.

But if one would master the whole scheme of general
and special adaptations necessary to promote the operations even of an extensive and complicated system of
modern machinery, he must study it long and intently, and
with powers well disciplined to that end ; for mental ability is indispensable to the cognition of any great creative
work.   Much thought is required to conceive and con-

The Text-Book.

summate the plan, and much intelligent insight is indispensable to an appreciation of the result.

Suppose a wild African, ignorant of any tool more complicated than his spear and hoe, to be transported suddenly into one of our large New England manufactories; he would be utterly dazed by the vast processes of carding, dying, spinning, weaving; and would doubtless go away firmly believing that this wonderful system of coordinated facts, allying many various modes of substance and properties to foreordained processes and results, must remain to him forever incomprehensible. Would he dream it possible, if left to himself, that he should ever be able to discover all these involved mysteries? He would stand in consternation, if this task were assigned him, and very likely would believe that he had been set to cope with the Evil Powers; as men in the early days thought it hazardous to question the Unknown; yet many a Yankee can perceive the operations of these fearful iron creatures as readily as he reads A, B, C; and the African could educate himself up to that point by steady culture. A shrewd mechanic, who had spent his life with his eyes open, in a paper mill, a foundry, or even a pin factory, if introduced into one of our great manufactories could perceive the relations and mutual adjustments in looms and spinning jennies at a glance, even though he had previously acquired no just conception of their plan of operations. The work of a large factory is no more comparable to the vast, intricate, most beautiful processes of universal Nature, than finite perceptive and constructive powers are comparable to the wisdom and power adequate to create a Universe and establish its limitless systems of coördinations; yet, if man was made in the intellectual likeness of his Creator, he must learn, through the use of his own powers, little by little to comprehend even the higher modes and processes over which he himself can exercise little or no control. Thus, one and another

— physicist, philosopher, moralist, and the sharp-sighted of all classes, — has seen and announced principle after principle, coöperative in the grand Cosmos. The many have accepted and tested these truths for themselves; and even the weakest mind is forced to perceive very much of the nature and operations of the vast number of things about him. When one can but compass the alphabet of any hitherto unknown language of things he may speedily become a proficient, for he finds the handwriting of the mother Nature as luminous as her own sunbeams.

PERCEPTIVE FORCE.

IF our text-book, in the present series of studies, is the actual universe, with its inherent, unchanging cofistitution as yet related to all changes, — to all modes of motion and emotion, and all processes of differentiation and development: given the universe to be studied, then each mind must perceive and appreciate it for himself. The so-called primary or first truths are patent, in their first forms of development, to the child who has hardly awakened into consciousness. They are as obvious to him as his own hands and feet, or his rattle-box. It would be as impossible to make him believe that the half of his rubber tooth-ring is the whole of it, as it would to convince the wisest geometrician that the whole is not greater than one of its parts. The principles of things are at least as self-presenting and as self-evident as any other of the facts of existence. But the human mind is coördinated with many, if not all the facts of the present universe.

The direct exercise of one's own Perceptive Force is held to be the only mode by which he can obtain a knowledge of anything. If this is affixing a grandly comprehensive scope to Perception, yet the theory seems to be necessitated by the fact. The intellectual forces of the mind are, I think, broadly divided into two classes; *Perception*, which apprehends or cognizes the existing facts of the universe by direct intuition, and *Conception*, which modifies and transforms those facts in thought, and reconstructs them into its own original theories and hypotheses. The normal product of intellectual force is thought.

Perceptive Force.

All intellectual activity, perception and conception, are included in the general act of thought; and each mind produces its own thoughts as each body originates its own movements; the number and variety of modes of motion produced by either being without limit; but neither can act wholly in and of itself, but is closely related to all the other properties of being.

Feeling is hardly a rational act, but rather the emotion of a rational actor; and volition is but the choice of the rational person exercising it; but thought is itself á rational or intellectual act. The same generic distinction does not exist, therefore, between perception and conception, as between thought and feeling, or thought and volition; yet the act of *perceiving* facts which really exist in the nature of things, and that of *conceiving* schemes which you suppose might exist, or which you think will best account for the facts which do exist, can never be confounded without the most hopeless confusion as to reality and hypothesis. The one is direct insight into the existing facts of nature — observation, pure, simple, and immediate, and nothing else; the other is combining percepts into schemes of thought, which may or may not have a reality in things, but which are not perceived as therein existing. The product of *perception* is philosophy; the product of *conception* is philosophizing; there can be but one school of the former, there are many opposing schools of the latter.

Perceiving is an experience unquestioned, whatever be our theory of the fact. We may maintain, with pre-Reidish philosophers, that through the eye we perceive nothing but the images or representations of things; with Reid himself that we perceive qualities and all material phenomena; with Reid's Editor and Critic that we perceive nothing but reflected light; or with the Belfast philosopher,[1] that we perceive the very substance of things;

[1] Dr. McCosh, now of Princeton, New Jersey.

yet we shall all equally admit the plain, undoubted luxury of vision. We see! is the unanimous verdict.

What sees? The blue or black eyes? or the mind which is looking through these living spectacles? *I* see! *I* perceive! here again there is general accord. Whether I perceive mental pictures, sunshine daguerreotypes, actual phenomena, or actual substance, yet it is the living *I* who is the acknowledged Perceiving Power. For the present, then, we assume the unity and personality of the perceiving mind.

Again, I perceive not through my eyes alone, but through all my other senses just as admittedly. I lay my hand upon the table in total darkness, yet by unaided touch I perceive all its dimensions, its form, its texture, its resistance to other bodies. Except as to color, I comprehend its properties better in every respect by touch than by the aid of sight alone. Thus, I perceive through my finger tips even more fully and reliably than through those wonderful telescopes called eyes. I also perceive sounds, odors, and flavors too subtle for eye or finger ; the whole living organism is eager to serve me, and its special senses are adapted to my special needs. The accompanying sensation is not the perception, for the perception is an intellectual and cognitive act; is positive, apprehending and comprehending the object perceived by direct intuition.

Most bodies are opaque to the human eye ; we see them from the outside, and if we would look into their hidden depths, we must divide them till we can bring the whole mass to the surface. We speak of seeing a peach or plum, though the eye rests only on the outline ; we perceive the form of the fruit, and the beautifully colored envelope in which the mass of juicy pulp and the kernel are concealed ; but we must open it, as we would open a sealed casket, if we would reach the mystery of its internal structure. If divisibility were not one of the prop-

Perceptive Force.

erties of matter, incarnated mind would be poorly adapted to cognize its existing constitution ; but depth and breadth can always be transformed into superficial area. Form, unless it is made to comprehend structure, can give but little aid to the student of natural science. Any attempt to classify by mere external resemblances can only produce dry and thin epidermic results. When Cuvier and Von Baer each made the independent discovery, that all animals are constituted in accordance with one of four distinct plans of general structure, they did this by penetrating into the complicated innermost recesses of large numbers of organisms, until their experience had become so comprehensive that they were each able, independently, to affirm that all known animals are actual realizations of one or other of these four definite plans of structure. These two discoverers, of different nationalities, about the same time, perceived and expressed essentially the same series of facts, which scientific men affirm to be verified in the animal kingdom, and if, perhaps, we except the Protozoa, to be complete and exhaustive of the objects classified. There is a literal perception of the internal structure of animal organisms, obtained by aid of the simple process of divisibility — incarnated mind being able to perceive nothing material till it is brought to the surface where it can come into relations with some of the organs of sense.

But there is something deeper in the percept than the mere fact of these bodily structures ; here are the four plans after which those structures have been made to grow. The mind perceives these, also, as actualized in their organisms, apprehending them intuitively, by virtue of its own intrinsic cognitive force. Ancient philosophers regarded perception as nearly coextensive with consciousness, in its broadest signification ; but the moderns have restricted it to the consciousness of material objects through the senses, and to self-consciousness. This is

Perceptive Force. 23

warping and narrowing the ordinary use of language ; the *people* speak, also, of seeing or perceiving principles and relations ; and they are right. If I can be said to perceive anything, I can perceive that two apples and two pears make four bodies, that the whole of an apple is greater than any of its parts, that extension is a necessary attribute of body ; these and all other actualized general principles or laws may be as clearly and positively under my vision as any material object can be. The principles are made persisting facts, through substances ; and can therefore be perceived in connection with them. As incarnated, I can only perceive matter, minds which are themselves embodied, and their several *rational* properties and *relations ;* but the percept is gained by penetration into the rational nature of their characteristics. There is no *intervening representative*, but a literal personal acquaintance with the object perceived. The organism is a transparency to the outlooking mind ; but in no sense does it *represent* the object. Neither does the mind represent the objective to itself in thought, but in perception it sees the very object.

When I attend to nothing but the relations of things, the likenesses and unlikenesses, specialties, or class characteristics, yet I literally perceive these facts just as the Creator has realized them in things. I have an immediate perception of the principles of an equilateral triangle, also those of an isosceles and a scalene triangle. I perceive the differences of plan in the three triangles, and the oneness of idea in the common scheme which includes them all. It is in and through things that I perceive these concepts to have become constitutional qualities of things. I perceive each of these schemes to be necessary parts of the general scheme, though, possibly, neither class has ever been perfectly exemplified in matter ; and although a representative triangle, which should be neither equilateral, isosceles, nor scalene, could not possibly be realized in matter.

24 *Perceptive Force.*

But my perception is not of the nature of a representation or mental picture. It is a direct apprehension of principles, and these principles are realized more or less fully as modes or relations, resultant properties of almost everything. They are modes also of thought and of general mental operations. The *percept* or apprehension of rational properties, is a real and positive somewhat, a cognition or knowledge which becomes a definite possession of the mind which has obtained it. The *percept* is not an *act* in any strict sense; the perception proper is the act and the percept the product of that act. Mind is the artist, but it obtains its materials from the object. This is true, also, of concepts; but in these, it elaborates and remodels its materials till they misrepresent the object. In pure perception the apprehension is one with the object: it is the immediate cognition of the embodied truth: it does not *represent* the truth, but *it is the literal principle introduced into the perceiving mind.*

A truth or principle, from its nature, which is thought, not substance, may exist as the same identical principle in any number of minds, and be actualized or substantialized in any number of substances. The principle is not, like substance, limited to one place and capable of being in the possession of but one person, but a thousand minds may each possess it at the same time: thus, a percept once obtained, the mind may turn to it at all times to find the truth presentatively, even in the absence of objective substance embodying it. It may not be always under the eye of consciousness; yet when it is recalled and perceived it is a perception of the very principle itself. Thus it is that all actual knowledge is intuition or immediate perception. "Memory," as Reid affirms, "is an immediate perception of things;" but not, as he says, of "things past," for the principles of things do not pass away; and memory is concerned only with the subjective.

Perceptive Force. 25

Concepts are possible principles not actualized in things; yet they, too, are rational plans, schemes, thoughts, which must be as indestructible as the mind which conceived them. All incidental and collateral proof is in favor of the position, that no thought ever is forgotten. In moments of great peril, great excitement, or great mental quickening of any kind, every occurrence of the past, represented by its ideas, comes into consciousness. We can perceive no past events, and know no past events in the present; but the events did once occur, and the mind, perceiving them, constructed its own thoughts of them, and these thoughts are imperishable; they recur to us when the events have passed. These thoughts, in so far as they were pure percepts, were literal transcripts of concerned principles, retained always for direct perception. They were also correct recognitions of the changeable and contingent.

It is necessary to assume that we are capable of perceiving substances and properties as they really are; that is, we must rely upon the credibility of our powers of perception, since we can have nothing else to fall back upon; if these fail us, we are left in outer darkness; but if they are trustworthy, our knowledge can be made reliable. The possibility of philosophy, as a subjective science, turns upon this vital pivot, — the trustworthiness of Perceptive Force. Let us admit the mendacity of this Power, and all knowledge becomes an uncertainty if not an impossibility; it ceases to be a *knowledge.* This can never be accepted without proof, and proof is impossible from the nature of the supposition.

There is a favorite theory that we cannot perceive things as they are in themselves; but only as they are in their relations to us. Doubtless things are to us as we perceive them to be, and not otherwise; but we may perceive them to be as they really are in their own specific natures and outgrowing relations. If we can perceive

Perceptive Force.

them as they are related to ourselves, why not as related to each other? Perception is a cognitive act, not a sensation. The above theory denies the essential nature of Perceptive Force, and robs it of its character of penetrating, simple insight. We can perceive nothing as existing without relations certainly, since nothing does so exist; and we must *perceive* things as they are, otherwise the act is not *perception.* Perceptive force can invent nothing; it can only read the existing somewhat, whether substance, property, or process. Whoever possesses perceptive power, in even the weakest degree, so far as he can perceive at all, must perceive correctly. We have no right to confound this mental act with that of conception, which is the process of originating theories and presumed truths; which may have no existence objectively.

All direct intuition must necessarily carry with it its own evidence. I am here looking into the object and recognizing just how much I perceive of it or know about it. If I would perceive more, I must look further and deeper into the object, till I have fathomed its whole nature; for, evidently, no perceptive knowledge can come to me at second hand; and a question of experience can have no proof outside of itself. An adequate percept must involve a full apprehension and perfect knowledge of an object in its whole nature and in its remotest coördinations, not with ourselves alone, but with all things whatsoever. Such reach of perceptive power may belong only to the Infinite; the finite act, if necessarily limited in its range, is yet sustained by a persisting faculty which may be exercised without limit.

The senses are used as eye-glasses, hence we must be mindful of their possible imperfections. While the material organism is called in to aid perception, the organism itself should be perfect of its kind, in order to the certainty of perfect results; and as it is doubtful whether the body is ever in absolute health, and under complete subjection to the observer, all perception of material facts must be regarded as possibly faulty, and as almost certainly inadequate. The intervention of extra-organic material aids still further complicates the difficulty; yet because some eyes see objects double, some eye-glasses distort forms and discolor surfaces, and some atmospheres deceive as to distances, few have been disposed to quarrel with the percepts of the physical world; but we have incomparably more ground for relying upon those of the self-luminous world of substantialized principles. Here there is often intrinsic evidence of the truth, till all room for doubt is absolutely withdrawn.

CONSTRUCTIVE FORCE.

WHEWELL says of the early Greek philosophers, "As soon as they had introduced into their philosophy any abstract and general conceptions, they proceeded to scrutinize them by the internal light of the mind alone, without any longer looking abroad into the world of sense. They took for granted that philosophy must result from the relations of those notions which are involved in the common use of language, and they proceeded to seek it by studying such notions. They ought to have reformed and fixed their usual conceptions by observation; they only analyzed and expanded them by reflection; they ought to have sought by trial, among the notions which passed through their minds, some one which admitted of exact application to facts; they selected arbitrarily, and, consequently, erroneously, the notions according to which facts should be assembled and arranged; they ought to have collected clear fundamental ideas from the world of things by *inductive* acts of thought; they only derived results by *deduction* from one or other of their familiar conceptions." The same error has influenced, in a greater or less degree, all attempts at science both physical and metaphysical, though the former, vastly more emancipated from this thralldom, has made comparatively greater progress. It is proper here to remark that all legitimate deductive reasoning is purely presentative; one may perceive step by step the positions taken, every point as clear as light and as true as its antecedent; for demonstration, throughout its entire progress even to its final inference, is a process of immediate perception. The syllo-

Constructive Force.

gism is the golden circle of intuition; but it is intuition of abstract principles, wholly without question as to whether these principles have been realized in nature or whether they have originated in the minds of men, having no actual existence in things. Herein is the great defect of logicians: they confound the constitution of things with their own concepts, and then reason thereon. Mathematicians may do the same; but from the simple nature of the truths with which they deal, there is little room for original theories, and so long as they confine themselves to pure mathematics, they can hardly go astray. The mathematical scheme of things is so clear and self-evident, that in the earliest ages, at the very first awakening of mind, there was little room here for doubt or difference of opinion, and the science of pure mathematics made accurate progress to a completeness which is admitted even at the present day; philosophers have, therefore, questioned whether mathematical truths were innate in the human mind, whether they were originated by it as baseless fancies are, or, like all other truths, whether they exist in and regulate the objective world.

Here is proof of a unity of perceptive powers in all men, and of the success with which the Creator has realized his ideals in his works in that men may thus intuit the simplest leading mathematical principles unerringly; and may go on elaborating less obvious truth in the light of their own minds with absolute infallibility. Indeed from the nature of mind, if deduction be absolutely true in its premises, it must be absolutely correct in its conclusions; but let philosophers attempt an application of mathematical truth or of general logic to any science, hoping thereby to arrive at unperceived facts by deduction, and it is then indispensable that they should perceive in things with perfect accuracy, in some cases even with entire completeness, the original data from which they take their point of departure. This it is difficult if not

Constructive Force.

often impossible to do, and therefore, deduction has become the most direct road to error; its remote conclusions, however demonstrated, intuited, and proved beyond possibility of cavil in the light of their own evidence, cannot be accepted safely till they are re-tested by existing objective facts. Early astronomers, assuming false data touching some of the simplest movements of the heavenly bodies, drew widely erroneous but perfectly demonstrable conclusions as to the entire system of astronomy; and men have logically proved every conceivable dogma which has ever been promulgated among mankind. Truth, then, to be accepted, must not only be perceived as evident, but as an existing element of nature, and true in its relations to other actualized principles. The book to be studied is the universe as it is, where all truth is clearly written out in its proper order, and occupying its own place; but since many of the characters are deeply hidden within their cloddish covers, and difficult to decipher when found, deduction is a beautiful art by which we create possible truth for ourselves; and, comparing these with the record, we may find, to our intense delight, that our thoughts are as God's thoughts, and that we are verily made in the intellectual image of the great Originator.

Hypotheses are rational scaffoldings which one may erect to enable him to observe from a new plane of vision: they may aid him in looking higher or deeper or farther then he otherwise could. Let us distinctly admit the fact that our powers are capable both of perceiving what is, and of constructing schemes of what possibly might be. This originative or constructive force is the mental power which we are now especially considering: it is *conception* as distinguished from *perception*, and includes fancies, imaginations, judgments, comparisons, inferences, arguments, proofs, notions, hypotheses, — every rational product, in short, except direct immediate percepts. The

Constructive Force.

self-acting energy in mind will not rest in the steady un-originative process of pure perception. It possesses, also, a constructive intellectual force, and the exercise of this power is ever varied and fascinating.

Fancy originates an endless wealth of mental pictures, in emulation of the countless variety of material objects ; producing at will not merely new combinations, but orig-inal and even impossible phantoms, often most beautiful and bewitching. This is the nearly irresponsible exercise of constructive power, the almost involuntary use of pent-up, irrepressible energy, which in children is riotous for exercise : they are no more content with merely perceiving the object-world, than with the patented amount of physi-cal activity prescribed by mammas and nurses. The young mind peoples its own kaleidoscopic play-room as the little body revels in the inconvenient restlessness of per-petual motion.

Imagination culls the principles of things and plucks its materials from thence ; but it builds up its new worlds, if not with the same perpetual eagerness, yet with even more cordial and appreciative love. It seeks, also, to express its concepts, giving them outward being tangible to others — a body, as it were, to the rational soul. Thus Powers originated the concept of his *Greek Slave* and embodied it in marble ; and Longfellow created *Evange-line* and incarnated his thought in language.

Probable hypotheses, as provisional suppositions, — at-tempts at approximation to the truth, to be tested and either accepted or set aside, — are doubtless inevitable. Mind gains command of its powers by this ceaseless ac-tivity of personal thought ; but as the mature man ceases to gymnasticize merely as an occupation, and exerts him-self towards the securing of definite, desired ends, so speculation belongs preëminently to the childhood of sci-ence. Matured science has planted itself on more stable foundations ; and is learning to be more content with the

Constructive Force.

study of existing facts. To the physicist who makes his hypotheses his ordinary working tools, they are of incalculable value; for they are good tools to work with, but poor material to work upon. In pure rational science, the chances are that one ultimately mistakes his hypothetical platforms for natural and legitimate foundations. Logic proves to him how strong and inter-dependent his hypothesis can be made at every point, till he really thinks it *should be* identical with the actual system of things: he would create the universe after this model undoubtedly!

Philosophy has been literally despoiled by the foolhardy enterprise of her handmaid, Logic. Seamstress by vocation, Logic should employ herself only in making up garments; but she interferes arrogantly in the production of the raw material, and the result is manifest in her numberless shining webs of mental shoddy. According to the great Anglo-Saxon godfather of the mantua-maker, Logic is properly concerned only with *the laws of thought as thought;* but, blinded by her autocratic dicta, he also has been led to confound her logical concepts with pure percepts. This vital error has crept in everywhere;—thinkers, now, as in the earliest ages, obtaining a supply of fragmentary half-facts, retire into some shaded mental corner and clamor vigorously for Logic to make them up. She does make them up; and with a thread of her own so strong that it absolutely cannot break or wear away! One is intoxicated by the consecutive, business-like tact with which she adjusts each part to all the others in an admirably symmetrical whole.

"Long live my system!" cries the philosopher, with enthusiasm; but new facts in the actual constitution of things are so many remorseless shears when brought in contact with the *system.* Logic patches and patches, until, at last, some vital breach is made, and the system drops in pieces. Here is an epitome of the history of specula-

Constructive Force. 33

tion. System after system had its perceived and incon·testable truths; but they were elaborated too much. Logic is invincible only when she uses her needle in the service of materials as enduring as her own thread.

Originality, in any valuable sense of that term, is not possible in philosophy. Who talks of an original Columbus, Linnæus, or Agassiz? The philosopher must stand by the universe as it is, precisely as the historian should by the events which have been; but while the latter deals with second-hand facts, and balances probabilities, the former should be an eye-witness to all he affirms, if not he will be but a blind guide. There is genius manifested in seizing upon the right facts; and genius in ordering a lucid arrangement of materials, and in felicitous modes of expression; but here its province ends. It would be as easy for us to *think the substance of an apple into existence* as it would to *think the law of gravitation into operation*, and as easy to create the material apple-tree as to create any of *its* already established modes and processes. Then, since all existing facts are beyond being tampered with by us, of what value are the systems of all the brilliant thinkers who are recreating the schemes of things in their mental laboratories, except as mental gymnasiums for the benefit of themselves and their pupils? One might as reasonably expect to learn the manners and customs of the Asiatics by blowing himself vigorously with a palm-leaf turned into a Yankee fan, as to learn the established nature of things through the ingeniously elaborated systems of the rival schools. The race has indeed made most wonderful and immense progress; and metaphysical discipline has given to many minds a marvelous sharpness and subtilty of perception and reasoning powers, as all exercise develops the appetency by which it is produced; but the vital hindrance to progress in assured knowledge has always been, not so much in the intricacy and difficulty of the truths to be apprehended,

Constructive Force.

as in *the fallacy that we can conceive and elaborate the principles of an existing universe by subjective processes of reasoning and reflection*. As we ourselves are coördinated parts of this universe, subjects of its laws, constituted by its principles, and made, apparently, with a strong mental likeness to the great Originator, even·these elaborative processes have not led us wholly astray ; but there is abundant evidence that no one has yet been eminently successful in "thinking" again the original scheme of things, or in "reasoning" it within the proper bounds. In the beginning, He actualized his own ideals — at least there they are to-day and forever, as matter of fact ; the Philosopher needs to be sharp-eyed and simple-tongued, that is all.

It cannot be that the *method* in philosophy must determine the system. Method determines everything only in system-making. If one is intent on discovering existing facts, his method becomes wonderfully simple : he begins by observing things, and ends by stating his observations. Nature's facts are not strung like beads on a cable of logic, and liable to be disarranged or entangled ; it makes very little difference what one begins to observe ; he may look where he will, at whatever class of facts he pleases, and may state his discoveries as they are made, with no fear of discrepancies, certain, if his perceptive powers may be relied upon, that he must be able to perceive realities. Of course he will make grievous mistakes ; he must first slough off his prejudices and educational traditions, for if he has been taught *logical philosophy*, he will be forever comparing, reasoning, drawing inferences, systematizing, and attempting originality with all the facility of acquired habit. A preconceived theory will adduce abundant evidence of its truthfulness from most unexpected sources and in perfect sincerity. It would be unfair to be unforgiving of educational mistakes ; our limitations must be charitably remembered !

PERCEPTION DISTINGUISHED FROM CONCEPTION.

WHEN the mind perceives only partially, it may then unconsciously misstate and misrepresent the fact, because it instinctively attempts to supply deficiencies; and is able by its innate *constructive force*, from the material already obtained, to create completed notions which seem consistent and truthful to itself, and which it easily but indiscriminately confounds with pure percepts. I am desirous to carefully indicate the differences between these two modes of mental operation and their results.

Perception presupposes an *object* to be cognized; and whether that object be simple or complex, substantial or affectional, material or mental, concrete or general, contingent or necessary, relative or absolute, the percept is nothing but a simple intelligent apprehension of the object. Conception, on the other hand, does not suppose an object to be directly cognized: it requires only objective raw material (if I may indicate the analogy between intellectual and mechanical processes of construction), which it makes up into original notions, ideas, or hypotheses — concepts of its own. It does this by processes of thought, fancies, imaginations, suppositions, arguments, and decisions of its own; by these various modes it can construct an endless diversity of widely differing results. The concept is not usually at one with any existing fact, though it may be so, as the constitutions of mind and matter have evidently the same origin; the laws of thought, therefore, if properly followed, will sometimes run parallel with the laws of things. I may *conceive* a

36 *Perception distinguished from Conception.*

truth before I can *perceive* it; but I shall not know whether or not it be an existing, objective truth, until I can perceive whether it is or is not such by really cognizing the object to which it pertains. If the truth be a general law of things, as the law of gravitation, I may trace it in many of its modes of operation; may determine its action under different conditions by mathematical calculations, and then carefully observe whether or not these computations are borne out by facts, as mathematical physicists have done so marvelously with the laws of motion; or, if the truth be one admitting of tangible quantitative demonstration, I may weigh and measure with the nicest accuracy, and under the widest variety of conditions, as all practical physicists are perpetually doing. But the majority of rational truths are not quantitative but qualitative; they are truths of *kind* or *intension*, not of *amount* or *extension*, and as they can be neither weighed nor measured by relative gravity, or numbers, or time, or space, or any quantity; they are dealt with by comparison, analogy, argument, and demonstration. Here is room for abundance of fallacy and honest mistake; and the only remedy is in a pure intellectual insight into the very nature of the modes and principles under consideration. That we are endowed with some degree of this perceptive force, it is necessary to assume, nor can we doubt it, any more than we can doubt the fact of our personal existence itself, for it belongs to the same class of truths — it is itself a question of pure and simple intuition.

By what tests, then, may we distinguish percepts from concepts?

1. The intellectual operations by which they are acquired are dissimilar. *Apprehending* an existing, *actual truth*, requires a widely different mental exercise from *originating* a *possible truth*. The one is observation, requiring an effort to look into the nature of the object under consideration, while the other is constructive and

Perception distinguished from Conception. 37

demands the building up and fortifying of a position by argument or otherwise. In the one case we shall find ourselves compelled to study the object, till we can fathom its nature by steady and direct insight; in the other, from such ideas as we have already acquired, we elaborate our mental structure with the same parental love for the result, that the artist feels in the construction of his handicraft. If we attend to the rational process by which we acquire any thought, we can thus determine the nature of the thought itself.

This is the subjective side of the test; we may apply it on the objective side also; and this is necessary, since our theories are so often educational or the accepted concepts of other minds like our own; or they have been held so long that we have forgotten the processes by which we obtained them.

2. If a pure percept be held up to its object we shall find it reaffirmed as the exact intellectual apprehension of that object; while deeper penetration into the nature and relations of a *professed object* will either convert a concept, logically obtained, into a direct percept, as it sometimes may, or the real object will give evidence that its presumed counterpart is only a sham.

3. *Self-evidence* has been given as the primary test of an intuitive principle. If by this is meant that when a principle is perceived to be an existing property of things, it must then be accepted on its own testimony, this obviously is correct. But if, as sometimes appears, it is meant that a rational principle must be accepted as truth on the intrinsic evidence of the principle itself, as an abstract or logical principle, I entirely demur. An incredible amount of error has arisen from just this source — from the failure to discriminate between the self-evidence of a rational principle, as a lucid possible principle, and its self-evidence as an existing property of Being. Many propositions seem extremely clear, probable, and reason-

38 *Perception distinguished from Conception.*

able; we perceive their faultless internal harmony, their unanswerable logic, and even their just relations to many accepted truths, we are charmed with their innate intellectual grandeur: they are symmetrical in themselves, and are self-evidently credible; but we cannot infer, therefore, that they are realized and self-evident in the objective universe. We can perceive all classes of ideas: we reason about both concepts and percepts continually; and draw logical inferences from them both, often without discriminating one class from the other; and thus it is, that in philosophy, psychology, moral, religious, political, and social sciences, we have only so many systems of mingled logical truth and equally logical error. Here, apparently, it is *method* which determines everything; only plant yourself at the right point of vision, and everything around you becomes self-luminous at once; but directly opposite theories, from their directly opposite stand-points, are equally lucid and equally self-evident. They have some of their deepest roots, too, in things; but, alas, obviously not all of them. There can be but one existing actualized philosophy, but one veritable *science* of psychology, one code of morals, one, both absolute and relative, religion, one political science, innate in the structure of related minds; and one social science, equally grounded in social natures. Principles must become the self-evident, literal properties of Being, and be perceived as really existing in the innate constitutions of their substances, or all their apparent self-evidence is only artificial light which can go but a very little way towards illuminating the actual universe. If man is really endowed with a reliable power or intellectual force for apprehending the nature of things, and for discriminating between the real and imitative, then ontology, including the ontology of rational concepts, which are the realities of finite constructive thought, is the whole of universal philosophy; and is a science which may be acquired by pure and simple perception.

Perception distinguished from Conception. 39

4. *Necessity of belief* has been adduced as evidence of an intuitive truth. If the truth is one of such primary character that the necessity of belief is positive and unconditioned, depending upon no other truth for corroborative support, like the truths of personal existence and the existence of the external world, the necessity of the belief is an evidence of its truth. Nothing but a theory upheld by logic can shake such a belief, and even that can never destroy it. But the necessity for believing many things is conditioned upon the belief in certain other things which stand to them in the relation of antecedents; thus, the ultimate question again is, whether or not the necessity of belief lies in the nature of things. In short, in every attempt to adduce tests, such as " Intuitive truths are incomprehensible, that is, we perceive *that they are*, without being able to perceive *how or why they are;*" "Intuitive truths are simple as opposed to complex," etc. we always return again to the same issue —the question of fact as to the nature of things; which is itself dependent upon the credibility of our perceptions.

Perceptive Force must have a vastly wider range of vision than has generally been assigned to it. Conception has been regarded as the process of abstract thinking which gives generic ideas — which classifies and comprehends under a general term everything which is common to every individual of the species. Thus the *conception* of the genus tree would be neither a first *perception* nor yet the mental reproduction or representation of such a percept; but it would be connecting together, in thought, the common qualities of trees into one general idea, which should stand for all trees equally well. But are generic ideas necessarily obtained by this elaborative process?

Conceiving anew the general scheme of any great class of natural objects! No hyperbole of Irish witticism seems

40 *Perception distinguished from Conception.*

to me more naive from its innocent suggestion of impossibilities. How is it certain that one has quite hit the true scheme, unless he can perceive the existing plan with which to compare it? Is it likely that all thinkers are to agree in even the essentials of the many schemes which each is thus compelled to originate or to accept on trust from his neighbor? Imagine a three-years old baby, for example, thinking out the generic scheme of so simple a thing as a leaf. It must be at once comprehensive and definite, must equally include the stiff needles of the pines and the webs of broadcloth on the palms; the ragged shreds on the pin-oak and the smooth flounces of the tulip, the green silk of the aspens and the yellow flannels of the old mullens. Can you believe he is able to think anything comparable to this, when he does not yet know that three and two make five? Yet he will tell you, without hesitation, that each of these widely different objects is a leaf. The explanation is simple: he looks through his young eyes and sees the material leaves, each the standing record of an actualized plan, which is common to them all; he recognizes a similarity of conditions and of functions; it really exists, and he perceives that it does; for it is no more hidden, or obscure, or difficult to be seen than are the leaves themselves, with their varied conditions and modifications. An older person might express the common properties and relations by a variety of words, while the child has but one word, leaf; yet that means something definite to him which he accepts on his own experience. He has personal observation enough to assure him there is a common bond which makes them all leaves. If a knowledge of generic terms is to be gained by elaborative processes of thought, this necessitates disciplined mental labor, yet the great fact remains that the child will lisp out the generic names of strange cats, and dogs, and trees, and horses; and he is .no more at a loss how to classify most objects of his acquaintance than his

Perception distinguished from Conception. 41

father is. Surely he *perceives* the likeness of type, perceives the actualized common principle, and readily associates the *name* given him with the *fact* which it represents.

The fundamental error of not discriminating *percepts* from *concepts* enters into many attempts at *classification*, creating endless confusion as to whether it is the province of philosophy to classify the *former* or the *latter*. The science of the actual can have to do with human concepts, only in so far as they evidence the nature of the mind which originates them. It is with the veritable *principles of things* that *Philosophy* is primarily concerned. These she would explain to us, classified and systematized; but it is no more Philosophy who is to do this classifying, than it is she who is to create the principles to be classified. The Creator has systematized, not his own *handiwork* merely, but his own *head work* also; He has not only classified substances, but He has classified the principles by which substances are constituted. What, then, is left for science but to take careful note of the fact?

All the generic ideas comprehended in general terms, such as triangle, parallel lines, horse, tree, mountain, world, solar system, or man, are contained entire in each individual of the class. A child, who had never seen any tree except one isolated maple, might obtain from it as full and correct a perception of the genus tree as he could have after he had seen a hundred oaks, willows, and pines; for everything which belongs to the generic tree is in the maple, and of course, may be perceived there. It is the individual and specific differences which he is unable to see in the maple alone; for these are not in the maple. In the individual we perceive the peculiarities which do not belong to the class.

Nature creates the likeness and analogy between the different species. She herself compares them; we have only to note the resemblances and differences. We may

42 *Perception distinguished from Conception.*

get both the specific and the general in the concrete; as in the solitary maple; then we may lay aside the individual and attend only to what is common in the species or genus, then to what is common in all bodies, then to what is common in all known substances; but we might possibly obtain as complete and positive a knowledge of substance *per se*, from one maple-tree, as from all bodies and minds collectively. I do not say that each person actually does get his knowledge of the general and universal in the concrete; but I affirm that the intrinsic nature of the universal, and everything except the fact of the universality of its actualization in things, may be perceived in the individual; and many, if not most minds, apparently perceive almost everything in the concrete. It seems to be the primary and normal process of knowledge-gathering.

Abstraction is the converging of attention upon the one property in question, to the exclusion of everything else. In classification of principles, subjectively, we fix the attention upon the given property till we perceive it distinctly, then we look for it in the wide range of objects in which it inheres, and putting aside all else we proclaim that nature has classified these widely differing objects by giving them, in this regard, an actually identical constitution. *Classification, then, is the abstraction of the common modes of things through perception.* As each object has many and various modes, of course it can be variously classified; and yet each classification be merely the product of so many differing yet veritable perceptions. The secret of a valuable classification would lie in the selection of fundamental and distinctive characteristics.

Why so much credit has been given to the constructive, that is, the reflective and elaborative processes of mind in abstraction and classification, it would be difficult to say. It is evident that perceiving the coördinations and ramifications of general principles, is only a more far-sighted ex-

Perception distinguished from Conception. 43

ercise of direct rational perception. Classification, to be successfully, systematically, and extensively pursued, only requires clear, disciplined, and penetrating insight, with the ability to perceive relations and coördinations with as much distinctness as we can perceive the things related and coördinated — for all relations and correlations are as veritable a part of the actual universe as any other. There must be an eye to real resemblances and differences, even of a most subtle and recondite character, and a gift of concentration to enable one mentally to abstract properties from their coördinations. All this only requires Perceptive Force of a high order, not differing in kind from that of a less efficient neighbor ; but broader in degree, either from native endowments or culture, or both combined. Of course, such a mind must not be wanting in judgment, the power of reasoning, or any other phase of Constructive Modes, for the two great modes of force are so practically allied as to be almost inseparable in every mental act. They coöperate in producing all the best results of mental effort, inasmuch as they are both modes of force pertaining to one indivisible mind, and are mutually adapted to the furtherance of its intellectual needs ; yet it is by Perception only that we can actually perceive or know the existing universe.

Whoever would penetrate deeply into a system of truths like those around us, which are at once simple, wide-reaching, beneficent, and instinct with a moral sublimity which no words may ever express, must himself possess a noble purpose and a large perseverance. Above all, he must be content to remain a simple learner, humble and self-forgetful — the recipient and not the donor. The eyes are servants of the heart, and whatever we look for, we shall find, if nature has it among her treasures.

H. D. Thoreau, one of the clear-sighted naturalists, says of himself: "In my botanical rambles, I find that, first, the idea or image of a plant occupies my thought,

44 *Perception distinguished from Conception.*

though it may seem very foreign to this locality,—no nearer than Hudson's Bay,—and for weeks or months I go thinking of it, and expecting it, unconsciously, and at length I surely see it. This is the history of my finding a score or more of rare plants, which I could name. A man sees only what concerns him. A botanist, absorbed in the study of grasses, does not distinguish the grandest pasture oaks. He, as it were, tramples down oaks unwittingly in his walk, or at most sees only their shadows." If this is true of the material, which is forced upon us sharply through every sense, how much more true of the rational, which has no reacting elbows to thrust out at us in mute appeal for recognition! All the noblest pearls of the creative thought are laid carefully away in their well-protected cabinets.

When one can fully recognize the fact that there can be no other *Teacher* than the great *Author* who wrote the work he is studying, and that all others must be mere *expounders*, he will find in everything traces of the loving mother teaching her children by the most winning processes ; wooing them to learn by holding out all her beautiful forms and colors ; her buds and blossoms, and birds, and ever beautiful changes ; but he will find, also, the inexorable purpose of the earnest Father, who, laying his principles deeply and unalterably beyond all created intervention, is thus ever rigorously but tenderly enforcing upon him the need of an earnest and most scrupulous application which alone can bring him an adequate reward.

WE PERCEIVE THE REAL OBJECT.

PREVIOUS to the time of Reid, it seems to have been almost universally held by philosophers, that, in *Perception*, it is not the real and literal *object* which is itself directly observed; but that we perceive the *representation, idea,* or *image* of the object alone. The representative somewhat was supposed to be either mental or extra-mental, according to the harmonic requirements of each peculiar theory. There can be no better illustration than this of the results of too much reasoning and speculation upon simple questions of fact; which must, in the nature of things, be decided upon the direct evidence of their own testimony; and by each perceiving mind for itself. A variety of highly ingenious, plausible hypotheses were constructed, in all of which it was held that we cannot immediately perceive real objects of any character whatever; whether of bodies, minds, or their properties. These hypotheses were, one or other of them, accepted almost without question by all the thinkers; possibly because such ingenious theories seemed so learned and *self-evident* that it was an intellectual delight to be able to appreciate them, and to feel that one had risen in intelligence above the masses, who still held implicitly to the certainty that they could directly and really perceive the very things themselves.

Reid says: "We have here a remarkable conflict between two contradictory opinions wherein all mankind are engaged. On the one side stand all the vulgar, who are unpracticed in philosophical researches, and guided by the uncorrupted primary instincts of nature. On the

46 *We perceive the Real Object.*

other side, stand all the philosophers, ancient and modern; every man, without exception, who reflects. In this division, to my great humiliation, I find myself classed with the vulgar."

On all questions of direct fact like this, it is pretty safe to stand side by side with the unprejudiced masses whose testimony is of necessity disinterested, they having no theory to support. An appeal to the general consciousness to give the simple narrative of its daily and hourly perceptions, is always of immense value; it is safer to credit it on any and every question of direct face-to-face perception, than to turn for aid to the constructive talents of the very wisest in all the ages. They may explain away the testimony of one's own very eyesight, till he really will come to doubt the assurances of his immediate vision. It is like being in the presence of a company of wonderful conjurers who show you so many impossible marvels, and who overturn the stability of nature with such astonishing facility, that you are left powerless in their hands, and, for the moment, are utterly at a loss whether to decide that everything which you see is real or whether everything is only a seeming.

After such an ordeal, one must unlearn all his former opinions and begin to look out upon the world again with the simplicity of a little child; he will see objects about him on every hand, and as he stands in their uncovered presence, as it were, face to face with them, he can have no doubt that he is everywhere looking at real things. To the skeptic's argument, that he cannot know there is an external world because we cannot directly perceive things, but only their representatives, he can answer boldly: " I do perceive things. The external world is here, and I am looking at it. I see both its physical traits, and its pure rational principles as existing and acting properties. I perceive all these directly, presentatively, and with positive assurance."

The affirmation of direct perception has its weight even among philosophers; theories of the necessary intervention of mental modifications, or of any other similitudes in the act of perception, belong now either to the dead past or to essentially un-English minds, who seem to be defective in matter of fact directness of insight. A representative perfume from a Lily of the Valley is unattainable to the most artistic Anglo-Saxon imagination; but the real perfume comes to us and presents itself. Ever since the founder of Scottish Philosophy arose, asserting the right of the thinkers to perceive things themselves, and not their mere effigies, the thinkers also have perceived certain classes of things, at least, just like all the commonest mortals. Thus much of progress has been made: it is an important step towards the general admission, that we can perceive objects not merely as they are in their coordinations with ourselves, but as they are in themselves and in their various other relations also.

WE PERCEIVE THE SUBSTANCE OF BODIES.

WE have been taught that we can never perceive substance; that what we really perceive is only phenomena, the changing modes and manifestations of substance; while the substance itself, standing under these phenomena, is known by us to exist only through a discursive process of reasoning.

Tell a downright practical man, who is looking at a rose-bush with its wealth of leaves and flowers, that he does not directly perceive the very substance of the rose-bush which is now present before him, and he will mock you. "Look here!" he cries; "I rend off this branch, and I see the very grain and texture of the wood from bark to pith. I crush these leaves; the whole of them lies here in the palm of my hand. Here is the very and actual substance of them all; do you tell me that I don't see it? Tell me, then, that everything in life is deception; for if I do not see the very ground-work of this rose-bush, I can see nothing whatever. I'd be a Punch and Judy in a puppet-show sooner than a man made only to be cheated!"

Your only resource now is to confound him with oracular sayings.

"Matter is incognizable in itself." — *Aristotle.*

"The objects of perception are the various qualities of bodies." — *Reid.*

"Mind and matter, as known or knowable, are only two different series of phenomena or qualities; mind and matter as unknown and unknowable, are the two different substances in which these two different series of phenomena are supposed to inhere." — *Hamilton.*

We perceive the Substance of Bodies. 49

"The essence, the being in itself, whatever it be, whether of bodies or of God, or of the soul, falls not under consciousness." — *Cousin.*

"The connection of quality and substance is not perceived but is thought." — *Hickok.*

"Matter as opposing our muscular energies, being immediately present to consciousness in terms of force ; and its occupancy of space being known by an abstract of experiences originally given in terms of force; it follows that forces, standing in certain correlations, form the whole content of our idea of Matter." — *Spencer.*

Shall not the practical man bow to this array of thought, attested by some of the highest names which have ever been joined to human authority? Poor, clear-sighted, untaught man! Let him learn to distrust his own senses, since through them all he gets the same positive affirma tion, that he sees, touches, and tastes the very substance of bodies, as variously modified.

Here is an apple! I hold on my hand the whole of its substance with all its innate properties. I taste it ; does this something which is related to my sense of taste, and is called flavor, — does this something which affects me, inhere in a substance or in no substance? If in a substance, then I must eat the substance to obtain the flavor ; if in no substance, then it inheres in nothing and here is a phenomenon with nothing underlying it. Can anything be more evident than that this bit of matter which is extended to nearly the size of my fist, of a roundish shape, a ruddy color, a delightful fragrance, and a pleasant taste — substance wedded to special properties in a common unity — together comprise this apple ; and that this apple with its definite size, shape, color, fragrance, flavor, and other properties or modes is so much organized substance, which I directly perceive. To my great gratification, I find the authority of my consciousness to this effect also confirmed by the catholic testimony of the vast

50 *We perceive the Substance of Bodies.*

host of unprejudiced observers. If human *Perceptive Force*, close and immediate like this in its action, cannot, without a learned elaboration of the Reasoning Powers, distinguish the grand kohinoor, real existence, from a paste bauble representing it, we might be expected to eschew its testimony altogether.

But at least one accredited philosopher of genius and position does maintain that we can perceive actual substance, immediately and literally. This opinion of Dr. McCosh came to me as the shadow of a great rock in a weary land, after I had for years maintained the same in public and private; seeking everywhere in vain for corroborating testimony. I have rested in its shade; finding strength therein for a more trusting reliance on intuition during all the subsequent investigation of kindred topics.

We cannot, indeed, perceive substance except as endowed with properties; for it does not otherwise exist, at least in our universe. Properties are forces and capacities, modes of present existence and action; and to perceive the property is to perceive the somewhat possessing and manifesting this property. We can touch a solid body, though we cannot touch a substance without body and solidity; but neither can we touch the abstract principles of extension and solidity. Evidently, then, we touch the real substance as extended and endowed with resisting force.

Smiles, dimples, and frowns are not wholly material facts; yet can there be smile, dimple, or frown and no face producing it? Do we perceive the smile alone? On the contrary, we perceive the face in the act of smiling, the substance in its present mode of a smiling face. Leaves and acorns are not the whole of an oak; the oak is not the whole of matter, and matter may not be the whole of substance; but when we perceive leaves, acorns, oak, and bodies generally, are we to believe that they are not real

We perceive the Substance of Bodies. 51

substance thus modified? How can they be merely the attitudes, changes, and processes of a something itself unseen?

Pure principles alone, as extension, divisibility, form, color, or all properties comprehending the total of actualized principles, cannot be the sole components of substance *per se;* but substance constituted by these coördinated and actualized principles must comprise the whole of existing or created substance. The determinate somewhat which is literally extended in this apple, which reacts when acted upon, resisting pressure and manifesting solidity, which has this color, this form, this fragrance, this weight; which is divisible, and which, in short, possesses a series of adapted properties, is the whole of the bit of substance constituting this apple. Substance, with its realized properties, we may directly perceive. It is not necessary here to dwell upon the influence and coöperation of the *organism* in producing sensation; it is enough that there is something in the object, which, by being modified in the organism, is thus perceived; something to be tasted as pleasant rather than disagreeable, to be noted as ruddy instead of black; and generally to be perceived as affecting us in some particular manner and not otherwise. The organism has its own material, quantitative relations with other bodies, and the mind must study these as objective facts, precisely as it studies everything else which does not belong to its own personality.

If we can perceive anything touching unconstituted, uncreated, absolute substance, we must do so by abstraction, by dropping out of view the existing nature of things and looking directly at the substance which remains in its own uncreated integrity. It would be premature to attempt this before we have obtained a far more complete and discriminating view of constituted substance — of the nature of the alliance between primitive substance and coördinated rational principles, and of the character

52 *We perceive the Substance of Bodies.*

of these adapted principles, which as realized in substance, are its existing rational constitution.

If it should still be denied that we can really perceive substance itself, as now endowed with a rational coöperative constitution, in the nature of the case there can be no mode of proving the position except by direct appeal to facts, and to one's own personal experience. If each person does not directly perceive substance, manifesting its various modes of property in all the many things about him, no one else can do this for him. He must wait for a more enlightened vision!

WE PERCEIVE BODIES AT A DISTANCE.

IT is currently maintained by philosophers that the field for direct perception is limited to the human organism. Nothing can be *immediately* perceived, they maintain, which is not literally within this organism, or in direct contact with it. Everything at a distance, it is held, is cognized *mediately* or *representatively*. Thus it is maintained that I do not, through the eye, immediately or directly perceive the paper and pen with which I am writing. I can perceive them directly only through the hand which is in contact with them. Looking out now upon the mountain and the wide plain, they insist that I do not directly perceive trees, houses, ships, water, land, or clouds; but what I do really and presentatively perceive, is only the light reflected from these several bodies; and that I *infer* from this the existence of the bodies thus represented.

"An external existence and an organ of sense," says Sir William Hamilton, "as both material, can stand in relation only according to the laws of matter. According to these laws things related, connected, must act and be acted on; but a thing can act only where it is. Therefore the thing perceived, and the percipient organ, must meet in place — must be contiguous."

London and San Francisco had not chatted together across the Atlantic and one continent when Sir William wrote the above paragraph. Electricity can make the steel hammers of the antipodes beat in cadence like next door neighbors — is it not possible, then, to suppose that light may establish its telegraph between the mind and

54 *We perceive Bodies at a Distance.*

the distant object? Since human constructive talent has practically discovered how to annihilate space in the material world, surely, if there is an Author of the creative scheme of the present cosmos, he may be credited as knowing how to do likewise; especially if, as in this case, the fact is positively attested by consciousness.

Certainly no laws of matter or mind need be violated. The mind and the distant body each acts and is acted upon by the other, and each in its own place, but through the aid of other coöperative forces. We know that a subtle material communication does really exist all the way between the organism and each distant object; yet why should this fact affect either the immediacy, the accuracy, or the distinctness of the perception? Neither the organism nor the undulations of light *represent* the object; it *presents* itself; and not to the bodily organ, but to the coördinated mental eye. It is not here, pressing its image upon the retina, but off there in the distance, establishing its relations with the perceiving mind. The material media are coördinated with the organism, with the perceiving mind, and with the object perceived; but as coöperative modes, not as a representative of either. Each organic sense has its especial extra-organic chain of communication with the objective world. Something material conveys the undulations of light from the illuminated body to the eye, conveys sound from the sounding body to the ear, heat from the heated body to the nerves of sensation, and odor from the odoriferous body to the nostrils. Something material reaches the coördinated organism in every case of sensation, producing a responsive modification in its special sense; but this organic modification is as much extra-mental as is the distant mountain or the far-off whizzing, rushing cannon-ball which produces it. The sensation is mental; so is its accompanying perception of the object which causes this sensation; but neither of these are represented by material

We perceive Bodies at a Distance. 55

forces. If, then, the mind can perceive an object directly, when the intervening organism and the object are in contact, why should it not do this also though there be a more extended chain of communication between them? The motion of heat, light, sound, or any other impulse from the object, enables that object to present itself to the living subject, who must then directly perceive through its own powers of insight or intuition.

The organic modification may be itself perceived and apprehended by the mind; but the perceptive act, even in this case, must be purely mental. Mental feeling — sensation proper — is produced in connection with the organic modification; but it is no more to be confounded with it than perception is. Consciousness includes both sensation proper and perception proper in the same act.

The mind can perceive also the extra-organic causes of the organic modification; it can distinguish and separate these, can follow them all back to the distant object, as the mountain or cannon-ball; which nevertheless, it immediately perceives and knows. Do you ask *how* the intellectual perception is conditioned upon the organic modification? This connection we shall consider hereafter. But whether or not we are able to perceive *how* or *why* the mind is incarnated and made dependent upon its body for its purely mental knowledge of material things, yet the fact that it is so is patent to us continually. The *reasons* for constituting anything as it is and not otherwise, and for coördinating many several processes in the way that has been done, are not actualized in things, and of course we cannot perceive them. We can only infer and reason in regard to them; but the *how*, the definite manner in which things are related is a legitimate fact, and can therefore be perceived, if we but possess adequate powers to that end.

It is self-evident that the eye could not aid us to perceive bodies if the sun did not assist also with his light.

56 *We perceive Bodies at a Distance.*

He lends us his powerful telescope, with which we annihilate distance. The ship yonder is sailing rapidly on its way. I perceive it, and therefore know that it exists. There are miles intervening; but the space, the atmosphere, the sunshine, the glass in my closed window, the color rebounding from every point of mast and sail into my open eye, and the eye through which I look, are all so transparent or so adapted to assist my vision, that I perceive the real ship: nothing represents it to me; it is there bodily, presenting itself. I might indeed be subject to an optical illusion, certain combinations of the forces of matter might produce an unusual mirage, or my eyes might be diseased and delude me; but we can test the instruments we use, can more thoroughly investigate the material media which seems partially deceptive, and in and through all this, may at length perceive the object by a more full and just insight into all its relations, as well as by direct cognizance of its substantial and constituted existence.

Can any one really doubt that vision may extend its perceptions beyond the calculable limits of space? If we perceive that it does this, what more can be said? Look at the Moon and you have specific evidence that you see the very planet herself, her broad changing face clearly showing you many of her quaint individualisms. A glass powerful enough would reveal as many characteristics of the dimmest fixed star, convincing us by personal experience that the eye and the light alike are normal telescopes practically annihilating distance between bodies.

Ancient philosophers, as we have seen, denied that we could perceive bodies at all; they held that we could only perceive ideas and compelled us to infer or think the existence of an actual world; the later teachers admit that we may immediately perceive such bodies as are in contact with our organisms; but they also compel us to infer or think the existence of all *distant* bodies. How much,

We perceive Bodies at a Distance. 57

then, have we gained? Very much, I admit. Under the former theory Hume could prove that there is no objective world; or at least that we can never be assured of its existence, since we can only perceive its effigies, which at best are only shadows, and may not represent anything substantial. By the later hypothesis we can know that there is an actual objective world, since the organism and everything with which it comes in contact is immediately perceived and distinguished from the *me* of consciousness; yet what a limited domain in which to exercise our boasted *perceptive force.* Our right hands should "touch the East" and our "left hands the West," if we must handle tree, and rock, and cloud, and lay our palms on the brow of distant mountains, to assure ourselves that they are not phantasms. Who is willing to blot out the science of astronomy from immediate perception? Sun, moon, and planets utterly without the pale of direct cognition! Let our heads reach the heavens if we can poke knowledge into them only by laying our foreheads upon the stars!

The ship, which I saw but a moment since, has disappeared behind the mountain. I can no longer affirm that it exists as a ship. I infer that it exists, for I saw it but a little while ago, and I perceive that percept by an act of memory; yet the ship is a perishable structure, and I can only suppose or believe that it still exists, though all probabilities are in favor of its continuance. Who shall convince me that my knowledge of yonder mountain, the clouds hanging above it, the young moon scattering them with its flood of light, and holding back the coming twilight — that my present perception of all these beautiful things is no more immediate or certain than my second-hand belief as to the vanished ship? Have I no present perception of the stars which steal out one by one into the field of my vision? I appeal from this decision to the common testimony of mankind, unprejudiced by a philosophic theory! I appeal to every unbiased personal consciousness, which must affirm the perceived present existence of distant bodies just as unqualifiedly as it affirms its own personal existence. Why may not the field of perception be as broad as the remotest material relations of the organism in which the Perceptive Power is incarnated? Who shall limit the possibilities of human Perceptive Force?

MENTAL AND EXTRA-ORGANIC COÖRDINATIONS.

WHO has ever held that heat and sound represent to us the heated and sounding bodies which produce them? Yet they do this in the same sense in which light does! Light is known to imprint the image of the body from which it emanates upon the retina of the eye; yet it is not this image which the mind perceives! Even though its attention be especially directed to it, it cannot perceive this image; it can only perceive the body represented by the image upon the retina. It perceives this body not in the eye, but off in the distance; in its real position, and with all its proper dimensions. The image itself is inverted and exceedingly minute; and there is a separate likeness printed in each eye.

An optician who would study this organic picture, who would investigate the science of vision in any of its material phases, must do this precisely as the physicist does in any other department of material science; he must study, not his own eyes from within, but other eyes from without. He must become the anatomist, penetrating to the facts of structure, studying them where they are to be found in their places, and investigating the nature of nerves and brain from the very organs themselves; and he must study the laws of light in their coöperation with these organic functions. When he can fathom all the joint mysteries of their action and interaction, he has then unraveled the secrets of vision in its material aspects. Next he must penetrate into the nature and processes arising from the connection between the mind and its organism, question

60 *Mental and Extra-Organic Coördinations.*

the mode by which material affections can influence mental perceptions, the character of mental vision, and the nature of the real observer. All this is within the legitimate domain of Perceptive Force; but there are two distinct departments of that domain. The one is wholly mental, the other wholly material; yet the modes of interaction between the two are all important to be determined.

The mind is competent to testify directly as to the nature of its perceptions, obtained through its organism in a normal state; but it is no more cognizant of the nature of that organism and of its coöperations with itself, than it is of extra-mental facts and processes. All its proper experiences are purely mental; and yet they are related to, and dependent upon coördinated activities, organic and extra-organic. These are adjusted to its needs in a system of pre-arrangements wholly independent of its knowledge or control. No one can discover the nature of his own organic growth, maintenance, or decay; can discover the processes of his digestion, circulation, or any other organic fact whatsoever, through the simple study of his purely mental experiences; yet he can just as well fathom all the coöperative processes which result in the digestion of food or the circulation of the blood, by merely attending to his own feelings as affected by these processes, as he can fathom the processes of vision by simply attending to his subjective perceptions. His sensations and perceptions are conditioned upon his organic modifications; but these modifications are as foreign to himself and as unknown to him except in the sense in which they affect his own personal modes, as are any other material changes. Vision enables him to apprehend distant bodies; but in that apprehension he wholly disregards the material media, and looks beyond into the nature of the things which they have brought him into the right relations for immediately perceiving.

A leaf, absorbing the red light and throwing off the yel-

Mental and Extra-Organic Coördinations. 61

low and blue, appears to us green ; the flowers by similar processes dress themselves to our vision in as many hues as there are colored rays in possible combinations ; and analogy must teach us that it is quite in keeping for the eye to gather up enough rays, thrown off from every point of an object, to give it the miniature fac-simile of the original. The beautiful experiments by which various substances are shown to arrest one or more colored rays of the beam of light and to be transparent to all the rest; and the still more striking processes by which Professor Tyndal proves that certain substances, opaque to all light, are yet transparent to heat, give us such enlarged ideas of the various adaptations of things, that we are better prepared to comprehend the elective processes of the organic eye in vision, or the ear in hearing.

Light and heat are modes of motion ; and each little wavelet must literally deal its own little blow against whatever it touches. As rays of light emanate from every point of the object, each leaving its mark, the whole together must print an impression like in form to the source from whence it comes, and thus, doubtless, impressions, reflections, or pictures of things are printed all over us — as we should perceive, if we had delicacy of vision sufficient to detect them. Such impressions are mirrored in every polished surface, and light must daguerreotype them upon every object on which it falls. They must be on our faces as really as in our eyes, although they do not here so modify the organism as to enable us to look through it at their originals. The impressions themselves must also be diffused, and doubtless also confused with other similar reflections ; while in the eye they are collected and concentrated.

But the millions of waves of light and heat which fall over us continually, dashing against us as literally as the sea-tides beat against the shore, must produce a visible impress upon the general organism, — visible, I mean, to

62 *Mental and Extra-Organic Coördinations.*

eyes gifted with powers which are able constantly to perceive it, as ours are not, except as to some of its coarser and more abiding effects. We may sit all day under the reflected light and warmth of the most beautiful objects, and yet we should know nothing whatever of their effects upon us if we were to remain with blinded eyes. When the sun or some intensely heated body pours his fiery flood over us, we can perceive that without eyesight. Each nerve of sensation, which is in the right angle to catch the beams, is like a separate sense in itself, advertising us of the storm of heat in which we are submerged. We can see the skin visibly redden under such an ordeal, we recognize the brown hue and the thickened texture which are the subsequent results ; and we have only to remember that the mildest light and heat radiated from every object about us, though less marked, is similar in its mode of action.

Sound, also, which is transmitted by motion of the atmosphere, must batter its impress of the sounding body everywhere ; and particularly within the ear, where the organism is especially adapted to concentrate the importunate little sound hammers. The ear can take no note of figure, yet since we know that these sound wavelets must smite us on hands and face, though we are not advertised of the fact by any coördinated organ, and since, aside from the ear, the whole dull mass of organism can help us to no cognizance whatever of sound, we may well believe that never so distinct an image of the sounding body might be battered upon our ears or our faces, and we be none the wiser therefor ! We must question general science ; which alone can determine whether every force whatever, when radiated from matter, does or does not, under the right conditions, produce on the human organism, and indeed on every object whatever, a literal imprint of the form whence it emanated.

Every mode of force is motion-producing, and everything

Mental and Extra-Organic Coördinations. 63

which moves, whether atom or mass, must leave some impress upon everything else with which it comes in contact. We know that there is a perpetual action and counteraction between the organism and its environment. Not only does every object perpetually radiate light and heat ; but it is interchanging electricity, magnetism, chemical influences, and all the other modes of force which are normal to it, so that the sum-total of change and general modification which it perpetually undergoes must be something incalculable. ▪A few special organs aid us in taking note of a few special influences and effects ; but these no more represent the objects producing those effects, nor do the resulting organic modifications, than the white drawing-paper, and the black lead-pencil together represent the artist. The whole system of natural coördinations must be studied, not through subjective experience, but by objective perception. We must immediately perceive these coördinations and their resulting processes ; cognizing them as far as may be through their actual operations. That all things are endlessly coöperative is perfectly evident ; yet the amount of molecular modification which everything constantly undergoes, seems yet to be very generally overlooked.

Physicians prescribe air, sunshine, and change of scene to invalids ; but there is a curious field for speculation (possibly even for mathematical science to determine quantitatively), as to the various proportions of the different influences producing the beneficial results. How much may be attributed to the direct mental stimulus thus communicated? how much to change of air with its modified states and new ingredients, whether absorbed through the lungs or through the skin ? how much to increased exercise, quickening the general activity? and how much is conveyed from the surface of the body to the whole system through the medium of the complete list of chemical, vital, and molecular forces generally, beating

64 *Mental and Extra-Organic Coördinations.*

upon the organism like a perpetual hail-storm — the organism in turn hurling back its overcharge of any mode of force modified and transmuted within itself? A bedridden invalid, stifled in his sheets and blankets, strengthened only by his unrelished food and by the changes of the pitying atmosphere, which will establish its currents of life everywhere more or less energetically, cannot at all perceive the prostrating influences which are at work within and about him. The room-bound sick man, whose vital forces have acted and reacted upon all his surroundings, till they have long since averaged a common level, is condemned a prisoner to inanity and lassitude; pitiless jailers, placed over him by the irrevocable laws of cause and effect. Even a poor fine lady, living in her shaded parlors, can be scarcely more alive to the keenest enjoyments of physical and reacting mental life; yet neither is advised of this, since no process of introspection will include organic cooperations.

All physical science, however, assures us that a sunbrowned skin is wholesome, and that every walk and drive has infinitely more in it than air, exercise, or æsthetic enjoyment. The half-naked children of poverty, when they do not perish of cold and too rude exposure, are hardened and invigorated by the vitality which pours in upon the naked limbs, in free and easy association with the surrounding elements. The weight and volume of atmosphere respired by a healthy pair of lungs has been estimated, and also the enormous amount of insensible perspiration thrown off by a single human body in a day; the results are so statistically and unanswerably given that they startle us into the imperative need of pure air and wholesome clothing, as accessaries to health. But no one has yet presumed to estimate quantitatively the influence of any natural force, as light, heat, magnetism, electricity, etc., in its interaction between the human body and its surroundings; yet enough is known even as to the quantitative rela-

Mental and Extra-Organic Coördinations. 65

tions of these forces to affirm that the action of any one of them upon the organism, and through that upon the mind itself, especially in change of scene and conditions, is so great as to be almost incredible. In the aggregate, they can build up, and they can destroy!

Going to sea, means more even than breathing fresh sea air! A year or two in Europe, South America, or any other remote locality, should have more and immeasurably better life in it than can be crowded into that interval of time at home. Other things being equal, a man who would have lived feebly in one place to the age of seventy, should live vigorously to seventy-five, if the added years could be judiciously spent, at intervals, among a wide variety of scenes. A Hollander, living to middle life in his quaint low-lands, would find the sharp arrows of light from the beautiful Swiss mountains, competent to shoot enthusiasm and strength into him through every pore. It is worth while to be saturated with the many beautiful forms and colors of nature, in various of her most diverse moods ; getting inspiration from them, not through the eye alone, but by becoming a recipient of their ever-varying phases, hues, temperatures, and outlines; and literally exchanging influences with them. Equal action and reaction is nature's law everywhere ; and though a child jumping from his hobby-horse may hardly expect to move the world perceptibly, yet he must produce some infinitesimal change in its center of gravity through his own change of position. The ocean and the mountain, in their greatness, may be but little modified by our interchange with them of coördinated forces ; while we in our weakness may yet be immensely strengthened and renovated thereby. We do well to remember that we are really quantitatively allied to every object about us; so that we are perpetually being acted upon and are unconsciously reacting again as unceasingly to our own good or hurt. The evils of poorly ventilated houses, school-rooms, lecture-rooms, and churches, have never yet been fully and emphatically enough stated; while the benefits resulting from frequent variety and change in all our conditions of life have never been sufficiently enforced. The destruction of the poor even in this also is their poverty; while the possessors of riches, with their frequent drawbacks of dissipation, are yet better practical learners of hygiene than their ever-toiling kinsmen. They who have neither poverty nor riches should be best able to study and practice the laws, not of disease, but of health; to seek not the cure of already acquired evils, but the positive attainment of waiting good. The time has come for a more earnest and careful attention to the conditions which are best suited to the health and vigor of the human body, and through this of the indwelling mind. These are to be found not in the organism alone, but in all its coördinations.

WE MAY PERCEIVE THE RATIONAL PROPERTIES OF THINGS.

WE may merely perceive the fact that matter exists in certain obvious modes, or, we may still farther perceive the rational nature of these modes!

A ploughman and his ox are in the field together; they see an apple fall from the tree, a stone removed from its place, and carried to a neighboring wall, and a child running to and fro in its play. The ox at his master's side perceives all these things in common with the man, as he gives evidence of doing in various ways. He has real intelligence enough to enable him to discriminate between the apple, the stone, and the child. He would step aside to avoid a blow from a moving body, or to reach the apple; but it would seem that he sees, hears, smells, tastes nothing but positive extended substance. All the qualities which he perceives are quantitative properties — are literally material parts of the one whole; but the man, unlearned and a plodder though he be, at once perceives, also, something of the abstract principle of motion; revealed to him through the moving bodies. Gifted with an insight into the rational nature of things, he need see but one body moving; when he immediately sees that not this body alone, but all other bodies must be capable of a change of locality, that the possibility of moving or of being moved must be an affection, not of the apple, the stone, and the child merely, but of all bodies generally. Without reasoning about it, without being able, perhaps, to state it clearly in words, the very weakest man not altogether an idiot, abundantly proves, by his practical

68 *We may perceive the Rational*

conduct in life, that he fully recognizes the beautiful abstract principle of motion, as an unchanging feature actualized in the nature of things. It is a feature, too, which he has not himself conceived, but which he has directly perceived.

This actualized principle of motion is a rational principle, — that is, it is a principle of intelligence or thought, a principle which, from the nature of it, could not have been actualized with its many related modes as an orderly consistent property of things, without the intervention of a rational mind. Regarding substance as self-existent or necessarily existent, we may also suppose that there necessarily existed in it the possibility of motion or change of locality; and also a possible motion-producing force. Property, whether capacity or force, if necessarily existent, must involve the possibility of change, and force adequate to produce change. Unsentient, self-existent force, could produce aimless, chaotic changes — motions requiring no foresight and produced to no definite end. But it is impossible to conceive that an unsentient or irrational force could originate a very complicated and perfect system of beautifully coördinated changes, — of motions always mathematically determined and most nicely adjusted each to all the others, and obeying always the most rigid quantitative laws, — processes all depending one on another, and all mutually adapted to secure the most desirable fixed results. All this at once elevates motion from the rank of a self-existing, unsentient, unwitting, absolute property, to that of a pure principle, abstracted from things by rational thought, coördinated in a system of relative, preadjusted, possible changes ; and thus definitely conceived, reapplied to things as a scheme of actualized rational modes, which is henceforth to regulate all actual processes.

Rational properties are those properties which have been, in thought, abstracted from things, as self-existent

Properties of Things. 69

chaotic possibilities, and coördinated to henceforth exist and act in a perfectly determinate, rational manner. Thus the *laws* of motion are not self-existent but created; and they are all definite and unchanging. They are the fixed immutable elements of things, and have been made such, as I maintain, through a scheme of rational or intelligent thought, applied to self-existent substance and property.

Again, self-existent substance must have possessed originally a latent possibility of becoming beautiful, of developing those fitting, adjusted combinations of things which are so eminently pleasing to every beholder; and yet, unintelligent forces could never have realized those principles of beauty, which we find everywhere operative! A rational mind, endowed with a sense of the beautiful, could alone have developed these elements of beauty everywhere; could have devised and established immutable laws of the beautiful in every department of being, coördinating all things in one æsthetic whole.

Substance must also have possessed the possibility of being everywhere mathematically related, of assuming specific forms, colors, texture, and of manifesting its various present phenomena; but as all these manifestations are definitely coördinated, as every change takes place according to specific fixed rules, all these results are of such a character as to furnish positive evidence that they must have been predetermined in thought. A power adequate to produce a scheme so eminently rational as this, must have been itself a Rational Power.

Rational properties are all those elements of things, which, having been obviously coadapted in thought, now comprise the whole existing rational or thought-constitution of substance, a constitution operating always according to established specific processes. This rational constitution is something which may be perceived and cognized by every mind whose powers are of a rational order, and have therefore been coördinated with its rational character.

70 *We may perceive the Rational*

Every item and detail of this rational constitution may be intuitively apprehended by related mental powers. There it is, a real fact, operative in things, and manifesting or presenting to us its true character perpetually. Thus, when one sees an apple divided in halves, a stone broken asunder, or a leaf separated from a tree, if he is a rational being, he cannot but perceive in the process the underlying general principle of divisibility. If he looks at an object which has a circular form, he cannot help perceiving that there is a principle of figure actualized in this object; or if he tastes a sweet flavor or a bitter one, he begins at once to have some idea of sweetness and of bitterness, as concepts which have been thus realized in concrete substances. No thoroughly rational being can help perceiving more or less of the nature of these thought-ideals which he sees actualized before him. One who has power enough to originate similar schemes of coördinated thought, and to apply them to tangible things, as the commonest man does perpetually in his handicraft and the most gifted in his higher art or invention, can also perceive the thoughts everywhere realized and conserved in the objective world. His own intellectual power is sufficiently akin to that higher power which is manifested in creation, to enable him to cognize something of the nature of the creative act. A wider vision may also apprehend the less obvious principles and their more complicated coördinations. They all exist, practically exemplified and operative in the existing cosmos.

To have an adequate perception of the rational properties of substance, is merely to have a sufficiently clear and comprehensive perception of the persisting rational constitution of things. Such a cognition would not at all differ in kind, but only in degree, from the simplest perceptive act. The magnitude of the creative scheme is indeed so far beyond our highest conception or perception as to be to us practically infinite; yet our powers, so far as they do extend, may give real and true percepts.

Properties of Things. 71

Obviously if there is a coördinated rational scheme actualized in the existing universe, some Rational Power must have originated that scheme, and established it as the persisting rational constitution of this universe. While we credit the present nature of things, it must be held that even Deity could no more have created something from nothing than man can. Self-existent himself, he must have realized or incarnated his scheme of thought in other self-existent substance and property. In proof of this position, we can only appeal to the universe itself; believing that it will be possible to indicate the preëminently rational character of all its constitutional laws, processes, and modes, as illustrated in the natures both of matter and mind. This universe is the only text-book from which we can study the science of the Rational Constitution of things.

Metaphysicians and philosophers generally have expended much time in determining the origin and nature of the ideas which are found in the human mind. They have talked of ideas, relative, contingent, and finite; and ideas, absolute, necessary, and infinite. They have derived these ideas from sensation, or from reason, or from both in turn, arguing endlessly about the real origin and character of their various concepts, and differing in their notions from the slightest point of divergence to even an infinite degree; but any philosophy which concerns itself chiefly with subjective concepts is certain of going widely astray. Thus we find one thinker maintaining with Locke, that the idea of space is finite, another with Cousin, that the idea of space is infinite, and still another with Hamilton, asserting that the idea of space is only an infinite negation. We can only cry out in self-defense, " Pray speak for yourselves, gentlemen ! You may be quite competent to expound your own ideas, but it is certain that you are not all in possession of the true idea. If you will help us to that, then help us to comprehend space itself. Our ideas

We may perceive the Rational

of space and of many other things are subject to revision, but every idea which the Creator has actualized in his creation is as permanent as is the substance which embodies it!" If one will look back into his own childish experience, memory may perhaps convince him that his idea of space was then most vague and indefinite. If he can recall the first philosopher whose works he studied on that point, he may remember the thrill of astonishment and delight with which he comprehended and adopted the ideas of his author; but if he has since read or thought still farther, he has possibly made three or four somersaults of opinion subsequently. The only remedy is the study of space itself. Space certainly exists in rational coördinations with things, and we must study it in both its persisting nature and relations; all of which must be immediately perceived. So of everything else. Children may go on learning by rote, but one must use his own vision if he would really perceive the existing principles of things. We should wonder at a group of naturalists, if, finding them engrossed in studying the daguerreotype of a rose, and explaining by what nice processes of light and various chemical agencies they had been able to make so perfect and beautiful a representation, we learned, also, that they were dogmatizing and contending, on the evidence of this picture, about the nature of a living rose!

All the rational properties of things must be studied at first hand, for they admit of no representation by another. They must present themselves! This is even more imperative than with the outward forms of things, for while one can gain some knowledge of tangible properties by description or representation of them, there can be no description or representation of a rational property. It can only be expressed. As the specific gravity of a fluid is present in every drop; or as the normal temperature of a body is all through and through it, so the principles of things permeate their substances, constituting their very and essential nature. There they may be found and apprehended, by whoever has powers ample enough and well enough disciplined.

THE CONSTITUTION OF MATTER.

IT has been already stated that Substance and Property are both assumed to be absolute, self-existent, or uncreated. *Absolute property*, for the sake of distinctness in ideas, is regarded as both active and passive, that is, as at once *force* and *capacity*. *Absolute force*, then, would be the innate, uncreated energy pertaining to self-existent Being, and *absolute capacity* the innate possibility of change in self-existent Being. I, for one, cannot conceive of even self-existent being except as possessing force or energy inseparable from itself, and equally self-existent; nor can I conceive that being could exist with absolutely no capacity for change: therefore I must regard *Substance* and *Property* as equally self-existent and forever inseparable.

In these Studies, *property* means a definite, persistent something, inseparable from its own proper substance; and as it is maintained that, in reality, each atom or molecule of substance and its property, are one and inseparable, and together constitute the self-existent unit, so also the *property* itself is one and inseparable, and the terms *force* and *capacity* indicate only the two ways of looking at the same thing.

In treating of the relative or present constitution of things, to avoid circumlocution, I shall sometimes speak of *forces* and *capacities* in the plural, though meaning by this only the various modes of the one indivisible *property* of each self-existent molecule. As language is already constructed this is almost unavoidable, and is sanctioned by usage. *Relative modes of property* may be classified as

The Constitution of Matter. 75

innate or *inherent* modes, or *properties proper;* and *resultant properties,* or *relations proper.*

The *innate properties* are the aggregate correlated modes of the one absolute property, and are all mutually convertible among themselves.

Resultant properties are facts arising from coördinated modes and processes, and are *transient,* pertaining to the changeable phases of things ; or *persistent relations,* pertaining to the persisting constitution of things.

I use the term *characteristics* as covering all distinguishing modes of being, general or particular, by virtue of which any substance may be characterized ; and through which it may be discriminated from all other substances. Thus each substance in its ordinary condition, has a group of characteristics which comprehend alike all its modes of property and process.

Process, in the present volume, means always a definite coördinated mode of action. It is maintained that every process of nature, sentient as well as unsentient, has been prevized in the Creative Thought ; that all unsentient or purely quantitative processes are so coördinated in things that they go forward always with rigid mathematical precision, and are always, taken in the largest sense, changes producing a real advance or progress towards a higher condition of things. Thus all unsentient processes are regarded as fixed modes of evolution, through which, from simple substance and property, by new combinations, the homogeneous is ever becoming more and more heterogeneous ; thus originating new compounds, new forms, modes, and conditions, with ever-increasing beauty and utility. Sentient processes, including both quantitative and qualitative coördinations, have their own special modes of process, which will be treated of at length hereafter. Their coördinations are also self-evidently fore-ordained, and are maintained inviolable in their actual operations. Sentient processes, also, taken in the largest related sense, are

76 The Constitution of Matter.

established modes of sentient development, through which higher and better living experiences are forever eventuating.

The term *Attribute* is a synonym for *property*. It has very generally been made to designate a dignified mode of property, as an intellectual or moral power — if I were to give it a special signification at all, it would be that of a *hypothetic property*, a concept not yet decided to be an actual mode of things.

Matter, it is believed, is constituted by the one primary abstract thought or principle of extension, as variously coördinated in things. All matter is coördinated through related capacities for being extended by various modes, and to various degrees; effected through its own innate force, also coördinated to act through preadjusted modes and processes. *How* this was all effected we do not ask ; we turn simply to the fact as we find it exemplified. It is found by experience that each particular kind of matter has a specific nature of its own, which is definitely established ; and which is always absolutely the same under like conditions. Gold is always gold, and all the characteristics of one ounce of pure gold are exactly equal to those of every other ounce of pure gold. The same is true of every specific substance, simple or compound. Of the forty-two or three supposed elementary substances, each possesses groups of characteristics very unlike those of all the others ; yet a given weight or volume of any one element, possesses all characteristics exactly equal to those of every other equal weight or volume of the same kind ; and double or treble the weight or volume of substance has double or treble the amount of all characteristics. This rule has never been found to fail in any instance, so that a knowledge of the nature of one piece of gold or one ounce of oxygen, is, in effect, a cognizance of the nature of all the gold and all the oxygen in the universe.

The Constitution of Matter. 77

The *element* enters into compounds, undergoes changes, and exhibits new phases continually; but its original nature is intact, indestructible, and always, under like conditions, exhibits like characteristics. Thus each particle of matter, apparently, has its own fixed special constitution, and is a definite centre of untransferable characteristics. All its properties follow the fortunes of their substance under all known circumstances, entering with it into compounds, changing with it and selecting new compounds, or dissolving all connections and standing again in isolation. Under all these differing conditions, each grain of any given substance exhibits exactly the same kind and amount of phenomena that every other grain of like substance does under like conditions ; and if it is hidden away for years or for ages in any compound, with all its modes of property as a simple, wholly or partially inoperative, yet when it is again brought to light in its elementary character, it is as fresh and vigorous in all its characteristics as though it were created only yesterday. This is the more remarkable because the modes of property peculiar to it as an element are often more or less inactive or at least unrecognizable in the compound ; and because each distinctive phase of the compound is endowed with a coördinated group of modes peculiar to itself, which are as well defined and intact, and as perfectly adjusted to that special phase of matter as the elementary modes are to the elementary type. Thus, water is altogether unlike its elements ; while they are gases, it is liquid or even solid. The dominant properties of a compound often baffle all *a priori* calculations based upon a previous knowledge of its factors. Sulphur is yellow, and copper red, yet their compound sulphuret of copper is black ; the sulphate of potash lays aside all the acrid characteristics of both sulphuric acid and potash ; and there are cases in which the compound bears almost no resemblance to its constituents either in density, in form, color, smell, taste,

78   *The Constitution of Matter.*

fusibility, volatility, or chemical affinities. But while there are examples of an almost total reversal of the characteristics of the simples, yet this is by no means a rule, for a large proportion of compounds bear a strong resemblance to their elements, exhibiting many of their characteristics in a marked degree. It is to be distinctly noted that when an element enters into widely dissimilar compounds, often combining in several different proportions with the same base, yet all these various compounds have each a perfectly coördinated constitution, differing from all the others, but never varying in itself. The properties of any one grain of a given compound are exactly equal and identical in every particular with the properties of every other grain of the same compound ; these specific characteristics, then, evince the specific, unvarying, predetermined constitution of that mode of matter.

This is not an hypothesis to be proved by argument ; but it is a question to be settled practically by physical science. They have invented instruments so delicate that we are able to weigh the thousandth part of a grain of matter, to measure distances by the thousandth part of a barleycorn, to measure heat by the thousandth part of a degree of Fahrenheit ; and to estimate properties and processes in general by various tests and experiments, almost incredible for the degree of nicest accuracy attained, and the above position is experimentally settled ; it has been *quantitatively proved* again and again, to all intents and purposes. Of course it cannot be asserted that every mode and process of matter has been actually weighed or measured ; but it is asserted that enough have been weighed, measured, or otherwise estimated, to make the induction as positive as in the nature of things it ever can be made by quantitative science. We will regard it, then, as settled by experience that each particular mode of matter is endowed with established, coördinated modes of property ; and that a given amount of matter possesses an

The Constitution of Matter. 79

unvarying amount of property. We may intuitively perceive these related facts, as we see them illustrated in things.

It is not intended to ignore the facts of allotropy ; showing that various elementary substances undergo remarkable changes while they are yet simple elements. These facts, on the contrary, are regarded as illustrations of various related modes pertaining even to the same element, but operative under differently coördinated conditions. Allotropic oxygen, phosphorus, and sulphur, are quite transformed in appearance, and changed in their manifestations of all physical and chemical properties. Similar transformations are equally exemplified in compounds. Water is either vapor, liquid, or solid ; and in the phenomena of crystallization the same substances assume a variety of crystalline forms, to be accounted for by a different grouping of conditions. On a similar principle can we comprehend something of the three several definite modes under which simple *carbon* is known to us ; namely, charcoal, diamond, and graphite,— all differing in specific gravity, specific heat, conducting power for heat and electricity, and in chemical relations. The brilliant hard diamond is visibly very unlike the black brittle charcoal, and the highly combustible coal is equally unlike graphite, which is so incombustible that it is specially used for furnaces and crucibles ; yet all three when pure, are simple carbon, and the three modes are as definite and invariable as any other established modes of matter. The whole subject is necessarily more or less to be settled by hypothesis ; but it is usually supposed by physicists that these elementary modifications are due to a difference in the grouping of the ultimate molecules.

In this connection I may refer to the phenomena of *catalysis*, in which two or more substances are made to unite, or to be decomposed by the influence arising from the mere presence of another substance, which is not

80   *The Constitution of Matter.*

itself, apparently, at all affected by the process. Certain metallic oxides, as those of iron, copper, and manganese, so greatly facilitate the decomposition of the chlorate of potash, that if a small quantity of one of these be mixed with the salt, it will be decomposed at a comparatively low temperature, though the oxide itself undergoes no perceptible change. Platinum possesses a remarkable influence in inducing the combination of bodies. If a little spongy platinum be thrown into a mixture of oxygen and hydrogen, it becomes incandescent, and the gases combine with a loud explosion. A special mode of force, called *catalytic force*, has been assumed to explain these and many similar phenomena; but explanations on better understood hypotheses are also given, and it may be presumed that with the advancement of science, all catalytic phenomena may be disposed of without the need of a special *catalytic force*. The only point which I wish to make in this connection is, that all similar inorganic substances, under similar conditions, are similarly modified. Every piece of platinum produces effects exactly like those produced by every other piece of platinum, under like conditions, and all ordinary sulphur can be converted into allotropic sulphur or allotropic sulphur into common sulphur, by definitely established processes. Thus each mode of matter, as well as each mode of force, is seen to be clearly defined and accurately realized.

The principle of extension has been *universally* realized as a capacity of matter; and all bodies have been variously extended according to a definitely arranged and rigidly executed plan. Solids, liquids, and gases are the general modes in which ordinary matter is extended; but everything has its own specific form and process of being extended. Thus, platinum, which is twenty times heavier than water, and hydrogen, the lightest ponderable substance, differ widely as to relative weight and volume. A rock and a tree, both solid bodies, have their specific

The Constitution of Matter. 81

modes of formation and growth; and these, again, are divided into persisting subtypes; as granite, slate, marble; oak, willow, elm, pine. The prearranged plan of extension is persistently realized in the constant succession of new forms, which follow each other in an endless progression. The modes and processes of organic growth will be treated of hereafter.

Let us look now at *crystallization* or *structure formation in inorganic matter*. Definite crystallogenic principles are known to govern all inorganic matter, whether brought together by nature or art. All inorganic compounds assume a crystalline structure, each according to its innate nature and to the influencing relations under which the crystallization occurs. The most shapeless masses of rock are found to have, even to their minutest grains, a regular internal structure, which is identical in character with the most regular crystals of like composition and conditions. In a single mineral, although the varieties of form are often very great, yet they are found to be referable to a single one out of several permanent crystalline types; so that from the first apparent complexness of like forms, one can trace, not only the most extreme simplicity in the fundamental form, but also a very regular, simple, and exact *system* of standard variations. Special variations arise as much or more from change in the coördinated modes of force as from chemical composition, so that whether there shall be a mass of crowded, imperfect, small crystals, or a few perfect large ones, and what special type of variation the whole mass shall assume, is a question of variously coördinated conditions. Thus all crystallizations belonging to the same locality, sometimes embracing even large districts of country, have usually the same forms; while in some remote region, the forms, though of the same common type, will be quite dissimilar. Artificial crystallization presents

82   *The Constitution of Matter.*

similar results. " Common salt crystallizing from pure water presents, almost invariably, a cubic form. But in a solution of boracic acid, it always occurs with truncated angles." [1] Rev. E. Craig, treating of microscopic chemistry, says : " If sulphuric acid be added to carbonate of copper, crystals speedily appear, presenting the form of six-sided tabular prisms. Add a little ammonia, the form is changed entirely to a long rectangular prism, with the angles replaced. Add a little more ammonia, and the form changes to several varieties of the rhombic octahedron ; a little nitric acid restores again the form of the rectangular prism. In all these successive changes, it is not that a few crystals of another form have been superadded, but each time the metamorphosis is seen to take place in the whole mass." Something of crystalline structure is found even in glass, and it is believed that all inorganic substances assume definite crystalline forms in solidifying. Professor Dana defines crystals to be " inorganic solids bounded by plane surfaces symmetrically arranged, and resulting from the forces of the constituent molecules." Each mineral has its own mode of crystallization by which to distinguish it as we distinguish plants. It is known by the constancy of its angles and by internal structure. Here, then, is evidence of a coördinated scheme of thought, embracing, according to the highest authority, six distinct systems of crystallization, each with its unlimited variety of forms and dimensions ; but all of them definitely symmetrical and illustrating the highest mathematical order in the whole of their internal structure. It is assumed, also, by mineralogists,[2] that the crystal is really already formed in the fluid state, and that fluids, as well as solids, have definite orderly arrangements of molecules. All molecular forces have well-established, orderly modes of process ; each acting always invariably

[1] Dana's *System of Mineralogy.*
[2] Griffin's *System of Crystallography.*

The Constitution of Matter.

alike under like conditions. We must, therefore, infer that the principle of extension is actualized in everything through distinctly prevised and predetermined modes.

Extension necessitates *figure* and *size;* for if a body is extended it must be extended in some form and to some dimensions. It must also have place to be extended in ; and there will grow up with it all the multiform relations of position and space in general. Degrees of density, solidity, gravity, and many other coördinated principles will arise from a logical or rational necessity ; and we find all these multiplied combinations realized in matter.

If matter can be extended, this extension can also be withdrawn, and the body be compacted or compressed again into smaller compass ; but the fact that there is extension at all necessitates a limit to the possibility of compression ; necessitates a property of matter which may be termed *incompressibility absolute;* which is, in fact, only the obverse phase of extension. Between *incompressibility absolute*, and the largest possible extension there is room for any amount of practical extension and contraction; and all bodies have capacities, not only for being variously extended, but capacities also for being again contracted.

These various capacities are furthermore all coördinated with *motion*. Every material process is a process of change in locality. The distinct modes of motion, recognized and described by leading physicists, are exceedingly diverse ; and produced by a large variety of the most wonderful, intricate, and beautiful combinations of force, till the mind is almost overwhelmed in its attempts to grasp the whole scheme of operations. Bodies not only change place in the mass, as when a ball receives a blow from a club, and is thrown off into the distance ; but their minutest particles are variously wrought upon, and tossed to and fro ; they expand and contract by perfectly systematical orderly processes, and are brittle, elas-

84 *The Constitution of Matter.*

tic, ductile, malleable, exercise chemical affinities and antipathies, and do everything, in short, according to established mathematical modes of motion. If a large cord were divided at a given point into a dozen separate and dissimilar strands, a movement communicated at the end of the cord would not only be carried on to the point of division, but it would be distributed to each of the dozen strands, and would move them all; but the motion of each, as in musical instruments, would be varied according to specific differences in their size, tension, etc. So if matter has almost numberless modes of capacity for motion, allied to as many modes of force, one or all of these may be at any time excited, and all possibly, at the same time; the right conditions for this being fulfilled. The ordinary movements of matter, as the swaying of trees by the wind and the passage of bodies from one place to another, are forms of motion obvious to all.

Organized bodies have capacities for growth and dissolution; processes of incessant change, carried on during their whole organized existence; yet all these are to the senses invisible and recondite processes, which we have not yet been able to altogether fathom. The little plant has made progress since yesterday; it is even perceptibly larger than it was an hour ago; it is constantly throwing off gases and absorbing nutritive matter from earth and air; steadily giving evidence of unresting modes of motion. These changes can be tested at frequent intervals; can be weighed, measured, and computed; and the mind can comprehend enough of them to feel as much assurance as to their phenomena as it does of the existence of the plant itself. There are modes of organic process radically unlike those of the inorganic world. These differences will be treated of in their proper connection. Matter in general can be appropriated by organic forces and used in the service of the organism; so that we may infer that all inorganic matter has capaci-

The Constitution of Matter. 85

ties for being so allied to organisms as, for the time being, to become itself organized and to aid in the discharge of organic functions.

But invisible or molecular motions of various kinds play a prominent part in all the changes of matter, organic and inorganic alike. The movements which answer to some of the most powerful forces of nature, as light, heat, magnetism, and electricity, are movements of invisible particles of matter. We perceive the net results; and in these cognize something both of the nature of the forces as properties, and of their resulting processes. Bodies are curiously constructed instruments, which may be played upon by the forces of matter; whatever be the mode of acting force, the instrument can respond only in its own way; yet every instrument is adjusted to various forces, so that each can control it to a certain degree, and can play upon it after its own method.

The science of forces has received an immense stimulus of late from the important discoveries of eminent men, verifying intuitions and hypotheses of equally eminent predecessors. In the language of Professor Youmans; " a pure principle (gravitation) forms the immaterial foundation of the universe," while heat, light, electricity, magnetism, and chemical affinity are, " an order of purely immaterial forces." There are efficient properties in matter which produce motion, and which are adapted, obviously, to the direct end of producing motion. Force may be defined as anything, which, the right conditions being supplied, is capable of producing motion or change of motion. No motion is ever destroyed, but like force itself, motion is indestructible. It is communicated from atom to atom; but the whole coördinated constitution of each atom, and its inherent amount of force, is not communicated. On the contrary, the atoms upon which any mode of force acts, producing a corresponding mode of motion in them, in their turn react again; and as all action and reaction

86   *The Constitution of Matter.*

are constituted equal and opposite, the reaction is a counter impulse exactly equal to that which was communicated to itself. Force, as a property, it is maintained in these "*Studies*," is not communicated; but simply exchanges one of its coördinated processes for another, so that the amount of force remains always exactly the same in every atom, and it always retains all its own special constitutional adjustments of forces and capacities. Nothing seems to me more evident than that force, considered as a property, is inconvertible and untransferable, remaining always with its own proper substance; but processes or modes of motion, correlated to like processes in other atoms, have power to excite these, transforming, for the time being, other modes of motion into this which it excites. Substances do not exchange forces, but they exchange modes of process. All modes of quantitative motion are mutually convertible into all other modes of like motion, both within any given atom and interchangeably between all atoms; but again, I repeat, that the property which produces these motions or processes is not convertible, but is so adjusted to everything else that it always receives again exactly as much as it gives, and thus through the universal principle of equal action and reaction, the balance of properties is always maintained. This is simply illustrated by the ball which bounds back again from the wall, making its angles of incidence and reflection exactly equal. The ball communicates motion to the wall, and the wall reacts again upon the ball with mathematically equal force.

Special modes of force can act, obviously, only when all the adjustments necessary to their activity are fulfilled. It is now generally assumed by chemists that the molecules of all substances in the gaseous state occupy the same volume. This conclusion implies that there are the same number of molecules in equal volumes of different substances, and that the elastic tension of every molecule

The Constitution of Matter. 87

is the same in all gases, and yet how different is the combination of forces in the formation of the various classes of objects.

There is at least one mode of force which is always in steady and uniform exercise. Professor Faraday says that, so far as we can perceive, gravitation is "inconvertible in its nature and unchanging in its manifestations." A permanent affection of matter, it undergoes no change, and the conditions for its activity being permanently realized, it is always in uniform exercise. But each mode of force, whether like *gravity*, so adapted to all other things as to be always operative, or like some special chemical affinity which pertains to but one specific form of its own substance, and can act only when in the presence of some other substance coördinated with itself; each *mode of force* is itself equally *inconvertible* and alike mathematically determined in all its convertible *processes*. All force in action will produce motion, and the same quantity of force will always produce the same amount of any given kind of motion under like conditions. The special motion is the special form of process which the force inaugurates ; and all process is continuous, indestructible, and merely a modification of something which has gone before, and is carried on under the law of equal action and reaction, to be again modified into something which shall come after.

Matter, apparently, possesses two broad types of constitutional forces : *extensive force*, by the operation of which all bodies are extended, and *contractive force*, by the operation of which all bodies are contracted. If the contractive modes of force alone were in exercise, all matter would tend to aggregation, to more and more cohesion and condensation, till the whole would be finally compacted into one unvibrating mass ; but the extensive modes are forever conjointly at work, expanding every molecule or projecting it into space ; working through a countless variety of processes. *Extensive forces* alone would dissipate all solids,

88 *The Constitution of Matter.*

diffusing the universe into unlimited space ; while the two coördinated types maintain the universe as it is, holding all processes in equilibrium. These two modes are in reality one, each being a reaction of the other. Light and heat are extensive forces, which pertain, apparently, to all matter ; but they can act vigorously only under adapted conditions, as in combustion or in the radiation of light and heat from the sun. The sunbeam has long been studied with utmost care ; it has been variously tested till science has determined that each ray of heat and color is a separate succession of coördinated waves of motion sent out by the radiating body, and communicated in straight lines to any other body which is so adapted to it in condition as to enable it to become a recipient. But it is the *motion* which is thus communicated, not the original, *motion-determining force*, which remains unchanged — a permanent mode of energy pertaining to its own substance. Heat and light, as modes of motion, are thus to be distinguished from the persisting modes of force ; which possess in themselves a permanent power to transform other modes of motion into these.

The medium which transmits the curiously adapted series of moving wavelets, which we call light and heat, must be itself matter, though incredibly refined and etherial ; it obeys the laws of quantity, possessing its own forces and capacities, and is the material bond between gross ordinary bodies. The same ether, or adjusted portions of it, must convey the converse line of motion produced by the contraction of substances largely endowed with gravity or other contractive forces. No line of contractive motion has yet been experimentally discovered ; but it must, I think, be presumed to exist, and we may yet make acquaintance with it as intimate as we have already done with the converse line of the sunbeam. Much evidence can be given in favor of the theory that gravity acts in lines, drawing in all directions from farthest

The Constitution of Matter. 89

space to the *attracting*, that is, the contracting particle. Many special molecules thus coöperating, as in a solid mass, the centre of gravity becomes the centre of the gravitative force towards which all bodies whatever are irresistibly drawn.

That two or more masses of matter can act upon each other at a distance, without some direct material communication, is in violation of all known laws of matter;[1] but motion may be produced in an elastic ether by the sudden contraction of molecules, and this mode of motion, reaching on into remote space, like a contracting cord, would draw with its own little power all masses which should lie in its path. Such a mode of motion, like gravity, could act only in direct lines, and could never turn aside for any obstacle; but would entangle everything indiscriminately within its tightening lines. The contracting of an elastic substance, as India-rubber when it has been forcibly drawn asunder, may convey some idea of the possible movement in the gravitating beam; but there must be successive wavelets of contractive motion, spreading outward from the dense body largely endowed with gravitative force. Gravitation is thus regarded as a reaction against *extensive* or *expansive* modes of force. Like all forces which act only in straight lines, gravity, running out from a point in all directions into space, from the necessity of the case, could produce effects only in an inverse ratio to the square of the distance from the attracting body. Heat and light, for example, are *radiated* from all points of the heated and luminous body and necessarily more and more diffused as they spread outwards; contractive motion would illustrate the same law — as all the lines of motion converged towards the contracting body, the less distance would they be apart from each other, and the greater the number in a given space; so that all bodies must mutually draw each other with a force inverse to the square of their distances.

[1] Dr. Faraday's *Conservation of Force.*

90 *The Constitution of Matter.*

The molecules of the inter-stellar ether which serves as the conducting medium, are supposed to have their own modes of force, so adjusted to ordinary matter as to co-operate readily under all circumstances. In the radiation of light and heat, the molecular forces coact always in the line of motion, ultimating in a polarity of the conducting medium; if the line of motion is changed by any intervening cause, the polarity of the medium is also changed. Why may we not, then, suppose that polarity of the ether results in the conduction of gravitative motion; each molecule of the medium coöperating in a definite direction with its next neighbor, thus drawing together the dense bodies which they connect. We must be content with more or less mere hypothesis in relation to most molecular processes until we can literally perceive ultimate molecules, and distinguish their motions through the senses, as we now perceive masses and their movements; but, marvelous as are the wonders revealed by the microscope, we are still very far from such an attainment. We must reason, therefore, from the amassed results, and correct our theories by the known facts. Some theory of contraction is evidently needed in explanation of the phenomena of gravitation.

I regard the coöperation of forces as comprehending not only the push and counter-push between atom and atom, but also the push and the withdrawal of that push by every atom singly and collectively, when not impeded in the completion of the process. Every molecule, it is believed, is itself endowed with the two reactionary types of the one identical force, which together keep it forever pulsing to and fro like the panting heart of a live creature, each atom a microcosm of the universe, with its eternal ebb and flow, its systole and diastole. We have endeavored to show that while extension is a universal capacity of matter, yet that there is a lowest extreme of extension, a constitutional minimum beyond which contractive force can

The Constitution of Matter. 91

produce no results. It is probable, also, that there is an established maximum of extension for each atom, and that, although every atom must be extended, yet that the greatest amount of that extension is not indefinite but definite. Extensive force, then, if not impeded in its action, could extend its atom only to a definite amount; there its ability would end, the atom being constituted for extension so far and no further. This maximum of extension reached, other atoms not interfering, the reactionary contractive force would carry it back again to its minimum; and thus it would beat to and fro in ceaseless unrest. Thus there are coördinated tides of action and reaction, flowing out to the boundaries and again beating back to the axis of the atom. We know that the law of action and reaction is everywhere equal and opposite; and it is at least possible that every atom is so constituted as to pulse to and fro forever if not externally impeded.

I have assumed that there are indivisible atoms or molecules, which are centres of properties. The various processes by which bodies are modified presuppose divisibility as a capacity of aggregated matter. The possibility of a division of masses is an integral part of the general scheme. While one body is a solid, another a fluid, and another a gas, here are necessary resulting divisions. Extension in one class of bodies is secured by growth and in another by accretions; then there are special constitutions and innumerable modifications, all grounded upon divisibility, as coördinated with other properties. Accordingly we find masses constituted for division and subdivision to such a degree that men have been unable to determine whether or not there is any limit to this capacity. Logicians have contended both for and against the infinite divisibility of matter; but, as a question of fact, it can with our present faculties be settled only by a logical intuition. As the principles of extension and contraction mutually limit each other, so the one force operative in

92 *The Constitution of Matter.*

these adapted modes must pertain inseparably to one substantial centre. I regard molecules not as mere centres of force, but each as indivisible absolute substance and property, constituted by coördinated modes of innate force and capacity! The principle of divisibility may well apply simply as between molecule and molecule, while each ultimate molecule itself remains indivisible. This, too, is the conclusion to which science may be said already to have arrived; at least it is now the prevailing scientific theory, sustained by many incidental corroborative facts. The doctrine of definite proportions, as accepted and explained by chemistry, leads to this conclusion. It has been experimentally determined that a compound, when pure, contains invariably the same proportions of its constituents; and this is true of every known compound, whether formed by nature or art. The weight of a compound atom is obtained by adding together the atomic weights of its constituents; and though two or more substances may combine in different proportions, forming a variety of compounds composed of the same elements, yet these elements though found to unite in different ratios, are yet always in definite proportions; either one atom with one atom, or one of one kind with two or more of another, or by any amounts of atoms which are integral multiples of unity. The proportions of the substances which act upon each other chemically, greatly influence the nature of the new compound. No adequate explanation can be given of this very beautiful system of definite combinations except that ultimate, indivisible atoms combine in various proportions. If there be indivisible atoms, these atoms must be constituted in groups, each group differing from all the others; but each individual of a group exactly like every other of its kind in all its characteristics, so that any combination of atoms will be, in every respect, like every other combination of its kind.

But each ultimate atom of matter is not only constituted

The Constitution of Matter. 93

by its own special characteristics; but it is also made eminently social, or coöperative with its neighbors in all its functions; so that, probably, no atom is left to expand and contract under the unimpeded action of its own properties. It is crowded against on every side by other atoms whose processes are so coördinated with its own that it may never be able to reach either its maximum or minimum of extension, but must vibrate always, by diverse processes, somewhere between the two, in response to kindred processes from without, as modified by its own proper modes.

It is the first law of motion, that "a body, if acted on by no external force, remains at rest; or if in motion, continues to move uniformly in the same direction." Simple expansive and contractive forces cannot change their own centres of gravity as separate atoms, nor yet the centre of gravity of a cohesive mass whose forces are all coöperative as one; so that if any body were left to itself, its centre of gravity would remain always at rest, and if started forward by some impulse communicated from without, its other modes being for the time transformed into this, there would be no power within itself to change again; but it must move on and on indefinitely till it should meet something else to which it could communicate this new mode, receiving in exchange some other correlated mode.

But the action of any force upon any other atom of matter than its own, does tend to change the centre of position in space of the foreign body; it is adapted, not so much either to enlarge or contract, or by any process to change the internal structure of the foreign substance, as to move it off into space, thus creating a new process — that of mechanical motion. The body thus moved, that is, some of whose forces are transformed into the mechanical force which carries it forward, if left to itself, would continue on in a straight line and with a uniform velocity; but, beating against obstructions, the mechanical motion becomes again

94   *The Constitution of Matter.*

transformed either into heat or some other correlated mode, or is thrown back again at an angle of reflection corresponding to the angle of incidence ; and thus the perpetual interchange of coördinated processes, among the variously adjusted classes and states of matter, produce the endless succession of change and variety in the existing universe. In this complicated and rigidly mathematical adaptation of things we find an endless widening of the facts indicating a broad, intelligent plan, combining unity of end with an admirable diversity of ways and means.

The conservation of all force is one of the great truths which modern science has experimentally as well as rationally demonstrated ; and closely allied to this is the doctrine of the correlation or mutual convertibility or exchangeability of all modes of motion, both in the same and in different substances. All modes of force and their processes are quantitatively related, so that one process is always exchanged for another in definite proportions. Thus heat and mechanical motion are mathematically correlated ; and it is found by elaborate, careful experiments, that 772 units of mechanical force are equal to one unit of heat ; that is, 772 pounds of weight, falling one foot, represents mechanical or mass-moving force, which, when transformed into heat, as it is by the fall, is sufficient to raise one pound of water 1° F. This is called the mechanical equivalent of heat. Heat, in its turn, can be transformed into mechanical motion, always yielding the proportion required by this law of quantitative relations. It is also shown, to the satisfaction of those best acquainted with the subject, that the modes of process produced by light, electricity, magnetism, chemical affinity, are all correlated with each other, and with all other modes of process, and are quantitatively convertible.

When coördinated substances are brought together, or are related through other connecting substances, the result is sensible movement, as in chemical, electrical, or magnetic

The Constitution of Matter. 95

action, or in the radiation and conduction of heat, light, or any other mode of process, or in the action of gravitation. It is not necessary for our purpose that we should dwell further upon the simple modes or the combinations of existing forces and capacities, and their resulting processes. It is enough if I am able to show that all these modes must have been planned in thought and realized in things; and that the *modifications of things*, therefore, *are not self-existent but created.*

I assume that atomic property is something intrinsically indivisible and inherent in its own indivisible atomic substance; but that it has been coördinated by thought and power in many varying but definite modes. The atomic substance and property, together indivisible and self-existent, has been wrought into ever-changing manifestations through a multiplicity of coördinated modes and their processes. Thus each atom may be studied by us either as comprising modes of force which can excite adapted movements in its own or other atoms, or as possessing capacities which are receptive to motions thus produced. All these modes of property are found to be mathematically related and belonging to two mutually limiting types — the one producing the ebb tide of universal movement, and the other the corresponding flow; together maintaining everything in virtual equilibrium, and within its preordained boundaries.

All extensive movement can be deflected from its course, or absorbed and transformed by adapted capacities. Thus, in passing from one medium to another, as from air to water, the direct line of light is broken. Every object absorbs its own adapted portions of the sunbeam, reflecting the remainder; and all *outward* motion, whether of the mass or molecule, can be turned from its course or transformed to some other mode by various resisting obstacles. On the contrary, *gravity* and probably all contractive modes of force know no obstacles, but they knit

96   *The Constitution of Matter.*

up everything alike in their imperative modes of regression. Hence we regard gravity as always operative; but in the broadest sense, all force is perpetually operative. All unsentient processes are necessarily reactions from something which has gone before. Neither new properties, nor new, that is original, unproduced movements ever begin to be; but one mode of motion is transformed into another through the intervention of constitutional forces and capacities, which must, evidently, have been coördinated for the very purpose of effecting such transformations. All quantitative modes are lifeless, unconscious, irresponsible, and they act always mechanically as they have been constituted to act. The *laws* of nature are immutable, but they are simply the established coördinated *facts* of nature.

Certain properties of matter, like extension, have a perceived existence as actual objective properties; but others, such as taste, color, sound, or resistance, are not simply effects realized in the object; but effects produced upon ourselves by something which does exist in the object. Thus colors are modes of objective motion in such relations to the human eye as to produce within it correlative processes, which, communicated to the mind, we call red, yellow, or blue. Sight, smell, taste, hearing, and touch; contact, in all its varieties; are so many modes of motion communicated from the object through material media to the percipient mind. There are coördinations relating mind and matter; and the living mind is necessarily the appreciative partner whenever it is itself one term of a relation. All unsentient force is simply quantitative or extensive; but sentient modes are also qualitative or intensive. We estimate the one wholly by quantity, but the other both by quantity and quality. We indeed speak often of the qualities of material things; but we really mean by it the quality of the effect produced upon ourselves. Thus sugar is said to have the quality of sweet-

The Constitution of Matter. 97

ness; yet everything pertaining to the sugar can be estimated by amounts; but the kind or degree of sensation which we experience in tasting it cannot be measured by any quantity. It is a mode which cannot be computed by amounts, but by the kind or intensity of the experience; that is, not simply by the quantity of the modification, but also by the kind or quality of it. This class of relations will be more fully considered in connection with mind and its coördinations. It is enough to say here that I use the term *quality*, in these *studies*, as *pertaining only to sentient or living experience, and the modifications of the conscious mind;* while it is held that all unsentient modifications can always be estimated by quantities.

There are relations subsisting between bodies in which mind has no other direct concern than that of an intelligent observer, in which it is as nearly a disinterested third party as is possible in a universe where all processes are correlated more or less remotely. The action of elements upon each other in a chemical compound are almost completely independent of the observing spectator; yet even here there exist relations which enable the mind to cognize the matter and its processes; and these relations are largely dependent on material chains of connection between them. The mind perceives through the senses of the body, and between these and the material object there is direct communication through adapted material processes. Thus mind is enabled to cognize matter in its essential nature and relations.

The pure principles of things pertain to mind as much as to matter; and the two are often coördinated in and through them. Thus the mind perceives all the principles of quantity, as pure rational principles rather than as affections of things; it is often able, therefore, to consider them impartially and with no personal bias. This impersonal method of studying the material world is of very great importance, as it enables one to study the re-

98 *The Constitution of Matter.*

lations of things independent of personal considerations, and purely as matters of scientific interest.

We can perceive, for example, that from the necessity of the case, *extension* could have been nothing but a pure rational concept, unless made real as a property of things ; and that force also is an immaterial somewhat, which could have no actual existence independent of substance. A force of nothing would be itself nothing. To assert that force or even extension had no actual existence in absolute being, before the present constitution of things was established, would be to transcend our knowledge on the subject; but if they were realities at all, they must have been absolute properties of being; and they have become modifications of the existing universe by special relative adjustments in the present order of things. Creation is a rigid mathematical coördination of modifications, superinduced upon self-existent being — that at least is the light in which it is regarded in the present essay.

It cannot be said that mathematical principles are actualized *in* any one substance, or indeed in all substances inclusive, in exactly the same sense in which extension and motion are characteristics of matter. Mathematical principles are realized rather as the *resultant properties* or *relations* of things. An innate property is something *in* the thing — its very and essential nature ; but the *relation* is only part of the comprehensive scheme or plan in accordance with which innate properties are made to coexist and coact. The distinction is obvious and fundamental. Thus *actualized relations* are elements of the *actualized schemes* in which all the concrete modes of things are contained and harmonized. The relation of parent and child, brother and sister, neighbor and neighbor, are actual relations belonging to the existing scheme of things ; but these relations are none of them the *innate properties* of parent, child, brother, sister, or neighbor.

The Constitution of Matter. 99

They arise as resultants from the general coördinations of the scheme, and embrace all parents and all children, etc. So all mathematical principles are actualized as an undeviating logical system, quantitatively regulating all possible modifications. Everything is found to exist coördinated in one established universal arithmetic!

This system of rigid quantitativeness not only coördinates all known substances and properties, with their outgrowing processes: but it also coördinates all outside contingencies and conditions, necessarily embraced in a completed, harmonious scheme of creation. These outside conditions or resultants arising from a logical rational necessity, are inherent and actualized parts of the existing scheme of modifications. For example, if bodies are extended, they must be extended somewhere or in distinct places or relative spaces. The place of a body is its relative position; and if the body itself is extended, then its place of being is extended also, of logical necessity. Extended place is space; and actualized extension originates actualized space. Then the mathematical relations of changing divisible bodies, extending to differing degrees, by unlike processes, under the influence of many modifications of properties, require also mathematical coördinations of divisible, related spaces. Thus spatial ratios and measures are as actual and tangible as are the substances occupying those spaces. But divisions of relative spaces cannot, in the nature of the case, be innate properties of relative being. On the contrary, they contain all substances. The sum of all relative spaces is space, as a whole — one actualized element of the creative scheme.

Time is another coördinated element. To say that anything exists, is to say that it exists *now* or in present time.

As all matter is constituted to exist in relative space, so it is also constituted to exist in relative time. Duration or eternity is only continuous present time — absolute

The Constitution of Matter.

time. The actualized scheme of time is an unceasing now with its relations of past and future; and duration is as really an ever-present continuous time, as being is an ever-existing somewhat.

Space, with its relative dimensions of length, breadth, and thickness, is inseparable from extended being; and *it must exist with being*, or else it could have no existence even in thought or as a pure principle. So time or duration, with its relative past and future, must be dependent for its actual existence upon actual being. The constitutional changes of the present universe, at once simultaneous and successive, are all mathematically coördinated in time; and the divisions of time are all measurable, and, like those of space, related in quantity to all the modifications of the universe. Every measure of any one of these quantities can be definitely expressed in terms of each of the others, and they are all so mutually dependent that neither can actually exist without all the others. Time and space are neither real substances, nor real innate properties of substance: they are simply the realized fundamental, rational facts of the existing creation.

To believe that either time or space, whether regarded as absolute or relative, can be anything purely in and of themselves, to me seems preposterous, however high the authority which asserts otherwise. As abstract principles or facts, how could they exist independent of a mind which originated them? Do you say that they may have an absolute existence, a self-existence independent of everything else, — then each of them is an absolute nothing, an infinite nonentity, if one might be allowed to join words so paradoxical. Without *Being*, either absolute and self-existent, or related as it is in the present universe, how could time or space or quantity acquire even the dignity of Hamilton's infinite negations; since there would be nothing positive by which they would be negatived. We conceive of them all only as the containing and con-

The Constitution of Matter. 101

trolling relations of things; and though we may imagine all real existences to be annihilated, and yet that time, space, and quantitativeness would remain, yet they would remain only as unrealities, as absolute nothings. Take away all *thought* of them, which is *something*, and nothing remains. True, there would still be unlimited nothingness; but can we call that something? can we call it a veritable existence? I can conceive of substance and *property proper*, as ,self-existent necessary realities; but I cannot conceive of time, space, or quantity as realities at all except as actualized relations of modified being, as resultant properties. Are they, then, infinite, absolute? They have, as principles, no limitations; they are unbounded; and like all pure principles, they are unlimited in the kind to which they pertain; and therefore as pure principles they may be infinite and absolute to any mind which can grasp the infinite and absolute; and they may, therefore, be infinite in the creative thought. As actualized relations of the present universe, and as perceived by ourselves, they are doubtless finite and relative. Infinity cannot be reasonably predicated of the contingent and relative. The practically realized scheme of things, even with all its vastness of perfect internal harmony, cannot properly be termed either infinite or absolute.

A faultless universal arithmetic has evidently been rigidly applied to the entire constitution of matter. Its whole mechanism, in every minutest part, has been built up on mathematical principles; and all its characteristics, from the most simple to the most complex, are mathematically related. If there is but little rigid adherence to primitive geometrical forms manifested in the growth of living organisms, it is because the principles of beautiful variety (shall I say of varied sentient good) transcend even the principles of quantity; but the one class never ignore nor annul the other. Each living thing has its own typical mathematical form and proportions,

102 *The Constitution of Matter.*

from which it never widely varies. The most highly ornate variations only illustrate a generic unity. Like a pictorial alphabet in a child's primer, with its wonderful departures from the original twenty-six letters, yet built up unmistakably on the old primitive groundwork of plain English vowels and consonants, so nature establishes all her embellishments on a very angular mathematical alphabet. Living organisms are under the rule of quantity; but a higher rule is also predominant. The ideal skeleton of every graceful tree, and leaf, and flower, of every roly-poly cherub baby, and of each ever-changing cloud even, is clearly made up of as many and rigid angles, triangles, and right lines as a whole book of geometry. A pine-tree, in its *tout ensemble*, and in every leaf, branch, and cone, is an illustrated volume of conic sections.[1] The leaves of each species of plant have a persistent order of arrangement which is peculiar to itself, and by which it may always be distinguished at a glance. "This order is subject to certain laws, and may be expressed by an arithmetical formula.[2] Flowers also are systematically placed; and provided for by prevised adjustments as beautiful as their own colors.

The little living mollusk in the building up of its shell is found to follow a perfect geometrical progression as to the size of the whorls, and the distance between contiguous whorls, winding its dwelling in a uniform direction through the space around its axis. Wasps, bees, birds, and even fishes, are instructed architects of the highest mathematical order. The ancient Platonic maxim asserts that Deity proceeds always by geometry. Since that early day the physicists have demonstrated that the forms, distances, and motions of the worlds are fixed in numerical coöperative relations; and that even imponderable forces, and the minute living creatures revealed only through the

---

[1] McCosh, *Typical Forms and Special Ends in Creation.*
[2] Figuier, *The Vegetable World.*

The Constitution of Matter. 103

microscope, are all alike mathematically coördinated. One of the most remunerative of human studies is the search after quantitative ratios and relations as we find them exemplified in nature under an endless variety of conditions. To find a determinate order of things cropping out in the most unexpected modes, regulating alike the colors of the simplest flowers and the wondrously complicated movements and structure of the grandest worlds, imparts a keen zest and stimulus to the mind which perhaps nothing else can parallel. Science has traced these mathematical analogies in many directions, and often with the conscientious accuracy of exact demonstration.

If a universal quantitative coöperation can be established between all modes of matter, coördinating all its properties and relations with their resulting processes, this fact must be the highest and most ultimate truth of physical science. Add to this the coördinations of the sentient world, of living minds, with all their intellectual and moral adjustments, and the cycle of interest is complete. It is not my present purpose to enter upon this subject. We need only remember here, that each organism is under the control of other than merely quantitative force, and that evidences of thought-adaptations are found equally in the organic and inorganic kingdoms. There is as much orderly arrangement resulting from unsentient, wholly mechanical force as from any other. We know that each mineral, when not disturbed in the process, assumes its own distinctive crystalline forms, each crystal bounded by plane surfaces whose sides are parallel ; and that all fluids and gases have perfectly orderly processes of modification. The only wisdom manifested in all these beautiful arrangements necessarily lies far back in the scheme of thought, and in the wonderful power which was able to consummate and maintain this scheme in things. Unsentient matter itself is only clay in the hands of the Supreme Architect —

The Constitution of Matter.

its innate forces being wholly unwitting and useless except as coördinated to act in furthering intelligent ends.

It only remains, then, to add that all *process* is found to have been *progress*, if judged by the steadily increasing sum of *results*. Science decides that there has been a gradual increase of heterogeneous bodies from homogeneous elements. This earth is now in a state of higher and more varied maturity than ever before; and this is not only true of its organisms, but it is equally so of its inorganic structure. There is found to have been an orderly, regular, and successive deposition of rock strata over the whole surface of the globe; and also, as a general rule, the more recent the strata the greater the similarity of its fossil contents to existing organisms. It is found that the whole crust of the earth is steadily becoming more and more rich and complex in varieties of all kinds, inorganic and organic alike. The old *Plutonic* rocks, supposed to have been hardened by the action of heat beneath the surface, and afterwards uplifted by volcanic or other influences, are being gradually *metamorphosed* or crumbled and deposited with other ingredients in *sedimentary strata*. We have the metamorphic crystalline schists of many varieties, probably transformed sedimentary rocks, and the processes by which these and similar results are secured are still going forward continually, producing more and more heterogeneity.

All known modes of force coöperate to produce changes. Heat and light seem at the first glance to produce only momentary influences; but the sum of their effects is to us absolutely immeasurable. Even the gentlest rains wear the earth into channels, and falling into the crevices and working their way down even into the deepest fissures, they abstract elements from the hardest rocks, depositing them elsewhere. Alternate heat and moisture weaken and perpetually crumble away all masses;

The Constitution of Matter. 105

chemical action is continually eating with a cankering tooth into already existing forms, and as continually renewing and creating others. Land-slips, avalanches, glaciers, volcanoes, floods, tempests, fires, and all manner of convulsions, have been at work since the beginning; and yet all geologists turn from such apparently chaotic actions to the innumerable evidences of a slow and steady, orderly progress with which even these violent actions are also coördinated. The steady encroachment of the ocean upon the land through the ceaseless wearing action of its waves, the debris deposited in it by streams of running water, the building up of land by the coral family and other inhabitants of the sea, and the growth and decay of vegetable and animal products on land and in the water, are all quiet, steady influences producing both change and advance. Higher and higher types of organisms have arisen in a very slowly ascending series since the beginning; and if the early dwellers in the soft, muddy world of very long ago — the huge reptiles and trilobites — have no successors of their kind, there are animals of a much more perfect organism inhabiting a more highly developed globe.

It can scarcely be believed now, by any one familiar with science, that the universe was instantaneously created by simple fiat, or that it could have been brought into nearly its present form and condition within six days, or in any short period of time. The most orthodox now reject this literal pre-geologic interpretation of Genesis. Vast periods of time, which must certainly be counted by many centuries, are known to have passed away before the world was fitted to become the abode of man. A gradual step by step process of change has gone on everywhere in both the inorganic and organic kingdoms; while the changes preceding any organism must have been even greater than these; so that no one, with the enduring evidences of all this accessible to him, can well intelligently doubt either

The Constitution of Matter.

that the present centre of the earth is still a molten, liquid mass, or that the whole solar system once existed in a state of vapor.

The interior rocks, which are generally, if not universally extended everywhere beneath our feet, are found to have been undoubtedly cooled from igneous fusion ; the globular form of the earth is such as would result from a soft mass revolving on its axis ; and the interior masses are found by careful examination in various metallic mines, salt and coal pits, etc., to be greatly hotter than the parts at the surface. The mutual action and counteraction of heat and gravity within the earth itself cannot well be overlooked. Heat, in all its modes of action an expansive force, prevents the great condensation of dense matter at the centre ; and yet pressure has produced greater density there than elsewhere, while at the surface radiation of heat has resulted in solidification to a large extent ; and thus are many modes of coacting force now maintaining essentially the present condition of the globe.

Almost everything now existing on the surface of the earth is in a compound state, which is preëminently a condensed or cohesive state. The single element, oxygen, composes almost half of the whole amount of the ponderable substance of the globe. If this gas alone were freed from its compounds, it would immediately occupy a space two thousand times as great as it now does ; and thus one entire half of the world, at least, would be resolved into gas. Other substances, released from combination under certain atmospheric pressures, expand in a similar degree, so that scientific authorities assert that it is not improbable that all the substances on the earth if freed from their compounds would enter into the gaseous state. There is much probability that our solar system was once a diffused nebula which has been gradually brought into its present relations through the continuous action of variously coördinated properties ; and we may even assume that all solar

The Constitution of Matter. 107

systems once existed undistinguished in one universal, homogeneous, exceedingly diffusive mass.

The *rational creative power* which could constitute every individual atom after its kind; and could so coördinate the whole as to secure a nett result so systematic, so perfectly orderly in its processes, and so obviously one great whole; with the most admirable, perfect adjustment of parts, as in so much of the universe as is even now comprehended by man, is certainly not inferior to that mere omnipotence of fiat which was formerly assumed to be the sole creative agency. To work by modes and processes is not only more philosophical, but also more intellectually and morally admirable, and more eminently appropriate to the character of a rational and benevolent Being. Descartes has his theory of "Vortices," Laplace his "Mécanique Celeste," and Newton his "Philosophiæ Naturalis Principia Mathematica;" each by theory or demonstration trying to show what might have been or what is and must be the explanation of various phenomena, if the universe is one general coördinated mathematical fact. Hypotheses can be made to cover almost every phenomenon; and even rigid mathematics has long since settled far more than enough to leave no doubt on any mind able to investigate the subject, that everything material is mutually adapted to everything else, according to the highest and most accurate principles of quantity and order; so that the sum of all merely quantitative processes is a continual increase of more and more variety, and of a steadily more complex, more beautiful, wonderful, and general unity. Considered in its still farther coördinations with sentient existences, we may add also, that it steadily eventuates in ever increasing utility and beneficence by immeasurably widening and ennobling sentient experiences. All this is accomplished, moreover, through no increase of properties, for there is found to be neither more nor less of these possible under the present constitution of things. Each atom, on the contrary, we have presumed to have its fixed amount and modes of property; and its established, definite coördinations of processes with other atoms from the beginning of creation.

MIND.

A GENERAL VIEW OF MIND AS DISTINGUISHED FROM MATTER.

THERE has been in all ages a general, almost universal belief that mind is something more than body; something which may be distinguished from the body even when it is incarnated within it; and which may continue to exist after the body has been laid aside. If this belief represents a truth, as I think it does, then it should be possible to study the constitution of mind till we are able to comprehend the nature of mental properties, and to discriminate between these and the properties of matter. The difference must be real, definite; and the properties fundamentally unlike in kind.

The forces of matter are all unsentient, acting mechanically and with not the slightest trace of an approach towards sensation, emotion, intelligence, or volition. They produce merely mechanical processes, motion in space, the ceaseless drawing together of unwitting particles and spreading them abroad again, or pushing them to and fro in space in endlessly varying combinations. All this is accomplished by processes so simple, so complex, so perfectly coördinated with everything else, that we stand in awe at the intricate, matchless scheme through which all has been achieved. We recognize the thousand phases of process, the more fascinating for their wide diversity, and we look on entranced in wonder at the magnitude and comprehensiveness of the results, tempted to cry out,

Mind.

surely here is life! here must be vivid conscious emotion in ever beautiful variation! Not so. We look deeper: there is not a vestige of sentient experience. In everything there is as much utter unconsciousness as in the movement of a clod or a stone. Though highest wisdom must have been exercised in devising the scheme, and infinite executive power was requisite to actualize it in substance and property, yet throughout all matter there is no evidence of even the weakest attribute of life. All these coöperating modes of force are wholly unsentient.

Whence, then, are these quick capabilities within ourselves, making us every hour the recipients of joys and sorrows? These acute sensibilities, constituted for enjoyment and suffering, can these arise out of a pure mechanism? These clear conscious perceptions and discriminations, can they be measured by quantity of force? These living powers which enable us to act or not to act in a thousand different directions, are they only modes of the dull unwitting pulses of action and reaction? Each mind is held to be an extended atom coördinated in continual action, reaction, and consequent perpetual interchange of processes; but in mind these processes when pertaining to itself are all sentient, felt, or experienced. Each mind is conscious of all its own characteristics, and within certain well-defined limits, is free to influence its own modes, and to determine the nature of the processes with which it will be associated, and to initiate new activities. Mental properties are living properties, mental forces are all appetencies, and mental capacities are capabilities for so many modes of sentient experience.

The properties and relations of simple matter can be measured, compared and discriminated as more and less, and even when they differ in kind can be expressed in the terms of a common quantity; but pure mental properties and relations can be neither measured, weighed, numbered, nor designated as more or less, nor expressed in

Mind.

terms of any common quantity. They can only be compared as weaker or stronger, as narrower or more comprehensive, as more or less distinct, or vivid, or acute, or clear-sighted, or noble or ignoble, or any other term expressing *intensiveness* or *quality* of characteristics. As mind is also related to extension with its quantitativeness, we often apply to its proper mental processes terms of quantity which are wholly inappropriate ; as we also apply terms of quality to matter with similar inappropriateness. This is calculated to bewilder and mislead rather than to assist us in comprehending the true nature either of mental experiences or of material processes.

There are few readily accepted, comparative terms pertaining to mental activities considered as intensive or qualitative. Science is literally almost undeveloped in this direction. Qualitative processes have usually been expressed quantitatively ; and this has misled us into a multitude of false hypotheses. Under the stimulus of fancied analogies mental properties have received names corresponding to properties of matter. We often hear people talking in good faith about the literal growth and enlargement of mind ; and minds are actually conceived of by them as adding to their substance in *quantity* or *amount*, in a manner quite similar to the growth of bodies, though nothing could be more fallacious than this. Many other processes of body are most illogically held, by implication, to be processes also of mind. This is the great inlet to confusion ; conducing to the popular belief that mental science, of necessity, must always be misty and speculative.

Mind, like matter, I maintain, has its own fixed and unvarying quantity of properties, coördinated with all other quantitative modes in the universe. Each mind has its own inherent amount of property, indivisible, and inseparable from its own proper substance ; but, *in mind, both substance and property are alive or sentient.* This life is not the product of lifelessness. Sentience is not one mode of unsentience, but the two are radically dissimilar and incompatible. Existence and non-existence can have no mean ; they can, in the nature of each, never be related through any third state or condition ; but everything supposable must either exist or not exist ; and nothing can do both at the same time. Precisely so nothing can be, in essential nature, both sentient and unsentient, or both living and lifeless. Intelligence is not simply another mode of absolute unsentience ; consciousness cannot arise as another phase of unconsciousness, and feeling is not merely a higher product generated from that which is utterly without feeling. Neither can volition arise from among the bond-servants chained in the eternal circle of reactions ; for all material action is, in fact, reaction, always dependent upon something which has gone before and produced it. No voluntary movement, therefore, could ever originate with matter ; but all the most subtle molecular forces, so like live impulses as they seem, are as really dead and unwitting as all the others. Inanimate matter is one vast, lifeless, beautiful mechanism. Free, conscious, and voluntary movement, on the contrary, is an attribute of many minds ; and sentience, or conscious, felt experience, is an attribute of all minds. Mind and matter, therefore, must be radically and constitutionally unlike.

Organic matter is still simply matter and nothing more , but each organism is matter with all its modes and forces coördinated with some mind ; and for the time being, under its directive influence and control. The mind is not its organism, but through the kindred element of quantitativeness in each, they are mutually coöperative ; all their processes adjusted each to each in a harmonious unity. Dr. Carpenter says : " When, therefore, we com pare the constant activity which we encounter in living organized beings, with the passive condition of inorganic

Mind.

matter, we are compelled to conclude, that to whatever extent the forces which control the latter contribute to the actions going on in the former, there must be additional forces resulting from the operation of properties, to which we know nothing analogous elsewhere." Does the physiologist discover so much, even in studying the material organism animated by its living mind? What, then, may the psychologist hope to find in his researches?

Mind is alive, so that all its constitutional modes are coördinated living experiences. Through its extensive or quantitative nature, if acted upon by matter, organic or inorganic, it reacts again; but the result in either event is *felt*, positive sensation in the sentient mind — a something experienced in the living consciousness. The greater the amount of acting force, the larger is the amount of mental sensation; but the kind or quality of this sensation, and of living experience in general, is not conditioned upon amounts or upon anything external to the mind itself. All qualitative modifications arise from coördinations in the sentient constitution itself, so that no one can be conscious of sensations or any sentient experiences unless his own nature is sentient and coördinated with that quality of experience. All minds are sentient, but different minds are widely and essentially unlike, both in the quantity and quality of forces and capacities, as related to all sentient possibilities. Thus *sensation* is one mode of mental modification, *perception* another, and *volition* still another. Each of these, again, has many differing qualities, adapted to unlike conditions both subjective and objective. A stone has no sentient mode of property, and therefore no coördinated external senses through which it acts and is acted upon by foreign matter; it could experience no sensation though it should be eaten up by corroding substances, or beaten with force enough to grind it into powder; but every mind, with its sentient properties, in this stage of being at least, is related to an

Mind.

organism through which it communicates with extra-organic substances, so that everything which it does, and everything which is done to it, eventuate in some quality of personal experience. The kind of experiences germain to it depends upon its own constitution, which is as definitely established in its special nature and in all its intensive coördinations, as matter is with its simple quantitativeness. Mind is living or sentient being. It is possible that even a vegetable may feel ; it is certain that an animal may both feel and perceive ; but it is evident that only a rational being can perceive, appreciate, and reason concerning the higher æsthetic and moral truths, and the abstract principles of things. Thus each mind has not only its own special quantitativeness of constitution, but its own special qualitativeness also ; each coördinated with everything else and mutually coöperative.

The increase of qualitative experiences, moreover, is something positive and permanent. *Emotion* is not like *motion* simply the unvarying product of equals derived always from equals, and admitting no possible increase of amount, but the sum of emotion, of intensive experience universally, is continually increasing. Thus is there an endless accumulation of more and more positive suffering or enjoyment coördinated with all modes of sentient process, and pertaining always to the sentient being experiencing them. If " a thing of beauty is a joy forever," so is every legitimate exercise of sentient property. I perceive a beautiful object, taste a pleasant flavor, run, think, choose, and act, all in accordance with the quantitative principles of equal action and counteraction which relate me to the objective world ; but the mental modes of sentient experience, also coördinated with these quantities, are mine alone. I gain these ; but I never return any of them again, at least to unsentient matter ; and if I communicate the like to any other mind, I myself lose nothing thereby. What I have gained of any experience, I have gained absolutely. I give back as much quantitative force as I receive; but the quality of the experience which waits upon the process is an ever new creation. It is not substantial existence, which, from its nature, can never be either more or less, of self-existing necessity; but it is a new mode of sentient existence arising from new coördinations. Sentient modes are not amenable to quantity, nor measurable by it; yet they never ignore or set aside quantitative principles, to which, also, they are coördinated; but over which they reign supreme as the master has authority over the senseless tools he uses for his own ends. Mind, in its highest modes, can exercise control over even the intrinsic passiveness or enforced quantitativeness of matter. It alone is intrinsically active or self-moving; and able, within fixed constitutional limits, to determine the nature of its own present modes and processes. It alone can act as *rational cause*, intelligently originating new events and coördinating adapted means to the furtherance of desired ends.

WE MAY IMMEDIATELY PERCEIVE MINDS; THEIR SUBSTANCES, PROPERTIES, AND PROCESSES.

MIND has no appreciable extensive properties; as weight, size, form, or color. It may possess all these on a scale quite appreciable to a more finely organized class of beings than ourselves; but our senses are not coördinated with quantities so exceedingly minute. It is, again, clearly impossible for us to reproduce an image or representation of any mind, either in language or by a visible likeness; since mind cannot be imaged by our coarse methods of representative art. But neither can any ultimate material atom present itself or be represented to us through sense. We perceive matter only in the aggregate, and every mind must be similarly studied, as related to its organism.

We cannot paint the likeness of an axiom in mathematics, and yet after a simple statement or definition of it, such an axiom is as clear to us as light; and as immediately perceived as any material object. Thus, "a whole is greater than any of its parts," is an axiom which needs only to be stated to be perceived. Statement is definition, at least in mental science, and with all abstract principles. Art can represent body by imitating its modes of extension; but it can only define mind by indicating the nature of its characteristics with so much precision that the learner can find them for himself, as existing in the object. To comprehend the simplest definition, requires the direct active insight of a highly developed, rational mind. An ox can see the picture of a tree as certainly as he can see

We may Immediately perceive Minds. 117

the real tree; but he has no comprehension of any possible definition of a tree. If, then, we perceive mind with its intensive properties, it must be through rational intuition.

Granting the existence of minds as living personalities, each possessing its own type of sentient properties, the question whether minds, like bodies, can be directly perceived by us, is first in order. Are we, under present conditions, and with our present development, as capable of directly perceiving and comprehending minds as bodies? Why not? Mental science is very much less advanced than material science — it meets with difficulties of a different class; yet perhaps not greater ones. The existence of sentient beings, as so many distinct, persisting persons, is ignored or denied by some theorists; yet we are not to forget that there are also rationalists who deny any proper existence to matter. In our efforts to perceive mind, we are restricted to self-consciousness, or the perception of our own minds as we find ourselves existing in connection with our bodies, and to the perception of other minds also existing in an embodied state. Apparently, as ourselves incarnated, we are not able to perceive, at least by ordinary processes, minds disembodied — if there be any such.

But can we immediately perceive minds existing in their material bodies? Can we discriminate between the modes of force which mind and body mutually exert; and directly perceive, in their joint processes, the coöperation of their several properties? The dull body, though in itself opaque to our vision, may yet be illuminated by the spirit within; the indwelling *energy* may render it transparent to the eye of a nature kindred with its own. I admit that we cannot, through the senses, perceive the ultimate atom, mind, as an extended isolated substance; but, in the same sense in which we perceive the ultimate atoms of matter, as they exist coördinated in any given body, in this sense may we also perceive mind as an extended ultimate atom coördi-

118 *We may Immediately perceive Minds.*

nated with its organism. It is a rational perception attained through material coördinations. Mind is part and parcel of its organism, as much as any molecule of matter is a literal part of any compound into which it enters as an integer. The mental properties coact with the properties of its organism, as really, as efficiently, and as harmoniously, as the properties of any special material atom coöperate with those of other atoms with which it is compounded. The processes differ as widely as mind differs from matter ; but they are equally accessible to us, and alike adjusted to our perceptive faculties.

Psychologists all admit that self-consciousness is an immediate perception. Who has ever held that he does not directly perceive his own thoughts ; but can he perceive the thoughts to be his own, and not perceive the act of thinking them ? How then would he know that they were *his* thoughts ? that he did think them ? His thoughts are a modification of himself, and if he perceives the mode, then he perceives himself in this mode. How can he perceive that they are his thoughts, and not also perceive himself as thinking them. Undoubtedly the whole organism is concerned in the process of thought. There is quantitative action and reaction between the mind and its body ; and matter, coördinated with thought, allows its forces to be used, transformed, and ultimately rejected and cast out of the organism, as having already served its purpose ; but throughout the entire process the mind is the only thinker. It alone has passed through modifications of sentient experience ; the whole organism beside, more or less actively coöperative as it has been in every part, has remained as unsentient and lifeless as the easy-chair in which the thinker sits.

Thinking is a sentient change — a conscious act on the part of a conscious person. From the nature of the case, there can be no sentient change unless there is a sentient *some-one* changing. To affirm, therefore, that we perceive

We may Immediately perceive Minds. 119

the change, and yet that we do not perceive the some-one changing, is to demonstrate that we do not understand the meaning of our own assertion. I hold it proved to one who asserts that he perceives his own thoughts, that he also perceives himself in the act of thinking. He may not be intelligently conscious of this; he may perceive himself confusedly, indefinitely. The newly restored blind man could see men only as trees walking. There is an ox-like state which looks out upon the material world, and can readily perceive extended, tangible, or measurable properties and modes of substance; but sentient modifications loom up before it like a dim, uncomprehended mistiness. The perception of one's own sentient being may be simply instinctive, unwitting — as it were, an irrational percept which has not fully cognized the nature of its own act. The young child sees that a whole apple is worth more than a half of one; when it stretches out its little hand for both pieces it asserts unmistakably its real perception that a whole is greater than one of its parts; yet its little head would be utterly bewildered at an attempt to comprehend the abstract principle. As the child readily perceives the applied principle, so there is a similar concrete, instinctive method by which we may perceive our real selves — by which, indeed, we must directly perceive ourselves, even while we are yet a great deal mystified by the complex nature of many of our modifications.

If I am accustomed to take the measure of everything, as I would measure a rock or tree, then, if I find my mind unmeasurable, I may easily learn to confound it with my body for the sake of arriving at something tangible. Unless I have some definite conception of the nature of the somewhat I am in search of, I may vaguely suppose that I perceive nothing but organic phenomena; but if I can really perceive any sentient process, then I must perceive also the sentient element coördinated with that process. By making one's self the object of his own closest study, the

We may Immediately perceive Minds.

perceptions must ultimately become clear and well defined. It must be possible to clearly distinguish every coöperating mode of force in the mental process ; and to comprehend much more than has ever been deemed feasible of the nature of the whole complex system of coördinations which contribute to every sentient experience.

I assuredly perceive my own conscious self, participating in every process which brings me another experience ; and I alone receive this experience. It is wholly mine, — a modification of my own living nature ; and nothing else, in the nature of things, can share in it. The testimony of my consciousness on this point is positive. I perceive the very substance of the *me*, as containing, as actualizing these living experiences. To perceive the sentient constitution of a mind, and yet not to perceive the mind thus constituted, would be as impossible as to perceive a physical movement, and yet not to perceive the moving body. We can never perceive properties or their processes except as existing in and through their substances.

I am often certain of obtaining an immediate insight into the minds of my neighbors. Are they not component parts of their own organisms — then why should I not be brought into direct relations with them ? Why can I not perceive their mental operations as really, though not as conveniently, and not always as distinctly or as accurately, as I can observe my own. Mental activity, manifesting itself through the energetic use of its own organism, is the normal condition of mind ; thus I am enabled to perceive in others all the details of a mental constitution kindred with my own, and coördinated with my powers of intuition.

But men may use disguises which I cannot readily penetrate ; the body may be made a cloak to conceal the mind, which deliberately withdraws itself from me. It is in no sense voluntary with a mass of matter whether or

We may Immediately perceive Minds. 121

not I shall be able to perceive any of its characteristics. My perceptions must depend upon my own powers of intuition as coördinated with the material body; but a mind, with voluntary powers like my own, may either help or hinder me in my efforts. Yet no one can altogether prevent my perceiving the involuntary and continuous facts of his mental constitution except by removing himself altogether from my presence. There are facts relating to his changing modes, — to his present volitions, intentions, and other activities, — which he is able, at least partially, to conceal from me, even when he is in my immediate presence. By judicious and persistent efforts he may do very much in that direction.

Generally we have only a surface perception of bodies, yet when we look at a rock, a cloud, or a tree, with even the briefest and most casual glance, the percept obtained is real, though not at all adequate to a full cognizance of the object. In a similar way we may obtain real percepts of friends and acquaintances, more or less adequate, according to circumstances. There is much room for moral deceptions, for voluntary and deliberate misrepresentation on the part of another who designedly appears what he is not; but there is much less room for intellectual fraud, or pretense and misrepresentation of personal abilities. Practically, in every-day life, we seldom doubt that we have a generally accurate knowledge of those about us — a knowledge obtained, too, directly from themselves and not at second hand. Probably we have never fully cognized anything in all its entireness — certainly not any mind; yet we have had distinct glimpses of thousands of different minds. Based upon our *perceptions* of them, we form very definite *conceptions* of the characters of many of these persons. Our *conceptions*, however, are only inferences, often doubtless, erroneous to a great degree, while our immediate *perceptions* carry with them such a weight of evidence that we cannot doubt their reality. We could

122 We may Immediately perceive Minds.

often as easily doubt concerning ourselves and our own modes of being and doing, as concerning those of our neighbors. All this is not a matter of reason to be settled by argument, but it is a simple question of immediate intuition.

Of course whoever contends that we cannot directly perceive matter, will be equally positive that we cannot directly perceive mind ; but if we can perceive the one, we certainly can also perceive the other. Our relations to extension and its various coördinations, enable us to appreciate like properties in matter ; but our higher sentient affinities relate us still more closely with all other sentient natures. The very essence of perception itself is sentience. I perceive another mind by the double aid of my own organism and of his through which he is made manifest ; but he is not represented by either organism — he presents himself to me, not as unsentient, like his body, but a sentient, personal mind, coördinated with an organism which relates him to the external world. We cognize this mental nature, looking out intelligently through the eyes, covering the whole face with its own glowing emotions, animating the whole form with its own vivid life. The sound of a voice in another room will sometimes enable us to distinguish the most delicate grades of emotion ; we know gladness from sorrow when the mind looks out upon us in either mood ; we see the whole being aroused and in earnest, and again lethargic or discouraged ; we see it vindictive or forgiving, self-seeking or unselfish ; and we often penetrate even the hypocrisies, shams, and pretenses, deliberately assumed to deceive us. Thus the one sentient atom controls the whole unsentient organism, coöperating with its forces both instinctively and reflectively ; relating all its passive or reactionary processes to its own active or voluntary modes. Mind can do no less than this ! Without body, in this stage of existence at least, it is helpless ; for sentient modes are so coördinated

We may Immediately perceive Minds. 123

with unsentient ones, that all qualitative experience is dependent upon quantitative coöperation. Why then should not the perceiving mind be also so coördinated with all these modes and processes, that its perceptions of them may be immediate?

The intuitions of most men give them a practical, unclassified knowledge of their fellows, upon which they act continually. They " read characters " shrewdly; and when some test arises, are found to have taken the measure of those about them with marvelous accuracy. They will trust *Deacon Honesty* in all questions of morals; but they never ask his opinion in a trade. The judgment of *Esquire Sharper* has great weight with them in politics; but none at all in the management of the Sunday-school. The most uneducated mother knows that her bright little Johnny can learn the multiplication table, though he does dislike it; and that half idiot Jamie is to be commended if he has mastered his A B C's at the same age. Illiterate day-laborers will look through their neighbors, as though they were so many open books, very legible on the whole, but subject to some perplexing contradictions, like most other books. How did they learn to read men at all? Obviously by simply studying them, precisely as they would study the nature of a new complicated tool which was put into their hands for the first time. The handwriting of the Creator is so clearly and broadly given, one part relating and illustrating all the others at every turn, that a great deal of it is often acquired almost unwittingly. It is the close connection and the endless repetition, with slight variations, which makes everything so intelligible, interpreted in the light of everything else.

When philosophers call in the aid of direct intuition in the study of other minds, both of their own class and of other types of sentient being, as they have long done in studying the personal *me*, many dark points will be illumined. It will hardly do here to rely either upon tradi-

124 *We may Immediately perceive Minds.*

tions and ancient theories, biased by long ago out-worn prejudices, or to construct all minds upon the principles of logical harmony, conceived in the light of one's own preconceptions and predilections. There may be many widely differing classes of mind, as there have been found to be distinct classes of elementary matter. If mind is sentient being, then it would seem that everything living should be accompanied with sentience, which is living experience. Every living atom, therefore, would be a mind. This is a question which can only be determined by the direct and most careful study of many classes of living beings ; and by a wide comparison of many of their characteristics. If every mind is not an ultimate atom constituted by sentient properties, coördinated with other properties both sentient and unsentient, then what is it? The only answer must be found in mind itself!

It is said that the reflective powers are the latest in development, and that self-knowledge is the most rare and difficult of all attainments. This may be true. I am convinced that much which was supposed to be derived from self-consciousness has been really acquired from other minds. Foreign psychological theories, when brought into our own mental laboratories for analysis, may become confused with our own mental processes till we believe we are studying the science of mind through self-perception, while we are quite as largely indebted to objective perception. What psychologist is not vastly more indebted to the theories of others for his mental science than to the direct cognition of his own mind? And who does not apply his philosophy quite as much to his neighbors as to himself, whether he is dealing with purely intellectual or with moral science?

COÖRDINATIONS OF MIND AND BODY.

THE constitution of the human mind and its relations to the body, involve interests of such vital practical moment that they cannot be safely overlooked. No mind can attain to the free use of all its powers through a defective body; and again, a defective body is often the direct result of a badly developed mind. The coördinated constitutions of a mind and its organism act upon each other so reciprocally that neither can attain to a perfectly harmonious development without a corresponding development of the other. There is a certain balance of forces, which, once inaugurated, tends to continue itself; coördinating all the new matter introduced into the system with its own status, and thus continuing peculiarities of an organism, not only for a lifetime, but carrying them on even into new organisms springing from the old; fashioning the descendant in the unmistakable likeness of his ancestor. This is as true of mental as of material coördinations, so that any peculiar mode or tendency of mental processes, such as the undue development or suppression of any group of sentient powers, usually continues itself, if not disturbed by foreign influences. On this point it will be necessary to dwell at length in another connection.

Mind and its organism are each mutually dependent on the other. A broken head may completely paralyze the rational activity of the mind; and a mind which grovels in the abuse of its intellectual and moral powers, can degrade its body even to the level of the brute; a body habitually pinched by want and starvation leaves the

126 Coördinations of Mind and Body.

mind fitful, inefficient, or imbecile in activities; while repressed and disused mental powers produce a gross and animal type of organism. The body can work stultification to the mind through intemperate sensual indulgence, and the mind can sharpen the body into unwholesome acuteness by immoderate intellectual activity. There is a type of fine animal development, resulting from excellent physical conditions and steady muscular training, which does not necessarily deteriorate the modes of mental activity, but tends rather to quicken and stimulate these also; as there is a judicious mental culture, which though perhaps excessive, and giving undue preponderance to merely rational activities, yet does not degrade but tends rather to elevate the body, and to refine all its operations. A truly harmonious development balances each against the other; seeking to build up the one strictly through its coördinations with the other. Of course the more we understand of their mutual legitimate influence, the wiser educators shall we become, both for ourselves and our children.

This mutual influence is found to extend to even the minutest details. Habitual mental habits are so externally patent to the eye, that he who runs may read. One can quite accurately point out the various nationalities in any crowd of men gathered on our streets. With nearly the same accuracy, he could group them according to their respective business pursuits. There is no need of the class-dress of the old world to aid physiognomic perceptions; for the mind is found to clothe itself in entire disregard of the fashions of the day. I have seen an imposing procession of well-dressed men in black broadcloth, with " Fenian " written more legibly on their faces than on their banners. In this country, where mistresses and maids are not always distinguishable either by the style or the materials of their garments, the expression and texture of the face is the best indication of social rank.

Coördinations of Mind and Body. 127

Even when this fails, "their speech bewrayeth them." Nor is it merely the *words ;* for we have but little provincialism of phrase or brogue among even the less educated of our own people ; while slang and doubtful grammar are largely accepted with us even among the cultivated ; but the *unconscious tones of the voice* are almost infinitely expressive of the degrees of general refinement. A dozen freely uttered indifferent sentences, in nine cases out of ten, would enable a close observer, whose attention had been called in this direction, to decide correctly as to about the mental and conventional status of the female speaker.

With men, the wider range of pursuits incident to a democratic business world, where almost everybody does a little of everything, develops in the male voice a complication of tones, to correspond with the widened and intensified male character, which is sometimes greatly perplexing. It only goes to show that perhaps a majority of our medium public and general business men are developed very much in stripes ; abounding both in mental and material incongruities, which arise legitimately from the somewhat heterogeneous character of their avocations and general conditions. All this still more strikingly verifies the truth, that each mind is the legitimate artist of its own body. It moulds it unconsciously, unintentionally, by the simple exercise of its own normal activities. It may still more powerfully affect it designedly, by a continued judicious care over it, as a rational and responsible protector.

Disease and deformity originate both from physical and mental causes ; so that a bodily hurt or a mental ailment are either sufficient to produce a like result. Idiocy may spring simply from arrested development of the body before or after birth ; from a hurt to some physical function of the brain ; or it may have its source in inordinate mental excitement, as sudden grief or fear. Anything which disturbs the adjustment of the organism to the

128 Coördinations of Mind and Body.

mental needs, and places it outside of mental control, must produce the effect of a mental incapacity or aberration. Thus if you can reach the imbecile's mind, it is found that you can most powerfully affect his body through this mental influence; and if the organism be not too feeble to bear the strain, it will strengthen and thrive thereby. It has been practically demonstrated that most idiocy is only negative, and like all other undevelopment, can be overcome by persistent efforts in the right direction. Where the mind has been hindered from action through some malformation or rudimentary state of the correlative organs, mental stimulants are found more efficient in overcoming the impediment than any amount of mere physical training can be; therefore the first care always is to arouse the mind to thought and comprehension, by any expedient which can be devised without too great a shock to the patient; but it is also true, that if you can strengthen and develop the body, through its direct influence upon the mind you may go far towards effecting a cure and benefiting the rudimental capabilities. On the other hand, if the first cause of the imbecility arose from some mental crisis, the mind should rest, at least for a time, and the body be made vigorous; and gradually the lost chain of relations between them may be found again, when the mind will resume its wonted intelligent action.

All forms of mental aberration, also, arise from some disturbance of the coördinated processes of the mind and its organism. The poor body, if persistently robbed of sleep, or worked with unresting excitement, or continuously goaded by a tortured mind, may well become at last so unnerved and discordant in all its various modes of action, that the mind will lose control over it; and thus lose, for the time at least, the control even of its own rational consciousness, and become insane. If when the mind thinks or feels, there is a rigid quantitative action

Coördinations of Mind and Body. 129

and reaction between itself and adapted portions of its organism, then all voluntary control over its own moods of thought and feeling must depend upon modes of coördination with quantitative force. Doubtless these may exist outside of its present organism, but so long as it is incarnated, it is coöperative with its organism ; and thus even its highest qualitative moods are dependent upon its quantitative relations. Keeping this fact in view, we can better comprehend how one mind may be wholly unbalanced, while another, sane on most topics, or under most circumstances, is yet entirely insane in special directions.

With our present knowledge, it is not easy to decide exactly where the disturbance arises. It is said, on the evidence of post-mortem examinations, that the brains of persons with whom insanity has been of long standing, do not always evidence a greatly diseased or a very abnormal state ; therefore the difficulty has been supposed to arise, not in the brain simply, — the brain being conceded to be the immediate organ of the mind, — but to originate quite as much with the more removed nutritive processes of the system, which fail to supply the right aliment in the right conditions for healthy mental action. However this may be, there is evidently some form of disturbance in the coöperative functions of mind and body.

But the abnormal phenomena attending insanity are not more strange or inexplicable than the normal phenomena connected with sleep ; and the one can no more be made to militate against the immortality of mind than the other. In sleep, some mental processes are inactive, while others are sometimes unusually quickened. I believe it will be found, as a general rule, that all modes involving discrimination, judgment, and moral volition, all modes in which mind is the self-determining and directive power, are partially or wholly inoperative ; while all those modes which are excited from without, either through the senses or by recollections of something which has

130 Coördinations of Mind and Body.

gone before, may sometimes be even unusually stimulated. Thus if we are disturbed by a noise, we often dream of sounds and the various objects suggested by them, or if in sleeping we feel any form of physical discomfort, we perhaps exaggerate it into other and greater discomforts. Also recent occurrences and those lately recalled to the mind, frequently dwell in the consciousness during sleep with a thousand fantastic additions. Of course the mind, governed as it is by quantitative laws, must be always in coöperation with its unresting, ever-changing organism, and as it is acted upon from without, the corresponding sentient modes are excited. The organism with its outer coördinations is in the ascendant, while in the vigilant waking moments, the mind is sovereign. Then it controls its organism and does very much towards choosing and directing its own modes of present experience; but in sleep it lays down the rudder and is drifted at the mercy of circumstances.

Sleep is mental rather than physical. Mind needs rest from its incessant activity with the accompanying vivid experiences; and more especially, when its rational and voluntary powers are in exercise, it is kept continually on the alert. But in natural slumber these are largely at rest. An equilibrium is established between this class of mental and their material modes, and active processes are for a time suspended. The exhausted brain has time to recuperate its spent energies from its adapted aliment, and when the mind is roused again to the use of its own legitimate functions, the renewed brain is again in vigorous working order, all its waste repaired from without. It is mind alone which sleeps; as it is mind only which is ever awake. Unsentient matter has no part either in the consciousness of mind awake, or in the unconsciousness of mind in its deepest slumber. Body, therefore, is never at rest. All its general processes of respiration, digestion, circulation, etc., are in continual exercise, and

Coördinations of Mind and Body. 131

though we speak of the senses as locked in slumber, yet, except in the case of sight alone, we have seen that this is only partially true ; and therefore, those modes of mind which are especially coördinated with sense, are still often responsive to the outer world with which the senses themselves are more closely related. In perfect health, that is, when all the various complex processes of mind and body are working in exact harmony, sleep is almost if not wholly dreamless, and the mind rests in total unconsciousness.

The sentient modes of mind are not directly coördinated with the general recuperative processes of the system. All these go on as wholly outside of our experiences as are the processes of fermentation which raise the bread we are to eat in the future. When circulation or digestion are impeded, we suffer pain, but if they act harmoniously, if the organs go on assimilating the prepared nutriment, as they do, sleeping and waking, then our sensations teach us nothing about these outside processes. We wake with a sense of immense refreshment, the various organs of the mind have all been renewed while we rested, the waste matter has been cast out from them into appropriate places, preparatory to a final exit from the system, or is already floating as noxious gases in the atmosphere; and with the new day there is born an ever new sense of vigor. Mind is found to be directly coördinated with its organism alone, and not with the outside processes of repair by which the organs are continually renewed ; yet if there is any disturbance in the latter, waking or sleeping everything is wrong, and attended with more or less of discomfort. Sleep is haunted by dreams and nightmares, and the waking comes, but without a sense of refreshment. Thus all the processes of nature are more or less remotely allied, and all things living are prone to slumber in the general peace and quietude of darkness and night.

In mental aberrations something akin to the condition of natural slumber is often manifested. The mind is not

132 Coördinations of Mind and Body.

now at rest as in sleep. On the contrary, it is generally most excitedly awake ; but, as in slumber the rational and responsible modes of mind have lost control over their adapted organs, through a balanced state of equilibrium, which for the time checks all action; so insanity is a loss for the time of the same control, through some break in the chain of coördinations. The rational powers have lost, for the present the conditions necessary to their proper activity ; while those modes of mind which are excited through the outer senses, as allied to foreign influences, may be unusually excited. All the more reasonable, sedate, and self-directive modes of force, have been converted into these. Hence the exuberance of fancy, and the boundless influence of imagination, in almost all cases of insanity. The special forms of the disorder must of course be as various as the complicated nature of the disturbance. Reason once dethroned, no vagary is then too wild to be conceived of or even acted on, in the utmost good faith.

The loss of sleep is an almost universal feature of the disease. A thorough rest of the mind would allow the organs time to recuperate, and when this can be effectually secured, sanity is again established and the mind resumes its wonted processes ; but while sleeplessness continues, those mental moods already in the ascendant are able to maintain the monopoly, and to occasion corresponding disorder in the whole organism ; so that the evil, like all others, tends directly to perpetuate itself. Happily the principles of order are too firmly established everywhere to be permanently overthrown ; and nature is always doing her utmost to effect a cure.

Insanity may also be produced by any physical injury to the brain sufficient to unsettle the direct coöperative processes between it and the mind, or by so great a disturbance of the general organism as will effect the same object. Hence some delirium is not uncommon in many constitutions, with even slight ailments ; and possibly, with

Coördinations of Mind and Body. 133

our present habits, very few of us continue to be perfectly well balanced. No physician can hope to succeed, in this involved nineteenth century, who does not understand more about the nature of the mind than of the body; since it is there that we are to look for both the causes and the cures of the larger half of all diseases.

All this is in direct evidence that there is an established system of normal adjustments between the mind and its body, and that upon the faithful maintenance of these, must depend not only the well-being of the mental nature, but also the health and refinement of the physical, and its adaptability to the uses of life.

But if mind and body are so intimately connected in all common interests, how do we know that they are not essentially the same? We perceive their different and unlike natures. We have each a personal consciousness of an identity which has remained unchanged from childhood. The same *me* who felt pleasure and pain long ago, is enjoying and suffering still, and all its experiences pertain to myself alone. My body does not enter into this personal consciousness. Its processes are not a part of my sentient life. It digests food and builds up its own organism in a way quite unknown to me. If I would observe its general operations, I must borrow the senses of the body and look through them to study the nature of body itself. Looking away from the conscious life of my proper self, I must study the body as something evidently foreign to me.

A soldier loses his leg or arm, but his mind is not diminished. He may lose both legs and both arms, and yet he will retain his personal identity entire. The child's body grows in stature and weight, yet his mind, though much more developed than in infancy, is the same mind still, having added nothing to its essential identity.

The body is changing all the time: it has less proper individuality than a mountain or a stone, since the moun-

134 Coördinations of Mind and Body.

tain and stone will remain for many years almost unchanged, either in substance or properties; while the organism is literally changing incessantly, and so rapidly, it has been computed that once in about seven years it exchanges its entire substance with all its forces. I myself am clothed upon by this ceaselessly changing organism; and yet I am able to so far extend to it my own character of personal unity, that it seems to us more individual than the rock or stone which remain to all intents the same for centuries together. This simplicity of nature is unmistakably in *me* — not in my body, which is so eminently complex and divisible.

The body is my indispensable medium of communication with other material substances, and my most efficient aid in the perception of other minds. Through its coöperation I acquire new experiences, and by its assistance I express these experiences to others; and yet it is mechanically subservient, always acting with me or reacting against me, through established quantitative modes. Thus I lay my hand on the table and it resists the pressure I make upon it with an exactly equal force. I feel the objective resistance — feel its influence both on my organism and through this on my living self. The sentient experience is certainly wholly in myself; but something communicated by the table and conveyed along the nerves of my body, awakens this experience in my coöperative mind.

A light ball is tossed into my hand : it communicates to me, through my organism, a peculiar slight sensation, and when my mind reacts against this with a force just equal to that which acted upon it, there arises in me, in connection with this act, the qualitative experience of perception, terminating in the object perceived. A heavy ball is tossed to me : it excites a similar sensation and perception ; but the sensation is intensified in proportion to the weight and velocity of the ball. Here, then, is quantitative action influencing the quality or intension of my mental expe-

Coördinations of Mind and Body. 135

rience. If I bring sugar into contact with my tongue, it produces a specific quality of sensation — the taste of sweetness. I take honey instead of sugar, and the result is a modified sensation of sweetness. Each sensation is wholly mental ; yet something as wholly objective in the sugar and honey contributes to produce the sensation, and the difference in the mental modification is coördinated with their different properties. If I take a larger quantity of the sweet article into my mouth, the increase of sensation shows a direct relation between quantity in the object and the quality of the experience in myself.

Quality, if used as meaning something pertaining to kind or intension of experience, cannot pertain to matter : but, it appears, that quantity or amount, measurable as more or less, does pertain to mind. The *quantity* of all coöperative modes of force directly influence the amount of the mental experience, not only throughout the whole range of sensations, but throughout the whole class of sentient experiences. The organism, as wholly material, must evidently obey all the laws of matter ; and, obviously a harmonious adjustment co-relates myself — my body, and every foreign body, allying us all quantitatively — precisely as where material forces alone are involved.

Not only are my experiences greater or less, according to the amount of coöperative agencies acting upon me, but I can also vary the quantity of effect which I am able to produce at will on foreign bodies. I toss a ball lightly, with so little force that it barely leaves my hand. I am distinctly conscious that it is I who *will* to toss this ball ; and yet I bring into exercise and hold under my control the material forces of my organism as essential instruments by which alone I can complete this act. The ball touches the opposite wall and returns feebly back towards me, its angle of reflection equal to the angle of incidence, showing that feeble as was the effort made by me it was subject to the quantitative law of all material movement.

136 Coördinations of Mind and Body.

Now let me send off this ball with my utmost force : it speeds like an arrow across the room, it beats heavily against the resisting wall, and flies sharply back into my face. Here, surely, are quantitative relations coördinating mind and matter. All my volitions, and everything material under their control, are most rigidly related in quantity. I perceive the same truth illustrated by every one about me. An earnest man with a purpose is one who accomplishes what he attempts ; while a fashionable lady, educated to aimlessness, must remain as guiltless of real achievement as her own little children. The most trivial details of life perpetually exemplify this law of inexorable quantitativeness. My friend, speaking quietly in the easy rest of his emotions, renders every tone of his voice calm and rest giving. We converse on topics in which he feels little interest, and his indifference comes pulsing back to me so palpably that I hurry on to a new theme — this perhaps moves him to the quick — a burning intenseness of feeling surcharges his lowest suppressed utterances, and I am moved too, as effectually as if he had dealt me a heavy blow. The effect is as different as the means used ; but not the less subject to quantitative restrictions. When I see a man in anger, beating the table or shaking his clenched fist in the air, I know that there is streaming on through his organism wave after wave of force, as fully governed by the laws of matter as are the heat and light radiating from the grate of glowing coals.

The mind may be presumed to unite its organism to itself exactly as throughout the universe one atom is joined to others, through the coöperation of their mutual properties — the only difference being that mind is conscious, and sometimes voluntary, in the use or disuse of some of its coördinated processes, and may in part choose its own modes and coöperative instruments, while each unsentient atom can move only as it is moved.

The body is not a clog or a burden ; but an ally relating

Coördinations of Mind and Body. 137

its mind to all the outlying resources of the universe. Without it, in this stage of existence at least, mind would be a waif in creation ; possessing possibly all its present sentience, but standing in unrelated isolation, apart from even all other sentient beings. We may safely infer that Creative Wisdom has made no mistakes in his adaptation of minds and bodies ; and that the highest good of the living being has been thereby secured !

Herbert Spencer has carefully discussed various material definitions of life, reducing them to a more comprehensive definition of his own. Life, as he views it, is " the continuous adjustment of internal relations (organic relations) to external relations (relations of the environment)." I should say, " Life " — that is the sensitive needs of the living mind — " causes the continuous adjustment of internal relations to external relations." Thus the organism is built up and maintained by ever repeated processes with ever changing materials — by a ceaseless " twofold material movement of composition and decomposition at once general and continuous." But indwelling in this shifting mechanism, there is a persisting mind, forever relating all these changes to its own sentient experiences.

THE CONSTITUTION OF MIND.

WE have seen that the very substance of matter is measurable in weight and in volume; that its processes are all measurable in time and in space; that all its remotest relations are quantitative; and that its conditions and possibilities, of all kinds whatsoever, are measurable in common terms of quantity. Matter can be neither pleased nor pained by any operations which can be performed upon it; its functions and processes are utterly lifeless. Its only social affection is quantitativeness — so much for so much.

It is now my purpose to point out in detail that all the attributes of mind, though related like matter in quantity, are also related in quality or kinds of sentient experiences; which are incomparably above all unsentient modifications in rank and worth. Matter is dead, mind is alive. Every mind is a distinct sentient being; so that all its activities ultimate in pleasure or pain within its own living experience. None of its modes are simply extensive, and to be measured only as greater or less spacially; but they are preëminently intensive, — are varied in kind or vividness of experience, or in the scope and comprehensiveness of its different experiences. Its characteristics cannot be adequately measured by amounts, but by values; as pleasurable or painful, worthy or unworthy, noble or ignoble.

An unsentient constitution is intrinsically an impersonal constitution. Each material atom may be individual and indivisible; but it has no basis for personality. A *mass* of matter can even have no proper individuality. One body merges in another, often with the most ludicrous avidity.

The Constitution of Mind. 139

The granite boulder dissolves itself into earth, earth organizes itself into tree, tree fructifies itself into apple, apple aspires itself into flesh ; then all flesh becomes grass ; and the round of incessant change begins anew. A sentient constitution, on the contrary, necessitates a personality — necessitates a true and proper unit — the indivisible subject of all sentient properties. To enjoy or suffer, implies that the somewhat enjoying or suffering be alive ; and the *simplicity* of its living nature is the vital pivot of its sentient characteristics. Two minds cannot combine to produce one and the same sentient act. If both should have identical thoughts or sensations at the same time, there would still be two distinct trains of experience ; for every sentient act must be felt and appreciated by one actor as its own. When two minds perceive the same thing at the same time, there are still two distinct acts of perception. There may be myriads of minds, myriads of beings each endowed with a living constitution ; but each must be in itself an indivisible person. Living force, because it does live, is inseparable from the personal mind constituted by it. Living capacity is the capacity of a live being. There can be no transfer of life as there can be no transfer of living experience. There is no quantitative basis on which to effect an exchange of qualities ; since all quality must pertain wholly to the mind experiencing it ; therefore *quality of experience* is not amenable to the law of quantities.

Even if mind could be regarded as only a temporary mode of matter, — as a form of consciousness arising from the organism and wholly dependent upon it, so that when the organism is destroyed the life or consciousness will also cease to exist, — yet even then, for the time being, all sentient experience must pertain to the undivided whole of the organism which has developed it. It would still be impossible that any two organisms could exercise identical functions. If both were perceiving the same thing

140 *The Constitution of Mind.*

at the same time, there would be two acts of perception and two distinct series of organic coördinations. Thus indispensable is it, in the nature of things, that present unity should be coupled with present sentient experience. Wherever there is positive sentience of any degree, from the lowest to the highest, whether this sentience results merely from a temporary coördination of matter or is a permanent property of a living atom, in either case, from internal necessity, it is related to an experiencing some-what, which, for the time being, is a unit ; and as such is equally sentient in all its parts. The present organism, if itself alive, experiences and acts in the present. Five or ten minutes hence the changing organism would have taken on a new sentience, and there could be no abiding self-consciousness. But the human organism is not equally sentient in all its parts ; and personal identity *is an abiding fact;* therefore it cannot be the changing, differentiated organism which is sentient, but the unchanging, homogeneous unit coördinated with its organism. If logic can prove anything, granting the premises, we must grant also the conclusion.

We might suppose, again, that any atom of matter elevated to the central and controlling position in an organism, would become sentient, and remain thus in unchanged identity so long as it maintained its ruling position, sustained by all the needful organic adjustments ; but losing these, the organism would be destroyed, and the deposed atom fall back again into unsentience. Consciousness here would involve a present conscious person, which is the point upon which we are just now occupied.

But can it be that life or sentience is simply one mode of otherwise unsentient matter ?—a mode so coördinated with organization that any atom falling into the authoritative position in an organism, would become sentient and continue thus so long, but only so long, as it could maintain its central post ? We have already seen that there is

The Constitution of Mind. 141

no mean between sentience and unsentience — that while everything must be either one or the other, yet nothing can be both at the same time. There are many modes of sentience, from the lowest feeling, pleasurable or painful, to the highest thought and volition, with their attendant emotions; can all these modes, many of them simultaneous, and, as a whole, persisting through a period of many years, together constitute only one mode of unsentience? The burden of proof lies with those who advocate this theory. It is not supported by a fragment of real evidence, while everything pertaining to the real constitution of things militates against it. Self-originated modes of living experience are so totally unlike the principle of endless reactions, emotion is so superior to motion, it is incredible that the one should arise from mere adaptations of the other. A new and higher element has surely entered into the constitution of living substance! All its modes are eager, personal impulses — appetencies and capabilities related always to qualities of pleasure and pain; which become perpetual incentives to its various modes of self-determined activity, as well as to all its instinctive operations. The quality of the sentience, in all its possible modes and capacities, constitutes the real and very nature of its mind, being indivisible in it, and inseparable from it. Thus each mind, because it is mind or sentient existence, must have simplicity of constitution and unity of experiences. Here is an entirely unlike, but not less real or self-evident series of coördinations pertaining to mind, in addition to those by which matter is constituted.

There are, apparently, two poles of sentience in every quality of experience which pertains to consciousness — not now a maximum and minimum of more and less; but two extremes or degrees of intensity related in kind. The current states of the sensibility are always somewhere between these two extremes; for one is usually neither

142   *The Constitution of Mind.*

suffering nor enjoying to his utmost, nor doing anything else with the whole might of his being; and there is also a negative extreme of apathy and inertness to which we seldom attain. Different minds differ in this respect. Some are habitually much nearer the negative pole than others; and a few are extremely erratic in their moods — examples of moral pendulums, always vibrating between the cavernous depths of depression and the mountain heights of enthusiasm. The mass of men are generally equable in their various moods, indulging in great extremes of any kind only on great occasions; but the most placid temper may become immensely exasperated; the most feeble will, may become grandly heroic on occasion, and the veriest sluggard may arouse himself to desperate deeds once or twice in a lifetime. The degree of intensity or force in qualitative experience of any kind, is influenced by the general state of the sensibility at the time; as all sentient modes are *quantitatively* correlated, so that an excess of one conduces towards a low state of every other. Sentient modes are also coördinated in *quantity* to external conditions of many kinds, so that more or less of force acting upon the mind or coöperating with it through any modes of process whatever, greatly influence all its degrees of intension. A heavy blow is more painful than a light one, and it requires much more conscious exertion to lift a hundred pounds than a single ounce; but the *kind* of sentience or consciousness is in nowise dependent on the *amount* of force or on anything pertaining to *quantity*. It is the *degree* of that particular kind or mode of experience which is directly affected by *quantity* of coöperating force. Thus an ox, like a man, can suffer more or less in the intensity of the pain which accompanies a more or less heavy blow; but the man, unlike the ox, may be excited thereby to think and reason on the subject; and thus be stimulated by the blow to the exercise of the higher but coördinated intellectual and

The Constitution of Mind. 143

moral modes, which also pertain to his higher and broader nature.

The qualities of sentient experience may be almost infinitely varied ; and not merely in degree, but still more widely in kind — in radical and distinct differences of grade, between which there is *coördination*, but not necessarily *correlation or the possibility of interchangeableness*. Degrees of sentient modes are quantitatively interchangeable in the same mind ; and also between one mind and another, and all the modes or kinds of property pertaining to any one mind are interchangeable or mutually convertible among themselves and with other minds kindred with their own ; but there are *kinds* of quality pertaining to unlike classes of minds, which are no more convertible with each other than the special modes of property pertaining to oxygen or hydrogen are convertible with each other or with those of carbon. They are all coöperative and mutually coördinated with the general scheme of things ; but as modes of property, they pertain to their own substances alone. Thus the simple content of satisfied vegetable existence is not correlated with the sublime joy accompanying a disinterested moral act ; and the one is never interchangeable with the other, although they may coöperate in common processes, and both possess one common feature, namely, that they are real and positive personal experiences, of the vegetable and the man severally.

If we admit that mind is substance constituted by living or sentient properties, which are at once both extensive and intensive ; or quantitative and qualitative in nature and in all their coördinations ; while matter is substance constituted simply by extensive or quantitative properties ; then everything which manifests life, manifests sentience, and must be either itself living, like the sentient mind, or like the unsentient body acting under the direct control of living power. There must be life or mind, then, in every

144 *The Constitution of Mind.*

vegetable or animal organism; and even vegetable processes must be coördinated with sentient personal experience.

It is comparatively easy for us to comprehend the minds of men, to interpret their thoughts and emotions, and to closely study the type of mind to which they belong. They are not only essentially like ourselves, in general attributes, but are somewhere in the same plane of development, experiencing like pleasures and pains, and influenced by like motives. To discern the exact nature of the ox, — to be able to appreciate and define the sentient type to which he belongs, — is much more difficult. We cannot enter into his experiences; we must observe him merely as outside spectators, judging him by the modes of sentience manifested to us. Is he a rudimental intelligence, capable under the right conditions of yet attaining to an active self-consciousness and to moral volitions? or are his capacities forever limited to sensations and to concrete perceptions? Who shall fathom the darkness of his instinctive activities — his patient weary waiting in a twilight of semi-self-consciousness, to us inconceivable, and as turbid as the outer darkness.

More remote still must be the experience of a vegetable life. We can trace in it but dimly, evidences of even the lowest attributes of a sentient, personal nature; yet surely we can discover, even in the poorest weed, that life is something intrinsically more than a product of " the double interior motion, general and continuous, of composition and decomposition " carried on under the conditions of " an organism to sustain the renovation, and a medium to administer to the absorption and exhalation," as De Blainville and Compte assure us. Sentience, or conscious, felt experience, is something known to us in many various modes; both as related to ourselves personally, and as manifested by others; and we find something kindred with this in even the lowest types of mind. If we can pre-

The Constitution of Mind. 145

sume to know anything of matter, to which we are only related through the principles of quantity, we can surely know still more of even the lowest mind, to which we are also related through quality.

We have analogies to guide us. There are kindred relations existing between all minds and their organisms, and many of the phenomena are almost wholly identical. All organisms are similar in their material processes and functions; they have numerous similitudes of relation and condition, which unmistakably group them together as a class. They are also distinctively unlike all inorganic, purely quantitative existence; is it not probable, therefore, that they are all similarly coördinated with an indwelling, sentient, organizing life?

I now take it for granted that we must each admit our own nature to be essentially living, and therefore, personal and indivisible. We have, then, a knowledge of two broadly discriminated types of being — the one simply quantitative, unsentient, impersonal; the other equally quantitative but also sentient and personal in all its characteristics. We have no knowledge of any substance differing from one or other of these two types. We know also that some animals are undoubtedly gifted with sentient properties; they suffer pleasure and pain as we do, manifesting this fact by unmistakable tokens. No one ever doubted that his horse or his cow could really suffer from a wound or from hunger or cold. Who has not perceived that a horse preferred fresh grass to stale hay, and good oats to dry chaff. Here, then, are evidences of sensation; but do our material senses experience the sensation? or is it the mind which feels? In ourselves we say without hesitation, it is mind alone which can feel; then it is mind alone in the animal which can feel! We see that a dog is more affectionate towards his master than to a stranger, and that many of his emotions approach more nearly to the lively manifestations of intel-

146   *The Constitution of Mind.*

ligent joy than do those of the placid and harmless sheep. There is, then, a difference in their habitual modes of activity, and we recognize them as belonging to different classes of mind ; but if sentient properties necessitate a person, indivisible and unchangeable in substance, in which these properties inhere, then the horse, the dog, and the sheep, must have each a special persisting mind indwelling in its ever-changing organism. It is equally probable that all animals have minds, and just as probable that all plants also enjoy personal sentient lives. Many of them may exist together in a compound organism ; but the sensations of each, if there be any such, must pertain to itself alone.

The capabilities of different classes of mind for varying states of experience may be almost infinitely unlike ; and the activities of the same mind in different stages of its development, may vary unlimitedly. In every human mind, there are modes of force possible to it, unused, undeveloped ; and, therefore, in their present state unusable to their fullest degree — thus there are capacities yet unfilled with the vivid experiences coördinated with them. How far, therefore, diversities which we usually refer to difference of constitutional properties, arise simply from the different exercise and general culture of similar mental powers, it must be quite impossible to determine with accuracy ; yet it is certain that there are radically unlike types of sentient properties pertaining to different classes of mind, and radical differences also in individuals of the same class. We have pretty strong evidence that a vegetable can never be cultivated into a man ; and there is almost as strong a presumption that all men could not be educated into Bacons, Newtons, Washingtons, Napoleons, or Humboldts. It is fairly presumable, however, that sentient capabilities are limited only as to the *quality* of their experiences ; while the amount of such experiences not only may but must go on increas-

The Constitution of Mind. 147

ing indefinitely. The vegetable must steadily accumulate sensations of vegetable content, though it can never rise to the experiences of rational thought ; and the rational mind must habitually go on increasing experiences of its own class, absolutely without limit. So long as it acts at all, since its activities are all coördinated with some mode of sentient experience, there must be an ever-growing new creation of living emotions, thoughts, and purposes. These living or qualitative modes of being are not strictly measurable by amounts, although perpetually increasing ; nor can they be created by amounts. Related to quantity, they yet transcend all quantity ; and while nothing new can originate among simple quantitative modes, where every action is invariably followed by an exactly equal reaction, something new is perpetually originated in the sentient mind, where both the action and the reaction awaken experiences higher than themselves, of new, living, felt, enjoyment or suffering.

Matter is constituted, apparently, in distinct elementary groups of individual atoms; as oxygen, nitrogen, carbon, gold — each atom of every group being exactly equal and similar to every other atom of its class, but different from every atom of every other class. There are also groups or classes of individual minds ; as plants, fishes, insects, quadrupeds, men ; but are all the minds of any one group, as in matter, originally exactly equal in sentient properties, so that every one of a given class would be developed into the likeness of every other of its kind, if from the first all the conditions of its development could be the same? As a matter of fact, no two minds are ever exactly alike in their development, and it is highly improbable that intensive properties should be extensively equalized in different minds. The coördinations of quantity require that every atom or mass of matter should be, in all its characteristics, exactly equal to every other like atom or mass. This is a mathematical necessity ; and if

148 *The Constitution of Mind.*

it were otherwise endless confusion would arise ; no one would be able to make reliable calculations, or to find any definite arrangement or fixed order in quantitative science. In qualitative science this is otherwise. Nothing in the general order or fitness of things requires that all the properties of each mind should be exactly equal with those of every other of its class. These sentient properties can pertain only to the one being possessing them ; and if every mind were entirely unique in sentient constitution, so much the more ample would be the richness and diversity of the whole hierarchy. We find no motive here for constituting all individuals of a class on the plan of rigid equalities ; and throughout the whole sentient universe they are not so constituted, or at least they are never exact equals in actual development. On the other hand, there are reasons of fitness arising from the intrinsic beauty which there is in endless variety, especially when found in connection with general types and resemblances, why each living being should be originally endowed with a unique, special constitution of its own; resembling in general traits the qualities of its class, but differing in those almost undefinable characteristics which distinguish it from every other even of its own species.

It is a well-known fact in organic development that each leaf and flower differs from every other, and that the higher the class, the greater and more numerous are the points of unlikeness. True, the material conditions are never precisely the same with any two living things, and as this must produce a reflex influence upon the life indwelling in the organism, perhaps it would be unwise to dogmatize on a subject so little investigated ; yet, while it is a fact that every lily, gnat, whale, and elephant is and always has been extremely like its progenitors ; yet that no two lilies, gnats, whales, or elephants have ever been found to be exactly alike, it is probable that the differences as well as the resemblances, arise quite as much from mental as from material conditions.

The Constitution of Mind. 149

There are very many more types of being, and greatly wider differences in kind in the organic than in the inorganic world. This is as it should be in order to an equally harmonious and more comprehensive mental than material scheme; required to perfect the symmetry of the *creative plan.* There is limitless difference in quality between mere vegetable sensibility, and the highest rational and moral attributes, with their conjoined emotions and volitions. Should there not, then, be radical differences of mental type, ranging all the way between the microscopic yeast plant, with its single-celled evanescent organism, and the beautiful human body with its simultaneous unity and heterogeneity of uses. Fortuitous combinations of matter must be subservient to the directive appetencies of sentient mind.

Sentient force may act either spontaneously or reflectively; but it acts always under the stimulus of some quality of pleasure or pain, affecting either itself or others. Spontaneous action is a reaction from something extramental which affects it, causing it to act in character upon a purely qualitative basis; but in reflective action it chooses the mode of sentience in which it will at present indulge. In both cases it is constitutionally impelled to seek the pleasure and to shun the pain — to exert itself to find the one and to avoid the other. The appetencies of one mind may be able to secure for it no higher good than that of the lowest sensation, while those of another impel it also towards pure intellectual and moral emotions. The one may blindly follow impulse, obtaining its good through processes as much uncomprehended by itself, as are the modes in which mineral crystals are formed, uncomprehended by the unconscious forces of matter; while the other may act consciously, rationally, reflectively, questioning every process, trying to fathom its whole nature and its relations, and selecting its means with direct reference to the end in view. Both methods ultimate in real

150

The Constitution of Mind.

sentience ; both are incited to activity by the present stimulus òf pleasure or pain. One appetency may be competent only to originate the feeblest effort which will build up and maintain the very lowest type of organism ; another may exercise control over a few insignificant foreign properties, using them and subserving them unwittingly to its own weak enjoyments ; and yet another may impel its mind to obtain clear rational perceptions, to cultivate admirable constructive talent, or heroic, unselfish, and general social aims — the incentives are still pleasure and pain — good to be gained, evil to be avoided.

The capacities of any mind for pleasure and pain are evidently coördinated in quality with the modes of sentient force by which its experiences are to be acquired. A low and feeble capacity is allied to low and feeble appetencies, and the quality of the conjoined experience is comparatively weak in kind and degree. A comprehensive capability for enjoyment is always associated with acute and powerful sentient force, with its widely diverse convertible modes or moods of energy.

All modes of sentient force are related both in quantity and quality ; and in the personal life of each mind are mutually convertible. We know by experience that pleasure and pain are nearly allied. The pleasure when too intense becomes pain, and from all extremely painful states of mind there is a natural rebound back again to the pleasurable. Overwhelming grief is followed by its wonderful calm, or even by spontaneous, almost unwilling joy. The sincerest mourner has often been shocked in the midst of his sadness by some cheerful thought streaming athwart him like sunshine through the rent clouds ; and whoever has known heavy affliction must remember the sentiment of vague wonder with which he was aroused to find life flowing on like a resistless river of duties and pleasures, himself drifting along with the current. Exceeding joy is equally supervened by its intense apathy, which sometimes

The Constitution of Mind. 151

becomes strongly painful; or by irritability which lapses into ready and active grief. Many degrees exist in the same class of experiences which are vividly *felt* in every mind; but for which we have yet no definite distinguishing terms.

The least attention to the subject will convince us that the mind is never at rest in any of its modes, but is perpetually vibrating between the two sentient poles of the existing mode, and that it exchanges one mode for another with ready facility. In gazing at some wondrously beautiful object, the whole mind seems to be absorbed in perception and all aglow with intense admiration. This is, perhaps, still more marked when the constructive or reflective mode is predominating—the mind is abstracted from everything except the one object upon which it is engaged; it feels neither hunger nor thirst, heat nor cold; its sentient activity is largely converted into the one dominant mode, and the whole being is in active, living sympathy. Moral and religious topics, long dwelt upon, will carry the mind up into spiritual exaltation, to the present exclusion of all earthly sympathies. These changes in mental states correspond to changes in modes of material motion. Several phases of mental activity may coexist, but every dominant mode necessitates the absorption of other modes into itself. One whose keenest and most constant pleasures are in sympathy with his intellect, is never a gross sensualist; and he who lives habitually through the senses cannot readily exercise high intellectual or moral powers. An adequately developed, strong intellect may not be incompatible with predominating sensuality, yet the two modes rarely or never exist coöperatively; they each rule in alternate epochs of activity. Almost every one must remember in his own experience that when he has been under the influence of some exalting moral emotion, he has been excited to intense disgust by some inopportune suggestion of sensual enjoyment. In an absorbing occu-

152 *The Constitution of Mind.*

pation he may have felt a positive loathing at food, and a general impatience at all interruption. It is always more or less painful, requiring a conscious effort, to turn from anything in which we are exceedingly interested — at least until satiety and weariness bring the reaction; when for the time we may be as much repelled as we had just now been attracted. It is with a kind of forced volition, an almost painful determination of will, in which the reason plays the school-master over the inclinations, that we turn back to any subject from which we have been thoroughly diverted — no matter how much it may have interested us previously. The more concentrated our thoughts, and with them our emotions, whether pleasant or painful, the more violent is the involuntary indignation at any interference. Anger and revenge, base passions and not at all pleasant in the exercise, are yet as peremptory as despotic benevolence itself. The angry or vindictive man, for the time, feels wronged and defrauded by any attempt to divert him from his stormily uncomfortable mood.

We might go on indefinitely, multiplying examples to illustrate the truth that there is a mutual convertibility or exchangeableness among all the modes of one's proper sentient energy. One and the same sentient force is variously exercised upon widely different objects, by different means, for unlike ends, and by differing but coördinated processes.

A similar relation exists between modes of force pertaining to different minds. Every one acts and reacts upon his neighbor continually. The orator plays upon the sympathies of his audience, swaying them to and fro at will, so that a whole assembly may sometimes be seen alternately bathed in tears or shaking with laughter. Responsive, and willing to be influenced, for the present they think and feel as he does, returning to him again his own modes quickened by their sympathy; but opposition once aroused, a public audience may become a very Babel of warring influences. All strong emotions are contagious. Great mental power in any direction is yielded to and acknowledged. Even the tamest person, like the coldest article in a warm room, is a centre of radiating influences. Evidently here are coördinations embracing all minds, all organisms, and matter in general. There must be a social order in mental adaptations as much higher than that which controls simple matter as sentience itself is higher than unsentience!

COÖRDINATIONS OF GROWTH.

THE mode of growth in all organisms is essentially the same. All growth is effected by the continued addition of minute, often microscopic vesicles called cells. All cells originate from fluids, growing either in the interior of preceding cells or developed free in the vegetable and animal fluids; as in liquids during fermentation, and in blood, lymph, and chyle. In all higher organisms, one cell goes on adding to itself another and another, and these yet others, all acting by entirely similar, though slightly differing processes, till from the original germ, the body of every living thing is gradually added or grows, particle by particle. Leaf, blossom, fruit, and wood are all formed by the aggregation of cells, equally with flesh, bones, hair, and nails. All secretions and products generally of every organism are effected by means of cells; food is introduced into the organism by cells, and even sensation, locomotion, volition, and in short, all action, is carried on through the agency of organized cells. With the dissolution of each particular cell the matter composing it drifts again out of the organism and is no longer a component part of it. The cell formation is the universal mode through which inorganic matter is organized and brought into active coöperation with the rest of the body. Material force in the already organized cell, attracts and modifies adapted inorganic particles, till it brings all their modes into coöperation with its own, they also assuming the cell constitution and becoming, for the time, integral portions of the organism.

Coördinations of Growth. 155

Just in this connection must we look for the distinctive influence of the mind upon its organism, and, if possible, discover the generic difference between organic and inorganic material processes. Is "the principle of life" or "vital affinity," which I maintain to be the distinctive organ-forming power, something which works on the same or a radically different principle from the simply unsentient forces? Chemical affinity always combines like compounds from like substances under like conditions ; crystallogenic affinity, with the same conditions, constructs only homogeneous crystals ; and all unsentient forces, from like causes, produce like results. The *living force* certainly has no more direct, conscious volition as to the structure of its body than have these other equally constructive forces. Who by taking thought can add one cubit to his stature? or can make one hair white or black? Which of us has predetermined to be a human being rather than a peacock, and has made himself such through his own volition? We exist by conditions higher than ourselves. We possess neither our sentient natures, nor yet our adapted organisms, from our own free choice. We may consciously develop and beautify both mind and body when we have learned to understand their needs, or we may willfully dwarf and weaken either ; being able, even, ruthlessly to sever the bond between ourselves and our present organisms ; but we cannot destroy the system of inherent coördinations through which our minds are forever allied to all other things whatsoever. We cannot permanently dissociate ourselves either from matter or from other minds. Vital force must co-work with vital processes.

Each sentient being is, apparently, intrinsically and radically an organ-forming being. To live at all, he must live in the exercise of his own proper appetencies, and to exercise these he must control coördinated matter to this end ; that is, he must build up an adapted organism. The lowest plants and animals, seeming to be wholly without ra-

156 *Coördinations of Growth.*

tional ideas or volitions, yet make for themselves bodies admirably adapted to their several needs. There is absolute *unconsciousness* of the relation of means to ends, yet the end is secured; the sentient atom, coöperating with matter as blindly as oxygen and nitrogen do in their atmospheric union, is yet clothed upon by an organism preeminently suited to it. The wisdom which alike coördinated all these " affinities " with the special work which each is to perform, is the only wisdom. Examples of chemical selection, of chemical marvels in general, are equally wonderful with kindred illustrations of organic action.

The grand evidence of a *generic difference* between organic and inorganic processes is found in the fact that while among inorganic substances every atom and mass of matter behaves exactly like every other atom and mass of its kind, in all possible relations, so that everything which can be predicted of it can be equally predicted of every other of its class — with organic substances the very reverse of this is true. The widest diversity of form and functions perpetually arises from substances identical in all known material properties : the most unlike, and, judging by quantitative standards alone, the most unlikely differences spring up continually ; so that it may be laid down as a universal rule that *from homogeneous material elements*, in all organic processes, *there arise heterogeneous results*. The simple cell itself is an organ ; and all organic processes are organizing or differentiating processes. It is an equally universal law, that *from homogeneous material elements*, in all inorganic processes, *under like conditions, there arise homogeneous results.* Doubtless this would be true also with organic processes, if with them, it were ever possible to realize the *like conditions ;* but as each organism is necessarily under the special control of a sentient being, with many special appetencies and capabilities pertaining to itself alone, these organize or differentiate the

Coördinations of Growth. 157

homogeneous elements in accordance with their own sentient necessities.

One piece of gold behaves everywhere exactly like all other gold in like relations, whether pure or in any of its possible combinations; one grain of sulphur acts always exactly like every other grain of sulphur, and one drop of pure water is, in every respect, and under all conditions, exactly like every other drop of pure water in similar relations. On the other hand, while the first material nucleus of every organism, vegetable and animal, is essentially identical; while all organisms originate under similar conditions, in connection with similar functions, differing only in the general variety incident to the wide range of varying economies pertaining to vegetable and animal life, and while their subsequent development is effected through the assistance of essentially the same materials, utilized through generally identical processes of composition, and rejected again by similar processes of decomposition; yet every sentient life is found to be coördinated with a unique organism of its own, constructed after a special permanent type of its kind, while the almost infinite diversity among them is a fact eliciting our endless admiration.

Neither the microscope nor chemical tests can, in the earliest stages of growth, distinguish between the germs of a reptile, an insect, a quadruped, or a human infant; if, then, quantitative influences alone were called into action, it should be possible to develope them all into similar forms, causing any one to assume the type of either of the others, or in any event to approximate towards this result. Supposing that we are sufficiently skilled in using the requisite material aids, on this theory, the insatiable crocodile should be actually transformable into the harmless ox; at any rate we ought essentially to vary the conformation of his organism by effecting a radical change of all his material conditions. There have been many experiments made in this direction, conducted with all the nicety

158 Coördinations of Growth.

of precision and perseverance which the exact quantita·
tiveness of physical science has cultivated in physical
investigators, yet no transformation nor considerable mod·
ification of type has ever been effected. The untypical
modifications, — and there have been many such, producing wide superficial variations and minor differences even
of structure, about which so much has been written by
the physical-development theorists, — are clearly referable
either to an abnormal development or repression of certain mental appetencies out of due proportion to others,
with their corresponding development of organs ; or, much
more frequently, to changes of food, climate, and other
similar material conditions, producing only insignificant
organic and coördinated mental results. To this subject
I shall refer again in its place.

The preëstablished organic type has not been found to
be essentially varied by external circumstances. The
organism may be dwarfed, weakened, and malformed by
privation, or strengthened by material comfort and abundance ; it may be distorted in the offspring by persistent
" selection " of parental peculiarities tending thereto, or
beautified in the posterity by a similar selection of beautiful traits in the progenitors ; and there is some rather dubious evidence that by persistent use or disuse, through
many generations, some organ might be produced or
suppressed in the posterity, or transformed and diverted
from its original use to some similar end better suited than
the original one to the subsequent habits of the family ; as
island insects have been supposed to lose the use of their
dangerous wings, which are perhaps gradually soldered up
in their cases, or converted into jaws or legs for their
greater advantage ; but however this may be, — and such a
result is not only possible, but probable, and supported by
analogy everywhere,— yet no creature, vegetable or animal,
has been known to develop into any other than his essential family type, or to lose or gain any mental property

Coördinations of Growth. 159

through any series of external influences whatsoever. If, as I maintain, it is the permanent, sentient type of the living being, which by its modifying influence determines the character of its organism, this must continue to be a universal fact. Crocodile's eggs, taken from their native sands and hatched artificially, will produce young crocodiles still. They are no larger than the eggs of a goose; but if the poor goose should incubate them she would rue the inborn dominant nature of her crocodile brood. Food, temperature, new surroundings, nothing can greatly modify the amphibious saurian organism. Innate sentient appetencies, to which there is nothing analogous among the properties of matter, will fashion the crocodile organism, just as all other like appetencies have built up similar organisms responsive to their needs, and will continue to use and maintain the same by continual repair, so long as it is able to perpetuate all the combinations necessary to effect this result. Thus, beginning at a common material starting point, the special sentient life in the mustard-seed, coöperating with its fellows, builds up the mustard-tree, the oaklet and its clan produce the oak, the clamlet organizes the clam, and the higher needs of the sentient human soul create the nobler human form. All this is done in unconsciousness; for the coördinations effecting it are outside even of human consciousness; yet the processes through which all is produced are carried progressively forward from the beginning, so that skillful embryologists claim to be able to distinguish the future mollusk, radiate, articulate, or vertebrate, in an almost microscopic organism, which the uninitiated could scarcely discern at all with the naked eye.

When we take food into the system, what combination of simply quantitative forces can convert that food into hand, or foot, or brain, or any other special organ? Foot and hand are essentially alike in all material properties. What agency, then, has made the one hand and the other

Coördinations of Growth.

foot? What simply chemical action can transform the same elements, chiefly carbon, hydrogen, oxygen, and nitrogen, into leg in the quadruped and wing in the bird? into ear that can hear and tongue that can speak? Chemical affinities might select ingredients adapted to become bone or skin or hair, but neither in chemistry nor mechanics are there enough pure unsentient principles upon which to construct the unlike bony skeletons of articulates and vertebrates.

The results are indeed quantitative throughout. A given amount of food will produce a like amount of organism, minus the residuum of rejected portions; but another and higher type of sentient forces determines the kind or *quality* of organs best suited to its needs. He who coördinated all things must have chosen the type of each class of organism, as He did that of each mineral crystal; but while, in the latter case, his plan can be actualized by combinations of simple matter, in the former, living, sentient experiences are the directive influence needed to consummate his designs. Each living thing, having its own inherent sentient properties, which, when either acting or acted upon, give it personal pleasures or pains of a specific character; these various sentient experiences are made the ever-recurring stimuli, impelling it responsively to energize in the direction which will build up and sustain an organism best adapted to its needs. The feelings of a small fungus must be equally unlike the mercurial pleasure of a dancing insect, and the reflective enjoyments of a human being. Each needs, therefore, a correspondingly unlike organism, adapted to its own quality of existence. A vegetable as highly endowed as man is with various appetencies, impelled by its innate powers to as acute sensations, as busy thoughts, as intense emotions, and to as wide a range of volitions, must become dissatisfied and even intensely miserable. Rooted to the earth, without locomotion, and with almost no material

Coördinations of Growth. 161

forces under its control, by which to gratify its desires or to execute its volitions, its whole life would be a hopeless mockery. Its seething, tumultuous passions, in unresting ferment, but with no outlet, would become intolerable torture. We find no such practical mistakes. Sentient demand and the adapted supply are everywhere commensurate. The appetency and its conjoined capacity for experiences are direct incentives to the growth of its specially coördinated organ ; so that fungi, insects, and men, ally themselves alike to responsive organisms, coördinated with the necessities of the living tenants.

Certainly we are now pressing closely upon the ground of sheerest hypothesis, and unless we can indicate the process by which an appetency can create its adapted organ, and sentience in general promote organization generally, it may count only as so much reckless theorizing. Any present treatment of the topic must be immature ; but it may point the way in the right direction ! Hunger is a well-known experience which excites directly to the taking of food. The gratification which attends the normal exercise of this function, as well as the discomfort of hunger itself, when excessive, alike prompt us to eat. These several sensations are, like all others, purely mental ; yet they are directly allied to the state of the body at the time. Under normal conditions, hunger is only felt when the organism is in need of material for growth or repair ; it is the appetency impelling to the search after a supply, thus serving as an ever-recurring stimulus to all coördinated organs, upon whose action depends the adoption and organization of the new matter introduced through the influence of its special promptings. Here, as it seems, the work of this special appetency (hunger) is at an end. It has accomplished the part assigned it, and is advertised of the fact by the sensation of content, pleasantly following the supply. The process is then taken up by related

162 *Coördinations of Growth.*

forces, sentient and unsentient, and carried forward to completion.

In treating of the possible nature of coördinated organic processes, it will be necessary to consider the subject from different stand-points, and to treat of it at length.

We possess a general consciousness of many various modes of physical energy, which it is pleasant to call into exercise. We are impelled to various kinds of unceasing activity by impulses which are not easy to define, but of which we are all distinctly aware, so that the body is never quite at rest, either as a whole or in any of its parts. We move a finger, we wink the eye, we breathe, we walk. We find ourselves made up of many different series of prompting energies, ever impelling us to act, act, act. These several modes of energy are perpetual stimuli to corresponding modes of exertion, and so also is the reflex enjoyment which springs from the normal exercise of every function, in a healthy condition of the system. Every natural movement has its attending satisfaction, while both inaction and excessive activity give proportional discomfort, and often positive pain. We are subject, therefore, both to the impelling force and its resulting experience; each in their very nature directive, by prompting towards the pleasurable and warning away from the painful.

If, then, we all experience a need for general unresting activity of the body and mind, often to no special end directly conscious to ourselves; but because we are incited thereto by an ever-active sense of force, prompting to personal exertion, is not this general restless impetus the universal prompter to all processes of organization?

Suppose the appetency for action, change, effort in general, to be first awakened in the nascent mind through some new coördinations adapted to excite it, this first new-born sensation would be accompanied by its appropriate satisfaction, and both experiences would react against co-operating forces, demanding more, more! To this demand

Coördinations of Growth. 163

the nascent organism would be responsive in turn ; the organic action would reawaken the appetency, and the reacting appetency adjust itself to new materials, bringing these also into the just forming organic germ-cell — thus sentient experience would increase, and under its influence, adapted atom be added to atom, till the appropriate mature organization was completed.

No new adjustment of unsentient forces can be supposed to awaken present active sentience in an atom, with a nature intrinsically unsentient ; but if every atom, whether sentient or unsentient, is constituted from the beginning, — all its properties, whether merely quantitative, or qualitative also, being definitely established with all their possible coördinations, and waiting only the conditions under which they can be merely exercised if simply quantitative, or exercised with their coördinated sentient experiences, if also qualitative, — then it is no more surprising that adapted conditions should first awaken and afterwards continue a distinct developed consciousness or sentience in the sentient atom, than that they should call forth the exercise of some hitherto unexercised mode of force in a material atom. No one would suppose that the mild drop of tasteless water might, under some conditions, become scalding steam, and under others freezing ice, if experience had not revealed the fact. Undeveloped mental atoms may exist in a state of semi-consciousness from the creation, or sentience may even be wholly latent and inoperative ; yet, being once awakened into active life by the right conditions, they can from the nature of things never relapse again into the undevelopment of the past. In the first germ-cell, life must begin already to act responsively, in conjunction with the material forces in its growing organism. Processes of composition and decomposition are already inaugurated, and must repeat themselves without cessation, or else the organism cease to exist. It must continue to be an organism capable of administering to

164 *Coördinations of Growth.*

the demands of a nature, which, as sentient or intensive, may act by repetition or by increasing intensity or variety of living experiences ; thus making upon its organism continuous demands of service, impelling it unceasingly to organize new substance, and as continually to cast out the old, which, having served its uses, is no longer available. The first series of distinct feelings must inaugurate the organized germ-cell, and continued sensation with other allied experiences continue the growth of a coördinated organism. On the other hand, the action of adapted external forces upon a mind not yet quickened to the exercise of sentient powers, is probably, in the nature of things, the ordained process by which the lowest phase of life, *sensation,* is first called into actual exercise, and in turn, sensation, type and fore-runner of all living experience, must inaugurate the reacting mental stimulus to all organic processes. Why should not the earliest appetencies act on matter from the first attempt at organism, instinctively adjusting it to its needs? At a later period, we perceive the coöperation of mental and material forces in a continuous process which we know began in the fluid drop, not yet assimilated into the first germ-cell, and will continue till the relation between the mind and its body is finally dissolved. We are justified therefore in thinking, that, from the first, the mind with all its nascent properties is a present and active partner.

Every mental act, in connection with its organism, seems to be as directly related to organic development as heat applied to water is related to steam, or as gravity is related to motion. The earliest mode of sentience produces the simplest and typical form of organic growth — the simple cell — which is radically alike in all organisms. But the modes of force may be many and various in every individual mind ; and still greater is the variety among the different types of mind. I am fully convinced that the kind and degree of each appetency, classed according to its

Coördinations of Growth. 165

present general state of development and activity, must be regarded as determining the character of its coördinated organ ; and as appetencies are associated in coöperative, harmonious groups, it is emphatically the mental constitution which not only uses but produces its adapted or ganism.

The bird possesses an evident most restless appetency for flight. Bred up in a cage, he beats his wings against the bars in impotent seeking after the gratification of this impulse ; once freed, he soars through the air in manifest delight and exhilaration. This appetency can be satisfied only by actual flight, as hunger is appeased only by its adapted supply. Can we not, then, appreciate the evidence, that here is a directive stimulus, energizing perpetually in one specific direction, and that the growth of the coördinated organ, the wing, is the legitimate result? Afterwards, use, the actual flight of the bird, strengthens and perfects the organ by a precisely analogous process. In both cases it is the controlling mental energy, using, and therefore coördinating matter with its own sentient ends, which both produces and maintains the organ. Use of the organ, in general, directly relates other material forces to it, by organizing their substances also. The disproportionate use of any organ, as wing, arm, brain, or any other part of the organism, directly relates the unassimilated food in the system to its repair, building up its waste, and strengthening *it* in particular. We can tie up an arm, hindering the mind in its action through that organ, and the arm will steadily wither and perish ; or we may strengthen and enlarge every muscle, as the blacksmith does, by incessant use. Thus any part of the organism may be weakened or strengthened by judicious use of means ; yet no system of external means can altogether destroy the appetency. No protracted disuse of any organ, even for many generations, has been found sufficient to suppress the organ wholly, in any animal belonging to a

166 *Coördinations of Growth.*

class possessing it. Nature makes at least a rudimentary attempt at forming it, and, doubtless, let the conditions at any time become favorable for this, the appetency and its organ would both develop alike. The goose retains its webbed feet, comparatively useless appendages where there is no water to swim in; but bring the poor goose into the neighborhood of any ditch or pool, and it immediately commences paddling therein with preëminent satisfaction. The appetency is sufficiently active, not only to maintain the organ in its proper development, but also to seek out every occasion for its fullest exercise. Fish in the Mammoth Cave, without light from the earliest generations, have at most but the veriest rudiments of eyes. *Amblyopsis spelæus* wants even the orbital cavity, yet here under the most unfavorable conditions the organism of the craw-fish (*Astacus pellucidus*) affords still the evidence of an unexercised but native appetency for sight. It would be a pleasant and curious experiment to introduce these fish into the sunshine, and watch for the gradual development of their organs of vision.

In the fitness of things, the kind and degree of sentient modes pertaining to any mind, should determine the structure and form of its adapted organ. The quadruped, whose appetencies are chiefly instincts, and whose instincts are related mainly to sensations, can do very well with legs alone; but man, whose moods are largely reflective, whose reflections connect means and ends, and lead to selection of modes, has need of arms also. His right hand is the complement of his head, and neither would be of much executive value without the other. He energizes as impelled in the direction of his many appetencies, and the material elements coöperate, adjusting themselves, cell by cell, in an organism much more perfect than that of any other creature. Spontaneously, rather than reflectively, he energizes as he is — a being of marked and various modes ; and the result is a growth and mainten-

Coördinations of Growth. 167

ance not of stomach, lungs, or heart alone, but of brains also, and a mind within, directive of the whole harmonious organism. A like correspondence is found throughout the organic kingdom.

We can trace the organism from a microscopic point, step by step, through all its processes of growth ; we know whence it came and whither it goeth, by following the elements which it borrows and returns again to the common environment ; but who shall point with no uncertain finger to either the beginning or the ending of a sentient existence? We perceive that new sensations are awakened within us by any modification of our organisms ; and that minds in the youngest organisms manifest like sensations with ourselves arising from like causes ; we must, therefore, infer that sensation was originally awakened in the nascent, but already constituted living mind, through the action upon it of coördinated external forces. But this mind must have been constitutionally endowed with life or sentience from the first, at least in the same sense in which we are endowed with the capacity for experiencing sensations when acted upon through the senses. The sensation may be something yet in the future ; but the appetency for it, and the capability of experiencing it, are inherent in the mind as the fundamental elements of its nature. Thus all sentient modes possible to any mind must have been definitely determined and constitutionally inwrought within it ; and perfectly related also to all coördinated elements. Sentience, that is felt or experienced activity, is the distinctive characteristic of all living things ; and if an atom constituted by a sentient nature has not yet experienced this, it is not yet actively alive, though it must exist, and being quantitatively coöperative with other atoms about it, unless perpetually in conditions where sentience is latent or at rest, as in sleep, there must be a general undeveloped sentient experience even from the first.

Living force and capacity may pertain to absolute sub-

168 *Coördinations of Growth.*

stance; but a created mind is a sentient unit, endowed with special created modes of sentient property, so coördinated with each other and with all coexisting modes of things, as to be enabled to exist and act with a predetermined nature. Just as gravity, heat, electricity, etc., are all created forces — that is, self-existent force related in definite modes, through established laws, regulating all their possible processes; or as carbon, oxygen, and other elementary substances, are created or constituted substances, with fixed related properties which must exist and act in special modes and motions under all like conditions; so minds are created or constituted each with a definite sentient nature of its own, with specially coördinated determinate characteristics. One mind is constituted a vegetable, whose sentience is to ultimate in sensations; another an animal, with both sensations and perceptions, and yet others with special types of unlike properties, rising higher and higher, till we reach man with rational and moral powers coördinated, like his Maker's, with the pure principles of things generally. A scheme of harmonized thought, embracing everything which is known to us, is thus seen to have been applied and realized in things, so that everything continually exists and acts in character. With such a definition, it is evident that our personal life not only may have had, but must have had a beginning; that there must have been to all created minds a first definite sensation as well as a first remembered experience. From this feeble commencement must gradually have arisen to each of us the many vivid experiences of our whole remembered existence. Originally we were constituted with sentient possibilities to be finally realized under certain conditions. Having found these established conditions, we live actively, consciously; we are coöperative sentient minds. He who gave us our original constitutions, determined also the circumstances under which we should begin the proper development of our sentient properties.

Coördinations of Growth. 169

An adjustment of many complicated conditions was evidently necessary to this wonderful awakening into active sentient being. In the existing economy of nature, the higher the type of mind, the more rare and beautiful are all the accessories requisite to initiate its development. The lower orders of being are often "asexually" developed. The new life seems able to spring up under even widely different sets of conditions; and one may even suppose that among compound organisms, whose offspring sometimes differ widely in form, two or more different sentient classes may really be found growing together under nearly the same conditions; each drawing material sustenance through the same organs. When a nectarine is found growing on a peach or a plum tree, or a real peach maturing on the stem of an almond; or a tree bearing peaches and almonds indifferently,[1] these and similar "sports" of nature seem to indicate that the sentient element in these beings is so similar that some living atom may easily arise abnormally in the circle of near kinsfolk; and yet that its own special mental properties, prevailing over its origin, have power to develop it after its kind. However this may be, the higher the sentient type, the fewer are the numbers reproduced; and the more complex the reproductive coördinations. This is as it should be in the fitness of things.

Sexual appetencies lead to reproduction — to that class of coördinations, mental and material, by which an organism originated in connection with parental functions, begins to exist, animated and directed by a life of its own. There is an eminent moral fitness in the prearrangement requiring the coöperation of the two sexes in this mental birth; at least of all the higher types of being, thus establishing a condition which will insure the new mind that it will be properly related socially to other sentient beings. Not only are the strongest mere passions and instincts called

[1] Darwin, *The Variation of Animals and Plants under Domestication.*

170 Coördinations of Growth.

into exercise through parental relations; but among rational and responsible beings, some of the sweetest, most unselfish social emotions are quickened in both parents and children. Desires and purposes seeking the good of others even dearer than self, are directly stimulated in the family circle; and while parents are quickened to unselfish love, and to the exercise of their highest moral appetencies, the child is also aroused to the earliest exercise of self-forgetfulness. Common interests arise between the parents, and these among rational beings descend to the children and the children's children, widening in many directions. Family love is the broad stepping-stone to universal good-will!

We have no reason to suppose that the proper mental constitution is in any sense derived from its progenitors, or that it receives from either parent anything except such preadjusted conditions as will secure its own proper development.

Does mind increase in substance? in amount of properties? Assuredly not! Then in what does the normal growth of mind consist? What is mental development? We know that mind cannot grow by additions to its substance, as body does, since mind is permanently unchanged and identical in substance. We perceive a persisting personal identity in ourselves and in others. The man is the identical being which he was as a child; and yet this persisting somewhat, unchanging in substance and in its sentient constitution, has acquired a continual increase of experiences of many different kinds. Thus mental growth is evidently growth or increase in the amount, strength, or variety of sentient experience; and in an acquired discipline of the mental attributes by which these experiences may be still farther accumulated! A child constantly perceives new objects, acquires new principles, learns to compare likenesses and differences, to observe, reflect, judge, reason, and choose wisely on many

Coördinations of Growth. 171

points ; and therefore we say that he has grown mentally, though he has added nothing to the substance of his mental nature. He has acquired no new sentient property or mode of experience, though he may have developed and disciplined many hitherto unused modes which were yet germain to his nature, existing potentially in his persisting constitution.

All actualized experiences constitute the mental wealth of their possessor. One's perceptions and conceptions, his joys and sorrows, his plans, thoughts, and purposes, remain as really and exclusively his own possessions, as does the personal consciousness to which they pertain. They are a perpetual new creation, a qualitative increase, which is forever accumulating, unlike mere quantitative values which must, from their nature, remain unchanged in amount. All quantitative values merely change their modes, but can become neither more nor less in consequence ; but every new sentient mode is a positive new gain to its possessor. He may or may not forget in time that he has ever enjoyed it ; but the present enjoyment was an absolute good. It could neither be measured by time, nor space, nor number, nor any other simply quantitative estimate, yet it had a felt value of its own, peculiar to all sentient modes, and which remains a thing actual in itself ; being never transmuted into anything else. The sentient mode may change ; one thought or feeling may glide into another ; but there is all the time an increase of sentient value, not an exchange of one kind for another, as among all quantities.

It is precisely this qualitative element — this endless increase of sentient good, which mind cannot get from matter *as cause*. But if the capacity for sentience preëxists — as we hold that it does from the first constitution of the atom — then a conjunction of quantitative influences may readily excite these qualitative experiences. Material coördinations are occasions or conditions conducing to

172 *Coördinations of Growth.*

the proper mental activity. Mental growth, therefore, is growth in mental experience, and in the consequent discipline of the mind through which similar experiences are acquired.

Hereditary traits and tendencies, apparently mental as well as physical, and transmitted from generation to generation, are a peculiar feature of lineal descent which we are called upon carefully to consider. The child possesses a definite unchanging mental constitution of its own ; how then shall we explain the often close mental resemblance to one or both parents? What satisfactory explanation can be given of inherited family traits, either mental or physical? Why indeed, need the offspring, since it preexists with a mentality of its own, even belong at all to the same type of mind with its progenitors? These are three several questions, each demanding a distinct answer of its own. The last, which is most general in principle, we will consider first. Why, then, if every sentient atom is a mind with an original fixed constitution of its own; on its attainment to the exercise of sentient powers why should every new life begin to exist in connection with progenitors of its own type? Why should not the rose-tree produce lilies and the lion give birth to the lamb ?

We might reasonably answer, Because He who coördinated all things prearranged otherwise ; but as we have never found that He apparently acts either without sufficient reason, or except through adequate means, we are bound to offer a more satisfactory statement of probable proximate causes and processes. The highest fitness of things, æsthetic, physical, and moral, requires that the existing broad principle of order should be maintained, providing generally that each living creature should produce seed after its kind. Each new life must necessarily find the most fitting conditions for its proper development in connection with its own class, whose sentient needs, and therefore all depending adjustments, are kindred with its

Coördinations of Growth. 173

own. The same principle which requires that appetencies and capabilities should ally themselves to an adapted organism at all, in order to their own proper activity, would require also that the nascent life should find proper conditions already prepared for it; and this, of course, could only be properly done in connection with beings intrinsically like itself. Again, the harmony of life would be destroyed if the rational parent were left in doubt as to whether the nature of his offspring would be kindred with his own, or whether he should give birth to some creature in a plane of life so remote that there would be, if not positive antagonism, at least but few common sympathies, and little common love. The bare thought is so utterly repulsive and subversive of all beautiful sympathies that it is the strongest possible argument in favor of the established order. Should the lioness find herself the mother of lambs, would she love them or eat them? Unless we would subvert the entire system of creative coördinations, we must maintain those which initiate the new life into the exercise of its new functions.

But, through what special adjustments has this almost universal order been established? Evidently through the mutual coöperation — the perpetual action and reaction of the mind and its organism, mutually stimulating each other by the simple principle of use or exercise. Each new experience gained by the mind is a discipline of its powers in that direction, continually preparing it for repeated, if not increasing, like experience; while the organism, also, once started in any direction, goes on repeating the tendency thereto by organizing new forces to coöperate with it, precisely as any other mode of material action tends to continue and communicate itself. As a blow from a club sends the ball forward in the direction it was itself pursuing, so the already efficient organs impel forward the elements continually introduced afresh, in the direction in which they themselves are tending; and as the club, com-

174 *Coördinations of Growth.*

municating its mode of motion to the ball, gives up so much of its forward impulse, accepting an equal reactionary mode in return, so the old organism transmitting its own modes of activity to the new elements, accepts others in exchange, gradually losing its organic coördinations thereby, and dropping back again into the inorganic world. No quantitative force is either gained or lost by the process ; but the continual change or renovation peculiar to all organisms is thus effected. There may be continuous and perpetuated processes of matter, and these would doubtless be effected in the organism if it could be coördinated independent of an indwelling mind ; but no series of simply material elements could give any positive gain, although there might be increased heterogeneity such as is effected through new combinations in inorganic processes. But just here, in all organisms, interposes the sentient influence. Activity in any direction having quickened coördinated experiences, this special quality of experience reacts, not quantitatively merely ; but, the largely developed appetency, once aroused to special vigor, diverts other modes of experience into its own. The appetency is a new and added element over and above all quantities ; so that although *they* still coöperate on the most rigid quantitative principles as hitherto, yet the new sentient element becomes at once directive of the unsentient. Thus does every qualitative or felt activity tend not only to perpetuate but to increase itself, though perhaps first excited by purely physical agencies. Given the sentient appetency as a preëxisting possible mode, and no matter what shall first excite it, its disproportionate activity in any direction, other things being equal, tends directly to perpetuate itself.

In the light of this principle, let us suppose that either parent possesses some marked mental trait ; this will naturally express itself in the parental organism with corresponding prominence. It must do so more or less, if, as we have tried to show, the mind is the proper architect of

Coördinations of Growth. 175

its own body. The new organism will thus begin with its material functions allied in the closest harmony with the parental functions, so that, unless the adjustments are disturbed, the physical peculiarities will go on developing in the child in the same ratios as in the parent. On the principle, then, that sentient properties are excited from without, tending thenceforth to repeat and increase themselves, we fully account for the apparent inheritance of even mental traits. Though the new being has its own immutable sentient constitution awaiting development, it finds the coördinated conditions for its development in connection with natures kindred with its own, and its various legitimate modes of sentient growth are influenced by the physical modifications already existing in connection with the parental organism. Doubtless no class of modifications can go any farther than to stimulate existing mental properties unduly in one direction rather than another, possibly to the retarding of other correlated or antagonized modes of power. Certainly no sentient attribute can be originated by any possible combinations of parental influence ; and yet, little by little, the child will normally develop under the same leading influences with which he first began life ; and will, therefore, grow both mentally and physically in the likeness of his parent. Especially if the parent had leading traits of any kind, will these be likely to retain the lead in the offspring.

But the balance of the new organism must almost necessarily be gradually more or less disturbed. All the surroundings of the child — the whole range of foreign influences as well as its innate sentient proclivities — will perpetually introduce new elements ; so that if an individual should spring from one parent only, and if parent and child were originally exactly identical in sentient constitution, they would, under the necessarily differing influences, develop unequally, and be still somewhat unlike in mind and body. Indeed, no one ever remains exactly like him-

176 *Coördinations of Growth.*

self from year to year, but is continually changing in manifestations while his real personality is yet unchanged.

Again, both parents have their special unlike traits which, conjoined in action, influence the development of the new being. The new organism, from the first, is started under the auspices of differing and sometimes warring tendencies, harmonized like all compound motion, by a mutual change and interchange of the various modes of force. The result, therefore, must be as we find it in actual life, the differences and resemblances both real, but highly variable. There is a universally recognized family likeness, always controlled and overruled by a clearly defined personality, transcending all common traits, whether pertaining to the whole class or to immediate ancestry. The most variously accumulated scientific evidence alike adds to the proof that each sentient atom has a directive sentient constitution of its own, which not only uses and controls, but also originates whatever is special to itself in its own organism.

Any mental or physical trait may be gradually accumulated by successive generations as a family heir-loom, or being accidentally acquired by either parent, may be reproduced in their child, or passing one or more generations, it will sometimes reappear even in a remote descendant. All similar "freaks of nature," as they have been called, are satisfactorily explained on the hypotheses of the reflex influence of coördinated matter and mind, mutually perpetuating all joint processes, and therefore tending to maintain acquired peculiarities of whatever character. Here is a universal principle necessarily applied under varying conditions ; therefore the varying results.

There is a natural tendency in every organism to cast off disease or imperfection, to recuperate and perfect itself. Organic processes are essentially renovating, improving processes — processes of perpetual new adaptations to perpetually new sentient needs ; and as disease is simply

Coördinations of Growth. 177

some form of disturbance to these natural processes, the organism must tend to right itself. Organic renovation is a physical necessity. Add to this the influence of mind, acting either spontaneously or deliberately; and in either case stimulating and directing the renovating process, because acting under the universal law of all coördinations, which requires that all joint processes, taken in the largest sense, should be harmonious and working to the same end, which end is a real progress or advance ; and we see how mind and matter everywhere coöperate for the highest well-being of the sentient life. Is disease hereditary? Nature, the universal physician, is far more hereditary still. Her treatment is unerring. We may coöperate with her ; but no sensible man will ever arraign her for malpractice ; for One wiser than she has instituted all her processes in beneficent harmony. Her treatment, too, is continuous, in sickness and in health, from the first to the last organic act. No room is left, therefore, for doubt that mind entering upon another life, will find nature — that is established beneficent coördinations — following him even on through endless existence. The established order of the universe is itself one perpetual curative process, ameliorating evil and increasing good forever. In a word, I repeat, that it is the universal law of all processes that they work together to the same end, to the perpetual increase of sentient experience, and to the highest good of sentient being.

The lower the type of life, the more gregarious and dependent seem to be its organic functions. The corals and hydras, like plants, grow in a common organism branching out tree-like ; new individuals springing from a common ancestor, and either remaining permanently fixed in the organic community, or dropping off to become in turn the progenitors of a new colony. Social ties may well rival personal endowments, with either the lowest polyp or the most exalted man. The little bud may be

178   *Coördinations of Growth.*

organically dependent for all its sentient good, which is doubtless as feeble as its own helplessness ; but man, in the multitude of his resources, is in reality no less dependent on others for his enjoyment. Plants and the lower animals propagate their kind by various and superficially unlike processes. A distinguished botanist[1] says, " It may be laid down as a pretty general rule, that the less seed a plant ripens, the more it becomes multiplied by buds, and *vice versa.*"

Probably a similar law exists in regard to those animals which are propagated both by budding and by self-division, or "fissigemmation." It is perfectly certain that an established *order of increase* exists among all ranks of beings, and that this order has been established in wisdom and beneficence. The lower the type of organism, of course the more helpless, the more directly dependent the indwelling life, and the broader therefore should be the range of conditions under which it may exist. This law of natural compensations will be found to be a very general if not a universal principle. Numbers of the lowest animals give birth to many millions of offspring in a single season. The Amœba and Hydra may, it is asserted, be divided into minute pieces, and yet each piece will form all the missing parts again and become itself a perfect animal. Normal self-division also takes place in different animals at all stages of growth, even before the formation of the egg ; and many eggs regularly divide into two, four, eight, or even twelve and sixteen perfect individuals according to the species, as in the Natica or sea snail, which, according to Professor Agassiz, divides into eight or sixteen, or in some varieties twelve parts, each becoming a perfect animal. Adult hydroids and worms also, self-divide after a very curious but carefully established programme, which evidently has been devised and is executed with the utmost precision. The season

[1] Schleiden.

Coördinations of Growth. 179

of the year and various other external conditions affect the normal processes of growth, so that the offspring of the same parent may take one form in the spring, and another in the autumn, or it may be perfecting two sets of offspring at the same time : the one to remain permanently on the parent stock, and the other to float out into the world independently, to seek its fortune and establish new conditions for its posterity. We are daily learning that there are more things in heaven and earth than men have dreamed of hitherto. Some of the normal modes of growth might strike one at first sight as highly eccentric. They certainly would have been regarded as extremely improbable if we had been called to reason upon them in advance, but being necessitated to accept them as facts, we are enabled to find a general unity of thought — a common plan with simply a good deal of variety in the details of its execution, according to the varying conditions under which it was intended to be executed. One of the well-known illustrations of peculiar modes of growth is that of the transformations in insect phenomena ; but if, with our great naturalists, we can generalize sufficiently to perceive that all creatures undergo some analogous transformation ; each always after the type of its own class, and manifested at different stages of development ; but real transformations from a lower to a higher grade of organism, we shall still find unity of plan everywhere, even to the minutest details.

The plant organism, generally lower in the plane of life than the animal, is also more prolific and may be propagated by even more various modes. Cuttings may be set directly in the earth or grafted into any kindred stock, while every vegetable bud is susceptible of becoming the beginning of a new plant of its kind, with its countless numbers of possibly self-sustaining buds. Schleiden even asserts that "the power is given to all plants, to develop new plants out of any of their cells, when they come to be

180   Coördinations of Growth.

placed in favorable circumstances."[1] Possibly; but hypothesis is not necessarily fact; no vegetable structure of a high type has ever been developed except by the normal processes of buds and seeds, produced by the action of legitimate functions. Among some of the lower plants there seems almost no limit to reproduction; and, as there are those whose whole organism is confined to a single cell, who shall say that there are not also compound organisms in which every cell represents its separate individual life.

Rapidity of growth in these types is as remarkable as their productiveness. It has been estimated that in the fungus *Bovista gigantea*, 20,000 new cells are formed every minute. The maggots of flesh flies, whose increase in numbers is almost limitless, have also been found to increase in size about 200 times in one day; but both these types are simply reorganizing already digested materials. There is certainly some relation between rapidity of growth and facility for propagation, and both characteristics belong often to the parasitic tribes, and very generally to low and dependent organisms. Thus plants do propagate in ways which seem to be quite abnormal, but which, doubtless, are as really legitimate as any other. "If, for example, a leaf of *Bryophyllum calycinum* is placed upon moist earth, young plants are developed from all the indentations of the leaf, and these can only derive their existence from the extraordinary development of certain appointed cells. The same phenomenon occurs on broken surfaces of detached leaves of the beautiful scarlet flowered Echeverias, and in many other succulent plants, as also in the orange-tree."[1] "If a notch is made in one of the thick veins of the splendid Gesneria, a new young plant is produced on the broken surface in about a week."

But because some plants may be propagated by these somewhat unique methods, it is surely no more legitimate

[1] *The Plant.*

Coördinations of Growth. 181

to infer therefore that *every* plant-cell may be made to originate a new organism, if "placed in favorable circumstances," than it is to infer that every organic cell, vegetable or animal, if placed in favorable conditions could be made to originate an independent organism. The hypothesis is a material one, and originates from a wholly material theory of development. Suppose one cell from the human heart, another from the brain, and another from the great toe could be each developed into a distinct organism, on this theory should it be in each instance a human organism, or should the one grow up into a gigantic heart, another to a powerful brain, and the third to one immense great toe? Every cell of a simple, yet many celled organism, with its several organs under the control of one sentient life, cannot, in the nature of things, become itself the centre of a distinct organism.

The whole range of appetencies and capacities acting through their appropriate organs are called into coöperation at the initiation of a new life. Imbecile and besotted parents too often beget children like themselves, because all their nobler energies being dormant, the latent tendencies of the new being are not therefore aroused and set in progress in connection with an adapted organism. It is easy to force the leaf-bud of a tree into bearing fruit, or to stimulate a branch to become a root ; because all the functions of a tree are essentially one, contributing as common organs to many kindred sentient lives, with but little varying experience. The several parts of a plant are all found to be simply transformations of each other ; the plant mind can be pushed into this or that form by external conditions ; but the several organs in every simple organism are the direct outgrowth of various special appetencies — all pertaining to one mind. Therefore the higher the type of life, the more nicely adjusted are all the many coördinations needful to its development. No one organic cell, not even the proper germ-cells, can develop the new organ-

182 *Coördinations of Growth.*

ism. It develops itself through the aid of the organism generally; it needs only to get the right conditions for starting; therefore, if its nature is feeble and almost uniform in sentient properties, the more easy are the terms of growth. A jelly-fish, but little higher than "an organized drop of water," may bud out almost anywhere into a new being, and so if the thick vein of the Gesneria is wounded, nature will surely rally to the breach; but instead of simply mending the hurt, as with us, she pieces on instead a new little Gesneria — all the conditions for its simple growth and prosperity being abundantly supplied.

A specimen of *Levisia rediviva*, collected in Western North America by Dr. Lyall, of the British Navy, on the authority of "Silliman's Journal," was "immersed in boiling water" before drying and pressing it, in order to stop its growing propensity, "and yet more than a year and a half afterwards it showed symptoms of vitality, and in May of 1863, it produced its beautiful flowers in the Royal Gardens of Kew." Such facts only indicate the wide range of conditions adapted to organic growth — the growth itself is one and simple, conducted after a uniform type, whether in the growing or the already matured structure.

Professor Clark of Harvard, thus describes a process of growth to which he was an eye-witness. A *Flat-worm* or Planaria was cut in two with a sharp knife. "The restored organs were not formed all at once, but gradually, as it were bit by bit, in this wise: From the anterior half a point insensibly budded out at the cut end, and within this projection a clear spot appeared, which eventually proved to be the retiring chamber, or sheath of the proboscis when retracted within the body; next the proboscis, with a gradually defining outline, made itself apparent, and at the same time irregular branching cavities became visible in the surrounding new tissue, and as they grew more distinct they could be traced along forward to the old branches of the intestine."[1]

This mode of growth, "bit by bit," is uniform with all organizations. Thus it is that organic functions everywhere, whether in repair or in original growth, coördinate inorganic matter; but the whole organism is coöperative in the process. The raw material is not immediately introduced at the point of growth, but is first variously modified and prepared for its special organic functions, through the influence of many coördinated simultaneous processes; conducted through the intervention of the whole adapted organism; each organ and each cell even, promptly responding in the performance of its own specific work.

[1] *Mind in Nature*, p. 93.

DIFFERENT TYPES OF MIND.

SENTIENT properties are evidently common to all animals, and there is no reason to suppose that they are not common also to all plants, while there are many reasons for presuming that all organic processes are conducted under the direct influence of some quality of sentient stimulus. We know by experience that appetencies are the direct stimuli to those processes in our own organisms which result not only in perpetual renovation but in general frequent activity; and as these processes are closely paralleled in the animal and vegetable kingdoms, we must presume therefore that analogous appetencies stimulate all organic operations. In brief, I maintain that the general quality of sentience is the only real and distinctive organic force — that it is the only mode of force which distinguishes between organic and inorganic processes.

Wherever the quality of sentience exists as a present and active property, there is organization. The sentience, whether acting spontaneously or reflectively, stimulates and directs the process which eventuates in the formation of the coördinated organ ; but wherever the process is wholly unsentient, no organization is formed, but the product of the process is homogeneous or inorganic. If this is true, then the character of the organism must be indicative of the indwelling sentient nature, and *vice versa*. It may even be possible, by studying and comparing their joint manifestations, by comparing the different types with each other, and by bringing everything into the light of our own experience and there carefully weighing resem-

Different Types of Mind. 185

blances and differences, to form some tolerably adequate idea of the natures of sentient beings very widely removed from ourselves, and agreeing only in possessing the one fundamental element of sentient or living properties.

A shaded house-plant reaches toward the light as if with a felt yearning after its needed treasures ; the roots of a tree penetrate to almost incredible distances and past untold obstacles in search of coveted water and necessary food, when these are not more readily supplied. What but vegetable sentience, but real and positive sensations, can impel the organic growth in exactly the needed directions? The whole tone of vigor and thrift which comes to a well-established vegetable is at least wonderfully suggestive of a condition of placid content ; while the faded, drooping, withered state of a starved or wounded plant is even painfully indicative of discomfort. It is strangely like this that we look when we are well or ill cared for, and enjoy or suffer accordingly. Now that humanity is waking up to "the rights of animals," it may be well to widen our banner still further and write upon it, " *The rights even of plants — the rights of every living thing !* " for life is sentience. I, for one, can no more doubt it than I can doubt that I myself suffer and enjoy, because I live.

The vegetable, like the animal, has its periodic seasons of normal activity alternating with rest. Animals, with more of locomotion and self-help, are more dependent on their own exertions for a supply of food and other necessaries. Their periods of active appetency and satiety, therefore, though ever alternating, are subordinated to their varying conditions ; but the vegetable, for whose fewer wants there is a much broader supply, is generally found to be steadily drawing upon some of its supplies by day, and habitually abstaining at night, when its coöperative organism still works on mechanically, precisely as ours does in sleep ; digesting the food, building up the organism, and throwing off the disorganized matter for which it has

186 *Different Types of Mind.*

no farther need. The *sleep* of plants is not a fancy, but an accepted reality. The botanist Linnæus first discovered the fact. He was, it is said, searching for some flowers upon a lotus, and not being able to find them, supposed at first that they had been gathered ; but as they reappeared the next day and disappeared again at night, he went out with a light examining his plant with care, and found that the leaflets had approached each other, concealing the flower from view. The appearance of everything in the garden was changed ; and so he learned that his beloved plants had fallen asleep. Some of the processes of the plant are quite reversed during sleep. While in the daylight they absorb carbon and exhale oxygen, in the night this action is reversed. There are also some night-waking plants, like night-waking animals ; and plants can be kept awake at night by artificial light precisely as in the case of animals.[1]

The dormant state of plants in winter is also closely analogous to hybernation, though there is a much larger class of deciduous trees than of hybernating animals. In both cases the normal functions are much more nearly suspended than in sleep, and in the dormant organism it is not the sentient activities alone which are more or less suspended, but all processes in general are greatly retarded—held in abeyance by the state of the temperature at the time ; so that both dormant plants and animals can be kept in an active state under the influence of the tropical sun.

If life is sentience and sleep the suspension of sentient activity, — being partial or complete according to circumstances, — then the periodical sleep of plants would indicate the existence of sentient activity with its constitutional need of rest, need of time for recuperating the organs which administer to the living experience. I have already tried to show that this is the true theory of sleep —

[1] De Candolle.

Different Types of Mind. 187

that it is the mind and not the body which rests, and that in disturbed states of slumber it is usually those modes of mind acted upon by external conditions which are wakeful. These are questions of fact which every one must test by his own experience; but whatever be the nature of sleep, it presents analogous phenomena in connection with *all* living organisms.

In a deep sleep, many things may be done to the body of which the mind is quite unconscious. A child is often carried from place to place and dressed or undressed without awaking; and many things may be done to an adult person of which he has no distinct consciousness, and often, apparently, no consciousness whatever. This sentient life is not usually, perhaps never, wholly suspended; but it remains either simply responsive to external events or it seems to retire into the internal chambers of being and resolve itself into a sense of rest, of passive content. The sensibility of the plant, also, seems to retire within itself; so that the leaves of the sensitive plant, for the time, lose their peculiar sensibility, which is still found to be active in the petiole. Whatever vitality consists in, then, it is seen that it is the vital phenomena which are more or less suspended in sleep.

Who shall say, in the face of facts like these, that there is not positive sentience connected with the existence of even the vegetable? When growing in a good soil, under favorable conditions, why should it not have some plethoric sense of the delights of the epicure? Basking in the sunshine may be as agreeable to the opening bud as to the little human child. These things are good in themselves, and why should not even these primitive forms of good be multiplied to their fullest extent? He who created good of all qualities, who established sentient experience with its joys as well as its sorrows, has taken excellent care that the plant, possessing but little or no volition, shall be able to find its appropriate satisfactions; while very little suf-

188 Different Types of Mind.

fering, apparently, can be inflicted on it. When wounded, it heals amain; are branches lopped from the tree, it is but a mode of easy, early death to some members of the family, while the instinctive *esprit de corps* of the whole community rallies in sympathy, thus converting the loss of the few into the gain of the many. Defenseless and dependent as the plant seems, yet its wants are coördinated with the most ample sources of supply. It can feed freely on inorganic matter, and on the decay of other organisms; it is nourished by ever recurring showers, by daily sunshine, and an unfailing atmosphere; and even if, by untoward circumstances, it be casually stinted in some needed supply, the privation seems to affect it rather as a negative loss of good than as positive evil.

Vegetation, in general, is so predominant a feature of nature's economy, it is so coördinated alike with the primitive inorganic elements upon which *it* alone can subsist, with the waste and outworn elements which higher organisms reject, and with these higher organisms themselves, to whom life itself would be an impossibility without the coöperation of these plant tissues, their humbler allies in the flesh, that we may well believe them to be humbler allies also in the spirit. The unity of plan running throughout all material details must surely indicate a like unity of plan extending sentient experience till it became as universal as organization itself. Why not? If good is good, the wider its latitude the better! Who doubts the general pleasures of a living existence — then is there poverty with the Creator that should hinder Him from bestowing it on the lichen and the potato-vine? We have been accustomed arrogantly to assert our own immortality, but the mortality of every living thing besides; and in the same spirit, while we could not deny sensation to the animal, we have contented ourselves by withholding it from the vegetable. Have we yet to learn that if *He* paints every flower as carefully and as beautifully as He does the eyes and cheeks

Different Types of Mind. 189

of childhood, that if He rounds every leaf and twig with as appropriate and well-executed symmetry in its kind as that even in the human form itself; it is a gratuitous mistrust of the universality of his beneficence to presume that it stops just short of bestowing the only thing which makes organization valuable? Little wild plants, growing under the protecting shade of the forest trees, flowers peeping through the crevices of the roughest rocks, and all shrubs and trees generally, seem so admirably adapted to their own private niches and special localities, that one is irresistibly convinced that they are the cherished darlings of an unstinted Providence, which has lavished upon them an almost unperturbed serenity, and an ever renewed positive enjoyment. It takes nothing from ourselves if it be so; but to them it is everything!

There are minds to whom all this will seem to be but a bewildered attempt at finding evidences to sustain a ridiculous theory; but if they belong to the class who can go out on a June morning, after everything has been washed tenderly and cleanly by one of Nature's shower-baths — adjusted expressly for the highest benefit of her vegetable children — without being able to perceive the visible joy of every bud, blossom, and leaf, as it lifts itself to the sunshine, to be dried and cherished by its warmth, and painted afresh in beauty by its light, I only pity him! Is not science maintaining to-day that the planting of trees is the only method by which men can woo and win the showers of heaven to fall on the now barren deserts of the earth? that the growth of abundant vegetation alone can insure to them the benefits of a moist and salubrious climate? If more trees, then, are the only salvation of now famishing, cannibal Algeria, are trees themselves likely to be of utterly no account in God's social economy? Just as a wrong done to the lowest of our kind reacts to the hurt of the very highest; so possibly we may yet come to understand that by the unchanging laws of cause and effect, a

190 *Different Types of Mind.*

deprivation of life to these the humblest of sentient existences, must react to the detriment of all intermediate grades, up even to man himself. We find no looseness of adjustment among all the innumerable coördinations of the universe; but everything, from the lowest to the highest, has been most definitely and systematically determined.

The term mind, with the idea which it represents in our thoughts, has generally been restricted to the reflective or rational mind of man ; but we have no word equally well adapted to comprehend all sentient personal life, as distinguished from the unsentient, impersonal existence of simply quantitative being. I have, therefore, extended the term to all sentient existence universally. It is no more derogatory to humanity that the mind of the perceiving, reasoning, rejoicing, almost omnipotent man is placed in the general sentient class with the fishes of the sea and the grass under his feet, than that his majestic body with all its pliant beauty and utility, to which no other organism can attain, is matured by precisely the same organic processes with theirs. A few years ago no one dreamed of that significant fact! Now, thanks to Karl Ernst von Baer, science accepts it as beyond the possibility of doubt. We are only called on now to discover a still vaster order, and a yet more beneficent generalization in the Creative Plan !

As each known element of simple matter has its own special properties — its own preëstablished, unique modes of force and process, so each class of mind is apparently endowed with its own special sentient properties, its preestablished unique modes of appetency and activity. Mental science has been studied. too unscientifically for me to attempt an exhaustive classification of even the most widely distinct types of mind. I can only indicate such unlike appetencies and capabilities as will be evident

Different Types of Mind. 191

to the most casual observer; and endeavor to show that each distinctive group of sentient properties constitutes a definite sentient type of its own.

One might suppose that there would probably be a wide unlikeness between vegetable and animal mental properties, but, in point of fact, the gradations between them as manifested in their organisms, and in their habits generally, are so insensible, that, at present, it is almost if not quite impossible to decide where the animal ends, and the vegetable begins. Some naturalists of high authority still believe in the existence of "plant-animals," or creatures having the characteristics of both kingdoms. Amongst all the higher orders, however, on either side of the line, the difference is very marked.

No vegetable is known to eat animals as food; while all animals subsist either upon vegetables or upon each other. Vegetables derive their subsistence either from the mineral kingdom, or from worn-out and decayed organisms which have fallen back into inorganic matter; while animals, in order to carry on the operations necessary to their higher organic processes, must consume other organic tissues. The decomposed tissue will not answer. It must be eaten while still in its organic condition. It is as though the vegetables and lower animals were employed to wind up the mainspring of each organic cell, getting its little system of coöperative forces all in working order; and, just at this point, that the higher animals, man inclusive, take the little organ into their own systems, readapting it with all its forces to their own more active and more complicated organisms. Here is a generic fact well established by physiology; and I can only draw from it the inference, deduced also from general observation, namely, that the most various and most intense appetencies are coördinated with the most perfect and generally higher, more available organisms. The carnivorous animal manifests fiercer impulses and a more available strength for all emergen-

192   *Different Types of Mind.*

cies tnan the herbivorous one of equal or even greater size; but strength and intensity of experience are not necessarily higher or even as high as the broader, more varied experiences of some of the more intelligent herbivora. Nevertheless there is an apparently direct connection between the nature of the food taken and of the organism into which it enters; so that one has only to be informed as to the character of an animal's natural diet, and he is able at once to classify his general sentient properties. If moreover a marble palace is better than a house of wood or brick, so an organism wrought out of already finely organized material should be comparatively better than one made of lower or coarser tissues. This theory may not be altogether in harmony with that of the strict vegetarians; but neither can it lead to cannibalism, or the eating of anything more highly organized in the way of meats than a good tender-loin of beef, or possibly in these enlightened days, *roti de cheval.*

There is an evident close connection between the appetency and the special food adapted to its uses. Most of the lower animals turn instinctively to the kind of food best adapted to their organisms; while man, with his varied appetencies, finds his physical and mental well-being best promoted by a variety of nourishment. The best of each class, and a generous variety of widely unlike viands, are probably the fittest conditions for a refined and healthy body, subservient to an active, elevated, and well-balanced mind. The prize-fighter should doubtless keep very closely to his under-done beefsteak, and the mild philosopher or humanitarian, living on fruits and cereals, may find himself best able to indulge in bright, clear, and placid states of mind; but variety for the variety-worker, is the undoubted law. There are but few animals who do not instinctively abstain from a repast upon the bodies of their own species. Probably the combination of forces in tissues too nearly like their own is not well adapted to their

Different Types of Mind. 193

purposes ; and coördinated appetencies advise them of this ; just as the seventy different species of insects, who subsist upon the oak, are all well apprised of the fact that the various oak-tissues are their legitimate diet.

It is said that all herbivorous animals have strong social instincts. Many of them are almost as highly gregarious as the plant, in which there are universally many individuals coöperating in a common organism (at least where the organism rises higher than a single cell) ; but carnivorous animals are highly unsocial, living often in the greatest isolation, as if their fierce appetencies were so intensely personal that they set them against every other creature, and every other creature against them. Thus do we find among organized beings a very wide variety of sentient manifestations with their coördinated habits and general outgrowth of results ; and everywhere the appetency and the organism are found to be closely coöperative.

Plants, in general, are rooted to the particular locality in which they grow, and are, apparently, without the power of voluntary movement towards any perceived object, while animals in general are endowed with powers of motion and locomotion, which they can exercise at will in the search after objects correlated to their appetencies. Some exceptions as to locomotion occur among animals aquatic in their residences. They are fixed to one spot like plants, or, being at first free, afterwards permanently locate ; but perpetual currents and other general agitations of the water, in connection with the voluntary motions of the little creatures themselves, are ample compensation to them for the absence of locomotion. A few plants, also, especially in their early stages of growth, move about in the water by the action of vibratile cilia or otherwise. All plants are freely stirred by the elements, many of them have a distinct power of what is apparently conscious and voluntary motion ; but it is believed that there is no plant giving any sufficient indication of *voluntary movement con-*

Different Types of Mind.

sciously directed towards an external object. I infer from this that plants have but a very small appetency for self-determined motion ; and probably no appetency for motion directed towards external things, which are either to be sought or avoided by conscious effort, while all animals have more or less appetency for motion of which locomotion is but one variety, impelled thereto both by their subjective impulse and by an objective perception of something desirable to be either sought or avoided.

Some facts stated by Mr. Darwin in his work " On the Movements and Habits of Climbing Plants," certainly go very far towards shaking one's faith in the position that plants have no objective perceptions, and consequently no power of voluntary movement directed towards external objects. He divides the movements of plants into two kinds : 1st. Automatic, usually continued movements, not set in action by extraneous invitation — as the gyratory movement of the small leaflets of *Desmodium Gyrans.* 2d. Movement in consequence of the contact or action of an extraneous body, as in the Sensitive Plant. Tendrils, he says, exhibit both kinds of movement, and they exercise a curious discrimination, coiling up into an open helix when lightly touched by a twig or a loop of thread, yet remaining impassive when the tendrils of different plants were dragged over each other even with much greater force, or when water was flirted over them, though it fell sometimes so violently that the whole tendril was moved. A still more striking fact I must give in the author's words : " I repeatedly saw that the revolving tendril (of *Echinocystis lobata*), though inclined during the greater part of its course at an angle of about 45° (in one case of only 37°) above the horizon, in one part of its course stiffened and straightened itself from tip to base, and became nearly or quite vertical. . . . . The tendril forms a very acute angle with the extremity of the shoot, which projects above the point where the tendril arises ; and the stiffening always occurred

Different Types of Mind. 195

as the tendril approached and had to pass, in its revolving course, the point of, — that is, the projecting extremity of the shoot. Unless the tendril had the power of thus acting, it would strike against the extremity of the shoot, and be arrested by it. As soon as all these branches of the tendrils began to stiffen themselves in this remarkable manner, as if by a process of turgescence, and to rise from an inclined into a vertical position, the revolving movement becomes more rapid ; and as soon as the tendril has succeeded in passing the extremity of the shoot, its revolving motion coinciding with that of gravity, often causes it to fall into its previous inclined position so quickly, that the end of the tendril could be distinctly seen traveling like the minute hand of a gigantic clock." Surely here are phenomena very like those which result from — not simple objective perception and choice merely — but from the highest reason, and a wise adaptation of means to ends ! Whether these phenomena can be satisfactorily explained on the theory that He who coördinated these wonderful results was able to effect them through the cooperation of quantitative forces with sentient properties wholly subjective, and therefore undiscriminating in their action, or otherwise, may admit of question ! One might gladly accord to *some* plants objective perception and choice, except that the admission, in this case, would prove so much as to be quite incredible. So high an order of intellect, pertaining to a being so dependent, and so unable to manifest it except in a single conjunction of circumstances, would lead us rather to suppose that in this conjunction of circumstances the action referred to is mainly effected through unsentient forces ; as in some of the almost equally marvelous phenomena of chemical and crystallogenic action.

Plants reach upward to the light and downward to the needed food ; some of them shrink from your touch, or move in various ways, influenced by no visible external

196 *Different Types of Mind.*

cause ; but a class of sentient properties wholly subjective, the mere sensation of stimulating appetencies and of gratified content when they find a supply, would amply account for all these, and for the resulting plant organization. The very young child gropes for its food blindly, impelled by a like subjective appetency, long before it manifests the slightest discrimination as to what it seeks ; farther than as finding the preadapted supply, it instinctively takes it. We must conclude, therefore, that these wonderfully revolving tendrils, like the planets, involuntarily follow the laws of motion assigned them with such rigid mathematical precision.

I should define the *plant-mind* as, *a class of sentient existence whose whole consciousness is subjective. The animal,* on the contrary, belongs to *a class of sentient existence whose consciousness is both subjective and objective.* It possesses not only sentient appetencies and capabilities which enable it to suffer or enjoy, like the plant ; but it is able, also, to perceive objects which are coördinated with itself and to exercise volition in the search or avoidance of them.

If the sentient properties of plants do all resolve themselves into sensations, and are so constituted that they can rise no higher than these, there seems no room here for memory. The plant may suffer or enjoy in the present, and it may go on with an endless repetition of its own proper sensations ; thus accumulating experience indefinitely ; but its consciousness would seem to be limited always to the eternal now. Helpless, without aspirations, or perhaps greatly higher possibilities than those pertaining to its present state, there is yet *One* who careth for it !

Nor is it necessary that we should look upon the primitive pleasures of a vegetable existence as of but little moment and scarcely worth possessing. Far from it ! While a large part of even the human race yet prize sensation as their highest good, and, possessing many far

Different Types of Mind. 197

nobler appetencies, are yet content to neglect these and to live almost entirely in the momentary pleasures of sense, there is little need of extending pity or compassion to the vegetable ! Its sensations, with all their many varied modes, are not of so tangible a character that we with our present faculties are able to indicate them, or even to form any just conception of their special characteristics. We find something akin in one department of our own natures ; and yet so different, also, that we may as reasonably expect to understand all the joys of a mind which has already left its human organism and is existing in some new unknown condition, appropriate only to itself, as to comprehend the distinctive pleasures of beings living, like the vegetables, in a compound organism, with all its possible, beautiful social compensations. What, except a most delicate adjustment of various sentient modes, could cause one class of these equally subjective lives to organize the huge trees of California, and another the low vegetable moulds ; and yet others all the intermediate grades of vegetable organization ? As each class works always after the type of its kind, thus producing its special formative influence upon its organism, we are as much bound to suppose that there are intrinsic differences in the qualities of sentient appetency as we are to accept the fact that the different characteristics of oxygen and carbon are the result of their unlike properties. If sentient force is the true organic force, and by the special quality of its appetencies influences the coördinated organs, determining the character of the organization generally, as I have elsewhere tried to show, then what nice distinctions and varied combinations of sentient experience must there be, even among plants ? What delicate shades of unlike sensations must be necessary in order to ultimate in oaks, pines, palms, ferns, and numerous other families with their varieties ! The several types of crystallization are indeed as distinctly marked, and yet these are admitted to be the

198 *Different Types of Mind.*

result of rigid mathematical law ; but the crystal has no organs ; it is essentially a homogeneous substance. How far special typical difference in plants may be effected by unsentient influences, it must be impossible in our ignorance at present to determine ; but so far as the various types are distinctive in organic functions, so far must they be under the control of distinctive sentient influences. Organs must be adapted instruments to be used by the sentient mind ; but the special size and forms of these organs, so wonderfully illustrated in the different species of plants, may possibly be effected rather through *quantitative* than *qualitative* force. Yet the latter must also coöperate, however impossible it may be for us to work out the limits of its influence ; and I find it most probable that an organism so graceful in kind as an elm or a willow, must derive its grace from coördinated sentient appetencies, energizing harmoniously within the myriads of little indwelling minds. Not even a stoic can doubt that the elegant, breezy happiness of a bird is real happiness, and that the little joyous soul has made to itself a body fitted to its own needs ; and I do not see that he can much more reasonably doubt that the self-poised enjoyment of the sturdy oak must be intrinsically different from that of the pliant, swaying willow.

It would not be easy to point out the specific differences of feeling and general experience in a wiry, dark-eyed, dark-haired man, and another light-eyed, fair-haired, and softly rounded in every outline ; yet that there is a very wide diversity in their habitual sentient modes, we are all perfectly well aware. They must be as really unlike in the whole general tone of their sensations, both in kind and intension, as probably are a red pepper and a banana. While the dark man is overstocked with a fund of unresting, narrow energy, either for his own comfort or for that of his neighbors, the other surrounds himself with an atmosphere of placidness ; which is quieting not only to his

Different Types of Mind. 199

own nerves but also to those of everybody about him. I might indicate a dozen or two typical temperaments among even Anglo-Saxons; while the different nations, and still more the various races, are unquestionably as mentally dissimilar as any dissimilarity of physical traits. The mind has a structure and coloring of its own, which influences its organic coördinations; which everybody tacitly recognizes, and which every physiognomist or student of human nature is able to reduce to a more or less scientific basis. Phrenology is by no means a wholly baseless science; though its professors undoubtedly may rely far more upon the general correlations between mind and body, than upon any special swellings in one brain as distinguished from another. Many physical traits may have a purely physical origin; and these may be able even to react upon the mind, influencing its sensibilities in a marked degree. I like to think of our carefully nurtured garden flowers as taking on a deeper and broader tone of sensations with their deepened hues and broadened petals. Their better care, and more varied food, though wholly material causes, and designed by the gardener simply to build their bodies in richer beauty, almost certainly produce a commensurate variation of sentient enjoyment — not of permanent sentient modes. Do we not know that a horse fed on oats manifests a more full and vigorous enjoyment than one who is compelled to eat chaff and stale hay? When we can feed *the poor* with the dainty diet of the sensible rich, we shall find their bodies, their brains, and the mind which uses them, elevated to a closer brotherhood. Ireland living on mush and potatoes must continue to be Ireland, improvident and unskilled in self-direction. Human tissue built up from turnips must be cross-grained and watery. The mind which attempts to work through it, is at as great a disadvantage as the body of the laborer is who tills his half acre with an old pick and a worn-out hoe, compared with his landlord, with his beef-fed brain and his improved

200 *Different Types of Mind.*

implements. Practical reform may begin anywhere ; but it must end by applying nature's coördination of means and ends.

Even color, the most variable organic characteristic, must possess a mental significance. The rich-hued pansies, tulips, and dahlias, I believe to be glowing with deeper, more various sensations than belong to their native stocks. Sensation is generally intensified in the tropics, while in the temperate zones vegetables mature slowly, and men become more reflective. There may yet be found to exist a direct relation between change of color in plants and animals, and change in the kind or activity of present sentient experiences. Since the various colored rays in the sunbeam move in different times and through unlike spaces, there must be a direct relation between color and the molecular activity of the colored body ; and as direct a connection must subsist also between the molecular activity in the organism and the effects produced upon the indwelling mind. Of course if we can deny to plants a sentient nature altogether, we have settled the whole question ; but if they are endowed with living appetencies and capabilities which are worth possessing, and therefore which it was worth while for Beneficence to bestow upon them at all, then why should He not have created all the charming differences of sensation which are naturally indicated by the diversity in their external dress? Has He taken such unlimited pains with the very least detail of organic arrangement, grouping kindred features and correlating every part with every other, with a minuteness and beauty of adjustment which can only indicate a most cordial and interested love for the work ; and has He not been equally careful as to all the nicest differences of coördinated sensations? To affirm otherwise would be to assert that Beneficence has less love and appreciation of varied living experiences, than of simple variations in structure, form, and color.

Different Types of Mind. 201

Agassiz, writing of the fertility of invention in varying even the same type, speaking of the Radiates says, they " Seem like the productions of one who handles his work with infinite ease and delight, taking pleasure in presenting the same thought under a thousand different aspects. Some new cut of the plates, some slight change in their relative position, is constantly varying their outlines, from a closed-up cup to an open crown, from the long pear-shaped oval of the calyx in some, to its circular or square, or pentagonal form in others. An angle that is simple in one, projects by a fold of the surface and becomes a fluted column in another ; a plate that was smooth but now has here a symmetrical figure upon it drawn in beaded lines ; the stem which is perfectly unbroken in one, except by the transverse divisions common to them all, in the next puts . out feathery plumes at every transverse break. In some the plates of the stem are all rigid and firmly soldered together ; in others they are articulated upon each other in such a manner as to give it the greatest flexibility, and allow the seeming flower to wave and bend upon its stalk."[1] The great naturalist was accustomed to amuse himself " by the introduction of some undescribed complication," and seeking for it among the specimens at his command, he rarely failed to find it among some of these ever-changing forms.

This evidence of working with a genuine artist's delight, is a feature which must very strongly impress every learner in nature's wonderful studio, but as His work is accomplished, not like ours through the direct handling of our materials, but is effected by complex, preëstablished processes, in which ten thousand forces are coördinated to produce the designed results, I shall not believe that the sublime satisfaction which He must have taken in elaborating His scheme of vegetation was not wonderfully enhanced by the pleasure of bringing every possible *quality*

[1] *Methods of Study in Natural History*, p. 222.

Different Types of Mind.

of sensation to exert its directive and coöperative influence in conjunction with unsentient forces. Shall one rob God of this highest prerogative of multiplying as many qualities and combinations of sentient experience, as of simple quantitative modes? We talk of "the human form divine;" but the living gem is how much better than the casket! All the wealth, then, of vegetable form and color is as nothing to the richer wealth of forever uprising and increasing vegetable satisfaction.

What folly to despise the sentient life even of a plant! Would Deity have multiplied it so infinitely if it were so valueless as we have believed? The world is beautiful this June day in its freshest garb of many tinted greens. Looking out from this elevated window, I can see many miles away, so that myriads and myriads of distinct vegetable organisms fall under my eye; and in many of these there must exist myriads of distinct living minds. What incalculable numbers, then, fall under the glance of a single eye! Was it worth while to give all these a sentient existence at all, and yet to make that sentience of so low a type as to be valueless to its possessor? We have been told that the whole earth was fitted up expressly for man. So, no doubt, it was; but it was also expressly fitted up for the little golden dandelion. Infinite resources require no stint or poverty anywhere.

> "Thou art as much His care, as if beside
> Nor man nor angel lived in heaven or earth :
> Thus sunbeams pour alike their glorious tide
> To light up worlds, or wake an insect's mirth."

Among animals, sentient peculiarities are either more marked or more readily appreciable by us; being more nearly akin to our own. The four (or five, if you group Protozoa as a separate class) grand divisions, are not more distinct in organic structure than in their manifestation of sentient properties. It would be a curious and perhaps profitable study to attempt to trace in detail the corre-

Different Types of Mind. 203

spondences between the several types and their organisms ;
but, besides requiring a very minute and practical knowledge of Zoölogy, even when fairly accomplished, it might
prove uninteresting to the general reader. It must suffice to refer only to more general and notable facts.

All animals, it is believed, give evidence of both subjective and objective appetencies — they evidently suffer
hunger, and in general, manifest clear discrimination and
volition in the search for food. Some of the microscopic Protozoa seem in their habits like infinitesimal
tigers. All one-celled animals are chiefly distinguished
from the one-celled vegetables by their evident discrimination in the choice of food, and by the contractile and
mobile organism adapted to that end. The fixed Polyps
and Anemones are known to hunt for their prey, managing
their tentacles very adroitly for that purpose. The possible
exceptions, are some of those compound organisms, like
the Portuguese Man-of-War, which are represented as composed of individuals possessing distinct functions — the
food-gatherers being each provided with a lasso which it
throws over its prey, after the manner of a Brazilian
hunter ; leaving its prize, however, to be digested by another functional member for the benefit of the whole community. This class of functional and special appetencies
presents very curious manifestations of sentient phenomena. The organic community abounds both among plants
and the lower animals, and in all such communities there
is a more or less distinct division of labor among the individual members. This must imply, either difference in the
original sentient constitution of the different individuals,
or difference in the development of the various sentient
modes possible to them all. The latter seems to me the
more probable, as a general scheme of vegetation ; though
exceptions to this rule may occur. It seems more natural
to suppose that one or more individuals, so placed as to
perform the functions of a leaf, with its corresponding sen-

204 *Different Types of Mind.*

tient life, under a different set of conditions could be developed into a fruit-bud, with all the differences implied in a quickened activity to a new group of coördinated experiences; than that beings with intrinsically unlike sentient constitutions should ordinarily be found growing together in the same common organism. We find an analogous functional character existing not only among animals dwelling in one organism, but also among all free individuals who exist together in a community, as among bees, wasps, and ants. The working or nursing bees can be converted into the queen-mothers by a simple change of food and other conditions; and we are forced to regard the whole class simply as undeveloped females. The appetencies developed by their ordinary condition, impel them to promote the well-being of the young offspring of the hive, and to the performance of a specific series of functional duties; but a new set of external conditions, first quickening a different group of appetencies in the yet nascent mind, would change their organic development, and give them an apparently very unlike occupation as members of the community.

Professor Steenstrup, the first expounder of the mysteries of the alternation of generations, says: "The circumstance of an animal giving birth to a progeny permanently dissimilar to its parent, but which itself produces a new generation, which either itself or in its offspring returns to the form of the parent, is a phenomenon not confined to a single class or series of animals; the vertebrate class is the only one in which it has not yet been observed. It would consequently appear that there is something intrinsic in this mode of development." Speaking of the Aphides, he says: "The propagation of these creatures through a series of generations has been already long known. In the spring, for instance, a generation is produced from the ova, which grows and is metamorphosed, and without previous fertilization gives birth to a new gen-

Different Types of Mind. 205

eration, and this again to a third, and so on, for ten or twelve weeks ; so that in certain species even as many as nine such preliminary generations will have been observed ; but at last there always occurs a generation consisting of males and females, the former of which, after their metamorphosis, are usually winged; fertilization and the depositing of eggs takes place, and the long series of generations recommences in the next year, and in the same order." Again he says, " It is peculiar to plants, and, as it were, their special characteristic, that the germ, the primordial individual in the vegetation or seed, is competent to produce individuals which are again capable of producing seeds or individuals of the primary form or that to which the plant owed its origin, only by the intervention of a whole series of generations. It is certainly the great triumph of Morphology, that it is able to show how the plant or tree (that colony of individuals arranged in accordance with a simple vegetative principle or fundamental law) unfolds itself, through a frequently long succession of generations, into individuals, becoming constantly more and more perfect, until, after the immediately precedent generation, it appears as calyx and corolla, with perfect male and female individuals, stamens and pistils (so that even in the vegetable kingdom the grosser hermaphroditism does not obtain, which is still supposed to take place in the animal) ; and after the fructification brings forth seed, which again goes through the same course." Thus free individuals, and those growing in a common organism, are found among all the lower orders of creatures to conduct themselves only as so many animated organs conducing to the common good of their community. This is a general and systematic arrangement from which, under ordinary conditions, there are no variations ; but which, under extraordinary circumstances, may be very widely varied, but always through definite and still very systematic processes. The leaf-bud will normally produce but

206   *Different Types of Mind.*

its single sterile leaf on the parent stem, but it may be stimulated into a flower with its several distinct individuals, and these into fructifying new seed which shall begin the organic round afresh ; or the original leaf-bud, favorably planted in the earth or grafted on a young sapling, may itself become the parent organism from which are to spring myriads of successive buds, leaves, and fruit ; and the sapling, cut off from its normal career, must see all its possible progeny suppressed, while the foreign bud goes on producing seed after its own kind alone.

My inference is that for sufficient reasons, which possibly may be inscrutable to us, most individuals of the low sentient types receive in this stage of being but a very partial and incomplete development — a mere functional development to which they are stimulated by the coöperative action of many others — of the whole allied fraternity in short ; but that there exist within them yet undeveloped appetencies which will doubtless be called into exercise in some other stage of their existence. Thus the sterile Aphides, wasps, bees, and all "neuters" generally, prompted by impelling appetencies, under better conditions may yet exercise their legitimate parental functions, and all other suppressed modes of activity which are legitimate to the sentient type to which they belong. How much they already share in all this through their social and coöperative natures we may not know ; but probably enough to quicken all their natural instincts in some partial degree. With the plant, or the polyp, I can believe that the whole fraternity may experience, without knowing why, a livelier joy when a new blossom matures its seed or a new medusa bud perfects itself, and breaks away with its fresh vigor to found its new colony. These higher culminating processes should rise to the climax of satisfaction in every member so closely coöperative in effecting its consummation.

We have seen that each sentient being, however low or weak the character of his possible living experiences, must

Different Types of Mind. 207

yet, in the nature of things, be a persisting and essentially unchanging unit. All his experiences are his very own; but they may still arise within him at every successive change which affects the general organism; and thus myriads of distinct living minds may be at the same moment overfull of the same pleasant sensations, whenever any genial influence produces a desirable effect upon the organic structure.

I return, then, from this seeming digression to the position assumed at its commencement, namely, that all animals evidence both subjective and objective appetencies — the animal in a compound organism, though not always manifesting such appetencies in his individual or functional capacity, being supposed to participate to some degree in all the sensations legitimate to his kind, or at least in all those manifested by any member of the common organism. We may, therefore, practically treat this class of organisms as each a unit, though really composed of multitudes of distinct living existences; but with their pleasures and pains so coördinated that they all suffer or enjoy together, and through the mediation of common organs.

All animals will turn aside from an obstacle, or shun an approaching danger, and are evidently cognizant of their own interests; but many animals evince no proper social appetencies, no care nor interest outside of organic needs, which may be regarded as personal needs. While they have objective perceptions and desires, as related to themselves; such as food, protection, or convenience to be sought, or danger or discomfort to be avoided, they evince no appetencies, no affections nor perceptions which are not strictly organic, and therefore in a large sense personal. Such animals even manifest no proper sexual appetencies; and while the multiplication of their kind, as with plants, may be accompanied by its appropriate satisfactions; yet, as it is dependent neither upon their own perceptions nor volitions, they are no more con-

208 *Different Types of Mind.*

sciously concerned with reproduction than with organization in general. Their appetencies in each case must be spontaneously directive ; but they are not consciously so in the one instance any more than in the other. It may, perhaps, be a pleasant experience for the hydroids to undergo the variously repeated normal processes of constriction and self-division through which their numbers are multiplied ; but if so, there is no volition or manifestation of any social affection connected with the process. Like the budding of a plant, if attended with any sentient experience to the parent, it must be analogous to the general content which results from the well-being of the organism as a whole or from the exercise of any special function. Hence I infer that perception, and therefore volition, to this order of mind, pertains only to relations directly affecting itself ; and that it is constitutionally incapacitated for taking a *social* view of anything whatever.

Another and higher class of animals possess appetencies not only both subjective and objective, but also both personal and social in their nature, and ultimating in a quality of satisfaction which has reference both to themselves and to others. This last class must comprehend all the higher animals, man inclusive ; but it also embraces many whom we have been accustomed to regard as very low indeed in the scale of being. Every creature who manifests strong sexual, parental, or social instincts of any kind, by which it is voluntarily influenced, must evidently belong to this class, however insignificant he may seem in his general uses or in his organic structure. The common earwig, whom we have been taught so much to dislike, is said to set on her eggs, and to brood her young like a mother hen ; and I have myself seen her little family gathered about her with manifestations of not only maternal, but also of fraternal instincts. Agassiz describes the action of a Gordius or Horse-hair worm, which looked like " a little tangle of black sewing-silk." It was twisted

Different Types of Mind. 209

around a bundle of eggs "about the size of a coffee bean," from which it was forcibly detached. "Immediately it moved towards the bundle of eggs, and, having reached it, began to sew itself through and through the little white mass, passing one end of its body through it, and then returning to make another stitch, as it were, till the eggs were completely entangled again in an intricate net-work of coils." This was a second time repeated; and the third time the little mother tried unsuccessfully to bring some loose eggs into the fold. The same naturalist represents some of the fishes of the Amazon as fostering their young, and evincing social instincts higher than have usually been credited to their family. De Geer says that a field bug (*Acanthosoma grisea*) conducts her thirty or forty young ones like a hen her chickens. The little ones follow her closely, and when she stops gather about her in a cluster. Bonnet threw the silken bag containing the eggs of an earth spider (*Lycosa soccata*) to an ant-lion, and she would have perished in its defense, but that he rescued her. She still remained immovable on the spot, as if disconsolate and heart-broken. That these creatures experience some emotion akin to parental instincts in ourselves, it is scarcely possible to doubt; and, at any rate, there is evidence of *some quality* of social appetencies which cannot be gainsaid.

Many of these creatures, so intensely interested in their offspring that, like the ants, wasps, and spiders, they will suffer mutilation and death for them freely, seem yet to have absolutely no wider range of sympathies, and no interest in anything beyond their own class. They, many of them, possess but little practical skill; they build no houses and lay up no provisions for the future, either for themselves or their offspring: but, rising and widening from these primary social and intelligent instincts, there is manifested by others almost every conceivable quality of sentience. Many creatures have each a special class of *in-*

210 *Different Types of Mind.*

stincts in which they are unrivaled, while yet they are deficient in all or most other directions. Thus the bird, the bee, the ant, the spider, the mole, the beaver, and multitudes of others, perhaps less well known, are each architects of a higher order after their kind than even man himself. They each evidence an amount of intelligent discrimination and choice, both in the selection of means and in the adaptation of means to ends, which must at least be accounted for on some more satisfactory hypothesis than that involved in the very doubtful term, instinct.

What is an instinct but a strong special appetency — a desire and a corresponding capability in the direction indicated? It may be, as I have assumed that it is in the plant, a mere appetency for various sensations, which perpetually recur to it through an incessant action and reaction between its sentient nature and its unsentient organism ; it may add to this an appetency for perceiving certain objective causes which affect its subjective states, and for choosing such objects as affect it favorably, and avoiding those which affect it unfavorably, as in the lowest animals, who seek food, protection, and personal comfort generally ; or instinct may widen into impersonal appetencies, which relate not merely to one's personal good, but to the good also of others more or less nearly related to one's self ; and it may rise by many and various degrees to a more distinctly intelligent apprehension of many contingent circumstances affecting various interests pertaining both to itself and others. The special proclivity which adapts an animal to the mode of life followed by all its kind may be either a wholly unthinking, simple feeling, or it may involve intelligence, thought, and discrimination in a greater or less degree ; from that in the simplest instinct which hunts for its prey, to the highest moral choice which is made between right and wrong.

Is man the only intellectual being? What then is the bird, with all its intelligent, cunning skill, and its beautiful

Different Types of Mind. 211

domestic sympathies? The spontaneous appetency for flight would be competent to develop wings by energizing in connection with the established coördinations adapted to that result; but what system of wholly unthinking co-ordinations can enable a bird to select the particular stick or straw which will best answer its purposes in nest-building? What, except intelligence of instinct, can enable each bird to build its nest after the general type adopted by its ancestors, and which is usually if not always that which is best suited to its own special needs?

In all inorganic processes, coördinated unsentient forces seem competent to produce the ordained results. Each force acts by mathematical rule, so that under the given conditions no other result is even possible; but in nest-building there are selective processes requiring judgment, skill, free volition, and locomotion in the sentient worker, which, however widely they may differ from similar pro-cesses in ourselves, must yet bear to them at least some distant analogy. It is certain that new elements have arisen here which must be higher in quality than those of mere sensation. If it is true that there is no adjustment of unsentient forces by which stick and straw can arrange themselves into the nest of a bird, it is equally true that no adjustment of simple qualities of feeling, which are competent to produce vegetable organisms, can avail here to give the oriole, the water-ousel, and the goldfinch, the requisite intelligence and skill to build the typical nests of their respective kinsfolk, or to enable the eagle, the sand-swallow, and the meadow-lark to choose the proper local-ities for their various house-building. In the execution of his plans each bird is compelled to make comparisons, to exercise judgment and choice, and to appreciate the dis-tinct objects for which he exerts himself. He is capable of varying the usual programme in many different ways, often adapting his work to unusual conditions with almost inimitable skill. It is not at all true that every nest is exactly like every other nest of its particular class, but on the contrary, each nest is specially adapted to its own location ; so that there is often as much intelligence manifested in the character of a robin's nest, considered in connection with its immediate surroundings, as there can be in a distinctly Gothic or Grecian structure which has been designedly modified to suit its special position. Birds, indeed, are never servile imitators, though they have a current reputation of being such, and of following as blindly in the ways of their ancestors as a shadow follows its substance ; but there is really great originality both of thought and action discernible in almost every bird's nest. One whose attention has not been called to the subject before, must be surprised on passing through any grove or orchard to perceive the considerable differences which exist in the different nests belonging even to the same species. Certainly all birds have the good taste never to combine incongruities of style in their house-building ; and they have also the instinct to perceive that the typical homestead common to their ancestors, is also the best adapted to their own needs.

Some adequate explanation must be found to account for results so remarkable as these. If instinct often works like intelligence, then why not suppose that instinct often is intelligent? Nothing less than real perceptions, discriminations, and choices, added to subjective appetencies, can account for the phenomena under consideration. Sensation and perception are conjoined in *our* ordinary experience. When any object affects us through the senses we not only experience the appropriate sensation, but we also intuitively perceive the object itself — perceive something of its nature, its relations to ourselves, and its relations to other objects ; then if we find these coördinations of sentient activity in ourselves, why not presume that they exist also with less gifted natures? If the bird evinces marvelous intelligence as to all the processes and conditions ap-

Different Types of Mind. 213

propriate to its special needs, why presume then that it does not possess real intelligence, real intuitions, as to the nature of all these things? All its notions seem clear and distinct as to the work which it has in hand, while everything which it undertakes is executed in a most admirable manner. It would seem that while we must admit that it possesses a real intellect, yet we must also concede that it is an intellect limited to a particular range of objects, and effective only in its own narrow department. While in its own range it seems almost perfect, and is certainly unsurpassed; yet outside of its limited family interests, it apparently knows nothing and cares nothing. The various birds have their strong special appetencies, which lead to their various modes of search after food, to their manner of flight through the air, to procreation, house-building, incubation, migration, and all personal and social concomitants, but here, apparently, both their appetencies and capacities cease together; while everything outside of their special bird-world seems utterly foreign to their natures.

Then if they do possess such marked instincts as all must concede to them, is it not highly reasonable that there should be associated coextensive mental powers, specially adapted clearly to perceive just how best to supply all their narrow but very imperative wants? Since the whole life of the robin is bound up in his little personal and domestic relations, what good reason can there be against his being endowed with a mental constitution which is adequate to take a lucid and rational view of his own personal and related interests? This is exactly what I maintain must have been done for him — judging from the evidences which he himself furnishes us by his whole general and special course of proceedings. If he furnishes no proof of either knowing or caring for anything beyond the concerns of himself and his own kith; yet he is abundantly shrewd in providing ways and means for their welfare; while he and all his are such jolly little inde-

Different Types of Mind.

pendent beings, so naive, graceful, and cheery under all reasonable circumstances, that it would be most ungracious to deny them so much acutely sharpened good sense as is coördinated with the skillful engineering of their various affairs.

Let us once admit that special instincts are special appetencies coördinated with a special intellect ; which is real, clear, and positive within its own domain ; and which works according to laws and processes of its own as intelligently and efficiently for its possessor as does the most comprehensive intellect in its wider department, and all difficulty as to the mode by which various instincts, so different in kind in various animals, are made to operate, at once vanishes. The intelligent skill with which all these are able to repair disorders caused by accidents ; their fertility of resources and the real discrimination with which often in emergencies they invent means to ends, making use of unusual and unexpected aids, has always been matter of astonishment for which there was no sufficient explanation in any current theory of instincts. Their palpable want of wit, also, in many instances where some feature of the matter in hand was just outside of the normal exercise of their powers, has been no less marvelous and mysterious. That they could do so much and yet should sometimes so signally fail, seemed incredible ; yet it becomes most credible if we regard their natures as at once both most clearly and most narrowly defined by coördination with their limited special appetencies.

Another marked difference between their apprehensions and ours is, that while we learn most things slowly and by experience, they know everything, not by gradual intuition merely, but as *a priori* or self-evident truth, which is perceived as soon as it is presented. Thus the youngest bird will build its nest as skillfully as the most patriarchal, and there is no need that the parent bird should instruct *his* child in what he himself has learned by laborious study.

Different Types of Mind. 215

We also have certain *a priori* truths of which every human mind is readily cognizant. Exactly as the child perceives that two apples and two apples make four apples; and that a fine apple is more desirable than a poor one; so the robin may intuitively perceive that an apple-orchard is better suited for its purposes than a dark hemlock grove; that one stick or straw or bit of wool would more nicely fill up the spaces in its nest than another; and that an orthodox robin's nest would better suit it than a tailor-bird's pocket of leaves. The young tailor-bird, also, may stitch his leaves together as cleverly as though he had tried a dozen times before, since impelled by his strong specific appetencies he is able directly to perceive in the concrete objects and conditions presented to him, exactly what is best suited to his own wants. Thus the eagle, the sand-swallow, and the meadow-lark, each is prompted from within to adopt the special scheme of life adapted to its species. With its appetencies impelling to this, are coördinated perceptions and resulting choices, so that its whole nature is harmonized to this typical scheme and its accomplishment. Each several scheme has its own innate truths and first principles, which become the fundamental laws of the bird-thought.

That there is a general bird-logic as certainly as there is a logic of human thought, can one seriously doubt when he invariably finds that all the races of birds are acting in conformity with it from the beginning? That their processes of intuitive reasoning, *i. e.*, perception of resemblances and differences, with the conclusions involved, can extend beyond the concrete objects immediately presented, is not probable; but that *somebody* has established principles of bird-logic as unalterable as the principles of logic or mathematics which we perceive and apply to our affairs, and that each bird intuitively perceives and applies the principles adapted to himself and his pursuits, as really as we perceive and apply those co-

216 *Different Types of Mind.*

ordinated with ours, I do not see who can disprove or even intelligently doubt! Still I do not look for a feathered Aristotle or Euclid, to become an expounder of the mental processes and theorems of this unique race of winged bipeds and songsters. Sufficient unto their warbling natures are the pleasant burdens laid upon them, and this is enough!

No one can deny that each of the higher animals has a sentient existence peculiar in a great degree to itself. We cannot ourselves share in its experiences, and can only perceive some of its special appetencies as manifested in action; but if their peculiar instincts do not often relate feeling, intelligence, and will, how then shall we adequately explain them? And why should not sensibility, intellect, and executiveness, work in concert through the merely animal organism as really as in our own higher natures? Why should not intelligence and volition in the animal be on a par with his admitted passions and sensations? We have always found analogous adapted coördinations in all other like things in nature.

The most highly developed man does not possess in perfection the special accomplishments of any of the inferior creatures. The fewer the number of gifts, the more special are they often in their action; the more intense, apparently, are the appetencies which impel to their exercise, and the more unerring are the coördinated perceptions through which alone they can be accomplished. We ourselves, though certainly higher than the bee in sentient endowments, yet cannot move from point to point in unerring straight lines as she does; and we cannot, without rule or compass to guide us, construct her waxen cells with every side and angle mathematically adjusted to every other. Mrs. Agassiz, in her "Journey in Brazil," has stated what is doubtless true, that many insects make their own bodies the measure which aids them in constructing some of their amazingly accurate mathematical

Different Types of Mind. 217

fabrics, instancing the bee as an example of this; but one has yet to be shown how the round softness of the bee can be a very accurate mould for her angular cell, so rigidly mathematical in all its proportions. I still prefer to believe that a wonderfully accurate intelligence is always at the helm, guiding all her occupations. How else shall we dispose of such facts as this given by M. Huber, known as one of the most conscientious of naturalists. He is said to have put about a dozen humble-bees under a bell glass with a comb of about ten silken cocoons so unequal in height that they could not stand firmly. Affection for their young, led the bees to mount upon the cocoons to impart warmth to the inclosed little ones; but the tottering of the comb making it impossible for them to stand in that position, two or three bees placed themselves against the comb with heads down and fore feet on the table, while with their hind feet they pressed against the cone, keeping it from falling. This they continued for three days, occasionally relieving each other. By this time they had manufactured wax enough to be placed as supporting pillars against the cone; and when these pillars were removed, they repeated the process till they could be again replaced. One would say that here were coördinated head and heart coöperative; and yet multitudes of cases are given in which bees are the veriest blunderers conceivable; showing that however acute their powers, they are yet wofully narrow in their operations.

It must be perfectly certain, also, that all the marvelous operations which we ascribe to instinct are not the result of intelligent action or indeed of any sentient experience whatever; for unsentient forces are coöperative here as elsewhere, effecting always their due share of results.

It has already been indicated that the most unerring instinct is never quite infallible; but that it often fails at points where we might presume it would be most accurate. Thus a bat, who in utter darkness can fly through a long

218 *Different Types of Mind.*

tunnel little more than large enough to admit his out-spread wings, without defiling himself with the pitch on its sides, is yet liable to miscalculate the movements of its prey; the mole, who knows how to build his subterranean palace with its convenient upper and lower corridors; its ingenious small water pits or its adopted great reservoir, the neighboring pond; its indispensable streets, tunneled higher or lower in the earth as is at the time best adapted to his vocation as highwayman; yet does not know how to do better when he meets a comrade in one of his narrow passes, than either to back out before him, or else fight with him for right of way; like two old-fashioned English noblemen on meeting with their unwieldly equipages in a narrow lane. Pierre Huber found that if he placed a caterpillar who makes a very complicated hammock, and who had completed its hammock to the sixth stage, in another hammock completed only to the third stage, that it would go on and complete this hammock also; but when a caterpillar whose hammock was only completed to the third stage was put into one built up to the fifth stage, it became bewildered and would perhaps build the whole over again. So we see an ant sometimes toiling over a difficulty which it would be vastly easier to go around; and multitudes of sharp-sighted insects flying in the face of danger when slightly confused. A bird will labor away in vain to thrust too long a stick through too small a space, when the slightest change in the position of things would remedy the whole difficulty. The sharp but narrow powers of these various beings must be not only especially liable to confusion by all sudden changes; but also to be easily thrown off the track by something, which, however trifling, is yet outside the legitimate range of their capacities. This must inevitably result from the exceedingly limited scope of their perceptions; admitting them to be, so far as they go, genuine intelligent perceptions. The fact, then, that instinct, though generally

Different Types of Mind. 219

accurate, is by no means infallible, instead of being a difficulty in our way is simply a confirmation of the theory that every instinct implies intellectual capacities commensurate with the appetencies involved. We have only to recollect how exceedingly nonplused some human beings become when there is but the slightest change made in something which they have been accustomed to do in a particular way, to find that it is quite credible for a mole or a bat to be similarly affected. I remember seeing a carpenter, who had an unusual reputation for ingenuity, standing in an attitude of the most dubious perplexity, trying in vain to understand the nature of some slight change required in a frame, which, according to his ideas, ought to be made only in a certain way. The clear preconception was most evidently in his way ; without this he would have been able to comprehend a much more difficult task. I fancy that difficulties of a similar kind must beset the poor caterpillar, when she suddenly finds her house built up to an extent outstripping all her preconceived ideas ; whereas if she finds less done than she had supposed, she is better able to go back again and remedy the defect.

The fact that one can see never so clearly in a certain direction does not at all necessitate his seeing clearly in other directions. On the contrary, with even human beings the reverse has been proverbially true. Only a few great minds have been remarkably gifted with very unlike powers ; but our geniuses are, or more especially were formerly, when general culture was less common than now, one-sided men, with clear visions only in the way of their vocations. Zerah Colburn, who could multiply by half a dozen figures at once, and who could at a glance take in whole groups of complicated numerical relations, as easily as most men can see that three and two make five, had no more insight than they in ordinary directions. He possessed simply a wonderful intuition into the nature

220 *Different Types of Mind.*

and relations of number, which was not only quite compatible with his being altogether a medium man in other respects ; but which would even tend to make him so by simply diverting other modes of sentient force into the one predominant mode of mathematical perception. Nothing is more common — and one might add, generally more disagreeable — than men of one idea. Nothing but the exceeding importance or the infrequency of the idea can ever make it excusable among *men*, whose powers allow them an unlimited scope of thought and action ; but among those creatures whose natures are largely confined to predominant instincts, whose feelings, thoughts, choices, and actions all centre about the one pivotal idea of their mental being, the case is different. They necessarily act chiefly from their personal stand-point ; while we, looking on from the outside, find in the whole arrangement an order, a variety, and a beneficence of thought which is beyond praise.

It is sufficient evidence that the different instincts of animals are not simply results of a different order of development, that even the most highly developed, not excepting man himself, is yet inferior to every creature in its own particular sphere of action. The male of a silk-worm moth (*Attacus paphia*) who delights in flying a hundred miles without resting, or the bumble-bee (*Bombus subinterruptus*) out-flying a railway carriage going at the rate of twenty miles an hour, by keeping pace with it in a zigzag course, are not more superior to man in locomotive powers than are that same moth and bee in the unique mental appetencies which enable them each to follow their own special vocations with their usual eminent success. What amount of development could endow us with the keen scent of the dog, who can trace the step of his master over leagues of earth, and for days after he has passed by ? Yet all appetency, all sentient experience being mental and not physical, there must be some unknown quality

Different Types of Mind. · 221

of sensation excited in the canine race, in some species particularly, which is as wholly removed from all our sensations as the canine or feline logic is removed from the laws of human thought.

Each type of being is too unlike that of any other to make it probable that by any amount of development in his own line, one could, on the strength of this, emerge from the constitutional bounds assigned to his own class into the possession of other or higher appetencies. Doubtless each bee may be developed in all possible bee-wisdom, and may enjoy all the many varied experiences possible to the bee nature; but can this take any of them a single step outside the circle of their own vocation? When they have all learned and practiced all the highest arts of the whole community, will they yet be one whit better instructed in the art of weaving the spider's web? Or will they know any more about her craft of entrapping flies? No general culture is involved in the exercise of special instincts; the little wisdom requisite for this is of so self-evident a kind that the youngest of its class seems to be as highly endowed with it as any of his elders, so that if he were to live forever exactly in his present condition, it is not probable that he could ever become greatly wiser than at first. Doubtless he must, like all other things, *exist* forever; and therefore, like all other living things, he must *live* forever if his life is to ultimate in his highest good; but if his constitutional appetencies continue essentially unchanged, as there is every indication that they both will and must, then his future life, though it may be more full and replete with experiences of its own class, must continue to be generically unchanged in character. Thus a plant would continue to possess the nature of a plant; the bee would continue a bee, the bird a bird, the spider a spider, and the lion a lion forever; just as literally as man must continue in the exercise of his human powers eternally. Their mental properties, like all other constitutional traits, are from the beginning.

222 · *Different Types of Mind.*

A sentient nature like that which we have supposed to be assigned to the plant, conscious only of its own present states as pleasant or otherwise, is at least possible. Life to its possessor would always be a positive good, while existing, as all vegetation now does, under conditions so generally subservient to its needs ; while if its experiences could be made as varied and beautiful as the variety of co-ordinated circumstances indicate, life then to every plant must be an incalculable good. Perceptions and volitions relating to the external causes which conduce to their pleasure or pain, since they have little or no executive power by which to effect voluntary changes, when allied to such incapacities, would be not only superfluous, but mischievous ; and therefore, as they manifest neither perception nor will, but feeling only, we may justly suppose that they are endowed with feelings or sensations alone. To this type of life there could be perpetual personal consciousness in an endless present ; but probably without memory of any past, or anticipation of any future. Such a being would be effectually shut up within itself, from the simple absence of any power or mode of sentient force which could take cognizance of anything beyond. Perceptions of the *not-me* could never arise from a consciousness of more acute or enlarged personal enjoyments, however varied and delightful these might become through improved conditions.

That objective perception might be developed in some future condition is not indeed impossible ; though we find no present trace of its existence ; while in all types of animal life perception is everywhere conjoined with sensation ; so that to endow the vegetable at any time with perception, would rationally necessitate the accompanying volition and executiveness, without which all perception must be a curse ; and would be to convert the vegetable at once into an animal. Nothing in legitimate vegetable development can ever lead to such a result ; and I find not a shadow of

Different Types of Mind. 223

reason for supposing that it ever will or can be effected under the present constitution of things. On the contrary, the plant-mind seems generically distinct from the animal, and nothing has ever been known to change in its intrinsic nature from the beginning.

A sentient nature like that which we have assigned to animals dwelling in composite organisms, with both a subjective and objective nature, but probably conscious only of the me and of the objective world as related simply to itself; yet experiencing all the sensations acquired through the common organism in its own personality, as really as though it were itself the only occupant of that organism, is also at least possible.

It is again possible that there should be myriads of distinct types of sentient being, each perfect and complete in itself; so that no one class could ever be merged into any other through any change of conditions or by any possible amount of development. This is the only hypothesis which will enable me satisfactorily to explain the facts of nature. To nature alone do I make my appeal for corroborative evidence of its truth; for it is the facts which she alone can furnish that must substantiate or refute this hypothesis.

I have spoken of the bird and the bee-logic, and the laws of canine and feline thought, as though there might be something in them antagonistic to those principles of things by which the human mind is governed in all its mental processes. Of course if there is one Author, and one comprehensive unity of plan, there can be no such antagonism! The same mathematics must underlie all perceptions, whether of bird, bee, or man; and the same first truth, that it is impossible for a thing both to be and not to be at the same time, must as much underlie the thought and action of the bird when it decides to build a nest, as that of the man when he concludes to build a house. I only mean that the bird intuitively both sees

224 *Different Types of Mind.*

and feels everything pertaining to its own scheme of life ; and is as mentally competent to pursue the course which will best conduce to its own good as it is to experience that good when it is attained ; aud that all its powers work together in harmony, exactly as they were coördinated to act.

So far as the minds of animals work in the direction with man's, so far they always coincide. It is the specialty of their differing vocations, and of everything conjoined therewith, which is impressive from the uniqueness which thus becomes inevitable to every distinct class of mental phenomena.

Many animals have but few marked special instincts ; they are not artisans of any special class, like the bee or the beaver ; and frequently possess little or no mechanical skill or ingenuity ; and yet they manifest a general intelligence of a much higher order, and in various degrees much more nearly approaching to that possessed by man. Some of our domestic animals are illustrations of this class.

The dog evidently dreams in his sleep, and, within certain limits, thinks and remembers in his waking hours ; he compares objects, judges and chooses between them, and manifests unmistakable, even intense emotions of joy and sorrow ; and he also possesses some degree of moral sense; but all his powers seem to be correlated to tangible objects and the effects which they produce upon him through the senses. He gives evidence of little if any perception of the abstract principles of things, rational or moral ; and apparently has not the dimmest perception or conception of the purely ideal. His associations and his reasoning seem always to be related to definite facts ; and it does not appear that either his reasoning or his moral sense can ever go farther than comparison or judgment as to things wholly in the concrete. Of course, therefore, there is no sense in which he can really be called a rational being, for

Different Types of Mind. 225

though he does sometimes make rational choices, he does this through a simple present perception of some difference in the things chosen between; instead of by a perception, not of difference merely in things as related to himself, but a perception of the rational nature of the things chosen, and therefore of the rational grounds for such choice. Neither is he properly a moral being, since he has not mind enough to lay hold of any of the principles of morality; for just as it requires a capacity which can lay hold of the rational principles of things to constitute a rational being, so it is requisite that there should be capacity which can understand the bearing of those principles upon general well-being, to constitute a moral nature.

Thus if a dog should bite his master he would manifest a *feeling* of guilt, just as he would show that he felt joyous or grateful at accepting a delightful bone; while at the same time he seems entirely unable to comprehend the abstract rule, Dogs should not bite their masters, or to get any idea of the nature of right or wrong, or joy or gratitude as principles. The feeling must of course be accompanied by some perception of the thing felt; but if the perception is wholly concrete, though it is not adequate to be called either a moral or a rational perception, yet, so far as it goes, it is akin to these. When a large dog refuses to fight with a small one, why not suppose that he really appreciates something of the intrinsic unfitness of the act? Since the unfitness does exist in the nature of the things themselves, why may he not directly perceive it in them? A large mastiff, brought into the presence of a troublesome small cur, sometimes manifests a great deal of self-respect, forbearance, and even a high nobility of character. Thousands of well-authenticated facts show that most of the higher mammals, under the immediate stimulus of the occasion, are able, under severe provocation, to manifest appetencies for some of the noblest virtues. They are compassionate, generous, forgiving, or magnanimous, as

15

226 *Different Types of Mind.*

the occasion requires ; they manifest love or hate, arrogance or humiliation, and many other impulses too often to allow room for doubt that their emotions are akin to ours, and that they possess intellectual appreciations commensurate with their sensibilities. I need refer to but a single fact in illustration of my position.

I once saw a cat, when suffering the pains of maternity, go to a lady who sat with her young child on her lap, and resting one fore-paw on the mother's knee, with the other pull restlessly at the infant's dress ; looking appealingly into the face of the startled woman, and calling to her in tones of unmistakable entreaty. It seems to me that no words could have said more plainly, " O, pity me ! pity and aid me ! By all the ties which bind you to your child, help me now in my anguish ! " Why might not this cat, seeing the mother and child, have intuitively felt and known enough of the relation to comprehend that here alone might she expect the fullest sympathy ? The poor creature had been caressed and petted by other members of the family who were present, while she had formed but little acquaintance with the lady and no personal attachment to her ; and yet this appeal was to the mother only ! It seemed to me, looking into these dumb but speaking eyes, that I could read in them a nature wonderfully akin to my own ; and that *she realized that fact*, at such a moment, perhaps as vividly as I did.

The patience and forbearance of cats generally towards children is proverbial ; and in this there is surely manifest some distinct appreciation of the weakness and innocence of childhood.

Suffering is a quickener not of the sensibility alone, but also of all coördinated faculties. Many persons must be able to remember, either in the mute expression of an animal's eye, or in the tones of his voice, some unmistakable appeal for aid or comfort in time of suffering or danger. The eye of a horse can ask for food ; and it can look

Different Types of Mind. 227

undoubted reproof or can flash with anger if it is withheld, or if in place of bread you give him a stone. There is a story told of a bird in Chicago (I think it was a robin) who was kept half famished in a darkened room, while a hand-organ played the same tune over and over in its hearing, till the bird, having nothing else to occupy its attention, learned to whistle the tune with the most astonishing perfection. It is well known that trained animals are almost always taught the nearly incredible feats which they perform, under the stimulus of some form of suffering; but who can believe that they acquire these things through the mere force of habit. Is it not more reasonable to suppose that they have intellect enough, when thus forcibly concentrated upon the matter in hand, to aid them in making even the most preposterous acquirements. . True, it is intellect coördinated only with the concrete fact. Feeling, intelligence, volition, all require the immediate presence of the object.

No animal lower than man himself, it is believed, has ever been able to manifest the slightest positive appreciation of purely abstract truth. If they possessed such abstract perception, notwithstanding their want of language-proper, which so distinguishes the human race from all others, they would surely discover some way of indicating this. Indeed, they would then invent language; for all articulate and written language is simply the embodiment of the purely abstract qualities and relations of things, and all animals do find some language of their own in which to express their real thoughts and feelings, as they are called into exercise. All their looks, tones, gestures, and attitudes show whether they suffer or enjoy. We see that they perceive the forms of bodies; that, in eating, they know just where to bite, making no mistakes by attempting to nibble at outlying corners which do not exist; they appreciate the place of a body, can generally determine its location at a distance by the eye, and walk directly up to it; and

228 Different Types of Mind.

they have a knowledge of color, sometimes showing their likes and dislikes in a remarkable manner. Thus while the stupidest swine will choose between a large pile of corn and a small one, not even the most learned pig has given the dimmest evidence of understanding the abstract relations of numbers. "The mother hen cannot count," is the children's proverb. The loss of a few eggs or chickens more or less, makes no apparent difference in the parental happiness, provided others still remain ; but remove her last chicken and the maternal grief is vividly manifest. While animals indicate so well that they know whether a body is round, or square, or oblong, if they could comprehend the nature of a circle, or a square, or any other figure, they would certainly manage to let us know it! though the fault, possibly, might lie somewhat with ourselves, so long as we can contentedly admit ourselves to be unable to classify or define the nature of their mental operations ; but indeed men have always given them credit for possessing instinct, feeling, and intelligence of some remarkable and unique kind ; and they have never been credited with a proper rationality.

It is not necessary to refer to the great sagacity of the elephant and his possibility of acquiring many remarkable accomplishments, or to attempt any further distinctions as to the different types of being ; though of course many of their diversities of gifts become more and more marked as we rise higher in the scale of being. But I cannot forbear remarking upon the rational symmetry of the different groups of appetencies ; considered each as a whole, distinct in itself. Every animal possesses a general harmony in himself. He may be either a lion or a lamb ; but he is not found alternating from one nature to the other : not only is he always true to his hereditary instincts, but each phase of appetency is coördinated with every other and consistent with it.

The general symmetry of the animal body indicates a

Different Types of Mind. 229

corresponding symmetry of the mind ; and we find with all races of beings that their looks and deeds are usually in close accord. For a sheep who is amiability done up in a fleece of softness, to snap and bite like a dog, would be incongruous ; or for a fox and a bear to exchange characters, each still retaining its present form, would be equally so. The race of serpents are undoubtedly very beautiful, yet the general prejudice against them is not at all mythological ; there is a stealthiness of nature exemplified in their forms, movements, and habits generally which it is impossible to ignore! Again the beautiful alertness and fleetness of a deer is manifested alike in his eye, and in his whole form and bearing. I will instance but one other example which may be found strikingly verified in the family of monkeys. They are proverbially *an imitative race*, delighting in nothing more than mimicry of everything which comes under their notice. In looks and manners alike, they are so many whimsical, merry effigies of their betters ; and though there are other animals with a higher mental nature than these, no others are so completely the apes of man.

The ludicrous and even the ironical have their own pleasant uses ; and may sometimes be made to teach their own lessons under a merry guise. I have been at various times startled, repelled, and amused, by seeing miniature suggestive likenesses of the human face, looking out from the countenances of the meanest worms. No one can possibly turn over an illustrated volume of natural history, go into a cabinet of stuffed specimens, or better still to any zoölogical gathering of the clans, without seeing in the curiously distorted features of many different grades of animals rather humiliating suggestions of kinsfolk many degrees removed. Nature undoubtedly has given many expressions to a genuine sense of humor ; for which almost every one finds some responsive appreciation in himself. My allusions to the birds have referred chiefly to the

230 *Different Types of Mind.*

graceful, pleasant types most closely associated with our civilization ; but He who coördinated all things, evidently was not one idead. Some of the bird-family have the queerest faces ; bearded, mustached, or somehow bedizened into quaint portraitures of human weaknesses, or their forms and attitudes express similar analogies ; teaching us that sedateness may sometimes be made subservient to fun. As we are the only beings who seem able to appreciate the correspondence, we may safely conclude it was intended that we should derive all possible benefit from the lesson.

The placid cud-chewing of the kine, healthful and time-occupying as it is in itself, has always stood as a ludicrous caricature of the higher processes of reflective thought. Our word *ruminating* indicates this idea, and, though of course it is easy to find plenty of fanciful analogies where-ever we look for them among the quaint similitudes of nature, yet one cannot help feeling that there is a standing joke in this repetitive, bovine relish of dainty morsels, it is so good a parody of the egotistical element in thought processes.

But if we are akin to all inferior sentient beings, we are yet almost infinitely removed from them all, by the possession of powers which must make us kindred also with even Deity himself ! Man alone, among all of earth's inhabitants, gives evidence of intellectual comprehensiveness enough to entitle him to be called a *rational* being — a being capable of perceiving the pure rational principles of things, both as established and operative in the physical universe ; and also as established and obligatory in the sentient or moral universe. Man alone, therefore, among them all, is a responsible moral agent ! The rational appetencies are all discernible in the youngest human child. Use, discipline, may develope them ; may accumulate new qualities of experience, varied feelings, perceptions of many objective realities, and one may thus acquire breadth, strength, decision, and moral integrity; but he has only developed and brought out the powers with which he was originally endowed. Man alone possesses discriminations broad enough to enable him to distinguish between the intrinsically right and wrong, the true and the false, the beautiful and the ugly; and as his volitions and sensations are commensurate with his perceptions, he only can intelligently make his own and other lives more and more desirable, by a closer conformity with all established coördinations. He alone can enter upon a course of unlimited improvement — of unending progress.

AN ECLECTIC DEVELOPMENT THEORY.

IT has been my aim to show, in each of the preceding studies, not only that there is a prevailing order in all change; but also that all the various processes of change have been so coördered or coördinated, that change generally is advance — that process in general eventuates in progress. Thus quantitative changes, involving continually new combinations of forces and conditions, produce more and more heterogeneity of compounds, and new states and conditions of the old; even while the universal rule still holds good, that like elements under like conditions produce identical results. The conditions have been so adjusted to preordained ends, that new and higher forms, both inorganic and organic, have arisen from time to time; so that the universe has been steadily carried forward from its first immature beginning to its present advanced stage of development; while there is every indication that it is still destined to undergo an entirely systematic and definitely designed but unlimited progress. Each specific thing has progressed, and will doubtless continue to do so, by established processes peculiar to itself. Its progress also is unique — a progress strictly after its own kind. Thus all inorganic progress is like a perpetual spiral, where no new forces are introduced, but the old ones wind continually upwards and upwards; producing other, more various, and more beautiful forms and states, each successively equal, quantitatively, to that of its predecessor; but, as a whole, growing continually better and better adapted to the higher uses of sentient existence.

An Eclectic Development Theory. 233

I shall presume that it is admitted, by every well-informed mind, that the present systems of worlds have been produced through gradual processes from some primitive state of matter. It will be conceded, also, that the organic kingdom known to us upon this earth, has arisen by steady gradations ; that while the first organic forms were of a very low order, every succeeding period has witnessed advancement in the prevalent organic types. We are led up at once, then, to the question: How were these different classes of beings introduced upon the earth? In what manner or by what process were they brought into actual existence? We have been taught that, " God spake, and it was done!" *That* hitherto has been answer enough ; but it is a solution which belongs to a period that supposed the earth to have been created from nothing ; and fully completed and equipped in six literal days.

Did the Creator probably depart from the whole gradual, progressive plan of creation, to make up a full grown Adam and Eve directly from the " red earth?" and has He, in a similar way, probably formed a mature first pair of every separate species, just at the time when it became desirable to introduce them upon the earth? It has been my plan from the first, to hold as closely as might be to existing facts ; leaving both the past and the future as much out of view in our present studies, as is consistent with a comprehensive and tolerably complete view of what I conceive to be the general scheme of the universe ; as illustrated by the universe in its present working order. Therefore it will be undesirable to speculate largely as to the possible " Origin of Species ; " and yet the whole question is too fundamental in its character to be altogether overlooked.

Judging by all analogies, Deity never does any of his work like an artisan ; taking part by part, and putting the whole together after the manner of a machine ; neither does He issue an arbitrary fiat which is straightway exe-

234 *An Eclectic Development Theory.*

cuted; but, in every instance, so far as human observation has extended, and so far as all rational inference reaches, He does everything by gradual, rigidly mathematical processes — in organic phenomena influenced and directed, but not superseded or in the slightest degree set aside, by the added element of an endlessly varied sentience or living consciousness, taking part in some of the processes in question. This progressive mode of working, is so inherent a part of the whole scheme of things, that it becomes highly improbable that there is, or ever has been, the slightest exception anywhere. To suppose such an exception, seems to me like supposing that the whole grand order of things has been partially subverted. Unless some adequate reason can be given for this, one cannot choose to suppose anything of the kind; for looked at in this light, it becomes too absurd and even monstrous a theory to be for a moment entertained.

We find that everything existing has now, and has had from the first, so far as we can know it, a definite and unchangeable constitution of its own. When we see a new compound we do not suppose a new creation; but a new change in some of the old elements; and when we see a new living being, even if it were a wholly new type of living beings, how could we any more infer a new creation, or even any really abnormal process of development? Every new organism grows essentially like every other, and every sentient being animating this organism manifests a nature of its own as radically unchangeable as is that of any inorganic substance. No circumstances, no development has ever been known to greatly change any sentient being, or any manifestation of sentient modes, so as to make it generically unlike that of its own type. The mere fact that mind was not always sentient, or at least that it does not remember always to have been sentient, and therefore, that this sentience or the memory of sentience in ourselves must have begun to be, proves nothing;

An Eclectic Development Theory. 235

for it is admitted that these sentient modes are dependent upon conditions partly outside of themselves; and that consciousness could no more exist in an atom, if it were isolated from all other substances, than water could exist if all the hydrogen, out of which water is in part made, were caused to exist in an uncombined state. The conscious state is eminently a state of process, and all mental process, in this stage of being at least, and probably in all other stages of existence, is dependent upon the coöperation of matter, in order to its own proper activity — as every material atom is dependent also on other atoms. Every atom, whether mind or matter, has its own unchanging possible modes of action; but it is dependent on social influences for the opportunity of exercising these modes, and this being a universal law, it is just as necessary that a mind should wait an opportunity for exercising its sentient modes, as that a hydrogen atom should wait its opportunity to combine with oxygen and become water. The great question is, does every sentient atom, like every unsentient one, possess a definite, fixed constitution, which admits of changing modes and conditions, but of no possible change in any of its inherent properties? My appeal is directly to living beings themselves; and I find that it is not more certain that unsentient atoms possess all their properties intact than that sentient atoms do also.

How, then, could a fish, or a monkey, ever become developed into a man? The answer must of course be, they never could become so developed. The sentient life of these three types of being must be eternally distinct. Their properties are as generically unlike as are the properties of lead, quicksilver, and gold.

How, then, if we deny to man the right both to these humble progenitors as his proper ancestors, and also to the privilege of a special act of creation to usher in the first full grown Adam and Eve, could the human race, or

236   An Eclectic Development Theory.

indeed any of the higher races of animals, have obtained a foothold in the earth after it was prepared for their reception? The *how* of every new little life to-day has something of mystery clinging about it. Must there be a union of two specific cells, a sperm cell and a germ cell, before a new organism can begin as the joint product of the two? or might every organic cell, under some possible circumstances, become the nucleus of a new organism? The best informed naturalists differ in opinion on this subject. There are those who believe in the spontaneous generation of some of the lower orders of beings, even at the present day; and they apparently originate such beings, producing them in sealed flasks which have been exposed to so high a temperature, previously, that all possible living germs are presumed to have been destroyed; but, on the other hand, living things are known to inhabit hot springs at a temperature even of 200° F.,[1] and glass and metal may be porous to infinitesimal beings, like some of the animalculæ; and so, in short, the powers of the human mind have not yet proved themselves adequate to settle the question of the origin of the first living being, and its organism; or of any living creature who has no parents of its own type to serve as the ordained medium for its introduction. We must necessarily infer, that when everything was prepared for the first sentient atom to begin its new phase of existence, — when the conditions under which it could become sentient were reached, — that then it began to live, and to develop its own inherent living constitution.

Myriads of atoms, of like or similar mental types, may all have begun at once, under similar conditions; and each thenceforward have gone on propagating its own species by the ordinary methods; or, possibly, but a single pair of any class of parentless beginners may have first begun to live; but in either case, we are compelled to assume that

[1] *Silliman's Journal.*

An Eclectic Development Theory. 237

both the mind and its organism must have *gradually* developed and *grown*, each as it now does from the lowest beginning. There must have been a first sentient experience — probably some weak mode of sensation, excited by external influences ; this, reacting upon matter, must originate the first germ cell ; and thus, little by little, would the mind become developed after the type of its kind, while the corresponding organism would be responsively inaugurated.

We know as a matter of fact shown by the geological record, that the first organic beings were of a low order ; and judging by all circumstantial evidence within our reach, we should expect such only to be first originated. The only point which I am ready to insist upon is, that every living being, whether originated with or without parental intervention, must have begun to be, as a living or organic being, *mentally*, through *a first sentient experience*, and *physically*, through *a first organic cell growth ;* both of which were gradually added to by coördinated processes, which are and must have been intrinsically unchanged from the beginning. Whether any or all classes of beings first found the conditions under which they could begin to live, through the coöperation of simply unsentient forces, as we suppose the first must have done ; or whether, with the higher types of mind, these conditions are so nicely adjusted that not unsentient forces alone, but some proper sentient influence also, exercised by the parent, is necessary for the birth of the new being, is a matter of comparatively little importance ; and one which, perhaps, we may never be fully able to determine. To me, it seems, however, that the weight of evidence is largely in favor of the hypothesis, that *all except the very lowest beings must have had their origin in connection with the reproductive functions of other living beings.* There is sufficient gradation among the different species to make this highly probable — more probable than that each should have arisen, successively, directly from the womb of inorganic matter.

238 *An Eclectic Development Theory.*

The animal body, in ordinary growth, must be built up from the plant, or from other animal tissues; if, therefore, the mature body cannot *maintain* its strength by drawing support from the mineral kingdom, it is hardly likely to have derived *its whole original sustenance* from that source! I infer from this, that even the lowest animal species must have arisen, originally, from a vegetable matrix; while many of the higher orders, certainly among the carnivora, were probably first nurtured by some other animal organism, sufficiently akin to its own to make such an origin at least possible. If each organism *is* the coördinated outgrowth from its own sentient mind, under whatever conditions a mind first became sentient, it would yet build up a body adapted, in general, to its own needs. Undoubtedly, such a body would have, also, a great general conformity to that of the organism from whence it sprang; but succeeding generations would approach more and more nearly to the ideal organism originally adapted to its own mental type; so that in a very few generations, the new species may be fairly supposed to have assumed its own proper character. We see something akin to this in the gradual fading out of foreign, national peculiarities, in descendants, all of whose ancestors, with a single exception, belonged to a kindred race. Thus the great grandson of a black man becomes essentially a white, if all his other progenitors have belonged to the white race; while the great grandchild of a white father has become a black, if all his other ancestors have been blacks. Therefore, if conditions were originally so coördinated, that the ancestors of the race of lions were to arise from among the tigers; provided each of these classes has a distinct mental constitution of its own, the descendants might be presumed to be distinctly lions, as early at least, as the third or fourth generation; while the mongrel, with the mind of a lion, still bearing the organic impress of the tiger, would speedily become extinct. The sudden introduction of a

An Eclectic Development Theory. 239

new species, or class of beings with no closely intermediate type between it and any known progenitor, would thus be satisfactorily explained ; and, taken in connection with the imperfect geological record, we should scarcely expect to find any trace of the few intermediate links, even if any such once existed between the old and the new species. Indeed, if such were found in rare instances, instead of proving that one animal is a gradually transformed outgrowth of another, it would only illustrate the predominance of native appetencies over the original material mould in which they began first to act. It is not impossible, and scarcely improbable, that so many distinct, carefully coördinated conditions were made necessary, in order to the ushering in of a wholly new species of beings, that when it once began to live, it would take on its own proper organism even from the womb of its foster parent ; though this would not, at a first glance, seem to be the plan most nearly accordant with other general processes.

We find, in the present, that while every creature produces seed after its kind, yet that there is a possible intermingling of varieties, and even of species ; and that new varieties and perhaps new species are introduced at the present day ; though it seems, that if left to themselves, all these would usually lapse back again to their original type. Most of these variations seem to me to be chiefly physical, or the result of changed physical conditions, as affecting the mental development, and thus, by simple reactionary influences, propagating the new order of development in the descendants.

Very much has been written upon the wonderful changes produced in plants and animals even since the memory of man ; the inference being, that if variations so considerable as these have so recently occurred, we may, therefore, reasonably conclude that all beings are the lineal descendants of primitive organisms, gradually modified by varying conditions and habits. To me this hypoth-

240 *An Eclectic Development Theory.*

esis expresses the real order of organic development ; but with the soul of the process wholly omitted. It states the grand principle of the orderly growth of species ; but with the proximate *sentient cause* of that order of growth left out. That every species has successively arisen from the matrix of radically differing species, is highly probable ; while that many very peculiar physical modifications may be superinduced by adapted processes has been again and again demonstrated. These two admissions, however, are quite distinct, and must not be confounded. The one is an inference. Such a scheme of lineal descent seems to be in accordance with all analogy ; it is more presumable that each class should have arisen from the womb of organic influences, than from that of merely inorganic coördinations ; but, in either case, so far as the mental nature of the new being is concerned, its material origin would not greatly affect its sentient development. In either case, its posterity would speedily take on the nature and development mental and material, originally adapted to its kind.

Possibly it has been so prearranged that certain crosses between different species would be most favorable to the new third character ; the one parental influence neutralizing the other, thus enabling the new being readily to assume its own proper functions and development. Many peculiarities in the growth of known hybrids point in this direction. Though such crosses are generally sterile, they are not always so ; and the exceptions might easily allow the origin of all existing types of being. Those hybrids, or their offspring, with which we are familiar, often revert to one or other of the original stocks ; yet if a distinct type of mind were to arise under a similar conjunction of influences, it would naturally go on propagating seed after its kind. Existing hybrids, generally at least, must be regarded rather as the product of *similar* mental types physically widely modified, and thus influencing the cor-

An Eclectic Development Theory. 241

responding order of mental development in each of the two parents. We have no examples of a fertile cross between very widely different classes of beings! The class of known hybrids merely indicates, that the advent of a really distinct type of mind might reasonably be presumed to be promoted by the union of two third types; from each of which it was itself intrinsically distinct, and yet no violation occur to nature's analogous processes of growth. The many acknowledged modes of reproduction, varying widely in detail, and yet all intrinsically one in principle, make *this yet one other possible mode of development* only the more probable. If I had not already dwelt on the subject out of due proportion to other topics also treated of, it would be easy to adduce analogy after analogy, to show that such a material beginning for all the different types of mind is altogether probable; but as, after all, it must be conceded that there are, in the present state of science, no admitted facts which can fully establish its truth, I forbear further considerations on this point.

But to return to the subject of the constantly recurring variations. These can be generally, if not always, shown to be simply material variations, with the commensurate influence which these produce on sentient development. Breeds of animals become larger or smaller, with or without horns or tails, more or less web-footed or winged, with some insignificant difference in their peculiar kind of outer covering, as hair, wool, or feathers; or of this or that particular form or color, etc., etc. In plants, closely analogous improvements, variations, and hybridisms occur. With both classes the amounts of known variations, though very great in some instances, are believed to be originally always of this outward material kind, which might readily arise from the changes of material conditions, co-working with the continued action and reaction between the sentient nature and its organism. Darwin, in his work on Orchids, has attempted to prove that there is a wonderful

242 *An Eclectic Development Theory.*

change in the form and functions of the various members of the orchid family, and that we can trace their present structure back to a simple original type, possessing its many distinct primitive organs ; but this being true, takes nothing from our present hypothesis. Orchids may have been removed from a likeness to their progenitors, simply by varying conditions ; but more probably they are a distinct class of plants, endowed with other mental and physical constitutions ; though arising as he thinks through the organism of those early progenitors ; while each variety has been most marvelously and beautifully coördinated with its present conditions ! So long as the grades of difference in vegetable sentience are entirely incomprehensible to us, being only vaguely held up to our perception as something which *must be*, as evidenced by their charming and so carefully coördinated outward diversities, we surely cannot yet, reasoning from scientific facts, dogmatically lay down the laws of their variations. With Professor Agassiz and his school, one may still believe that each species of being is perfectly distinct in itself ; that it cannot in any proper sense be mentally hybridized with another ; that it is formed after an original type which preëxisted in the mind of the Creator, and is intrinsically invariable ; and that each species was introduced into the world nearly or quite perfect of its kind from the beginning of its career : but I do not believe with them, that there could have been a special act of creation necessary in order to establish the new class ; that their introduction was effected by a special fiat or edict, resulting in their creation, or that they originally began as full grown pairs, from which all others were to arise by reproduction.

On the contrary, it would seem to be almost undoubtedly certain, that the development theorists are right in supposing that each successive species sprang by physically lineal descent from their predecessors. Yet it seems to me also incredible that any change of material conditions, of

An Eclectic Development Theory. 243

advantageous material development, or habits gradually inherited from ancestors, could, in themselves alone, have produced the wide diversities among living creatures. Dropping *mind* out of the organism, they attempt to account for diversities simply through the influence of quantitative coördinations. Whether or not they have generally left Mind also out of the original creative scheme, one need not attempt to determine, since these studies are in no sense a review or criticism of others. To me there is no blundering, blind, unforeseen modification of organic beings, ultimating in the final perpetuation of features which will most advantage each in the struggle for existence ; but everything, to the most insignificant details, first coördinated in the Creative thought, is legitimately realized in existing things.

Mr. Darwin's theory of " Pangenesis," — in which he supposes that each cell or " unit " of the body casts off its special " gemmules," and that these, by coördinated affinity, under the right conditions, coöperate together to produce new offspring after their own kind, thus accounting for the facts of inheritance and " reversion " with their multiplied variations, — seems to me a preëminently material theory. If even a crystal may supply the deficiency of a broken angle through the coöperative polarity of its atoms as influencing any kindred fluid ; then, surely, an organism may go on building itself up in any determinate direction, through the action of its coöperative forces upon matter generally ; without making it necessary to suppose that there must be multitudes of already manufactured gemmules, which are required to act as germlets for every special part of the future organism. On the contrary, there is evidence that the sentient life in the new organism possesses a potency of its own, which is superior to all preëxisting processes, and can modify these according to its own needs, calling in the aid of any generally adapted substance to that end. The material "affinities " or adaptations of quantitative

244 *An Eclectic Development Theory.*

atoms may account for many of the phenomena of organization; but not for all of them ! Just as a living sentience must inaugurate the first development of the germ-cell, though acting under a preordered conjunction of circumstances; so the same living sentience is alone adequate to build up its whole organism in connection with the adapted elements which come under its control. Let us once admit the existence of an indwelling, independent sentient life in every organism — an indivisible mind so coördinated with it that while perpetuating its quantitative processes by qualitative influences, it also modifies these processes; and we render all the many conflicting facts of inheritance harmonious, and at once self-luminous. Whether the new mind is started in its sentient career through the aid of general organic influences only, whether it is dependent on one isolated germ-cell as parent, on the coöperation of two parent cells, or on a whole group of parent gemmules; and whether the parent cells or gemmules must pertain to its own species or otherwise, is of comparatively little moment, provided there be a real mind quickened in conjunction with an organism of its own, which both acts upon it, awakening continually within it new sensations, and can be in turn reacted on, and built up to maturity in accordance with the indwelling sentient needs. Reproduction is both sexual and asexual, and is known to be conducted through a variety of processes; but in all of them alike, the mind must ultimately develop its own proper appetencies. The higher and stronger these appetencies, other things being equal, the sooner will the new being assume his own proper character, whatever be his material beginnings. Man therefore, from whatever matrix he may have sprung, and through whatever coöperation of cells or gemmules, must be always the master-architect of his own organism. His sentient powers are so incomparably higher than those of any mere animal, that they should become, at once, unconsciously directive of all organic processes, and should speedily build up the human organism in all its ordinary strength and beauty. Low and unrefined as the wild man may be in comparison with the highest types of civilization, yet we are not necessitated to regard him as a being who was ever obliged to grovel on hands and feet! He is preëminently sentient; while between the rational and irrational mind there is a great gulf fixed which is impassable.

THE "STRUGGLE FOR EXISTENCE."

EVERY animal organism is built up and renewed from the remains of preëxistent organisms. It must feed on other organic tissues, vegetable or animal, if it would maintain its own organic life. The vegetable derives its supplies from the organic debris which has fallen back into the inorganic kingdom, and from various substances not previously organized; but even the vegetable must compete with its fellows for the common nutriment which is supplied to them from earth and air; and the animal must kill and eat its neighbors or itself die. There is no alternative; and man is no exception to this law which is absolutely universal.

Everything connected with organic life is correlated with the fact that one organism must be built up at the expense of another. A very large majority among both plants and animals never reach maturity. It has been shown that if the offspring of even a single pair were all to survive, they would soon so fill the world with their descendants, that all others would be crowded out. The majority, then, must die prematurely; while the minority must feed upon their remains. It is also true, that the greater the variety and the differences between the various organic forms in any given region, the larger the number who can find subsistence. The various classes of being, requiring such different conditions of life, and feeding upon such different states and elements of matter, the more easily find a supply for all, the more unlike they are in their demands.

We find, also, that the nicest adjustments everywhere exist between the nature and uses of the organism, and of

The " *Struggle for Existence.*" 247

the materials from which it is to be sustained. The good cow would die if she were required to feed on flesh, and the noble lion would equally die if you attempted to nourish him upon a pasture of grass. Most of the strong special instincts of animals are related to the obtaining of a supply of the proper food for themselves or their offspring. The spider weaves her beautiful web as a snare for her prey, and the ant-lion constructs her pitfall with the same intent. Their organizations are coördinated with their precarious modes of subsistence. Kirby, in his " Entomology " says, that an ant-lion will live six months uninjured without food ; yet when it can get it, will devour daily an insect of its own size. The camel, then, is no more wonderfully fitted for his desert-life than is this little hunter for her avocations. M. Vaillant kept a spider under a sealed glass ten months, at the end of which time it was as vigorous as ever, though thin. Other insects have lived for years, apparently fasting, yet when they do eat, they must find an animal tissue exactly adapted to their peculiar needs. The most curiously-related facts connected with parasitic animals have long excited the astonishment of naturalists. That a little insect-mother should know enough to deposit her eggs in exactly the situation in which they will obtain a supply of the food adapted to them, even though she would abhor it as nourishment for herself, in her present state of development, is a striking phenomenon. Whether she is guided by mere sensation, or by an intellectual sense of fitness and adaptation, is not material in its bearing upon the fact that all organisms are coördinated with all others, through the most various and peculiar relations ; as food mutually for each other. There is wheel within wheel, but all working together. Darwin says, " we see on every side of us innumerable adaptations and contrivances, which have justly excited in the mind of every observer the highest admiration. There is, for instance, a fly (*Cecidomyia*), which deposits its eggs within

248 The "Struggle for Existence."

the stamens of a Scrophularia, and secretes a poison which produces a gall, on which the larva feeds ; but there is another insect (*Misocampus*) which deposits its eggs within the body of the larva within the gall, and is thus nourished by its living prey ; so that here a hymenopterous insect depends upon a dipterous insect, and this depends on its power of producing a monstrous growth in a particular organ of a particular plant. So it is in a more or less plainly marked manner, in thousands and tens of thousands of cases, with the lowest as well as the highest productions of nature." [1] If the highest animals feed upon the more lowly, yet the highest of all, man himself, his organism once fallen into decay, becomes food for the very lowest, the plant.

Here, then, is a cycle of perpetual change — a most complicated system of economy for the utilization of matter ; allying it, through the utmost number of states and conditions, and a most remarkable series of correlated expedients, to the largest variety of sentient needs. So far from being repelled at the thought that all organic matter is the common servant of many different minds, we should rise up in admiration at the fertility of invention evidenced in a scheme so full of multiplied utility, and yet so replete with the harmony of mutual adaptations. We are not feeding upon other living beings when we make use of the tissues which they, through their sentient experiences, have wrought up into special states exactly adapted to our needs ; we take from them their organisms, because He who created us both has designed this, and has adjusted all our appetencies accordingly ; because He saw, as we also may see, that thus only can the highest good of all be attained. To be thus socially related, through our bodies as well as our minds, is but another evidence of the unity of the whole rational plan of creation. By no other conceivable scheme could so many living beings, who can attain to active sentience only through the coöperation of matter, have lived and enjoyed at all.

[1] *Animals and Plants under Domestication*, p. 5.

The "Struggle for Existence." 249

The more we give our attention to this subject, the more and higher evidence shall we find that the seeming cruelties and sufferings incident to the existing organic scheme, are only *seeming* cruelties, and that the highest beneficence has ordained them all. When we find the bees destroying their drones, and the wasps in autumn slaying their helpless young, we are at first shocked and repelled; but when we remember that if all the drones continue to eat, younger and more useful members of the community must die of want, and that, if the young wasps are left to the mercies of cold and starvation, they must miserably perish with far more of suffering, we become reconciled. We are justly shocked when the mother passes her child under the car of Juggernaut; but if her premises were correct, that by so doing she would secure to herself and to it, eternal happiness, then her conclusion would be correct. No one can intelligently doubt that a larger number and a higher type of sentient beings may exist under the present system of interchanging organisms, than by any other which can be devised. If the young are cut off in their still exuberant life, and in all stages of development from the very earliest, yet each life has been a good; and it was better to live for even so brief a space than not to have been at all.

The sufferings of those who die early are probably not greater than if they had lived to the end of their full term of present life; and we must remember that sooner or later, they are all to die — that this is an essential part of the system. But we cannot, on our hypothesis, suppose that they are to cease to exist — that their mental constitutions are to be annihilated, or that, having once attained to the exercise of sentient powers, they will be compelled to permanently lose the possession of this free gift. The great desideratum must be to begin to live, even if, in connection with its first organism, for ever so brief a space! Living experiences once gained, become ever more and more easily renewed. Exercise develops the appetency;

250 The "Struggle for Existence."

so that it continually becomes more and more strong in itself; and, instead of requiring to be first awakened by external conditions, it becomes itself an active power, seeking conditions! If, therefore, we may trust to the beneficence which originally conferred the sentient constitution on each primitive atom, and which subsequently ordained the conditions under which it began the exercise of that sentience ; the coördinations necessary to the continuance of the only boon which makes existence of any value to its possessor cannot be imagined by us to have been either overlooked or wantonly neglected, and the plant and animal shall live again. The great point, then, is to have already lived at all ; and this point is immeasurably better secured through the interchange of adapted organisms among the coördinated varieties of sentient beings, with their diverse sentient needs, than by any plan which we, with our limited powers, can suggest. Since it has been adopted as an integral part of the creative scheme, it seems not unreasonable that we should be willing to lay aside our first repulsions, so far at least, as to be able to freely exercise our rational powers in discovering the incalculable advantages of the present method, its multitudes of exceedingly involved, but always admirable adaptations, the marvelous beauty of every detail, and the matchless symmetry of the whole.

So long as we believed that every plant was without sentience, and every animal perished utterly at death, a warring of instincts was inevitable ; and every vegetarian was respected if not imitated. It seemed hard to rob the poor dumb creatures wholly of the little enjoyment which they were evidently getting out of life, and hard to give them pain to satisfy our own hunger, or to gratify what might, after all, be only a depraved appetite in ourselves. The hunting instincts of the panther or the cat seemed detestable, and those of the vulture, or of the flesh-fly and her grubs, simply disgusting ; but if we are sensible beings,

The "Struggle for Existence." 251

we must be conscious that a wider range of view, which even we ourselves have powers adequate to obtain, may transform all these into wonderful adaptations, subservient to the highest needs of the most varied sentient experience. If the animal will live again, we take nothing but his body which has been specially adapted to our best development; if we cut him off in his prime, we make the more room for his successors, and they, with their exuberant young life, will enjoy more than he whose organism is already becoming less and less subservient to his needs, and which can at best, however well fed at their expense, serve him but for a very brief term. If we give him pain, we do this unwillingly, incidentally, and for but a brief moment, — probably, on the whole, much less than he would have suffered if left to die of old age.

There are many compensations, also, connected with pain and suffering of all kinds. A wise man passes through few experiences, however painful at the moment, which he would afterwards willingly forego. They all help to broaden and deepen his nature, revealing him to himself as nothing else could have done. Even physical pain has its coördinated, elevating, and softening mental effect; for the suffering is in reality itself mental, although caused by the relations of the mind to its body; so that we may well suppose, that, with irrational beings as with ourselves, the suffering, which is a necessary experience, is not wholly without its salutary results. That it is the instinctive warning away from dangers, we know; that it is a natural stimulus to all appetencies, we know; that even when extreme, as in excessive want or acute pain, it may perhaps be an initiation into the exercise of higher possible sentient modes, we may at least hope, with some assurance that we are not ourselves more benevolent than Deity; and that that which He desires, He may know how to accomplish! At any rate when the cat seems to be torturing her prey, or when we watch the spider who has been so beautifully instructed in the art of entrapping her flies, remembering how excessively ignorant we are, we need not in our hearts accuse God of malevolence! We may be content to leave the irrational creatures to the free exercise of instincts which we find to have been so carefully coördinated by the highest rational thought, while we ourselves use our best endeavors to regulate our own conduct by the impersonal principles of rational and moral equity.

The struggle for existence, then, regarded in its whole scope, is but a perfected system of coöperations in which all sentient and unsentient forces mutually co-work in securing the highest ultimate good. Appetencies and organisms are found to be all alike coördinated with this end. The round of nutritive processes is simply the winding, material stairway, by which successive generations of the many types of being are mutually aiding each other to mount into higher stages of existence.

THE RATIONAL MIND.

A RATIONAL mind is a mind which is able to perceive and appreciate the pure principles of things actualized in the existing universe. It is more than this; it is a mind coördinated with rational principles, as such; so that it can comprehend not only intellectual and moral thought, as related and actualized in things; but it can originate thought, conceiving other rational principles, which might possibly exist, and which, within certain established limits, it can even cause to exist or become actualized as facts. Perceptive and conceptive forces are both modes of insight into the nature of principles, actual or possible. Perceptive force is competent to discover existing substances, with their existing properties in their actual states, operations, and relations; it creates nothing; but perceives and knows realities of all kinds. The constructive mode of force, on the contrary, originates thought, that is, it originates fancies, imaginations, hypotheses, and various possible principles which may or may not be actualized as the real principles of things.

These two modes of intellectual force are both appetencies. The intellect desires to perceive the true nature of things. It hungers after a knowledge of everything which exists, to satisfy the purely mental appetency, as really as it hungers for the food which is to build up its organism. The satisfaction which follows when it first perceives the character or effect of any new rational fact is a delightful experience; of a correspondingly higher character than the gratification of any appetency connected only with the material or quantitative elements of things. This appe-

254 *The Rational Mind.*

tency, like all others, recurs again from time to time, and strengthened by exercise, it becomes ever more and more imperative. A dull man may become content, much like · the animal, with the outside surface of things ; neither perceiving nor expecting to perceive very much as to their rational qualities ; but one whose native insight is quick, or who has been well disciplined, often becomes excessively eager to *know*, and his gratification at any new discovery is supreme. The consciousness that one is able really to perceive the inmost principles of the universe, as realized and operative, must be coördinated with the most fascinating and exalted of all purely intellectual capacities. The moral appetencies alone can be more sublime in their demands, and accompanied by yet more ennobling emotions.

Perceptive force, like any other appetency, may be overwrought, or rather the mental instinct may overwork its material servants, and thus suffer reactions. One may be surfeited, also, with a multitude of unsystematized facts — facts which are not comprehended in all their general bearings, so that the intellect is cloyed by them, as the stomach is wearied in indigestion. Perception, from the very nature of it, can be wholly satisfactory only when it extends to the whole scheme and relations of the property in question. It has nothing to do, and everything to see.

Constructive force is the instinct of personal intellectual power — the spontaneous assertion of innate rationality, which must seek for gratification by the legitimate exercise of its appetency. Here is the imperative need supplying itself through the very strength of that imperativeness. One always loves the ideal world which he has power to create. His mind-craft is more interesting to him than any possible handicraft, because it has more in it of his very life. He demands that it should be beautiful ; or at any rate that it should have an internal fitness and harmony of its own, and be generally conducted according to

The Rational Mind. 255

the ordinary laws of thought, if not of fact. The child, with his little men of straw fancies, which he accepts as he does his dolls, knowing that they are only pretty effigies, is yet unwilling to have them discordant with his ideas of propriety, or of right and wrong. I have seen two little girls contend seriously for the right disposal of an imaginary pair of scissors, each taking a slightly personal view of what was required by impartial justice. A poet would be in despair if his work were not faultless when tried by the rules of poetic logic ; and all speculators and reasoners would throw up their vocation in disgust if they might not ally their thoughts to the four fundamental laws of thought universal. Thus are we created in the mental likeness of our Creator ; so that the principles which He conceived and actualized in things generally, are also realized in our mental constitutions. We can no more think that anything can be and not be at the same time, or that the same object can be at once round and square, or that two and two make anything more or less than four, than Deity can produce such contradictories as literal facts.

Moral force is appetency for sentient good, allied to perception which can discriminate between the various qualities of good and thus become directive of the volitions. The moral appetency would be wholly spontaneous, acting impulsively instead of reflectively, and therefore not constituting a moral act, if it were not directed by moral perceptions ; making rational distinctions between various classes of good, and choosing accordingly. The appetency, the moral insight and the volition, together constitute moral force or "the moral sense," and neither could be anything without the other. A *free-will* or power of rational choice is simply the executive force pertaining to a sentient rational being, who is free to use or not to use it as his appetencies dictate. The *will* is one mode of force, and the person to whom it pertains, if himself a rational being, renders the exercise of this will a rational or moral act.

The Rational Mind.

Every rational mind has a moral sense — has an appetency for right moral choices. It delights one to be able to perceive and to choose the best, the intrinsically most valuable; not for himself alone, but for others also. Many of his purest joys arise from the consciousness of thus perceiving and choosing, in despite of contradictory appetencies. Any good, of whatever kind, brings a still higher good to himself, if he can voluntarily relinquish it in favor of another. Thus has he been created with a moral constitution — a nature which can both perceive and choose the best, because it is the best intrinsically, and not from any personal considerations. His moral appetencies are directly dependent upon his rational perceptions, which are able rightly to discriminate between relative values ; for, having thus discriminated, the unselfish moral appetencies are ready to accept the best, however his own personal interests may be affected thereby. Many of his lower appetencies will rebel, but these must be brought into subjection.

Every appetency impels towards its own legitimate gratification. Appetency is force, which, when in exercise, is actively seeking its object, and is *choice* or *will* to itself and in itself. I see no more necessity that choice should necessarily be selection between two or more objects, than that thought should always consist of comparisons between two or more things ; but I maintain that as perceptive force may directly perceive any object by itself alone, so the power of willing or choosing at all, may enable one to determine in favor of any single object for itself alone. But moral perceptions and choices necessitate comparison of objects, and the accepting of that which best commends itself. A moral being, then, is one who, possessing many diverse appetencies, has yet a dominant appetency for the intrinsically highest and best ; regarding things impersonally or in their abstract, intrinsic relations. His freedom to choose is made possible by his

The Rational Mind. 257

appreciation of the moral or qualitative order of things, thus releasing him from appetencies which are nearest and most personal in relation to his present individual state. He is able to perceive and choose the obligatory principles of moral equity in preference to personal gratifications, which become ignoble and wrong when brought into conflict with these. Principles of justice and right, established for the general good, are intrinsically higher, broader, more beautiful than any others; and all rational and moral properties are coördinated with these! Many of the deepest and sweetest emotions are also allied to them, so that the exercise of personal self-denial in favor of impersonal justice and right, is often rewarded with its own exceeding present recompense.

Every one is conscious that he can both perceive and choose any form of sentient gratification, directly, as something desirable in itself; but also that he can and often must select between two or more qualities of experience, either of which is desirable in itself, but which are incompatible together. If, then, he is willing to act irrationally, to close his eyes to the highest good; choosing the lowest because his appetencies are more clamorous for it, he can do so! This is precisely the way in which the masses of men generally act; yet each one is conscious of possessing a dominant appetency for the intrinsically best or right, which, if it were allowed fair play, would impel him to choose according to his own best judgment, uninfluenced by conflicting desires. One's real freedom lies, then, in his power to decide whether he will be governed by his reflective, rational, and therefore impersonal appetencies, or by appetencies which, simply acting spontaneously and being wholly personal to himself, are, like all unreasoning instincts, liable to lead him into injustice toward others, and corresponding harm to himself.

The principles of moral equity, which are as fully established as any other actualized principles of things, are

258

The Rational Mind.

the only motives which should be allowed to influence rational choice! But every rational mind may choose its own motives, may choose which shall be its dominant appetencies! The reasoning powers are coördinated with the moral appetencies, but even these may be subverted and used in the service of the irrational propensities. Since man has many properties in common with animals and plants, let him beware how, by making these dominant, he too, becomes to all intents a merely irrational being ; while his highest prerogative is the exercise of rational and moral attributes.

We have seen that all sentient experiences, though the appetency for them is in ourselves, are yet wholly dependent upon external influences for their development. For all our joys, for every sensation, for every one of even our deepest and most personal emotions, the subjective appetency must wait on its objective coördinated supply. Are we hungry, food alone can content this desire ; do we delight in the enjoyment of beautiful forms and colors, material nature must furnish the objective world to gratify us ; are we eager for the knowledge of the rational scheme of the universe, this universe itself must be our only teacher ; would we even create new schemes of thought, yet we cannot think without the coöperation of our material brain, and our thoughts are only a recompounding of the established principles of thought. They are the immaterial, qualitative elements out of which our fabric is to be built up, like in kind, but not in structure. Our social joys, far more thrilling and exquisite than either sensation or intellectual action, are yet coördinated with all other sentient activity ; so that all one's richest experiences are but a free gift from his fellows. A being, alone in time and space, even with the richest sentient endowments — since these would exist in him only as subjective possibilities to be awakened by objective coördinations — would be no better than any senseless clod. Let us cease, then, to regard even matter as contemptible. Our bodies are not clogs to be borne with in patience; they are the ordained ministers of every good. Nor is it a most praiseworthy thing that we should remember the interests of others, since we owe every good which is most worthy of being possessed directly to them. We may well thank Him who has made all our social appetencies as much more remunerative in higher enjoyments as the powers of a rational mind are nobler than the personal or concrete faculties of any irrational being.

We may rest, also, in the assurance that the principles of morality, which regard all sentient interests impartially, and as wholly independent of the mere personal desires, are the principles to be studied by every rational being, and to be applied everywhere and under all possible circumstances. These principles are the natural outgrowth of coördinated sentient relations. It is not more certain that every event must occur in time, that every extended substance must exist in space, and that every mind must think according to the established laws of thought if it would form correct conclusions, than that every rational being must conform himself to the principles of moral equity, if he would reap the full benefits which are coördinated with the exercise of his rational faculties!

THE RATIONAL MIND AS CAUSE.

SENTIENT force may consciously direct and control material forces, and through these it may influence other minds ; thus one is able to greatly modify existing states and processes, producing new and otherwise impossible events. Human beings are able to produce endless modifications in the normal routine of nature. It is not the author, the artist, the inventor, the agriculturist alone, who becomes the *rational cause* of important new events ; but the commonest man is continually and designedly modifying the processes going on everywhere about him.

I am conscious that I can raise my arm, that with it I can lift up an iron mallet, and that by beating with the mallet against a rock I can probably rend the rock asunder. I decide to do this, and do it. Thus I have designedly inaugurated a distinct new series of events. I am conscious of the whole process as it advances ; for it is so coördinated with my sentient nature, which is coöperative in the process, that the whole is literally felt by me as sentient cause ; and I maintain that there is no break in the chain of conscious process. Philosophers may think otherwise, — one's only appeal is to experience ! Physiologists treat of the conformation of nerves and tissues generally and their modes of use ; we concern ourselves only with the fact that mind consciously and designedly uses coördinated bodily organs, and also extra-organic matter, to introduce changes and produce new events. The force which I employ is not simply my own proper sentient force alone ; but it is chiefly the unsentient force under my

The Rational Mind as Cause. 261

control, which I act in conjunction with, and which, reacting in its turn upon my sentient nature, produces in me the completed consciousness of the entire process.

The intelligent control which mind exercises over matter continually, causes new material improvements, so that the whole civilized world has been remodeled by the rational power of man. The more intelligent this power becomes, the more admirable are the changes effected. Mistakes are necessarily made; for there must be various misconceptions in different minds as to the true principles of things, and of the objects to be attained by improvements; but when men have fully learned that all the rules of æsthetics, of utility, and of general progress, are already actualized as the properties of existing things, and are to be directly studied and perceived therein, they will become apt scholars, and be more ready and able to apply all these principles in practice. We must accept all classes of rational principles as the established, unchanging laws, in accordance with which alone can any desirable results be produced; but by the coöperation with which all desirable results may be accelerated. The creative latitude thus conferred on us is not inconsiderable. We may well content ourselves with an endless modifying power, which can produce rearrangements and conformations innumerable. We may make the whole earth blossom as the rose; and by doing so we shall undoubtedly confer an incalculable increase of pleasant living experiences upon all varieties of the most beautiful vegetable forms; for if all things are coördinated in wisdom and beneficence, the most cultivated types of the great plant family are those which attain to the highest sentient good! Why, then, is it not reasonable to suppose that we may assist them to a better development of their own distinctive appetencies, that their lives may thus become more ample, more free from the discomforts of their class, more replete with varied satisfaction, and possibly even better prepared to animate some

262   *The Rational Mind as Cause.*

future higher organism. The flower of a plant is generally the most beautiful not only; but also contains the most highly individualized organs in the whole structure : when the world blossoms therefore in beauty to our eyes, one would be glad to know that we have produced also the culmination of vegetable enjoyment! The more highly vegetation flourishes and becomes civilized, the higher and less noxious are the types of animal life which feed upon its adapted tissues ; and, it may be presumed, is man proportionately nourished and made harmonious, mentally as well as physically, with his improved surroundings.

The human mind may become the rational cause — that is, the forecasting author and designer of new sentient experiences — both to itself and to other minds of all classes. Any rational being can almost remould himself or his child, through a persistent use of the right means to that end. The sculptor is not more truly the rational cause of the statue which he creates ; the chemist of the water which he manufactures by exploding gases, or the gardener of the apple which grows upon the tree which he grafted, and in the soil which he cultivates ; than the teacher is of the thoughts, emotions, and purposes which he awakens in his pupil. The *statue* could not have *grown* in the *garden*, nor the *apple* have been *chiseled* from the *marble*, even if the artists had expended infinite thought and labor to these ends ; for they must each co-work with the persisting nature of the things which they seek to modify. Effective human causality lies in producing legitimate changes and improvements in substances already existing with their immutable properties. The chemist must discover the right key to unlock the mysteries of nature's hydrates and oxides — must free the gases according to her laws, and marry them afterwards according to her fixed statutes. Each inventor must realize his plans in her materials. If he would produce a self-moving machine, which is almost alive, he must blend the forces of her wood

The Rational Mind as Cause. 263

and iron into his steel; endowing it from her treasure-house with projectile forces which are at least equal to her inexorable gravitation. Perpetual-motion makers may be certain, in advance, that Nature will always maintain her balance of power; for all her forces are correlated and coördinated with all possible events. Thus the educator, either of himself or of another, must comprehend something of the nature of the being whom he seeks to modify, before he can be in any sense rational cause of such modifications. A person, with intelligence and volitions like his own, free to change or to resist changes of mode, must divide with him the rational responsibility. When the blow falls upon it, the glass *must* be shivered; but if influence falls upon a rational being, he *may* resist its legitimate effects.

Mental appetencies exist, requiring nothing but exercise to secure development in any direction. Sensations and emotions respond to every coördinated appeal from without; and you have only to co-work with the native appetencies, stimulating or repressing as is needful, to realize your wishes. Many of your efforts may be counteracted; but a steady purpose will almost surely accomplish some portion of its designs. A rational man will perhaps stand at the helm and mark out his own course; but an infant, on its early life voyage, must float at random, almost wholly at the mercy of circumstances. Its mind is as plastic to exciting influences as matter is to the moulding touch. As the sculptor fashions the clay after his ideal, so the wise teacher unfolds the powers of his pupil in any direction by the use of adapted stimulants. The mental process is no more recondite than the material, and all its details are equally well established; yet the world certainly is not yet so far advanced, either in the theory or practice of sentient culture, as in physical improvements. Education has been largely conducted as an empirical process. We have been content to follow precedents;

264 *The Rational Mind as Cause.*

making but little inquiry after the principles of mental development. Doubtless example is the most efficient, and therefore the most scientific of all mental stimulants; but we do well to remember that the science of rational causes and effects has as definite and well-established principles as any other branch of actualized thought; while it is evidently higher in importance than any other or all others combined.

He who gave Nature her innate constitution, and established all her coördinated processes, is her Rational Cause and Author, doubtless, in a higher sense than that in which the chemist is the *cause* of the water generated by the meeting of gases in that fiery embrace in his glass tube, or the gardener of the improved apple produced by intelligent high cultivation; for He established the laws for the formation of water and the improvement of the apple, and His broad, rational design must have comprehended in its scope all possible events. Just as He forecasted events, adapting means to ends, so fore-ordination is a necessary element of every rational scheme. A rational cause is a forecasting cause, who, designing the end, uses in view of it the appropriate means. Rational causation involves a perception of how to originate or modify events, volition deciding to do this, and executive force able to accomplish it. A rational mind causes new events because the mind is so coördinated with their causation that it becomes a part of its daily vocation to do this. The rational mind has an appetency for acting as rational or forecasting cause, experiencing many qualities of satisfaction and delight through its exercise. A father hands his child a fine peach, that she may experience the sensation of a new and pleasant taste. He carries her to the meadow where she may see the grass and the lilies, that he may enlarge her experience and procure for her a new pleasure. He teaches her some of the relations of numbers, that he may discipline her intellect, and give her the use of her rational

The Rational Mind as Cause. 265

powers — in all this he is intentionally working through existing forces, and according to preordained processes, to produce desired results.

Any finite mind, by causing a conjunction of circumstances, may occasion events undesigned and undesired; these are wrought out through his materials which are constitutionally true under all conditions. He miscalculates the forces which he employs. Since he must co-work with Nature in her vast store-house of many but partially understood elements, there must frequently arise new and unexpected complications; and dealing with sentient beings, themselves possessing the power to wholly or partially resist his efforts, his uncertainties increase. Of course his sole remedy lies in a wider knowledge of all the forces involved, sentient and unsentient. This alone can enable him to obtain over them a more complete influence. Meanwhile, he cannot be held fairly responsible for all the untoward results of his interference. He is rational *cause* of so much only as he has intelligently planned; but by his wisdom or folly in dealing with the powerful and but illy cognized powers to which Providence has related him, must he also be held to moral account, for Rational powers are coördinated with commensurate responsibilities.

A *rational mind* can be the intelligent designer of events, and in this sense he is cause — *rational cause. Matter*, on the other hand, can be nothing but *substantial* or *quantitative cause*. It is something which passes into its effect, so that every quantitative effect is exactly equal to the sum of its causes. The effect literally is the cause or causes, existing under a new mode. Of course there is a radical distinction between *rational* or *qualitative cause* and *quantitative cause*. Deity is the rational cause of the present universe. He planned or designed it, so coördinating means to ends that all the details of his design shall be ultimately consummated; but He is in no sense the sub-

266 *The Rational Mind as Cause.*

stantial or quantitative cause of the universe! He works with existing materials, as man does ; the difference being that while He established originally the rational nature and relations of those materials, and his ends are both proximate and ultimate, man must accept that established nature and its relations, contenting himself with designing new proximate ends, to be secured by appropriate means.

If man, therefore, as rational cause, can accomplish so much, shall we doubt that the ultimate ends of the great First Rational Cause will be attained? Gardens, parks, conservatories ; cottages, castles, cities ; roads, and railroads, in the cultivated old world, are notable improvements upon marshes, jungles, forests ; barren prairies, sandy plains ; wolf-paths, and Indian trails, in our great unkempt West ; yet the Oregon of a thousand years hence, will doubtless wonder at the record of crudities in the England of to-day! And can we doubt that social progress — the progress of the human race with its rational and moral attributes — has been coördinated with physical progress? The Infinite Mind as Cause has not so irrationally constituted his Universe !

The human mind is cause also of *pure qualitative values.* It creates these, perpetually increasing the sum-total of sentient experiences. Pure principles and relations of all kinds, and the correlated personal appreciation of them, which in its various modes we call perceptions, conceptions, emotions, and volitions— that is, thoughts, feelings, and choices generally, are not convertible into quantitative values, nor can the material nature of the one represent the immaterial nature of the other. Mind may be the originator of new material events by the intelligent reordering of material forces ; but when a mind excites or directs a new mental process, either in itself or another, the mental experience is a positive increase of sentient values.

The standard of all values is purely qualitative, so that

The Rational Mind as Cause. 267

each mind must affix its own estimate of them, which it does according to its powers of relative appreciation. A teacher may explain some series of natural events to his class, as for instance the nature of light, its undulations, and the general relations of color. One pupil is filled with admiration at the nice adjustment of forces which can enable every ray of the sunbeam to act always in character, performing its delicate work with mathematical accuracy. Another regards all this as super-refined and unpractical ; but is deeply interested in the effect of light upon the various arts ; while yet another is feeling that an hour in the sunshine, with a young friend and a fast horse, would be better to him than the whole philosophy of light, useful or beautiful. All values are thus immeasurable, because no two minds can have a common standard, and it is only when you bring them down and ally them to quantities, that you know how to apply the principles of justice and equity. Yet just as there is a perpetual increase of new material events, although there is no increase of the materials entering into those events, so there is a perpetual increase of sentient good or evil, although neither the experiencing mind nor the co-working unsentient forces are increased. Any rational mind, then, may become the intelligent cause or designer of such experiences, either in himself or others. He may elevate or degrade the character of such experiences. He has only to comprehend the nature of his forces, coöperating with all that is intrinsically highest and noblest, in order to render every life about him more beautiful for his influence. Indeed, one has only to be truly noble and unselfish in order by his social influence to infect others with his own character ; so that even a child, with no intent of doing good, and with his rational powers too undeveloped to know how to act discreetly, may yet be the moral benefactor of all who meet him. Thus the simplest natures, if only self-forgetful and thoughtful for others, are always the most beloved ;

268 *The Rational Mind as Cause.*

for they appeal to our best moral appetencies, elevating our sensibilities unconsciously to themselves. The graceful chamois has no turn for æsthetics, though himself a gem of beauty, in his picturesque setting of mountain and crag.

One mind may communicate with another almost wholly through the medium of the senses; but in all intellectual and moral communion, the material coöperation is comparatively small. When the mind is occupied with the purely rational character of things, it becomes comparatively independent of the ponderable elements. An exalted divination enables one mind to interpret another; thoughts, feelings, and purposes are given and received without an intervening tangible medium, so that words and even looks become superfluous. In our ordinary conversation, while we listen to each others' voices or exchange looks, yet the rational principles about which we converse, are, by the one mind, embodied in words or looks, and by the others, directly perceived as thus made visible to them. The quantitative can *represent* quantities; but everything qualitative must *present* itself. It has no extended form that it should be imaged, but is a pure mental creation which can be represented by nothing else whatever. We can either embody it in language or in things generally, and we may lead one's mind in the direction for perceiving it by referring to analogous or parallel properties or their opposites. One phase of thought or emotion may be made, in some sense, to represent another; that is, it stands in the place of another or imitates it; but is not its true representative. A musical instrument may be made to suggest the song of birds, the chirping of insects, the sounds of the winds and waters, the peal of thunder, and almost every other sound natural or artificial; but sound alone can represent sound. A blind man may fancy that a brilliant scarlet is like the blare of a trumpet, but it is very unlike it nevertheless. Neither does the sound repre-

The Rational Mind as Cause. 269

sent the sentiment which is embodied in it; but for the time being it gives expression or actualization to it, and this is directly or presentatively perceived. Sound, therefore, is but the medium of communication — not the representative of the thought communicated.

Nor is there necessarily a quantitative relation between the two. The lowest whisper, freighted with an important thought, produces infinitely more impression than a thoughtless shout. Two persons may listen to the same message, and yet one will be almost unimpressed by it, while another is thrown into the utmost excitement. The quantitative force used was identical, but the two persons were differently related to the quality of the communication. During the terrible prevalence of cholera some years since, a lady and gentleman were conversing on the subject with the quiet thoughtfulness of people in a rural neighborhood, remote from the scenes where it prevailed. The lady remarked with some solicitude: "I have a brother who is probably now at S."— naming one of the infected cities. "I shall feel anxious till I hear from him!"

"Your brother!" exclaimed the gentleman; "the Rev. Mr. B. of S.! He is dead! I was told so not fifteen minutes ago!" It was thoughtlessly uttered; for he did not yet realize the force of his own words, his strongest emotion at the moment being a simple surprise. But he smote the listener's heart with a blow the strongest arm could never have given. What quantitative force here was suddenly transformed into the dull, terrible chill of that first mental shock. The effect was mental and the producing cause qualitative. The related material elements were insignificant, though the shock, once received, reacted upon the whole organism. Any strong emotion exercises strong control over the body; the mind uses its correlated unsentient forces in the service of its sentient experiences; but this class of emotions is originally excited by qualita-

270   *The Rational Mind as Cause.*

tive — not by quantitative causes. This is true of all the higher orders of sentient modes; sensation and the perception of material forms alone being quantitatively correlated to material elements. A little later this young lady received authentic assurance that it was another Rev. Mr. B. of S. who had fallen a victim to cholera, while her brother was still in health. The sudden reaction of her mind to a relieved and grateful joy naturally expressed itself in a lightened step and a bright eye ; for these wait on a glad heart as naturally as languid movements and the dimmed eyes are responsive to a weary sorrow ; but the sentient emotion is not transformed into the unsentient movement. Say rather that when mental force is concentrated largely on any one mode, that this mode exercises a correspondingly strong control over coördinated material forces, not that it is transformed into these forces. Because a man in a terrific passion will sometimes stamp or tear his hair ; because a wood-chopper expends muscle, and thus stimulating the organ by exercise causes it to be still more vigorously renewed ; or because a man who thinks, uses brain, producing coördinated changes in his whole organism, we are not, therefore, to infer that passion or the exercise of will in the use of mechanical force, or of thought in intellectual processes, is transformed into mechanical force. There is undoubtedly a quantitative action and reaction between every mind and the matter coöperative with it ; but the kind and intension of sentient experience are not necessarily dependent upon this quantity ; but may be more or less, indefinitely, while yet the quantitative elements remain unvaried. Thus one mind influences or causes changes in another by occupying it with rational principles or with various social and moral emotions, though the physical agencies used may be few and unimportant. Indeed the most purely rational causes use the most purely rational agencies, so that the best educator is he who can bring to bear the highest and best motives. Yet if he would cause these to become motives, he must present them in a form adapted to the appetencies and capacities of his pupil. To become the intelligent, judicious cause of new qualitative events is therefore one of the highest arts to be acquired by a rational being. It requires far more wisdom and address to steadily improve the habitual modes of a rational mind, without arousing opposition on its part, than to deal with any other class of properties. Be ye wise as serpents and harmless as doves!

MEMORY.

MEMORY brings past experiences back again into present consciousness. That it can do this in some sense and to some extent, no one doubts. It only remains to discuss the nature of memory, its province, and its mode of action.

Memory is a sentient power, and like all other sentient forces it has its own keen appetency, impelling it into frequent exercise. It delights us to recall past pleasures, to revive again the experience which charmed us on its first occurrence, or to trace connections between it and other events by which it was preceded or followed. We are self impelled to this, and to rejoice in the results, as certainly as we are mentally incited to eat, to relish our food, or to look out upon the world, rejoicing in its beauty. Even painful memories have their fascinations, by which at times they attract; and their still stronger repulsions, goading us on to seek more pleasurable experiences.

The appetency for remembering is also coördinated with its objective stimulants, and is incited by them into exercise. All the associations and adaptations of objects among themselves are so many mutual stimulants to memory; which is thus able the more readily to recall them in connection. The utility, and the charm of so widening the scope of consciousness as to take in all past experiences at will, are perpetual and ever present incentives to the activity of "reproductive energy."

Memory is simply that mode of personal force which recollects or revives past personal experiences of all kinds; if then, we can decide how these experiences were first

Memory. 273

awakened, we may find a clew which shall guide us to the modes through which they are reawakened.

Perception arises through the presence of the perceived object; the visible traits of the object are daguerreotyped upon the mind, or the rational scheme of it is read and interpreted by the perceiving mind, and is thus made its own — an element of its own personal thought. A concept, also, is a personal experience — a modification of the mind; so is a sensation, an emotion, and a purpose. All these are more or less dependent upon the objective world to furnish occasions for their exercise; but having become the veritable experiences of a continuous personality, they are so many modes or phases of that personality itself. As affections of the persisting being, they must pertain to it thenceforth; and need only to be remembered or recalled into present consciousness, to be realized as themselves persisting. Anything, then, subjective or objective, analogous to the original conducing means to any particular modification of mind, will tend to reawaken that experience.

Space and time, as two different measures of processes both mental and material, severally relate all mental experiences. Events connected in place or time are likely to be also mentally associated and remembered together. The more remote, also, an event is in time, the more removed is it likely to be from present experience, and the less readily, other things being equal, will it be recalled. Old age, passing in thought the intermediate active life, and remembering again the events of childhood, is not an exception to this rule, but a most striking illustration of its truth; since the sympathies and occupations of childhood and extreme age are more nearly akin than those of business-troubled, active middle life. The fact that an aged man does recall even the trifles of long past boyish days, is a striking proof, if any were needed aside from the nature of the things themselves, that all

18

274 *Memory.*

experiences of the mind are its own personal treasures forever.

Again, events bound together by any chain of cause and effect, rational or material, must naturally stand related still in memory. Resemblances or contrasts, and, in short, all associations, intrinsic or accidental, are mutually suggestive ; and the same or similar conditions with those which originally excited the experience will again recall it into present consciousness. Different classes of associations, also, variously affect different minds, modifying the general process of remembering by individual peculiarities. Thus one person, with a strong sense of the grotesque, will recall events through suggestions of the oddest analogies and the most whimsical or ludicrous incidents ; while another can remember dates, and groups of events. Of course our modes of remembering must be as unlike as our modes of thinking. Memory is also largely a matter of habit or practice ; for exercise of this mode of mental action, of course, strengthens and develops it like that of every other. A disproportionately good memory seems sometimes to absorb other modes of the mind into itself ; but large retentive powers are also compatible with the most vigorous and well-disciplined mind.

It is necessary to understand fully that memory gives us only the *subjective element of events* ; and that the objective is as wholly outside of its province as it is outside of the intrinsic personality of the *me.* I have the memory of a quiet country church, at the mention of which there rises before me widely different eras of thought and feeling. I can see hundreds of faces, from those of faded, withered elders to the plump cheeks of long-ago young children. Again I see these once children grown into bronzed and sallow middle life, and sitting in the old pews, with their stalwart, blooming youths and maidens. Among the shifting groups there are ruddy faces, which to me will never change ; and there are the still white faces

Memory. 275

of an ever young brother and sisters, in my memory sleeping forevermore in that front aisle ; and yet the old church is now burned to ashes, while changes more than I know have fallen upon the scattered people. All the objective elements have changed or passed away ; and the changes of subjective experience have been greater even than any of these ; yet those early memories must always vividly recur, because gained when life was young, eager, and all its powers alert. They are living gems in the mosaic of memory which destruction cannot overtake, if I abide forever! *Objectively, the transient perishes* while the *permanent is conserved ;* but *our percepts of each alike endure.*

Distinctions must be made also between different classes of experience. Any pure principle — a thought, or a purpose, or anything closely connected with the rational powers — may often be recalled as clearly as at first, while sensation or emotion is very rarely felt a second time with all the intensity of the first. The philosophy of this difference is evident. Our cognitive powers suffice, in any ordinary condition of mind and body, to recall in thought any pure rational principle or any past purpose. Such a principle, first perceived in the object, is incorporated in the intelligence of the perceiving mind — abiding there thenceforth for easy reference. The process of acquisition was almost purely mental in the beginning ; therefore, the stimulating mind and its organism can co-work in the absence of an extra-organic object. Hence one is able to realize in his own experience that thought is indestructible. The same truth recurs to him again and again. When an idea which he remembers something about, seems to have been utterly lost to him, perhaps for years, suddenly, it may be, to his intense astonishment and delight, it recurs to him in all its vividness, distinct as though it had never passed out of his consciousness. This is especially true of what has been termed a "philosophic memory," or a memory of associated principles. There is no one who dwells much

276 *Memory.*

among abstract ideas and their relations, whose heart has not jumped for joy with some such experience as this. Our choices, too, being largely determined by our own mental states at the time, are easily recalled; but not so easily rechosen; for our purposes are often almost as variable as our sensibilities. Volition may be in subjection, either to our rational powers or to our desires, and on this depends the stability or instability of our purposes. The sensibility is always much more dependent than the intellect upon present modes and habits of feeling; upon organic and other external conditions, and also upon the presence of the object or exciting cause of the emotion; and, therefore, emotions, sensations, and all states of mind which depend upon these, are seldom reproduced with all their original zest. We recall a past choice, perhaps with no desire to rechoose it, or some former intense desire or emotion is remembered with the utmost present indifference. Even the strongest attractions of the past may only repel us in the present. The more new experiences intervening, the less likely are the old feelings to be again brought into ardent action. Emotions which are dependent upon intellectual and moral principles, must wait upon habits and appetencies of the mind; while sensations are dependent on material coördinations. The mind may have adopted a wholly unlike emotional attitude from that to which it is now habituated, and from which it is not again easily swerved. It cannot fall back into sympathy with emotions which are outgrown. Those affections which are most nearly universal, and most germain to every sentient constitution, such as parental love and other social instincts, are most easily revived in memory.

Since mind and body both enter into new phases so continually, and external conditions so constantly vary, although past modifications of the sentient life are all real and indestructible, like the life itself, yet those experiences which are largely dependent on adjustment of conditions are

Memory. 277

never fully reproducible in present consciousness without a reproduction also of those conditions. Pure principles are intrinsically comparatively independent of matter, while sensations and their correlated perceptions are almost wholly dependent on it — dependent moreover on the most careful adjustments, mental, organic, and extra-organic. All the way between these extremes, thought and feeling blend in the sentient experience in varying proportions. It is the universal law that those experiences most dependent upon external conditions for their original production, are, in the absence of those conditions, most difficult of reproduction in memory.

All classes of feeling are necessarily in close relations with their objective occasions. The knowledge of a truth in the abstract is distinct and clear in perception, in proportion as it is disencumbered of its factitious acquired relations, through its embodiment in things ; while the reverse is true with all experiences of the sensibility. Knowledge of suffering, in the abstract, affects us but little ; but the presence of a sufferer will awaken the tenderest pity. To know that a whole army are bleeding and dying on a distant battle-field does not move us so deeply as one wounded soldier brought home to our active sympathies. We can weep with the heroine of a story because her griefs are present to our imaginations ; but we sit idly calm, though we know that the real heroines of life are suffering far more deeply and variously than language can depict.

Every good cause is inevitably promoted by agitation and discussion, because its intrinsic merits are thus held up to present view, and in contrast with conflicting demerits which only heighten the effect. Indeed, agitation promotes every cause which is not absolutely baseless and irrational ; for as its plausible features are always presented, they are generally readily adopted by the unthinking, simply because the mental appetency demands the stimulus of new thought, and is ready to accept anything which for the moment seems obvious. This is the strongest of all arguments in favor of an ever-active promulgation of important truth. Anything to be accepted, or to produce a present influence, must be brought home to the present consciousness.

Memory is that mode of force which can bring into present consciousness past phases of experience. All pure rational experiences are most readily reproducible as they are at once most independent of all external coördinations, and, being rational or impersonal in character, are also most independent of personal changes of mode; while sensations and emotions are least readily recalled, because closely related both to objective conditions, and to subjective modifications. In other words, memory, like all other forces, acts only in conjunction with its established coördinates. It is the present and immediate perception, not of the objective, but of the subjective element in past events; and it is as necessarily immediate in its action as any other form of self-consciousness.

LANGUAGE.

SENTIENT life instinctively learns to express audibly its own varied feelings. Sound is produced by a coördination of material forces; and even inanimate nature has its own variety of appropriate normal sounds. We can hardly call the murmur of leaves when stirred by the wind an expression of their content, though one might easily fancy that even they have their own little articulate expression of vegetable satisfaction; but the insects, the birds, and the higher animals unmistakably express their feelings in sound. There is as much joyous welcome to his master in the glad barking of a dog, as in the ringing voice of his little human playmate. The cry of a wounded animal is sometimes as touching as that of a child; and the cry of a grieved child is as pitiful as any sound with which the human ear may ever expect to be greeted. A spring-morning carol of birds is a *jubilate* of innocent excitement. Cries of rage in a wild animal, and even in our own domestic bull and stallion, are terrific; while the lowing of kine and the whinny of the horse, may be as peaceable as their own meadows. Insects have their notes of love and general rejoicing; and though they are not known to use the voice, yet they have their own modes of speech, and ring out their harmonic roundelays, making the summer evening at once both jubilant and sentimental.

The human voice, unless artificially schooled into a false tone, instinctively expresses every variety of human emotions. The laugh of a little child is a spontaneous poem; and the merry prattle of a group of children more

280 *Language.*

really musical than the artistic singing of any professional glee-club. While a boy is still too young to find fitting language for expressing his feelings, you can readily gather them from his look and tones. Even at a later period, when caution and insincerity have begun to creep into his *words*, his *tones* are still the best interpreters of his desires. In later life, after long training in the school of conventionality, his emotions are not so patent in his voice ; yet even then it is only by the most determined effort that any strong passion can be wholly suppressed in expression. If he deliberately disguises or falsifies his emotions, the mental force expended in accomplishing this, for a time suppresses or suspends the emotion itself, transforming it into the sheer, hard effort of will. His struggle to control the emotion will thus tend directly to subdue it ; and if the exciting cause be removed, it will never return to him in its first intensity ; but if the cause remain in all its original force, the suppression, followed by a strong reaction, may rekindle the emotion even greatly intensified.

The voice is certainly the natural outlet for every mode of feeling. A sigh is generally quite involuntary, and a groan is often a great comfort — even almost a necessity in very acute suffering. If not restrained by a sense of personal dignity, backed by education and some consciousness of the rights of others, there is no reason why grown men and women might not go on crying like children over every hurt, physical or mental; or why a gentleman might not scream, like any fine lady, at the unexpected proximity of some poor little insect.

The changes of the countenance and the attitudes of the body are all more expressive of *feeling* than of *thought*. Smiles and frowns are nearly universal. Each class of emotions or passions has its own coördinated looks, gestures, and attitudes. A child's face, like his voice, is a truer index of his present feelings than the man's : his eyes are little beacons always alight with the spontaneous,

Language. 281

internal warmth. Anger, pity, joy, sorrow, and all the other impulses to which his young life is subject, radiate from his face as though it were a mirror, reflecting out to you the phases of the soul shining upon it from within. Thank God that his whole carriage is usually as jubilant and bounding as the young life which has learned but little yet of weariness or retribution! Thus all things have been tenderly ordered everywhere for the inexperienced! In after-life the habits of a person are so inwrought in the features, and in the whole form and bearing, that however possible it may be to conceal any given emotion for a time, it is next to impossible to disguise all the tokens of a customary frame of mind. The smooth serenity of a genuine Quaker, and the wiry unrest of a Yankee trader, are not mere caricatures of the real men; they are embodied facts — the permanent language of habit. The step of habitual weariness will not become elastic even at the close of the longest holiday. Crushing dependence, or independent ease of position, each become personified in their subjects. Deep sorrow leaves its gentle, mournful signet on eye and brow, disappointment graves its mark in bitterness, and darker passions bespatter the whole man with an outer stain of contamination.

Even animals typify externally the nature of their sentient internal life. There is more wary alertness in the beautiful tiger than in the soft, mild-faced sheep. One can hardly see an ox, — that toiling, emasculated bond-servant of men, — without getting a new suggestion of the worth of patient, strong endurance, even under great wrong. It would be easy to indulge the illusion that every plant, rooted in the nurturing soil and reaching up to the affluence above, is a type of a sentiment far better than that we express by the ignoble word *vegetate*. To me plants personify acceptance, trust, serenity, contentment.

Words are correlated to thoughts. The appetency which impels us to the expression of thoughts, as instinc-

282 *Language.*

tively uses the adapted organism to effect this, as the appetency for seeing uses the eyes, or hunger the mouth. An infant of a few months will smile and crow back in response to its mother ; at a year it has generally mastered some easy and expressive words, and at ten, a well-trained, intelligent child has become quite a linguist in its mother tongue, and possibly in several other tongues which it habitually hears pronounced. The facility with which children master a language which is spoken to them is proverbial, and the philosophy of this seems to be very evident. Instinctively seeking expression for each new experience as it arises, on hearing a word used to indicate any present object, or any existing feeling, they grasp it with an almost single-minded avidity. Their range of experiences is narrow, and as it widens, the use of language is thus easily acquired as the vehicle needed by their enlarging ideas. In later life, association has already joined the word to its idea ; and the range of experience has become so extensive that the mental energy and attention are diffused. Memory, too, making the past a shadowy perpetual present, leads often to a lessened interest in current events, while anticipation and hope open a new deceitful present in the much desired future. Memory, in general, is thus made to appear much less tenacious in matured life than in childhood ; for divided attention is favorable neither to new acquirements nor to a systematic command of the old. Learning a language late in life, it is as though an innate jealousy of the accustomed tongue, made it a perpetual rival of the foreign one. Thus many a family, resident in a foreign land, is surprised to find the elders far outstripped by the little children in their efforts to acquire the current speech. Acquired discipline, including the habit of concentration, is found to be an offset which with most minds, at least in the study of a spoken language, is scarcely an equivalent for the fresh directness of a young being whose life is all in the present ; and

Language. 283

whose whole soul drifts as a unit into the mood of the moment, whatever it may happen to be.

Words are evidently in part *imitations* of *natural sounds;* as in the terms *ma, mama, maman, papa, pater, fader, vater;* which simulate the natural cries of the child in need of care. We have other examples, in the *bow-wow*, the *moo-cow*, the *ba-sheep*, and many active verbs and their derivatives, as *whiz, whirr, whirl, whip, boom* — in short, the whole group of buzzing, trilling, rough sounds in all languages. Their quieter kindred, such as *murmur, gurgle, tinkle, hush, hist, still, listen*, seem suggested by the lulling monotony of blended summer sounds, in which noise and quiet are at once harmonized. *Gesture* and *pantomime* arise also from the intrinsic harmony and fitness of things, and are essentially the same among all peoples, of however different habits and modes of thought. Philologists find more and more similarity between all languages, the more the subject is investigated.

Modern language is of course largely derivative; but the most ancient tongues evidence an unexpected likeness, which can be accounted for only by supposing, either that they grew up independently, equally arising out of the natural relations of things, or that they were mutually derived from some still older dialect. Probably both sources have aided in the production of every language now extant; as we find them to-day both enriching and modifying every living tongue, still in the process of normal growth. *Representative* language may be said to have had a simple growth by accretion; for it deals with the *obvious elements* of things, producing similarity in all tongues as the legitimate result; but it is combined with *a purely mental process of thought*, seeking to embody enlarging experiences in symbols and words, arbitrarily defined and arbitrarily harmonized with the already established modes of expression.

The growth of language, presenting the innumerable

284 *Language.*

phases and degrees of sentient experience, is something nearly as wonderful as the creation of physical nature itself; and it is at least closely analogous to it even in kind. It is the physical or embodied expression of sentient experience, whether feeling, thought, or purpose, and is created progressively ; many minds acting toward a common end, and adopting, by general consent, series of given signs as embodying corresponding series of recognized experiences. All language may be regarded as one magnificent structure, well built and harmonious as a whole, but with incongruities and discrepancies of detail when viewed from different stand-points. The real marvel consists in the essential unity of the thought attached by many minds to the same term ; rather than to the shades of difference affixed to it by different minds, and by the same mind on different occasions. Language is itself the highest evidence of the *unity* of all like sentient experiences, enabling each mind readily to comprehend the thoughts of others through its own personal appreciation of them. Ears and eyes are severally the channels through which the body of language co-acts with one's own organism ; but the recipient mind perceives directly the rational element embodied.

Each author is creator, not so much of original thought, as of new combinations and expressions of thought. Spoken language is a present process, vanishing as it passes, but written language is as enduring as the material used. Deaf mutes can read the thoughts expressed through the eyes and fingers ; and the deaf and blind, like Laura Bridgeman, by simple touch. Smell and taste also are in some instances exceedingly useful to the blind ; and in scientific pursuits they often lend important aid to perception when grosser senses are in default.

Every mechanical invention is the language of its own scheme of thought, expressed in some combination of matter and its forces. Painting, sculpture, pictures, hieroglyph-

Language. 285

ics, are so many modes of language embodying their appropriate ideas. Art produces its carefully elaborated concepts of the beautiful, homely, grand, ludicrous; forever seeking a more suitable form for its ideal than any present natural embodiment. A perfectly mathematical crystal is a rare product of nature, though the ideal theory according to which all crystals are evidently formed, and to which they all approximate more or less nearly, is perfectly and mathematically accurate in all of its several types. Thus everything in nature is more or less varied from its normal ideal; the most successful artist is perhaps he who can best perceive these ideals and embody them most perfectly in his creations; the language of highest art may thus be more beautiful and expressive than even nature herself. In composition, one may ignore the malformed and the commonplace, which nature everywhere tolerates and propagates. A painted landscape, or a landscape garden, representing only the harmonious, and seeking the most perfect ideals, may appear even more charming than nature herself; as well as much more suggestive, and more readily understood by ordinary minds. Men are placed here, undoubtedly, to cultivate the earth and to subdue all its imperfections, material and rational; but it is indispensable first to attain the perfect, one's-self, before seeking to give it expression. Language embodies experience. A parrot or a monkey is as worthy to be called an artist, as is one who attempts to create any language or embodied expression of any kind, without first perfecting it as a living, personal intuition of his own.

The appetency which impels every rational being more or less strongly to seek adequate expression for all the modes of his sentient life, is not only innate in his constitution, but is so inherently coördinated with the material elements which are adapted to embody and present his experiences to others, that language, regarded as an ultimate fact, must be as much a legitimate part of the general scheme of creation as is crystallization or any other result of a predetermined process. In the one process, the acting forces, unsentient, irrational, and involuntary, act mathematically, as they are coördinated to act ; in the other, the force is sentient, rational, and free to choose its modes, not only as between this and that form of expression, but as between expression and but partial expression or non-expression, in any given instance — therefore here, certainty, or mathematical precision as to nett results, is impossible. In the one case the product is always fixed and absolute ; in the other it is a perpetually varying result, both in quantity and quality. Humanity must needs perpetually seek expression for its ever-widening experiences, because such expression is coördinated with some of the highest modes both of primary and reflex satisfaction ; but the form and extent of such expression is necessarily dependent at once on the choices and the rational ability both of individuals and of the social whole. Therefore, like every other process pertaining to mind, language is not a fixed, but a perpetually varying quantity, so far as it can be quantitatively estimated at all. The point here is, that language, like any other product of mental force expressed in matter, must be regarded as the normal outgrowth of the inherent constitution of mind. Human language is the legitimate expression and product of the experiences of the human soul, in the use of its proper powers as coördinated with material forces. Each mind at once embodies thought and perceives the thoughts of others when similarly expressed. Thus has originated *language proper* — an elaborated system of expression, to be regarded as at once the spontaneous outgrowth of nature, and at the same time as a highly artistic creation of the human intellect.

THE CONSERVATION OF MATTER AND ITS PROPERTIES.

SINCE Lavoisier invented the balance, experimentalists have practically tested the fact that matter is indestructible. Nothing is created and nothing annihilated. It is found after every change in the modes of matter that the same quantity permanently exists, though perhaps under widely different forms. Skillful chemists have been enabled to trace every thousandth fraction of a grain from one transformation to another, and thus to prove by actual weight that matter is never annihilated. There is no wearing out of the substance itself, but only of the fabric, scattering its undiminished particles to the four winds. Rocks may crumble to sand, but the sand remains; sand may be melted into glass, the glass ground to powder, and the powder mingled as ingredients in a dozen several compounds; yet the substance, unchanged in quantity, continues to exist. When the candle burns, its substance is not consumed, but is only converted into gases. Not since Priestley's time, when the theory of Phlogiston was believed in, has any naturalist for a moment admitted even the possibility of the detruction of matter. Neither is it found that substance is ever added to, or by any possible process increased in quantity. When plants and animals grow, they gather the materials used from the earth, sun, air, or from other organic structures; but no atom is brought into existence or created from nothing, under the existing order of things.

This great fact, that matter is a fixed, unvarying quantity,

288 *Conservation of Matter and its Properties.*

once established by science, has led to great exactness and care in all analyses. It has resulted in the discovery of unsuspected elementary substances, which, though small in quantity, perform perhaps most important work in the economy of nature : it has confirmed the habit of mathematical exactness in experimental science, applying the nicest varied tests, and compelling the most careful attention to the minutest details. The ingenuity and beauty of many of these experiments is something wonderful and well-nigh incredible. This nice practical skill has arisen directly from the assurance that no atom of substance ever has been or ever can be either originated or destroyed. If this fundamental fact could be disproved, inductive science would lose its zest, and fall back again into the slovenly inaccuracy of early days. When an experiment failed, it would again be supposed to fail because of the destruction or creation of some residuum of matter ; thus all quantitative science would stand paralyzed and virtually dead. But the truth remains. Matter is inherently existent. It is superior to time — every atom a perpetual fact.

A still greater advance in science was made by the discovery that all the *forces* of matter are also persistent. They change their modes of action, and are correlated with each other or convertible from one mode into another ; but they are all alike absolutely conserved. Mechanical force can be changed directly or indirectly into heat, light, electricity, magnetism, cohesion, and every other known mode of force : these can be again reconverted into mechanical force or into each other. The relation between them is found to be so strictly quantitative, that a given amount of one mode of force will always produce a given amount of any other, under like conditions. Though the definite relations between all the various modes are not yet well ascertained, yet enough is known to assure us that all the forces of simple matter can be

Conservation of Matter and its Properties. 289

estimated in quantitative values, and that the smallest fraction of force can no more be destroyed than can matter itself. It is equally true that no new force can be originated ; but that a definite, fixed amount continues and must continue absolutely, under the existing constitution of things.[1]

Scientific men accept the doctrine of the conservation of force with great unanimity ; and are ready to admit its consequences even when most rigidly applied. The fact that matter with all its constituent properties is indestructible, lies at the root of every natural science, of all departments of physical knowledge. To suppose that it could be destructible, either as to its substance or its forces, would be to suppose that its whole present constitution could be destroyed ; for pure matter is constituted wholly by its rigidly quantitative properties. No hypothesis can find a shadow of favor with science to-day, unless it adopt the truth of the conservation of all the constituent properties of matter. They all remain the same from the beginning — neither more, nor less, nor different, however many their continued changes of mode and process, or changes in any of the non-essential elements of being. If any property of matter disappears, physicists are bound to search for it, and to account for its disappearance ; or at least to leave room in any hypothesis which is adopted on the subject for a final explanation of the nature of its changes and the mode under which it at present exists. No thorough student of nature can rest satisfied till he has explained the connection between the transmutations of all the activities of matter, tracing them through all their various modifications.

We may admit, then, that matter with all its constituent properties is indestructible ; that nothing pertaining to its constitution is either added to or destroyed. It simply *is*.

This far-reaching truth is as much a question of metaphysics as of physics. A metaphysicist, Herbert Spencer,

[1] *Correlation and Conservation of Forces.*—Youmans.

290 *Conservation of Matter and its Properties.*

has shown that the "persistence of force" is a primary truth in all philosophy — a truth which transcends all demonstration and is "deeper even than definite cognition — deep as the very nature of mind." In the language of the present essay, it is one of the necessary, fundamental, or first truths, which every one must as certainly immediately perceive as he must perceive his own existence and personal identity. He may not be able to reason about either, and if attempting to verify his perceptions, will perhaps stumble and doubt the evidence of his own consciousness ; but they are truths which he always assumes and acts upon nevertheless. But I hold that the persistence of force alone is *not* the *most fundamental* intuitive truth. Mind perceives the persistence also of the substance, as constituted by forces or coördinated properties. Each mind accepts the fact of the existence, persistence, or conservation both of matter and its essential properties. Every child, even, instinctively relies on this great, most comprehensive truth of science. The steady, unchanging existence of matter is the one central point which is above and beyond any question of time. It exists in the eternal present. Past and future are nothing to it : it was and is, then, now, and forever.

It is not enough, either, to affirm that matter and its properties, as a whole, cannot be destroyed. Each atom as constituted by its own special properties is equally indestructible. There is evidence that the atom and its inherent properties are one and inseparable — one and indivisible. Undergoing a variety of modes and combinations, it is yet conserved, with all its properties, as a distinct indivisible atom. Its forces are acted on and react again forever, through all possible changes and transformations ; for force, as a property, is found to be never separated from its own special substance. Each atom or molecule of matter, then, in all its entireness of essential properties, is indestructible, and must exist while the present constitution of the universe is still maintained.

IMMORTALITY.

IF matter and its forces are found to be indestructible, is it possible to believe that *mind can be destroyed?* Mind is, it exists. If it existed merely as a resultant of material forces, if it were only the outgrowth of an organism, then, with the dissolution of the organism, it also would fall into nonentity. But if mind is itself substance, constituted by its own properties, and existing in its own right, then, under the present system of things, it cannot be destroyed. Like all essential being it must be superior to time, eternal or immortal.

We have first to settle the question of life. Is it, as we have tried to point out, substance allied to its own distinctive, innate, coördinated sentient properties? Then life cannot, in any sense, be regarded as the opposite of dissolution; which is what we mean by death as applied to the body; but it is opposed to annihilation or absolute destruction. We have seen that under the present constitution of nature annihilation does not and cannot exist; but that every substance with its innate properties is equally indestructible. Does life belong to these real existences which have received an inherent immutable constitution? Then life cannot become a nonentity. The term death, in ordinary usage, does not mean destruction, but decay and dissolution. The body dies in the sense that, all the nice adjustments of its parts being destroyed, its forces no longer work in common: it decays and falls asunder — its particles scattered and converted into other modes of being. But neither substance nor property is destroyed. There is change of adjustments and modes, and a readjustment of

Immortality.

new phases of things. If a quartz crystal is pulverized and scattered far and wide, its destruction as a crystal is complete. Nothing short of a miracle could ever re-gather all its particles, group them again in precisely the same order as before, and thus reunite them in that particular crystal. The almost rational coördination of crystallogenic forces which coacted in that particular crystalline formation, as though with innate intelligence all working toward the same end, is presumed to be forever destroyed. In all probability just that conjunction of forces will never exist again ; but the forces themselves are none of them destroyed. They all exist still in their own proper substances, ready to enter again into any possible number of new alliances.

The analogy between the dissolution of the crystal and the dissolution of the body is complete : it is as striking as we find the analogy of process to be in the formation of the crystal and of the living organism. That conjunction of adapted atoms which built up the organism, which digested its food, and kept it in continual repair, which worked through its brain in thought, and through its arm in muscular force — that special coöperative whole is destroyed, though the atoms themselves are each still unchanged in permanent nature. Why should not the sentient atom be equally conserved ; equally indestructible with all the others? At the dissolution of the body the sentient mind is separated from it, but is this mind therefore incapacitated for new alliances of a similar or higher type ? Is the mind destroyed, or are its sentient properties annihilated, or does it exist still — of rational necessity, as part of the present system of things — with its whole sentient constitution unchanged ? If each life *is* an ultimate atom, constituted by immutable sentient properties, as material atoms are constituted by definite unsentient properties, then each mind is surely as indestructible as each material atom. This is immortality ! Life, then, is

Immortality. 293

continuous life, immortal life ; and the adjective adds no force to the substantive. Life is something superior to time — is simple, sentient existence in a perpetual present.

The experiences which the mind acquires while dwelling in its body have no necessary dependence on its relations to its present organism. It perceives by direct vision ; and whether it perceives through its material eyes, or, if disembodied, a similar perception were produced through some kindred process, is not essential. Perception is an affection of the mind obtained through some conjunction with the object perceived ; and whether the organism intervenes to aid the mental act or otherwise is of no consequence. It is only essential that there should be some adequate coördination between the perceiving mind and the thing perceived. If the perception is presentative, when the mind is allied to its organism, there is no reason why it should not still perceive presentatively when separated from its organism. The same is true of all mental activities usually performed in connection with organic functions. Mind is the self-poised sentient power, whose proper experiences are all personal to itself, even when it acts through its bodily organs, and is acted upon through them by the material world. Because a mind is now coördinated with its human organism, and this again with the external world, is no reason why the same mind, with its own proper innate constitution unchanged, should not hereafter, on leaving its organism, enter into new relations with yet other elements, and thus continue uninterruptedly in the exercise of its own proper activities. When one sees an object divided, he immediately cognizes the pure principle of divisibility ; but if nothing in the material conditions *represents* the principle, then, whether the present organism, or indeed any other, intervene between the mind and the principle is not important ; and the perceiving power may perhaps exercise its proper function under a wide variety of conditions, with equal facility. He who adapted

Immortality.

minds, organisms, and inanimate nature, in all the phases of existence to which we now belong, has shown no want of resources which should lead us to doubt his ability for the future. Unless He has failed utterly at the very point where the chief value of life just begins to be appreciated by its possessor, He must have prevised adapted conditions of being, after the separation of the mind from its body, so as to secure the highest use of its legitimate sentient powers. The negative supposition is wholly incredible and contrary to all analogy. There is no more shadow of evidence in favor of the annihilation of sentient properties than of any other class of forces in the universe; but, in addition to those which demand the conservation of merely mechanical force, there are an infinity of added reasons why sentient forces should be conserved! The beautiful, rational scheme, embracing sentient existence as its crowning glory, would be shorn of all its grandeur, if consciousness were to be dissipated and to end with the dissolution of the organism. But this is a consideration distinct in itself. I wish in the present paragraph to show that all the normal powers of any mind are legitimately its own, of unchanging constitutional necessity; and that so long, therefore, as it exists and can find conditions under which it is possible to exercise them, that all its experiences must continue to be conscious experiences — that its activities, whether feelings, thoughts, or purposes, must continue to be personal or self-realized activities.

Doubtless mind with its sentient properties may sleep, may rest or lie inert for a time, there may be a state of mental equilibrium or balanced mental and material forces which is total unconsciousness; but this, from the nature of things, can be only temporary. It would seem to be quite as likely to occur while the mind is incarnated as in any other condition of its being. We are subject to at least partial unconsciousness in the state of natural slum-

Immortality. 295

ber ; and a patient under the influence of chloroform or any other anæsthetic, is apparently totally unconscious. The mental and organic forces are not, for the time being, in working relations with each other ; so that the body may be cut in pieces while the mind has no cognizance of the fact. In some of the modes of *matter*, certain of its unsentient forces seem to be wholly inoperative ; but when they do act at all, they act always in character. Let us grant that *mind* has also its *static phases of existence* — that it can be even wholly inactive and therefore unconscious, yet it must be also true, that, in the moment when its proper activity recommences, its personal consciousness must be again continued. Since all its special properties are sentient, while its present constitution is retained, all its proper activities must involve a personal consciousness, under every possible state of its active existence. When the mind leaves the body, therefore, though we can know but little concretely of its relations in the future, — we ourselves being limited by our own organisms, — yet we may be certain, not only that this mind is still conserved with all its innate properties, like all other classes of being ; but, also, that if its relations allow it any proper activity whatever, it is then in possession of its own personal consciousness, and must be accumulating new sentient experiences continually. Its largely developed sentient powers will be able to seek conditions in which it can act. If we concede, then, the point that minds are, like matter, indestructible, and persist with all their constitutional properties intact, we are ready for other considerations bearing upon the question of immortality.

We turn to arguments from the nature and fitness of things ; and to various social and moral considerations. The whole subject is so important that we may be justified in treating it from every point of view ; since some minds are likely to be more impressed by other trains of thought than by such reasoning as has just been presented.

296 *Immortality.*

A belief in immortality is so universal that it must have originated in the very constitution of the human mind. It is adopted under circumstances so diverse, that I can see no other way of accounting for it. It cannot be regarded, as some suppose, as a truth given exclusively by revelation; for heathen nations, who lay no claim to a revelation upon any subject whatever, also believe in it. All their religion is often based upon that belief. They try to propitiate their gods, and do voluntary penance to secure rewards after death. Every nation, without one exception, which can be admitted as such by the careful historian, is more or less confessedly occupied with "laying up treasures in heaven, where neither moth nor rust can corrupt." Nor can a truth so generally accepted be regarded as a mere tradition. Mankind do not so unanimously accept any doctrine in which they find no evidence of inherent truthfulness; the man himself tries the tradition, and accepts or rejects it as he is able, in the face of sufficient evidence. It is this very intuitive evidence that I am desirous of examining, and testing to the utmost.

A man's life is himself; and the one is not without the other. He feels this without reasoning about it. It is the irrepressible first consciousness: he cannot help the assurance that he is a veritable living person. The idea of his ever losing this life may not occur to him for years. Why should it? It is as foreign to think of losing his life as it is to think of losing himself—of being divided or parted from himself; for he cognizes his life—his sentient being, as inseparable from his true existence; and he can have no thought of ever laying it down till this thought comes to him from without. The consciousness of life originates within the living soul: it is the idea of death which comes wholly from without. This is what is meant by the affirmation that a belief in immortality arises from the mental constitution; for immortality is life and it is nothing more than this. It is life, without a cessation of life. The being

Immortality. 297

who is conscious of past and present existence can believe in future, in unending existence, which is only the duration of his present self. It has already endured in his consciousness for years; and it could only be some violent outrage to his nature which should suddenly compel it to cease to exist. He could not believe this possible without the strongest external proof. The very thought of it is a shock to him: he shrinks back from it, his whole nature rises up in rebellion, and he refuses to admit anything at once so incredible and so undesirable. He cannot be conscious of death, of non-existence; but meantime he is conscious of life, of present, actual existence. Can you bring any conclusive proof that he will ever cease to be? If not, he will cling to his belief in continuous life. In the absence of such proof all nations, heathen and Christian, have trusted the internal evidence in favor of immortality. The youngest intelligence must perceive the intuitive logic which assures him of a sentient, persisting, personal identity; and therefore humanity has asserted its dogma of immortality almost universally; but if it has been its first unreflecting and most childish decision, it has been the decision also of its wisest and best philosophers!

Death, if there be any essential death or destruction of the living person, is the encroacher; whose power to destroy must be made manifest before we can believe in it. Men have reasoned by a false analogy from the dissolution of the body to the annihilation of the mind, or at least to the destruction of its continuous personal consciousness; but the argument grew up in the speculative era, before men saw, intelligently, that all substance and force are alike indestructible, while the present constitution of things continues. There can be no question now as to whether the substance of mind is indestructible, when science has settled that everything is quantitatively conserved; but it can hardly be said to have decided that each conscious personality is indestructible. On the contrary, it is still

298 *Immortality.*

halting between that opinion and the doctrine that mind or sentient experience is only a transient mode of matter, and may therefore pass away like other similar modes. It is only those who reason and observe — the thinkers among the masses of mankind — who are intelligent skeptics as to the future life ; but these have learned to doubt also as to the distinct mental individuality of the present life. It is as easy to doubt the one as the other, and as easy to prove the one as the other. If we cannot believe in a persisting personal identity, distinct from the changing organism which it inhabits, belief in an indestructible continuous life is of course impossible ; but if we admit the one, we must concede the other.

The moral argument in favor of immortality is perhaps more convincing than any other. Life is desirable. Sentient experience, with all its drawbacks of pain and suffering, is full of general satisfaction. Everybody instinctively loves life and clings to it. The possessor of sentient powers is keenly alive to the good they bring him : he is able, in a great degree, to appreciate the increasing value of his sentient experiences and to desire their continuance. Every human soul craves an immortal conscious existence, and must do so, because sentient life has been so ordered that it is felt to be intrinsically desirable. Apart from the doctrine of endless and irrevocable future punishment, every rational being cries out instinctively against the blank, black evil of future nonentity, and holds up his protest to God himself against it. " I live ! and life is good ; then I shall live forever ! Why not ? Who shall prevent it ? Will the Creator take my life from me ? Then why did He give it at all ! He might have prevented my existence at first ; but now that He has given it me, and I prize it, why should He take it again ? He must have given it me because it is good, and if so He will continue that good ! " So reasons and protests the intuitive logic of all humanity.

Immortality. 299

When the cold dogma of annihilated consciousness first intrudes itself upon the credence of the philosopher, he feels it as the blade of torture severing his dearest hopes. He sees it pruning away the earliest loves of the soul, and knows that his childhood world of intuitions and beautiful undoubting trust, is falling in ruins about him. Show me one who has become reconciled to the idea, who has become content to cease to be, and I will point to one who has suffered what no words can tell of doubt, protest, agony, despair. He may turn for remuneration to physical science, with all its admirable processes and adaptations, may go into dream-land as poet, logician, or ideal philosopher, may become a humanitarian, a sensualist, or a speculator in stocks or dry goods, as his tastes dictate ; resolute to find good somewhere ; but at the best his existence is to him life with the very essence of life omitted. He has need to be a man of resources, if he would find social existence in its present stage of development even bearable. Is he to look calmly on suffering, outrage, and wrong? to see myriads of his race doomed from infancy to wretchedness, ignorance, hopelessness, and vice, and to death with no more of good in store for them ? It is well that when one can disbelieve in an immortal life, that he must disbelieve also in a free, rational Creator and Ordainer of life, or otherwise he must curse Him to his face, arraigning Him for his cruel malevolence. If it is granted that neither substance nor force are ever annihilated, then the annihilation of a sentient existence would be the most utterly monstrous anomaly which could occur in the universe !

Life, with all its ills, is yet intrinsically good ; with all its possibilities of suffering, it has infinitely higher possibilities of enjoyment. If its sufferings, as I have tried to show, react upon it, impelling it ever to higher good, and if its ultimate destiny is the attainment of ever increasing and nobler enjoyment, then life is the incomparably highest boon which it has entered into the heart of man to conceive. We may well believe that He who gave it to us will not take it away again. We desire it above all things, as the only basis upon which all other things can be brought into our cognizance, and as it is He who made this desire the strongest appetency which we can possess, we may rely upon the infinite parental tenderness which will satisfy the demand. If his arm is not shortened that He cannot help, nor his heart hardened that He cannot love, then while his resources prove commensurate with the existing scheme of things, which He himself has ordained; then while every atom of the clay we walk on, of the air we breathe, and of the flesh and blood in our own organisms, with all its unchangeable properties, is conserved, shall not mind still exist also with its higher sentient properties immutable and indestructible? His wisdom, power, and benevolence are our all-sufficient guaranty! But it must be true, also, that all these things exist of innate constitutional necessity, and that not one of them can be destroyed without the destruction of the whole rational fabric — of the whole actualized existing universe. We may be content if, so long as the present nature of things continues, we too must continue our immortal life with its unending consciousness!

SELFISHNESS IS A QUANTITATIVE VICE.

WE all possess appetencies for every enjoyment. Each mind must desire to possess every possible good, every experience which would bring pleasure to itself; and as this desire is the spontaneous outgrowth of the mental constitution, it is to be cultivated rather than repressed. No appetency should be despised or wholly disused; and yet, when its present gratification would run athwart either one's own or his neighbor's best interests, obviously, from these manifold relations must arise various natural checks to self-indulgence. If, then, we could discover the relative value of all appetencies, settling everything as between ourselves and others from a rational or impersonal stand-point, we should be able to settle all the practical questions of social science.

All sentient experience is qualitative necessarily, even when, like pure sensation, it is excited simply by material properties; but the higher qualities of experience, which are coördinated with rational principles, being objectively qualitative also, excite in us only impersonal or unselfish sensibilities; while those experiences which are coördinated with quantities of all classes, depending upon our personal appropriation of these quantities to our own ends, and to the consequent exclusion of others, all tend directly to selfishness, that is, to the unjust appropriation to ourselves of what more properly belongs to others. For example, here is a fine apple which would both satisfy my hunger and gratify my taste, giving me various pleasurable sensations; but if I eat the apple, I destroy

302 *Selfishness is a Quantitative Vice.*

its present mode of being, appropriating its substance and properties to my own organism. Very naturally I desire the apple ; but my neighbor desires it also ; and we cannot both have this identical quantity. Then shall I seize it at any cost, and enjoy the good which I covet? The temptation to this is evidently very great.

Money is the general representative of all those values which are closely related to quantity. It can buy almost everything which has a substantial existence ; and therefore is money desired and sought after as the highest material good. Men often become exceedingly unscrupulous as to the means by which it is acquired. They are tempted to overreach, defraud, or rob others outright, that they themselves may possess this potent symbol of all material values. The spirit of fraud is the lust for material things, at the expense of others. Theft secretly and meanly appropriates to itself some quantity which belongs to another. Avarice, covetousness, the pride of wealth, of ostentatious display in dress or other equipments, the pride of position, of power, and of caste, all representing gradations of the acquirement of material goods, are as deeply rooted in the simply quantitative phases of things, and are as grossly material and earth-bound as are the very lowest vices ; such as gluttony, drunkenness, unchastity, or any other debasement arising from excessive sensual indulgence. The grasping spirit is simply a muck-rake for gathering up *material* things ; low and base-born in its nature, it can grope only in the dust for the gratification of its desires. It knows nothing of qualitative objective values ; but it looks only at quantities, ignobly trying to seize all it can get. Quantitativeness is the fulcrum for all selfishness! It is the sole law of matter.

It is a first necessity that every habitually selfish man should be low-minded. Since self-seeking is a direct seeking for only quantitative values, and as these are allied only to those lowest appetencies which man shares in com-

Selfishness is a Quantitative Vice. 303

mon with irrational animals and even plants, he goes down in feeling to their primitive level; while his rational powers, unused, remain shallow and narrow, as a legitimate result. Any life devoted chiefly to amassing simply quantitative values, of whatever class, even if it be regulated by the principles of the strictest justice, is yet miserably ignoble. All fraud may be ruled out, both in theory and practice; and the man be even rigidly conscientious, yet if his chief aim is the accumulation of quantitative things, which can pertain to himself alone, he is of the earth, earthy. He is reaching after those forms which of necessity must perish with the using; and when these are gone nothing remains. He must start life over again as a bankrupt.

All self-seeking in an odious sense, is a seeking after quantitative values. The love of power, of strength, of knowledge as a means of controlling the forces of matter or mind, is the love of that which, if possessed, will give precedence over another. It is the selfish abuse of those normal appetencies, which, as directly related to material things, must appreciate material values. There is nothing intrinsically ignoble in our relations to quantities. All our appetencies are in themselves desirable and beautiful. A pleasant flavor, a delightful scent, a fine dress, or a fast horse and handsome carriage, are in themselves unobjectionable; and to be sought for according to their relative value as compared with other things. It is the elevating of material things to an undue rank which is objectionable; for it either diverts too great a share of our own energies in the pursuit of them, or it renders us unjust and oppressive towards others. Of course, anything which can be quantitatively estimated, or in any way so related to quantities that its value can be made to depend upon them, must come under the strict law of equity or impartial justice. The rational mind must weigh all relative values impartially, and from a purely rational standpoint, if it

304 *Selfishness is a Quantitative Vice.*

would reason correctly, or act in accordance with the principles of moral order.

But if it is ignoble habitually to degrade one's self to the sphere of quantitative temptations, it is supremely base to lead another into the same vices. To educate a child to live chiefly through the senses, appreciating only the grossest quantitative things, is a shocking perversion of one of the most beautiful of moral trusts. A stream never rises higher than its fountain, and an unworthy parent can hardly be expected to nobly train his children; yet, since he really possesses the highest appetencies, though chiefly unexercised, he may raise his children far above his own level. Warned by his own disadvantages, by his own ignorance, by his own debasement even, and the fearful powers of developed evil tendencies, he may, and sometimes does, lift his child above all this; and surrounding it with better influences, secure to it a better development. The careless educator, who is himself ordinarily moral and intelligent, but who yet neglects those young beings confided to his guidance, is under the control of a far more callous selfishness than the misguided man who from his babyhood may have fallen into evil, but who would yet tenderly preserve others from the same fate. If it be a great wrong to defraud any one of his houses or lands, it is incomparably greater to keep him out of a part of his birthright as a rational and moral being.

Excessive personal indulgence is a vile thing. The frame of mind which it engenders is radically irrational. Everything held up in the light of personal interest, and looked at exclusively from one's own stand-point, is stultifying to the moral sense; but to lead another into a similar frame of mind, and to the indulgence of like propensities, is doubly criminal. A social vice is, therefore, immeasurably worse than a solitary one; for by degrading another, it acts and reacts between the two with a tenfold debasing force. Viewed in this light, the hail-fellow latitude

Selfishness is a Quantitative Vice. 305

of young men at a convivial club is blacker than they know! Each, unwilling to be outdone by his fellows, will indulge in excesses of which he would be heartily ashamed if he were himself the only witness. All this is strictly philosophical. Our social appetencies being largely qualitative, and comparatively above the relations of quantity tend always, through reflex influences, to a manifold increase; if these, then, are subjected to the dominion of the senses, are forced to become the bond-servants of quantity, they multiply evil influences; as they would have multiplied good ones if left under the legitimate sway of our rational powers. A deliberate seducer may be less brutal; yet he is a criminal far more deeply dyed than the coarse wretch who could commit a criminal assault. There is no gentility in any form of selfishness, however refined its assumptions and disguises. Its essential feature is robbery of others to enrich one's self; so that it is intrinsically irrational, and in direct violation of all the principles of social and moral order. If the reins are once given over to sense, all the beauty of upright moral action has departed; and the most fastidious wrong-doer is brought down to the level of the most vulgar. He may seem to be floating gently out with the current; but he will soon be adrift and rudderless on a wide ocean of surging passions. The sinfulness of sin has been much dwelt upon; but the degradation of it is a much more revolting feature, and may well warn off one who is pleasantly coqueting with wrong-doing, from its more disastrous stages. The daughters of the horse-leech always cry, Give! give!

20

UNSELFISHNESS IS A QUALITATIVE VIRTUE.

PURE qualitative values are immeasurable by quantitative standards. Every act of simple thought, whether percept or concept, is one and indivisible; but the rational idea about which it is employed is of such a nature that it may be possessed by hundreds of minds at the same moment — that is, the objective of all qualitative values is wholly impersonal, — is some kind of pure rational principle actual in things or possible in conception. It may belong to each of the hundred or more persons in all its entireness, and yet no one will be the poorer for his neighbor's possessions. Thus an apple, whose quantitative properties one alone can appropriate, has also purely qualitative properties, which many may possess. It is a beautiful growth; we admire its form and color, and it gives us pleasure merely to see it as it hangs in its red and russet beauty amid green leaves. It is perfectly unnecessary to monopolize this beauty to enjoy it; for it is realized in the apple; so that any number of other persons similarly related to it may perceive it at the same instant, without in the least degree diminishing our enjoyment. I have a divine right to possess all the truth, all the beauty, all the excellence, there is in the whole universe — if I infringe no quantitative law thereby; and my possession can rob no one else, for every one is alike entitled to the whole, if he but knows how to attain it. All possession of objective quality is simply appreciation of it — it never monopolizes.

Indeed, the beauty of the apple would be far more en-

Unselfishness is a Qualitative Virtue. 307

joyable if a friend stood with me to admire it. What landscape is not doubled in interest if there are two to rejoice in it; or what truth that is not more prized by ourselves, if we find that it is also valued by others? One therefore, may be greatly the richer for giving all that he has of the pure objective qualities of things to his appreciating neighbors. Each, with his own personal powers coördinated with these rational values, will almost certainly perceive yet other relations, draw yet other deductions and conclusions, and be only too eager to return him in kind, treasure which he might otherwise never have possessed. Selfishly withholding here would tend to poverty; but freely giving returns him his own again with interest. All qualitative action and reaction is important in its working; for it is infinitely more munificent than the measure for measure results of quantitative law. That gives as it receives; this returns a hundredfold! The more persons to whom one can give any rational truth the better; since, not only does the giver lose nothing himself, and yet multiply the value of the knowledge each time, but the mental discipline which the truth gives, and the social stimulus which it becomes to every mind thus socially and rationally coördinated with it, are so great, that untold related discoveries somewhere in the vast field of universal coördinations are inevitable. The great body of natural science as it now exists among men, is a wonderful illustration of the proverb, "There is that giveth and yet increaseth." Each new discoverer records the fact which he himself finds; other hundreds receive it, test it, add to it, follow out its relations, group it anew in most unexpected categories; and hand it back to its original possessor incalculably increased in value. Thus the work goes on! If each possessor of the rational principles of things should monopolize his treasure, as the owner of material values does, there would be but a sorry pittance for any one. Even if each learner were forced to commence at the beginning, dis-

308 *Unselfishness is a Qualitative Virtue.*

covering everything for himself, we should be little farther advanced to-day than the Bushmen of South Africa. Has not giving, then, in this mental world which is concerned with the rational qualities of things, returned us even a hundred million fold ? It has created all our arts and sciences, our improvements, our inventions, our comforts and luxuries — everything beyond the barest necessaries of life which we enjoy in common with the animals. The body of well-tested science is already so immense that no one lifetime will suffice to master it ; so that we shall all be forced to carry over our studies into another condition of being. The rational principles of all sciences, physical, intellectual, and moral, are thus found to be coördinated in all their relations ; giving us their ever-repeated testimony that One Beneficence created and coördered them all.

Narrow-minded persons have sought preëminence by attempting to keep knowledge as an exclusive possession for the favored few. Tyranny and oppression have feared always to educate the masses whom they seek to control, and this is precisely because they seek control of a monopolizing character. They apparently confound the nature of qualitative and quantitative values. Because nothing pertaining to the latter can be possessed by more than one person at the same time, they unconsciously degrade the former to the same necessity, in their thought. The result is a niggardliness of sentiment which is not only unphilosophical in theory, but is incalculably pernicious in practice. It is extending the mantle of selfishness, which even the utmost greed should widen only far enough to cover all material values and their immediate relations. If the lust for over-reaching is contemptible even in the province where measure for measure is the only law of equity, it is most pitiable in the domain where to give is to receive again so much more abundantly. It becomes a ghastly force when seen to be thus palpably over-reaching

Unselfishness is a Qualitative Virtue. 309

itself. In this light, nothing seems more hopelessly besotted than all self-seeking at another's expense.

The legitimate tendency of the whole constitution of a rational mind is directly towards all unselfishness. Its social appetencies are all perpetually proclaiming the one great truth: it is better to give than to receive! Every one knows that to share a pleasure with a friend is to heighten the zest with which we ourselves partake of it. Who would enjoy a pleasure excursion so well alone as with a few valued companions? Many delightful experiences would entirely change their character, almost wholly losing their relish, if we were compelled to accept them in miserly isolation. What artist could ever have created his grand masterpiece if he positively knew that he only in all the world would ever appreciate its beauties. Every good author probably enjoys and prizes his own work more than any one else ever will; yet could he plod on so steadily, or with a fraction of the same thoroughness and effectiveness, through years of unremitted toil, if he had no hope that others should one day recognize and share with him the value of his work? Humboldt could never have lived in his "Cosmos," giving it the best love of his eighty or ninety years, if he had had no friends to enjoy with him his researches at every step, and no appreciating public to accept his munificent legacy to science. No one can imagine Dickens, Charlotte Bronte, or Mrs. Stowe as deliberately sitting down to write Pickwick, Jane Eyre, and Uncle Tom, merely as a personal treat to themselves. The delicious stimulus of social sympathy is needful to quicken even genius in putting forth its best efforts. In their normal condition all social appetencies are eminently unselfish and ennobling — the true stimulants to all laudable ambition.

The eagerness with which a little child runs to its parent or its playmate in the importunate desire to share all its simple pleasures, presents the most unsophisticated ex-

310 *Unselfishness is a Qualitative Virtue.*

ample of the legitimate increase of pleasure to one's self by giving to others. So long as the good is purely qualitative, or as there is so much in quantity as to suggest no considerations of self-denial, a very young child never wishes to do anything alone ; but once let him realize that to give his cake or his ripe peaches to his playmate is to be deprived of them himself, and you will see him stealing into a corner, to slyly munch his tidbits, with a zeal worthy of any miser. The little animal in him, unchecked by his yet undeveloped rational powers, impels him to adopt the most obvious " principle of grab." Thus all our social instincts, when degraded into the bond service of any form of sensual vice, become, like all other best things, the most grossly despicable.

There is a natural hierarchy in all the qualities of sentient good. Even the lowest is good ; but there is a long series of better and better, till we arrive at the best. These relative values *differ intrinsically ;* so that we have only to contrast them one with another in order to decide on their relative merits. It is not a matter of indifference whether one remains ignorant and debased all his life or whether he learns to use his rational and moral powers ; thus making the most of his higher rather than of his lower nature. He owes it to himself to make his noblest appetencies his dominant ones ; though he can wholly neglect none with impunity, because his whole nature is coördinated with them all in a general symmetry. But if a man existed alone in the universe, with the same nature that he now has, he would yet owe certain duties to himself. He would be bound to develop his powers in the utmost harmony, and to increase his own happiness. He would be bound to maintain his own self-respect ; to meet his own self-approval. Do you ask to whom he would be thus bound ? Of course to himself, if there were no one else. He would be bound to his own nature to develop it in a knowledge of the principles of things, that he might secure

Unselfishness is a Qualitative Virtue. 311

to it its best good. If he were to study the physical world and to master its properties and laws, delving into its mysteries and unraveling its secrets, his soul would steadily exult in its acquirements just as the myriads of men do to-day. It would acquire power over nature just as men do now. This isolated, sole intelligence, if it were to live long enough, might in time acquire all the knowledge which has actually been acquired by associated humanity. It might also subject the elements, making them its servants ; it might ride up and down the universe in solitary state, with the steam or even the lightning harnessed to its car, and it might make the world more and more beautiful—varying the order of events and producing desirable results through the agency of its own rational causality.

All this would surely be better for the poor lone being than to sit down in inglorious self-indulgence. It would be better than over-feeding upon dainties. Because these intellectual pursuits are intrinsically more noble than mere sensations, it would be vastly better for the poor solitary to discipline both his body and his mind to the utmost perfection ! It would be base and contemptible to lie down tamely with the brutes, becoming one of them ; or to live like a savage in filth, ignorance, and self-neglect.

The laws of fitness, of right, and duty to himself grow out of the nature of even the isolated being. His intellect is intrinsically superior to his body ; it can discriminate between the class of goods which he is capable of enjoying, and guide him to the highest possible happiness under his isolated circumstances. Do you doubt whether it would be better to elevate himself by knowledge and by judicious and conscientious subjugation of all his passions, appetites, indolent and unworthy tendencies, and every mere present indulgence ; which would enervate his body, pull down his manhood, and lessen his strength, and his uprightness of character ? It would be better to constitute himself the rational monarch of his universe, than to

312 *Unselfishness is a Qualitative Virtue.*

allow himself to live the mere victim of circumstances, like everything else around him. The laws of his being are within himself; if he obeys them he will rise towards Godhead, if he disobeys he will fall to the dust; for his only salvation is in making his rational powers the guide of his whole conduct.

The laws of our being are also within ourselves; and they carry within them the same rewards and the same penalties. Every rational element of things is so intrinsically higher than every other, that it has power to attract us continually into appreciation of its merits, to elevate us to its own level; lifting us out of our narrow personality into the contemplation and the application of all the coördinated principles of the true, the beautiful, and the good. A truly rational being becomes perforce unselfish; for the interests of others necessarily hold as high a place in his perceptions as do his own. They are as intrinsically valuable as his own, and he sees this. His appetencies for the divinely constituted social and moral order yield to him so much more beautiful compensations than any possible gratification at the expense of another, that he is naturally led out into unselfishness, almost without the exercise of any will of his own. When he finds that all his best good, when shared with others, is also increased to himself, it can but win him into an attitude of social benignity; and like begets like, as truly in the moral as in the material world! His influence will be contagious, and men who have rational and social appetencies like his own, will all tend to become magnanimous like himself. All those appetencies which are allied to quantity may also be freely exercised, since an adequate supply exists for every need.

A true discipline must consist not merely in pitting one class of instincts against another, thus developing and giving strength to the nobler, as is sometimes attempted; but one should be made to comprehend in theory, and

Unselfishness is a Qualitative Virtue. 313

gradually habituated to apply in practice, the principles of *justice* to all *quantitative values;* and of *benevolence* and *good-will* to all *qualitative ones.* The law of justice is the outgrowth of all quantitative natures and relations, and must be rigidly applied to one's practical every-day affairs ; while the corresponding principle of benevolence is the outgrowth of qualitative natures and relations, and may rule supreme in the coördered realm of rational being. The two also are coördinated, working coöperatively under the system of universal order, while the innate supremacy of the latter may often beautifully enable us to elevate justice into the domain of love ; finding that it is often better to give than to keep even in material values. Self-sacrifice meets always with its own beautiful rewards. Self-approval, and the approval of every rational mind, is better than any quantitative value. Ye have heard that it hath been said, "Thou shalt love thy neighbor, and hate thine enemy: But I say unto you, Love your enemies, bless them that curse you, do good to them that hate you, and pray for them which despitefully use you and persecute you ; that ye may be the children of your Father which is in heaven : for he maketh his sun to rise on the evil and on the good, and sendeth his rain on the just and on the unjust." Thus would He win us all to the practice of a beneficence like his own! The ægis of unselfishness is broad enough to cover all values, even the most material. As selfishness draws everything down into its own dark and narrow pits, so unselfishness elevates everything to its own mountain heights. The one is the vice of a narrow-minded greed ; the other a rational virtue which has learned to gauge all social values, applying the innate principles of things to their outgrowing practical relations. The one is blind, irrational instinct, struggling to circumvent social equity and social love ; the other is the social and moral appetency which is able freely and intelligently to group all interests in one indivisible unity.

LAW AND ITS SANCTIONS.

ALL Divine *law* is one and harmonious, whether it be a law of physical or of mental nature; for the same creative Mind originated and enacted it, with all its manifold coördinations. A law of matter is an expression of the rigidly quantitative modes in which nature exists and acts. Such laws are, therefore, unvarying or uniform in their action under like conditions. Since they are merely statements of nature's quantitative modes, they are necessarily most rigidly accurate mathematical statements. On this subject there can be no difference of opinion; but it is not, perhaps, equally evident to all, that mental laws are also nothing but the expression of existing mental facts — that they are simply condensed statements of the principles of mental action. Using the term mental in this its most comprehensive sense, as covering all sentient nature, and including both intellectual and moral facts, I mean, of course, by *principles of mental action*, the principles according to which minds of all classes, whether irrational or rational, have been constituted to exist and act. These principles I hold to be as definitely fixed, and as continuously operative in the universe, as are any of the laws of physical action.

We are not to conceive of the Great Moral Lawgiver as, first, having withdrawn apart from his subjects and devising his moral statutes; then, like our human lawgivers, coming forward and publishing his code, with all its attached penalties. On the contrary, when He created his subjects, He did this by giving them mental and moral

Law and its Sanctions. 315

constitutions coördinated with the laws or rational principles by which they were to be governed. The principles being devised in the Creative Thought, the natures were constituted in accordance with these principles. The simply quantitative, unsentient natures of material atoms were constituted according to quantitative or mathematical principles ; sentient but irrational natures were constituted according to sentient or qualitative rational principles, coördinated with mathematical ones — all alike incomprehensible to the irrational natures themselves, yet made the laws of their being and action nevertheless ; and sentient rational natures were constituted according to sentient rational principles coördinated also with quantitative or mathematical principles ; but all alike comprehensible to these rational natures, and existing for them as the established rules of life and conduct. The rational principles of the universe are thus many and various ; but all harmonious and coöperative.

These rational principles are all realized in things. So far as the scheme of matter permits, they are applied or incarnated in matter ; and so far as mind will allow, they are realized in mind ; but the principles being more comprehensive than the natures constituted by them, cannot always receive a literal embodiment ; and yet a rational mind is able to discover them as operative and controlling influences in the general processes of creation. Thus mathematical principles are not all literally embodied in things, though all things are created according to their laws ; and Time and Space are not *in* existences or their changes ; but all existences and changes are in time and space. Gravity, on the other hand, seems to be a universal innate *property* of all substance ; and the laws of gravity are the laws under which substances move or are mutually drawn together by this property.

A mind endowed with rational powers is simply a mind adapted to perceive, comprehend, and adopt pure rational

316 *Law and its Sanctions.*

principles. Human powers are adequate to perceive all the various classes of principles, apparently, which pertain to one's own well-being and to his various coördinations with other beings. Possibly he may hereafter even fathom all the laws of the Universe; for his incapacities arise, it would seem, not so much from his perceptive powers themselves, as from the amount of aid given him by his material organism. As soon as man had invented the telescope, his mind was able to use it in obtaining a knowledge of remote worlds which were entirely shut out from him before; and when he had constructed the microscope, he opened up a new world about which hitherto he had never even dreamed. So when he has won to himself a new and finer organism, there may be no limit to his perceptive abilities. Now he is limited everywhere by his standard of spatial measures, and whatever is too far off or too near, too large or too small, he can only speculate about, but cannot directly perceive. He does not even know assuredly whether or not there be any inorganic kingdom; or whether every mineral atom may not be itself constituted from innumerable infinitesimal organisms.

But profound as his ignorance is in some directions, his knowledge may be clear and distinct enough concerning other matters. He can comprehend both the principles of justice and of benevolence, and need be in no more doubt as to the laws of impartial equity and right, than he is as to the fundamental principles of pure mathematics. The application of moral laws, also, aside from selfish or too strongly personal desires, is no more difficult than practical arithmetic; and if men, by long study, can become practical surveyors and astronomers, by the same kind of diligent application they can become practical moralists. Unfortunately the delusion that the moral code, unlike all other systems of principles, was to be studied not in moral natures and their coördinations, but was to

Law and its Sanctions. 317

be sought outside, through expounders and interpreters, has occasioned a wide-spread doubt as to whether social and moral laws do really and unchangeably exist in things as absolutely as do physical laws ; and whether the penalties for their violation are alike certain and irremediable.

There can exist only two classes of laws. The one class is inherent in the nature of things ; it is made up of the innate principles of the whole rational constitution of the Universe.

The other class of laws is factitious and arbitrary ; they are rules made and announced to meet special exigencies, or to protect the public and promote the general weal by particular enactments, to which are also attached special penalties. They may be at any time promulgated as laws, and at any time abolished, as seems best according to the best judgment of the law-maker.

To this latter class belong all human laws ; and to the former, as I believe, belong all of God's laws.

Thus the law, or coördination of things, which requires a human being to breathe and eat, under penalty of death, belongs to the class of natural and inalienable principles. His body must breathe and receive nourishment, or die ; because this is the only mode by which any body can be built up or sustained ; and if you set aside the law, you must set aside the very essence of all physical being, not only, but of mental being also, which is coördinated with the physical. Again, the law of justice which requires that one man shall not defraud another, has also its inherent penalties. Justice, as he himself perceives, is a true principle, which no moral being should ever violate ; therefore if he commits an unjust act, he degrades his rational and moral nature into the service of his irrational instincts. Of course he loses his self-respect, and the respect of every other rational being who is cognizant of the act. This penalty cannot be remitted without destroying either the principles of morality or the moral natures which appreciate these principles.

318 *Law and its Sanctions.*

The penalties of all factitious or arbitrary laws may be at any time remitted. The originator of the law attaches just such reward or penalty as he sees fit ; for there is no necessary relation between the law and its sanction, or between the law and the subject who is required to obey the law. At one time the law may fine a man ten dollars for driving over a covered bridge faster than a walk ; the next month the penalty may be made five dollars, and a year afterwards it may be ten days' imprisonment for the same offense. The penalty, also, need not necessarily be enforced. If a man in a light carriage should drive never so rapidly across the bridge to save himself from being run down by a pair of unmanageable horses attached to a lumbering stage-coach, no one would dream of exacting the penalty. Or, if the son of a poor widow deserved the penalty — if he had driven furiously across the bridge in mere wantonness, yet it is possible, that, in considera-tion of the mother's dependence on the earnings of her son, this might decide the humane executors of the law for once to dismiss the youth with a reprimand. Or, another might voluntarily pay the fine, or suffer imprison-ment for him ; and the court might accept the substitute in the place of the youth who had incurred the penalty for himself. It is evident, then, that all penalties attached to factitious or arbitrary laws may be remitted, at the option of the proper authorities. Laws which require an execu-tor to enforce them are not necessarily enforced !

As all human laws are factitious, and may have their sanctions remitted, we have reasoned, as it seems to me, from these to the inherent constitutional laws of Nature. Human laws are often valuable, and one would not depre-ciate the dignity which they have acquired in the eyes of men, or diminish the reverence with which they are regarded among us, who are eminently a law-abiding people ; but as well might one compare a living child to a wax-doll, or Niag-ara to one of its own stereoscopic likenesses, as a law of im-

Law and its Sanctions.

mutable Nature to a law of changing circumstances. The very term *law* has become a misrepresentation of the *principle* which it is intended to represent. The rewards and penalties of Divine Law are as really a necessary part of the nature of things as the laws themselves ; and can be no more changed or destroyed without disturbance or destruction to the whole coördinated system ! Doubtless the power which could establish a certain system of coöperative principles, might afterwards destroy the same ; but where would be the motive ? Neither could He destroy so essential a part of the system as that which pertains to the nature of law and its sanctions, without destruction to the whole fabric ! Practically, we may conclude, therefore, that the penalty to any law, physical, intellectual, or moral, will never be remitted.

If one cuts off his right hand, it is not restored again ; if he puts out his eyes, he is left sightless as long as he lives ; if he besots himself with drink, he becomes, for the time, a madman or an imbecile ; or if he wrongs his fellows, he carries about the soil of evil-doing in his soul. The burned finger pains, whether it belongs to a dove-eyed child or a blear-eyed man ; and the cut finger bleeds, whether cut by accident or design. If the system seems severe, we have but to remember that its chief aim is not *cure*, but *prevention*. When the little child tosses painfully on its bed of fever, it seems difficult for finite tenderness to look up trustingly to the All-Father, believing that He watches the little sufferer with boundless compassion. The piteous baby-moan smites us to the heart. We would so gladly give a portion of our own cool life-blood to soothe its hot little veins ; would so gladly suffer in its stead ; and God, who is so powerful, seems pitiless. The heart is tempted to cry out : " He could spare it, but He will not ! " No, He will not ! His wisdom is too wise and his compassion too all-embracing to set aside the very being and constitution of all things to spare this one little sufferer ; and to its

320 *Law and its Sanctions.*

own hurt! Shall He dispense with his salutary thunder storm, least some one, with his self-responsible freedom of action and of locomotion, should put himself in a position to be smitten with its lightning? Or shall He destroy the freedom of the man's soul forever, for the sake of saving his perishable body for a day? Even we ourselves are too far-seeing to dispense with our steamboats and railroads because of the frightful accidents which they incidentally occasion.

God never remits a penalty, whether it is incurred by guilt or innocence; by ignorance or willfully, with wide open eyes. A murderer may deeply repent the murder, but the life of his victim is not thereby restored. If, from the depths of his remorse, a self-denying purpose spring up in his soul; and, seeing that it is useless to live lamenting the past, which he cannot undo, he lives to make reparation for his fault, and to elevate others and himself to nobler deeds, then God co-works with him; not by absolving him from the consequences of his fault, but by aiding him to bring forth better fruits meet for repentance. This, as I understand it, is *His* forgiveness; and it is all the forgiveness which He has to bestow. If a parent has ruined his child by neglect or evil training, though he may since have repented of it in dust and ashes, guiding all his younger children in wisdom and goodness, yet in so far as he was guilty of the ruin of that one, it must be forever true that it was he who caused those bitter consequences. He need not continually upbraid his present self — that would imply that he was still in fault, and perpetually recommitting the wrong. On the contrary, he is doing all that in him lies to counteract the evil long since produced; but no one can take from him the authorship of his fault, nor can assume for him the consciousness of having committed it! The whole nature of sin is such that it is impossible to save the sinner from the effects of his sin, while he still persists in sinning; and for a like

Law and its Sanctions. 321

reason it is impossible for another to assume those effects for him, even after he has stopped sinning. He himself, and every generous and good mind everywhere, may and must work together to undo and counteract those effects, if they would see good prevail over evil; but no one can, in the nature of the case, take either his transgression or its outgrowing necessary effects, either from him or for him. There is *forgiveness* in that there is *love* and *compassion* for him in his repentance; but there can be no remission of innate consequences. Nothing flowing from the transgression of any natural law can be remitted without setting aside also the law itself, which would be setting aside a part of the rational constitution of the universe. Deity is not, therefore, to be regarded as implacable in his anger against the evil doer! On the contrary, even the penalties of broken law, inevitable as they really are, are yet better for the transgressor than any remission; and Divine love is more manifest in establishing these painful effects, than it would be in taking them all upon himself, even if that were possible under the present system. He chasteneth whom He loveth.

Even the innocent must bear the unvarying penalties of broken law; and broken not by themselves, but by others. An intemperate father maims his little son in the frenzy of intoxication, and the innocent child suffers excruciatingly at the time and must hobble about on his crutches a poor lame man all his days; or a whole family suffer to the very soul's quick through the ruin and shame of a beloved daughter of the household. A portion of this suffering may be factitious — the results of the unjust prejudices of society, ready to brand innocence with a disgrace merited only by the guilty; but another portion grows necessarily from the close social tie, which binds the wronged and the wrong-doer inseparably, compelling them to enjoy or suffer in common. All humanity is bound together by these potent sympathies which make the weal or

322   *Law and its Sanctions.*

woe of one, the common heritage of all. Our bodies must either have been made so that they could neither be maimed, killed, nor otherwise hurt ; our minds incapable of emotions, either pleasant or painful, all our powers unsentient, and therefore without rational perceptions or volitions, and unable either to distinguish or to choose between good and evil — in other words, we must have remained without life and its sentient experiences ; or else suffering must result from everything which violates the conditions of our well-being.

The innocent suffer, but they are never punished ! While guilt says, " I deserve it, I caused it, and the penalty is just," innocence, bearing up its sufferings to heaven, can be assured of nothing but the tenderest compassion. A good conscience can transform all evil, pain of body, sorrow of soul, and even the sharpest temptations, into elements of good ; helping forward its own moral advancement. This is the natural effect of any suffering which we bear for another ; bearing it worthily, as only rational and moral beings may. Years ago I met a little child in the Randall's Island hospital who had long been there a confirmed invalid from early exposure, want, and hereditary disease. She had been neglected and forsaken by her intemperate mother, who had visited her only two or three times in as many years. The doctor had just amputated her limb ; after waiting since the time of her first coming, lest he should give her needless suffering while she was so almost hopelessly ill. When the operation was over, the little creature looked up into his face with a smile of the most touching gratitude, and said, " Thank you, Doctor ! You will tell mother that you have cut off my leg, wont you? She will be so glad ! " I have never seen expression on human face so full of heavenly beauty, pathos, and love, as that in the countenance of this mother-forsaken, homeless little girl. Strangers cared for her, little invalids lay all about her, and her smile rested on

Law and its Sanctions. 323

one and another sometimes with an expression of almost maternal pity. So God " giveth to his beloved rest " — peace in the midst of suffering, and exaltation of soul through suffering !

The only fearful evil is that the innocent so often consent to be contaminated and debased by the crimes of others. Little children, reared amidst ignorance and vice from babyhood, feed greedily upon the evil influences with which they are nourished from the cradle ; and men and women not only follow the lead of their betrayers, but they often pass beyond them into yet lower depths of iniquity. Time in this world is not long enough to right such wrongs ! That penalty of evil doing, unrecognized by him on whom it falls, an increasing stultification of his better nature, forever haunts his footsteps like a black shadow of himself. One enduring the worst of retribution, but knowing it not, stands as a warning to others who can see the desolation of his soul better than he himself. He is a living monument, illustrating the ruin which is allied to all transgression ! If the lesson is fearful, yet it is just, and salutary both to the beholder and the sufferer. Though the latter knows nothing of the immeasurable width of the gulf between himself and the good and great, yet he sees that there is such a gulf, and that he is on the wrong side of it. If anything will lead him to ask after causes, and consent to renounce his degredation, it is this.

All who have aided in his debasement see their own crimes mirrored in their victim. Can a father who has trained his child to unworthy pursuits see the dark soul looking out upon him reproachfully, without sometimes awaking to the anguished thought, " I have done it ! I have done it ! " Is there comfort in that, think you? Can a man look upon the wreck of womanhood, standing abject and degraded before him, and say, " I caused it ! " and then sleep sweetly upon the reflection ? Not so !

324 *Law and its Sanctions.*

God is the creator of men and not of demons. People do things from selfish and thoughtless impulses, from the depths of blind debasement into which they have themselves fallen, from revenge or hate, which seem at the moment as sweet as they are fierce, and from many other motives no higher than these ; but pure diabolism is not one of the attributes of humanity. Precisely as no one can choose misery for its own sake, because he loves misery, so no one can choose to entail it upon others for the love of seeing them miserable. If the desolation which he has wrought in the lives of others cannot arouse his better nature, then nothing on earth can do it. He must wait! But so surely as he and they all have immortality before them, the moral lessons so terribly enforced must be learned at last ; for the appetency for acquiring them is inwrought in their coördinated moral constitutions. It is because moral right is intrinsically better than wrong, that rational beings must ultimately choose it !

All humanity suffers loss or gain in the woe or weal of its humblest member. "Bear ye one another's burdens !" is the inwrought constitutional requirement of Him who coördinated all rational natures. Go labor for the worst and vilest, willingly and cheerfully, reaping an abundant recompense ; or by the eternal laws of humanity, their burdens must be laid upon *you, to your hurt!* There is no perfect rest to a good and noble nature till the heavy chains of society are lifted up from the weary shoulders of the weak, whether wronged or wrong-doers, and until all men are taught to walk in just and upright ways, and to inherit the birthright awaiting them as moral and rational beings. The way of the transgressor is hard enough. Show him the character of his guilt, and the nature of its penalties, and make him realize the infinite loving-kindness of his Creator. He may still refuse to improve, but why should he? Mind has been coördinated with motives.

Law and its Sanctions. 325

Though no penalty of broken law will ever be remitted, yet if in this world or the next there is true contrition for past wrong-doing, every just man, and therefore, surely, Deity also, must be ready with sympathy for the contrite, and aid in his future well-doing. But just as one who has lived all his days in vice and ignorance, when he does reform, is far below a noble philanthropist like John Howard, who has spent his life in doing good ; so may no one hope here or hereafter ever to overtake lost opportunities. If he has voluntarily gone back along the road of progress, just so much time has been lost irretrievably.

Here arises the important question, Are the penalties attached to constitutional law always or indeed ever commensurate with the desert of the wrong-doer? Who shall answer in the affirmative? One can find no worthy reason why in constituting the present scheme of moral government, it should have been determined to attach the utmost penalty which the crime deserves. What worthy end would be attained by this? Far be it from a beneficent mind to say, " Let men suffer because they deserve it." There is in such a spirit a spice of human vindictiveness. It is hot with the flavor of headlong revenge and retaliation — impulses as blind and irrational as that which possesses the mad bull. We may well infer that no other penalties are affixed to broken law than such as must follow inevitably from the established nature and relations of things, and that the whole question of *merited* punishment and *desert* was left out of view. The law of justice requires that no injustice shall be done ; but it does not forbid the conferring of the free gifts of benevolence and universal good-will !

Yet there is a moral sense in us which requires that an unjust or evil-doing man shall be awakened to a full sense of the real blackness of his offense. What we call justice is sometimes the committing of a second wrong in the irrational expectation that this will somehow right the first,

326 *Law and its Sanctions.*

for two wrongs often make one right in Anglo-Saxon morality, just as two negatives make an affirmative in Anglo-Saxon grammar. But in the science of universal morals, right and wrong are not convertible terms.

It must satisfy every instinct of moral justice to have the culprit fully appreciate the real nature of his crime and of its outflowing consequences. I cannot see that it would make any one morally better to inflict upon him some horrible retaliation, or that the spectators, if they had rational and social instincts, would be either edified or benefited by the spectacle ; but if the criminal could be made to look into the very eye of his crime, until he felt its meanness and realized the ignoble depths to which he himself must have fallen before he could be guilty of it ; and if he could be made to feel the moral reprobation not only of the best and noblest, but also of those as self-ish and vile as himself, this universal condemnation of his course would be enough ! This I believe to be the true end of all Providence ; and the true legitimate penalty for all willful and deliberate wrong-doing. Can one ask for the offender a keener or a more terrible punishment than this ? — a punishment which sooner or later, too, is inevitable, if we are to continue to be rational and moral beings forever.

But in the midst of this retribution let us not forget the possible healing. Tears of penitence must wash white the soul, that all may be able to shower back upon him the blessings of their fullest sympathy.

I can imagine a master and his slave blundering together into a new world, where they have practically learned the creed that all men's rights are equally sacred. The slave, abject, dark-minded, and revengeful in soul, his school-masters all his life having been fear, ignorance, and want ; and the master, arrogant, selfish, vindictive, and obstinately willful, and they stand in the new moral light about them, looking at last into each other's faces as man

Law and its Sanctions. 327

to man. Now let all men and circumstances rally and tear off the veil, forcing them each to see distinctly. The poor slave is totally unfit for his new conditions; but shall no pity be felt for his past sufferings, and nothing be forgiven him that he has made no better use of his powers? Will there be no one found to teach him now? No one to share with him the burden of his incapacities? And what of the master? Malevolence itself would not call now for scorpions to sting him, or for scourges to lash his already bleeding wounds! Forced to contemplate the injured soul of his victim — a desolate waste, overrun with hateful passions, and an unspeakable poverty of good! Forced to look into his own being with its even deeper darkness, the shadows and mildew of despicable wrong-doing and its blighting effects! Ah, this is enough! And every eye condemns him. Let his remorseful penitence bite and devour him till he is willing to confess and forsake his long injustice, and to begin the holy, atoning work of reparation. To this he must turn at last; and can justice ask more? Or can benevolence give more?

I can see this master now kneeling by his slave, and with manly sincerity revealing to him the barrenness and guilt for which they are jointly responsible; and, beginning with the simple truths which have been so long hidden, teach him some of the sublime principles of universal science, physical and moral. All things in nature and Providence seem to me alike coördinated with so desirable a result.

SOCIAL PROGRESS.

IT is now quite generally admitted that both individual and social development are the legitimate outgrowth of constitutional facts, variously stimulated by external conditions. When everything else is found to act according to the innate properties of its essential nature, as acted upon and modified by other forces, mind can scarcely be regarded as an exception to this law. One cannot doubt that a normal unfolding of mental powers is secured by an innate necessity. Mental growth is generally as unpremeditated as growth of the body; since the exercise of all the functions of mind, in infancy, and to a large extent through life, is quite involuntary. The direction of development depends largely upon the stimulating external conditions, thus originating peculiar, one-sided characters, individual and national. Ancient Sparta raised patriots, heroic and self-forgetful, but untrained in the gentler domestic virtues; while Athens moulded her nobler sons into artists or philosophers.

An aggregate public sentiment, which we call the spirit of the age, is the great educator. It re-casts whole races of men, literally re-creating them; it is perhaps more potent than innate constitutional bias. We talk of metaphysical Germany as if no other country could have given birth to Kant, Fichte, Schelling, Hegel. If this be true, it is so, possibly, because no other land has so persistently clung to the delusion that the scheme of the universe can be fathomed by thought. While they ignore the objective phase of philosophy, they are necessarily lost in the mazes

Social Progress.

329

of ideality. By way of reaction the material side of German character, especially as developed in the masses, is grossly and amazingly materialistic. Again, Americans, largely casting aside precedent, and striking out a new order of practical democracy, have developed self-confidence, ingenuity, invention, resources in every direction ; till every man is more or less sharpened into an individuality, and I am sorry to add, also, often a vanity of his own. The Chinaman, on the contrary, has been exactly the opposite of this. He aims to step as carefully into the footprints of his father as his small-footed wife does into the small shoes of her mother, — of course century after century passed, and China seemed to ride at anchor on the ocean of time. The spirit of the Chinese age seemed perpetually becalmed ; but we shall soon see, since they have begun to accept intercourse with other nations, and have opened a university for the cultivation of modern science, how all this will steadily change their nationality, how progress will glide in at every opening, till its leaven permeates the old senseless stability which has so long defied the Christian era.

A nation is but an aggregate of persons ; and we know that a child trained by educated parents is nearly certain to acquire something of the parental tastes ; while the unfortunate offspring of the vicious or the vulgar are moulded, as a rule, into the likeness of their surroundings. The most plebeian boy will often become a gentleman under favorable conditions, while the son of wealth and culture is almost certainly degraded to the level of his training, when the position of his family has been shipwrecked. Now and then a genius overleaps the barriers about him, and, once started in a new direction, he moves on with increasing ease and freedom. While on the one hand it is certain that mental traits are often hereditary, on the other it is no less certain that education dwarfs or stimulates, so that the progress made both by persons and communities

330 *Social Progress.*

has been that of a ship driven onward under the combined impetus of counter forces, and the real advance made has been due rather to the inherent coördination of things than to the direct intentions of any human agency.

How far personal and national characteristics are attributable to external stimuli and how far to properties pertaining to each type of mind, is still an open question. It possibly may be shown, hereafter, that of the five or six typical races of men, each is as unique in mental as in physical traits. The African is by some of his best friends believed to be the highest human type of a social and sensuous temperament. By his long suffering, his patience, docility, and teachability while in slavery — by his forbearance, magnanimity, and courage during our long war, and by his self-poise since he has become a freeman, he certainly has given high evidence of a wonderful susceptibility to some of the sublimest virtues. His hilarity, his love of music, his religious fervor, and his enjoyment of tropical warmth and harmony of color and outline, make it at least presumable that he may yet lead in a civilization of gorgeous artistic beauty, of social good fellowship, and generous fraternity, such as the world has not known hitherto. External conditions must greatly affect a child or a savage ; but a cultivated man in his maturity may rise above his surroundings ; and in the end, every race of men must find its inherent constitutional traits more and more potent to determine its social status. Various orders of civilization, each charming and perfect after its kind, and nicely harmonized with all the others, may yet arise in the natural course of human development, in illustration of the wide variety of typical minds. Analogy certainly points in this direction, and so also do all indications derived from existing nationalities, with their peculiar broad diversities. Enough of likeness pertains to all human races to insure to each a keen appreciation of the special excellences of all the others, with a desire to emulate their

Social Progress. 331

preëminent gifts. To this end, there needs not only what we are now so rapidly attaining — a free intercommunication among all nations, but above all there must arise in each of the yet semi-civilized races a belief in the possibility of superior endowments of its own, awaiting only cultivation and development to enable it to be the leader of every other in the direction of its own specialties. The most barbarous peoples may yet manifest special talents, now undreamed of by either themselves or others; and if so, this reserved force, once awakened, will immeasurably stimulate all human progress.

Typical differences seem also to exist in the mental natures of the two sexes. Such a distinction has been largely insisted on as an argument for keeping women within their proper spheres. Instead of allowing woman to develop any peculiar gifts which she may possess, freed from conventional restraints, a predetermined sphere has been marked out for her, and she has been rigidly enjoined to keep within its precincts. Granted the fact of her peculiar feminine gifts, this obviously is a direct argument in favor of her developing all her powers untrammeled; and finding for herself her own level in society. So only can the world attain to its highest possible advancement. Variety built upon a substratum of unity, is the order everywhere in nature. The two kingdoms, vegetable and animal, are one in physical structure and growth; and, as we believe, also possessing a common mental unity no less conspicuous. The beasts, birds, and fishes have each their innumerable species; why then should men be the sole exception to this law of diversity. If they differ widely in physical conformation, it is presumable that there is a corresponding difference in mental endowments or development. Every special type of sentient being adds only to the exceeding richness and value of every other capable of appreciating it; and each is "very good" in its original constitution; whatever may

332 *Social Progress.*

be said of the mode and direction of its present stage of development.

The attainments and achievements of each mind are also designed to be a free legacy to the race. Discoveries of the principles and processes of nature expressed either in language, in machinery, or in art; the whole body of science, and the whole realm of improvement, constitute the wealth of all mankind. It belongs to no one alone, however exclusively he may have been the discoverer or the originator. Where, then, is room for jealousy, envy, or aught but appreciation and generous emulation of the best powers of every other being? No man possesses the whole of even human knowledge; each must be content to gain steadily, in common with his fellows, and to know that the great residue is parceled out to the universal multitude. Science arises from the achievement of some benefactor of all the rest; but even he is in advance of his fellows in but one, or at most in only a few special directions, while all around him are pioneers far in advance of him in discoveries perhaps equally valuable with his own. Thus no one liveth to himself alone, but for the benefit of all mankind. However selfish and misanthropic his desires and purposes, he must give and take unceasingly, from an innate necessity of his nature. The mere love of personal gain may lead to the coördination of winds, waves, steam, or electricity to machinery, and this to human control; but the result inevitably quickens the progress of the race many fold. A world spanned with telegraphs and railroads is impelled on in intellectual and moral advancement by the simple correlation of forces. The scheme of the universe so binds all things together that a forward move in any direction enlarges all other capabilities. This has been beautifully illustrated in almost every department of science.

All movements which combine the coöperative energies of many persons, and thus closely bind together the inter-

Social Progress. 333

ests of the community, point to a new era of progress. The more varied the talents and functions of these joint workers, the better for the amount and breadth of their accomplishment! Doubtless socialism may have sought too eagerly for an air-line route to the desired goal, for nature approves of but very few straight lines! Yet even the mistakes of the past are an earnest of good for the future! When we become nobler as individuals we shall find better modes of co-working for mutual assistance ; for the best good of one is the best good of all. Woman must become a broader and more rational worker ; more self-forgetfully remembering the well-being of the whole community ; while man must equally learn that charity begins with the necessary, unending, small details of home and its inmates ; so shall their several talents interweave far more beautiful and perfect results than those which their separate efforts have yet achieved.

The code of social amenities has always been refined and elevated in common with other branches of science, however strong may have been the popular inclination to dissociate all higher morality from business relations, and from every-day life. Laws of qualitative value have been found so personally distasteful and self-subjugating when applied to quantitative affairs, that the world will not yet believe that they are bound together from an inherent unity in the general scheme embracing both ; and not till it fairly grasps this thought as a fixed reality, and applies it to practice, shall we have entered on an era of progress which can at all realize the ideal, ultimate good which humanity is yet destined to attain. When the masses can perceive that it is an unvarying fact, established in the whole coördinated nature of things, that every mind must learn to subject all quantitative values to the sublime law of the qualitative, or suffer grievously in default of so doing, then we shall soon progress into a literal earthly millennium. We shall simply begin to apply a moral code,

334 *Social Progress.*

noble enough for heaven, but not too noble for earth ; the code which is so indelibly wrought into every phase of the human constitution that it can never be changed without an entire change of the whole nature of man, material and rational ; and moreover, which is so thoroughly part and parcel of his social being, that if he breaks this code either knowingly or ignorantly, not only he himself must suffer, but with him must suffer also more or less directly, his whole race.

Humanity is assuredly so constituted as to be guaranteed a ceaseless ultimate progress — an unlimited development towards perfection. Nations may retrograde, individuals for a time may tend downwards under the stimulus of adverse influences ; but so surely as good is intrinsically better than evil, as enjoyment is better than suffering, and as there is an inherent difference even between positive values, men will steadily learn to make better and better choices, as they are more enabled to discriminate between comparative intrinsic merits. The scheme which includes all qualitative correlations is immeasurably more exalted, comprehensive, and incomparably more admirable in its operations, than any scheme of mere quantitative adjustments can be ; and it is as unerring and inevitable in its final results. Every sentient and rational being must needs choose to better his condition perpetually ; and this instinct, as an ever-active incentive, is a pledge of unending progress.

Perhaps this is the most difficult scheme of thought to express fully in language, and make comprehensible to another, of which we have yet treated. It is a scheme, which, though now in actual operation, is yet only in process of realization, and not, like most other schemes, already fully embodied, and illustrated in things ; and only repeating itself under new aspects. The schemes of crystallization, of growth, of the equal action and reaction of all material forces ; in short, of every known quantitative process, was long since exemplified in full. There may be new applications in other details; but each entire scheme is already not only completed in thought, but actualized in fact. This cannot hold true of any scheme of perpetual progress for either the individual or the race. It may be complete as a thought in the conception of the Originator, and the conditions necessary to insure its accomplishment may be incorporated in the mental constitution; but it is necessarily incomplete in its consummation. In quantitative processes, no new element is introduced from the first — there is only perpetual repetition of new definite combinations of matter and force; but in mental process there is a perpetual new creation of sensations, emotions, perceptions, and purposes — an endless, *endless*, increase of all sentient experiences. If life, to a rational being, is a good at all, it must be, then, possible to make it forever better and better; and if He who ordered all things has not so ordained it, his work would be then a comparative failure. Thus, though the scheme which comprehends this distinct order of development must be itself incomplete as an actualized fact, like the experiences with which it deals, we may perceive all the elements of it, as already operative constitutional data; and we may turn to logic, to all valid inference and analogy, to aid us in the conception of an ultimate perfection in human development, which, from the nature of things, we cannot now literally perceive as already attained.

SUBSTANCE AND FORCE AS UNCREATED.

IN endeavoring to get any idea of uncreated existence, or Being wholly without the present constitution of things, we must let the whole rational framework of substance drop completely out of view. The mind must rest upon the one fact of Being — existence, something which is, but without any of its present modes or correlations — pure absolute Being, the self-existing, the indestructible. So much we perceive was and must have been of innate necessity before time began, else it would not be now; else it could not have been transmuted into existing and possible conditions. Something absolutely from nothing! The conception is too incredible for minds constituted like ours to entertain it for a moment.

Being must have existed before the present cosmos began, with its limitless series of rational coördinations; nor could it have existed as a total stagnation — an eternally unchanging whole. It is as incredible that change could ever begin to be, that force could originate from nothing, as that substance itself could begin to exist. Change, then, and the *substantial cause* or force which produces change, must be as absolute, as self-existent and eternal, as Being itself. We can fall back upon absolute substance, possessing absolute force; but here we must find a check: it is impossible for minds constituted like ours to go any further. We have lost sight of almost everything which we know either of matter or mind, and see only that absolute existence and its absolute force are alike necessarily existent and uncreated. They are the

Substance and Force as Uncreated.

basis, the unvarying and original facts of the present system of things. When physicists, therefore, demonstrate to us that all substance and all force are alike uncreatable and indestructible, they only bring us to the same conclusion with psychological deduction.

CREATION.

IF we first contemplate simple being, absolute existence with its simple absolute force, how then can we conceive of the present complex constitution of things as having arisen from this original data. But prior to this question of the how, let us contemplate the fact. There really does exist a complex nature or constitution of things, fixed and unalterable in all its essential properties, and comprehending all known substances. We turn to some of the prominent features of this existing constitution and find that the indestructible, uncreated force which produces all material changes is made to act under a great variety of related modes, so apparently dissimilar in process that it is only a recent discovery that these modes are correlated and mutually convertible. Each of these modes is definitely wrought out after its own specific type, and is always unvarying under like conditions; and the relations between them are also perfectly identical under identical conditions. We can admit that substance exists and that force exists, of simple inherent necessity; for we perceive that such must be the fact from the essential nature of each, and that no intelligence or exercise of rational power was needed to call them into being; since they are themselves the simplest and first facts underlying all perception and all conception — the primary starting-points of everything actual and everything possible! But we cannot intelligently admit that the present complicated system of related, definite, and ordained changes is necessarily existent, or that it is self-existent! On the contrary,

Creation. 339

we may conceive of it as non-existent — as even entirely annihilated, and another and very different system of modes and changes reigning in its stead. The present scheme of inherent relations must have been first carefully and elaborately devised by rational thought, and practically applied to the present cosmos, else it could not be now in successful operation. It is intrinsically a rational scheme — a scheme of applied thoughts, of pure principles actualized in simple self-existent substance and force. Our present comprehension of this scheme of creation is doubtless both meagre and faulty. We catch glimpses of it here and there, and probably misinterpret many of its details; but we surely perceive immeasurably more than enough to enable us to determine that Creation, or the present Cosmos, must be the product of an elaborate, thoroughly matured, and perfect scheme of thought, applied and wrought out in primitive Being.

Substance is not now homogeneous, but heterogeneous. We are conversant with sixty-two or sixty-three supposed simple material elements, each of which differs widely from all the others; but with every molecule of every given element, under all known conditions, exactly identical with every other molecule of the same kind. No rational scheme is involved in simple necessary existence; but when substance has been so intelligently constituted that all its innate properties act invariably according to the most rigid mathematical principles; when more than sixty specific kinds of substance have been created, each with a very complex but definite character of its own, which remains unchanged in all inherent properties amid a thousand changes of mode and condition; and when all these elementary substances are found to be so perfectly coördinated in all their many processes that from given data we can predict with unerring certainty the inevitable results; we are certainly compelled to admit that here there is evidence of a scheme of adjustment relating all these many elements,

340 *Creation.*

forces, and processes, with all the actual and possible combinations resulting therefrom. When to these we add still another and higher type of substances, whose properties and processes become sentient and self-appreciative ; and in the highest orders of which there is not only self-consciousness, but perception also of the characteristics of the not-self, and distinct cognition, not only of the existing coördinations of things, but originality to devise new adjustments and other conditions, similar in kind, involving also schemes of connected rational thought ; are we not then compelled beyond question to admit the existence of a Rational Thinker, who ordained all this? There is a positive necessity for rational thought to originate the conception and actualization of so stupendous a system of things! We are not, as rational beings, self-existent ; and we have not created ourselves ; yet here we are, feeling, thinking, rational minds. Nothing but intelligence could have created us thus. We can immediately perceive principles of thought as incarnated in things. We can comprehend these principles, can express them in language readily understood by other rational minds, and can apply them ourselves under new but analogous conditions of things. Can all this arise from mere unreflecting chance, or from pure necessity — like that which compels us to accept the fact of primary, simple, uncreated, and to us unknown Being? The supposition is totally incredible. The present Creation, that is, substance with its existing nicely adjusted system of constituent properties and processes, is known to us, and is so evidently the outgrowth of an intelligent plan, that unless men strenuously denied any sufficient evidence of rational thought in the constitution of the Cosmos, it would seem impossible to suppose that they ever could deny this. As it is, we must believe that they simply misunderstand the nature of the Creation, or they could not persist in denying to it an intelligent, forecasting cause. It is indeed impossible to con-

Creation. 341

ceive of thought as originating either substance or force *per se*. Absolute Being must be independent of everything but itself; but we know that thought could originate the scheme of principles which it would be necessary to apply in order to regulate the action of gravitation; that thought could settle the question of the proper adjustment of the motions needed to produce the revolutions of the planets; that thought could plan a general scheme of structure and growth for all organic bodies, vegetable and animal, and that it could devise the details of mental and physical likeness and unlikeness between the various classes of creatures. A rational mind could originate these and similar plans for controlling the processes of nature; but nothing except intelligence could do this! The distinctive work of creation would seem to be, the originating and actualizing a system of related thought, through the aid of already existing substance and force. To take away the element of intelligent design from the universe, would be to take from it not only all that is beautiful or noble, but everything also which is credible or intelligible. This universe, with its persisting constitution, cannot be shown to exist from internal necessity. We can reasonably suppose no intrinsic, unintelligent motive or cause why each elementary substance should possess exactly its present immutable constitution rather than any other; but we can see that the consideration requiring this or some other related scheme must lie in the necessity for establishing and coördinating all things in order to secure a harmonious, coöperative, orderly, and progressive whole. The necessity for each special mode is found in its relations to all the others, as part and parcel of one common unit. The *necessity* is a purely *rational* one, like the necessity that two and two should make four. Under the present nature of things, two and two must make four of *intrinsic* necessity. So every substance must continue to possess and exercise its properties of a like necessity.

342 *Creation.*

Pure gold, under its present conditions, will be always extremely malleable and of a yellow color; but there is no *absolute necessity* that gold should possess these special properties. In short, the present constitution of things must be regarded literally as a system of pure principles, harmonized in one all comprehensive scheme of thought, and actualized in the existing Cosmos. This scheme of rational, related thought, realized and maintained in things, constitutes the great work of Creation.

With the progress of science, widening and ramifying in every direction, there grows up a mass of ever accumulating testimony to the intrinsic unity of the whole scheme. Nothing is more firmly established. The details of all sciences lead to the same wide generalizations, and are found to be based upon the same fundamental principles. Most unlooked-for kindred features manifest themselves perpetually in departments of learning to superficial view, the most widely removed; one discovery leads to another, often by apparently whimsical and quite unexpected links of connection. No one would have supposed in advance that a few old bones, accidentally found in the rocks, would prove to be the key which should unlock the temple where Providence had so long hidden those tables of stone containing the laws and chronicles of the pre-Adamite ages. No one would have dreamed that every bone was to help repeople a new valley of vision reaching back through a vista of immeasurable time; and that all science was to be illumined anew by the old light which was to come streaming down upon it from those remote centuries. No one dreamed once that every coal glowing in our grates was to be like a living witness to corroborate the testimony of the old dead bones, that they all grew successively, ages and ages and ages ago, when no human mind was there to witness and record the fact that the same identical constitution of things was in operation then as now!

The different branches of science no longer admit of

Creation. 343

any other than an arbitrary division. Every student, if he would be a master in his own department, is forced to know something of almost everything else. No one attempts to write an exhaustive treatise upon any topic, who does not, of necessity, trace its relations more or less directly to almost every department of human knowledge. The zoölogist surely has a wide primary field in the whole group of larger animals on land and sea, and the more than 500,000 known species of insects, to say nothing of the infusoria ; yet the zoölogist finds himself compelled to study the plant as well as the animal, that he may distinguish their points of resemblance and difference ; and even after the nicest prolonged observation he is unable distinctly to draw the dividing line separating the animal from the vegetable kingdom. He must study structure, and thus he becomes a physiologist ; composition, and he is enticed into the beautiful mysteries of chemistry; he must study the forces operative in the animal organism, and is led on by their correlations into mechanics and out into the universal domain of all force, till there is no resting-place for him anywhere. But if he comes back with an olive-branch into his original ark, and throws his heart into the work immediately about him, he soon finds himself investigating the influences of climate upon the animal, of location and comparative elevations ; and the influences of atmospheric pressure, and the pressure of columns of water upon sea and fresh water fauna, and the relations of the infusoria to the various mediums in which they live ; he will be guided into embryology in pursuit of the mysteries of growth, and into psychology in search of the secrets of related life ; he will delve after fossils, and perhaps wander very far off into the intricate stony paths of ancient geology, till he loses himself among the extinct moraines of the old glaciers. Thus even while he is still in the direct pursuit of his own scientific specialty, he will almost necessarily become largely imbued with the whole of universal science.

344 *Creation.*

A mathematician, feeling no necessity to limit his studies in any direction, vibrates like a shuttlecock between mechanics celestial and terrestrial, and applies his arithmetic to almost everything, from animalcules "not larger than from 1-1000th to 1-2000th of a line in diameter," and so crowded together that a single drop of water will contain five hundred millions of them — "an amount perhaps nearly equal to the whole number of human beings on the surface of our globe" — to the sun whose diameter is found to be "upwards of 880,000 miles," and which is so far away from us that "a man travelling in a railroad car on an air-line, at the rate of thirty miles an hour, would be three hundred and sixty years in reaching it." He determines that "a cheese-mite can jump twenty-four times his own length," that "a fly so minute as to be almost invisible can take 1,000 steps during one pulsation of a healthy man's blood;" that "Mercury at her perihelion moves along her orbit thirty-five miles in a second;" that "in an inch length of a ray of violet light there are fifty-nine thousand seven hundred and fifty-six vibrations;" and "if a single second of time be divided into a million of equal parts, a wave of violet light trembles or pulsates in that inconceivably short interval seven hundred and twenty-seven millions of times." If he finds himself confounded by the growing incredibility of his facts, he may recover himself by remembering that practical science everywhere confirms theoretical; that even improvers of telescopes learned to adjust their various lenses first in mathematical theory, and applying this in practice that they obtained anticipated results ; that among all the many variations in the movements of every known member of the solar system there is a rigid agreement between the fact as it is and as it should be on mathematical principles ; that the planet Neptune was twice discovered mathematically before it was found in reality; and, in brief, that everything material is found, after re-

Creation. 345

peated and multiplied tests, to be rigidly and unvaryingly quantitative, adjusted in "measure, number, and weight;" that organic beings constitute the "higher geometry of nature," and that all successful arts or handicrafts are only so many new modes of applied mathematics!

When the most superficial student reads on any topic, it perhaps suggests more to him about some other, with which he had hitherto supposed it to be only remotely allied, than even the information he gains as to the matter directly in hand, and he is thus compelled to follow on and on through the whole round of known science. Finding himself still in the same endless cycle of inquiry, and seeing that everything true or valuable which he has learned has been drawn by some one directly from the same open book of nature, which is forever repeating and illustrating universal truths under their great variety of aspects, how can he do otherwise than conclude that the Cosmos is a Universe? It would seem sheer perversity to doubt a fact which is becoming forever more and more clear with every fresh discovery.

The several parts of the universal science are all so mutually confirmatory, that to prove and illustrate any one important fact, it is almost necessary incidentally to demonstrate a score of others. The whole infinitude of adjustments and adaptations, innumerable as we find them to be, are yet all classified under a few simple general principles. The widest range of details are massed under a common type. It is not more true that gravitation alike moves worlds, draws down the floating leaves, and sends Niagara tumbling over its ledge of rocks, than that the organism of a lichen, a lizard, a forest-tree, an elephant, and a man, are all modeled after the same universal organic type. The most superficial observer is struck by the mere external resemblances of the insect tribe; but when we trace them, family after family, through all their various

346   *Creation.*

transformations in the larvæ, chrysalis, and perfect states, we recognize the curious, simple, yet recondite plan after which, by these distinctly marked stages, all of them are similarly constructed. A little knowledge of embryology still widens our view, and we find that all organizations undergo very similar transformations. Winged creatures, whose life is to consist largely in the delights of rapid, airy flight, apparently need that their growth should take place almost wholly in the sunshine, that they may gather up its light and warmth into their intense and concentrated vital energy; but the reflective mammal may complete the early stages of growth in the placid warmth of the parental bosom, growing into the perfect form of its kind before it emerges into the prying daylight; yet a general unity of plan for all organic growth is perfectly evident, and is illustrated even in the vegetable. The progress of science has always been a progress towards wider generalizations!

All the *first principles* of the philosophers are in perpetual working order everywhere. Not a nook, or corner, or side bit of effect, whether in the deepest wilderness, the most barren desert, the highest mountain, or the most populous city, has ever been discovered where a different order of things prevailed. Even in the minutest details, there are absolutely no exceptions anywhere, to any one of the established principles of nature; apparent exceptions, on a more careful investigation, are found to be only superficial; and a better understanding of the matter proves them, often, to be striking and peculiar illustrations of the very law to which they at first seemed to be exceptions. As the same mother-earth sustains all the fauna and flora which grow upon it, so a grand *unity* of rational scheme must have originated all the adapted principles of creation. Thus *Gravitative force,* universal and unceasing in its operations, performing important work in the economy of all things, from the smallest to the largest, *must have been forecasted in all its minutest bearings upon its infinite range of objects, before it could have been adopted as the unchanging law to which everything else was to be adjusted;* and all these various adjustments are themselves established, immutable facts. How can we do otherwise than conclude that the same Author originated the entire rational scheme which we see exemplified equally in every department of being? If creation must be regarded still as finite; yet one who could devise and execute this creative scheme, must be himself in the possession of powers which are infinite!

THE NATURE OF THE CREATOR INFERRED FROM THE CREATION.

VERY much has been said and written on the subject of Cause; and many kinds of cause have been distinguished and defined; yet there are but two essentially different classes of causes. These two are coöperative; but generically unlike in character. The one is *substantial* or *quantitative cause*, which is literally converted into the effect, — the sum of causes in every instance being exactly equal to the sum of their effects, and *vice versa*. The other is *rational* or *qualitative cause*, which, through intelligent and designed modifications and combinations of substantial causes, produces new foreseen or desired events.

There is almost nothing in a civilized town which is not the direct product of human calculation, foresight, will — effects produced by rational, finite causes. Each mother is a special providence to her own child. The Esquimau clothes her little one to give it warmth; the Congolian lays hers in the shade to cool it; an English princess enfolds hers in soft linens in summer and in softer woolens for winter; and the Irish peasant wraps hers in its few rags for July, and in its many rags for January. They are all rational causes, seeking means for securing the well-being of their children. We all admit that the curious great clock in the Strasburg Cathedral must have been planned by some mind; and that the minute watch set as a gem in a lady's finger-ring must have been the product of forethought and design; can we not, then, fully perceive that

The Creator. 349

nothing less than Mind could have planned the present universe? There must be an adequate rational cause for so preëminently rational a scheme of coördinations!

I, for one, do not claim that God is the substantial or quantitative cause of Creation; or that He is Himself, in any sense, the totality of things; but that He is the personal, rational Being who constituted the present cosmos, and who is Himself manifested in his works. I find proofs of one infinite, consistent, beneficent design in the whole system of coadaptations — in the whole constitution of every atom, sentient and unsentient. Everything testifies, not only to an intelligent cause, but to a Cause adequate in comprehension and power. Not until I can believe that the thermometer, which it is self-evident has been planned and beautifully adapted for the measurement of heat, had no rational cause; but was either self-created or the work of chance, can I believe that the solar system was self-created or the product of chance. We are all ready to give credit to the inventor of the planetarium, which is only a puerile, aping mechanism, but faintly illustrating the original! If there is no rational cause manifested in the vegetable and animal economy of this earth, no design shown in the growth of new vegetation from the decayed tissues of the old, and of the higher animal tissues from the low, then there can be no design indicated in anything, for there is no evidence more conclusive of anything in nature! We ourselves are but so many stupidities, not capable of deciding upon any question of causation! If one might challenge the assent of an intelligent mind to any proposition whatever, surely he might do so to the assertion that Nature is one vast compilation of internal evidence as to the forethought and purpose which coördinated all its properties and processes. I claim, therefore, immediately to perceive that Creation had, and must have had, a rational Creator.

But *rational powers*, as we have already seen, can only

350 *The Creator.*

pertain to a *personal mind;* and if God is a rational being, then He is a real and true person. He thinks, feels, and acts ; possessing a living, sentient nature of his own ; and however different may be his type of mind from ours, however above and beyond us, and therefore to us incomprehensible, yet his nature like ours must be indivisible and indestructible.

What then can we learn of his attributes? His wisdom is so manifestly great that we must assume it to be Omnis·cient. We can define his attributes only in relation to the corresponding attributes of men, existing simply in finiteness. Infinite wisdom must be the knowledge of all things actual or possible — of things existing not merely, but of all possible creations and combinations — knowledge actually unlimited by anything actual or possible ; but even Omniscience would be limited by impossibilities. For example, God cannot know to be true what is not true ; or he cannot know to be false something which is not false.

Infinite wisdom, of course therefore, must know everything which is known to all finite minds. If our knowledges were all added to His, they would not increase it; and if all finite knowledge were obliterated from the universe, this would destroy nothing which is in the intelligence of Deity. This suggests the question, Is our knowledge, so far as it extends, identical with God's, and a part of it?

" If God is omniscient or infinite in wisdom," it is said, " then He is the totality of wisdom ! If He is omnipotent or infinite in power, then He is the totality of power! If He is infinite in all his moral perfections, then He is the totality of moral perfections ! If He is infinite in his essential being, then He is the totality of being ! All knowledge, all power, all perfection, all essential being is then a part of God !" This is the logical result of one mode of conceiving of those absolute attributes which we call infinite ;

The Creator. 351

and by which, in reality, we mean absolutely boundless or limitless. But the nature of all personal properties and modifications is such that no being can by any possibility possess them for another!

For example, knowledge is a personal modification, subjectively considered. Deity may know all things and man only a few; but these few are in themselves, or objectively, exactly the same, and neither more nor less, whether known to God, to one man, or to many. I know that two and two make four; Deity knows this also; but from the intrinsic nature of knowledge, you cannot add these two knowledges together and thus increase the amount! It is already complete — absolute in itself; so that the knowledge of a million people on this point would be no greater and no clearer than the knowledge of the one. This knowledge, then, cannot be objectively increased or diminished. We learn from this simple illustration, that if Deity knows all things actual or possible, the knowledge of all finite minds together cannot increase the total amount; and if there were two Infinite Beings, or indeed many of them, yet the sum of actual knowledge could be no greater! Our personality is no more merged in that of the Creator, because we may have a knowledge of some of the same things, than it is merged in that of our fellows for the same reason. Light is always light; yet the little flame of the burning candle is its own, belonging in nowise to the sun.

Again Omnipotence may be defined as, the power to do all things actual or possible; for Omnipotence, also, must be limited by the impossible. It could not, at one and the same time, both establish the existing nature of things and also destroy it; or do any other rational impossibility. Finite power sustains exactly the same relation to infinite power that finite knowledge does to infinite knowledge. All things which man can do, God can do also. His power to accomplish everything actual or possible is already per-

The Creator.

fect, so that all our might added to his could not enable him to do anything more. If I am perfectly able to lift a feather or to make a simple choice, then nothing can add to my ability in this respect. Subjective knowledge implies something objective to be known, and subjective power is also allied to the objective; but the personal element in it pertains to the one personality alone. If God has given me power to choose right or wrong, as I myself will, then He cannot compel me at the same time to act against my own choice — that is, He cannot make me free to choose and necessitated to choose at the same time and in the same sense. He is limited here by the natural impossibility; and having decided to give me freedom of action, he must henceforth influence me through motives.

We turn, then, to the moral perfections. The evidences of unlimited Beneficence are so manifold, his attributes as manifested to us through his works are so wholly beautiful and good, that we are compelled to ascribe to the Creator infinite goodness. Yet He has not, therefore, absorbed all virtue in himself; for goodness, like knowledge and power, is a subjective or personal attainment — a mode of the very being itself. By becoming good ourselves, we take nothing from the Creator or from any other being. No one can take my personal goodness from me, or assume it for himself, any more than he can so take upon him my vices, or than he can assume my personal identity. This is, as we have seen before, true of everything qualitative or pertaining to mental experiences. Each mind, whether of plant, animal, man, angel, or Deity, must act for itself, know for itself, *be* for itself; possessing all its own mental properties and treasures of whatever character. Mind is like the widow's cruse of unfailing oil, and the barrel of meal which should never be diminished! Draw from its stores and give to others abundantly; yet the immortal well-spring is in the soul, the

The Creator. 353

granary is within the mind. You may add every day possibly to its riches; but you can take nothing away. This is the distinctive difference between matter and mind; between quantitative processes and the qualitative. How, then, can God be the totality of all personalities? He can possess no more than his own personality intact! He may possess infinite wisdom, infinite power, infinite goodness; but He does not therefore possess, in his own experience, any finite wisdom, power, or virtue! My consciousness cannot be a part of the consciousness of even its Author and Creator! My personality is not a fragment from Himself; though it may, in a finite degree, have been made in his own likeness.

"He that teaches man knowledge, shall not He know?" is the old Jewish argument; and it can stand the test of ages. Nothing but an intelligence could have created us intelligent. One who could appreciate the dignity and excellence of a conscious personality, could alone have given me a personal identity, inalienable from myself. There must be a Creator possessing conscious, personal attributes, or *rational effects exist without their adequate causes;* which is incredible!

We have found that for every appetency there is always its coördinated supply; but the strongest man feels weary sometimes, helpless and impotent; there is no human power mighty enough for him to rely upon it; and there is a craving after reliance upon the boundless love which is above him. The little child may be content with parental tenderness and affection, clinging with instinctive trust to any one who manifests these in its behalf; but the same instinct in man must look higher for its satisfaction — as high as the Infinite, upon whom both its affections and its rational demands can centre. An atheist, like a motherless child, may be comforted by all the kindly influences about him. He may reason himself into the stoicism of privation, and may feel, at times, in himself strong and all-

354 *The Creator.*

sufficient ; but there come moments when if he could find such a Creator as even he himself is able to conceive of, it would be an infinite relief! His filial soul yearns for the universal Mother.

There are wrongs which a good man cannot right, and they burden his soul! The more noble he is, the more he suffers from a sense of his own incapacities, and the boundless need of a Beneficent Helper. To be able to fall back upon a being wise and powerful, even if no better than himself, would afford him immeasurable satisfaction. To be able, then, to find one, infinite in all his attributes, who is really ordering all things ; and as far as may be, bringing evil out of good, must give a sense of boundless content! His weakness is coördinated with the strength of the omnipotent Father.

No one could rationally choose to live in a universe which was simply under the control of blind, irrational, quantitative properties, if he could find one governed and guided by a rational mind. To think of countless systems of worlds, whirling through space with an inconceivable velocity, each revolving on its axis, and rolling in groups around a common centre ; and all, probably, circling still more rapidly about larger centres — an almost infinite, moving, but soulless mechanism, of frail, poorly adhesive materials, is rather less satisfying than to think of yourself as floating alone in mid-ocean at the mercy of the elements. Catastrophes may be less near ; but they would be more grandly awful. To be assured that there is an Almighty Arm and a Sleepless Omniscient Eye, able to see all things and to reach everywhere, cannot fail to bring its own comfort!

Think again of the myriads of ignorant, free agents — rational minds indeed, but sunk in most irrational pursuits ; and not content with blindly sacrificing their own best interests, but everywhere periling the well-being of others, till the world has become a "vale of tears." Amid

The Creator.

all the disorder incident to this system of rational action, where the strong are often too cruel, and the helpless suffer too acutely for us to find for them in this life any compensation, .there must be a wonderfully sustaining power in the consciousness that an All-sufficient Helper is continually adjusting and re-adjusting all complicated interests, with all the impartiality of absolute justice and of infinite benevolence.

While He allows mankind, as finite rational causes, to continually intervene for the creation of new events, He, the Original Cause of the whole complicated system, could not have intended to sleep meanwhile; allowing by any possibility his ultimate ends to be disarranged! Nor does He sleep. If there was a Creator of the whole adapted scheme of things, there is also a continuous Providence, forever aiding in the consummation of his own designs. The constitution of his universe was long since fixed; but its destinies are yet in abeyance; and He who inaugurated the processes of nature, must be unrestingly superintending them still. So far as man is permitted to be rational cause of new events continually, coöperating with the established principles of nature, so far, at least, may the Creator of those principles, He who actualized them everywhere in things, also superintend their processes, even though He should work no miracle. A wise sculptor may trust to his assistants the marble which is to realize his ideals; but in the important moments when all may be lost or won, does he leave his directive duties to another? With his own hand he may work out the final results!

A *Creator* necessitates a *Providence;* and nature as it is necessitates a Creator. If the Universe were all quantitative, and must consequently move forward in the very grooves which were marked out for it, the case would be otherwise! The nature of things, then, being essentially fixed and irrational, might have a supposed self-existence, which would work out precisely the results which do accrue; but when the whole is complicated with living

356 *The Creator.*

beings, with their continual increase of sentient experiences, when the universe is no longer merely a fixed unvarying quantity, but is allied to forever increasing qualities of good or evil, it becomes far otherwise. The interests at stake are then too far-reaching for any mere fortuity to have invested itself with them. The beautiful coördinations of things become too self-evidently adapted to the highest well-being of all sentient experience not to reveal the intelligence which coördained them — the beneficence which was the underlying element of the whole creative scheme. If the rocks and rivers *may have a Creator*, all sentient beings, irrational or rational, who have been made capable of suffering as well as enjoying, *must have a Father*. Our sense of moral fitness and of moral justice would be utterly shocked otherwise.

Deity, if He exist, a Being unlike ourselves, Infinite in all his attributes, must of necessity be to us incomprehensible in the fullness of his perfections. If we cannot altogether fathom the nature of the bird or the insect, because they are so far removed from our own experiences, and their capacities so unlike ours, it must be hopeless to reach immeasurably above and beyond our own powers. Is the Creator himself self-existent? He must be! At least so far as our universe is concerned, He is apparently absolute ; personally independent of it and all its concerns, except as He voluntarily chose to interest Himself in its creation. There we must leave the subject ; for we may as well, with our present powers, hope to find the outermost world and the pure space beyond in which all existence ceases, as to find the mental conditions or limitations of the Infinite, Creative Mind. We know Him only as He is revealed in his works!

The inherent *need* of every sentient being for a Protecting Power who will sacredly guard all his interests ; who will practically maintain the principles of equity which He himself has established, is to me the strongest possible proof of his existence!

CPSIA information can be obtained
at www.ICGtesting.com
Printed in the USA
BVHW082045200622
640215BV00001B/183